THE
GUARDIANS

ALSO BY JOHN GRISHAM

A Time to Kill
The Firm
The Pelican Brief
The Client
The Chamber
The Rainmaker
The Runaway Jury
The Partner
The Street Lawyer
The Testament
The Brethren
A Painted House
Skipping Christmas
The Summons
The King of Torts
Bleachers
The Last Juror
The Broker
Playing for Pizza
The Appeal
The Associate
Ford County
The Confession
The Litigators
Calico Joe
The Racketeer
Sycamore Row
Gray Mountain
Rogue Lawyer
The Whistler
Camino Island
The Rooster Bar
The Reckoning
Theodore Boone
Theodore Boone: The Abduction
Theodore Boone: The Accused
Theodore Boone: The Activist
Theodore Boone: The Fugitive
Theodore Boone: The Scandal
Theodore Boone: The Accomplice

NON-FICTION

The Innocent Man

John Grisham

THE GUARDIANS

HODDER

For sale only in India, Bangladesh, Nepal, Bhutan, Sri Lanka and Pakistan.

First published in Great Britain in 2019 by Hodder & Stoughton
An Hachette UK company

This paperback edition published in 2019

1

A CIP catalogue record for this title is available from the British Library

A format ISBN 978 1 473 68461 4
eBook ISBN 978 1 473 68445 4

Typeset in Bembo MT by Hewer Text UK Ltd, Edinburgh
Printed and bound in India by Manipal Technologies Limited, Manipal

Hodder & Stoughton policy is to use papers that are natural, renewable
and recyclable products and made from wood grown in sustainable
forests. The logging and manufacturing processes are expected to
conform to the environmental regulations of the country of origin.

Hodder & Stoughton Ltd
Carmelite House
50 Victoria Embankment
London EC4Y 0DZ

www.hodder.co.uk

To James McCloskey
"The Exonerator"

THE
GUARDIANS

1

Duke Russell is not guilty of the unspeakable crimes for which he was convicted; nonetheless, he is scheduled to be executed for them in one hour and forty-four minutes. As always during these dreadful nights, the clock seems to tick faster as the final hour approaches. I've suffered through two of these countdowns in other states. One went full cycle and my man uttered his final words. The other was waved off in a miracle finish.

Tick away—it's not going to happen, not tonight anyway. The folks who run Alabama may one day succeed in serving Duke his last meal before sticking a needle in his arm, but not tonight. He's been on death row for only nine years. The average in this state is fifteen. Twenty is not unusual. There is an appeal bouncing around somewhere in the Eleventh Circuit in Atlanta, and when it lands on the desk of the right law clerk within the hour this execution will be stayed. Duke will return to the horrors of solitary confinement and live to die another day.

He's been my client for the past four years. His team includes a mammoth firm in Chicago, which has committed thousands of pro bono hours, and an anti–death penalty group out of Birmingham that is spread pretty thin. Four years ago, when I became convinced he was innocent, I signed on as the point man. Currently I have five cases, all wrongful convictions, at least in my opinion.

I've watched one of my clients die. I still believe he was innocent. I just couldn't prove it in time. One is enough.

For the third time today, I enter Alabama's death row and stop at the metal detector blocking the front door where two frowning guards are protecting their turf. One holds a clipboard and stares at me as if he's forgotten my name since my last visit two hours ago.

"Post, Cullen Post," I say to the dunce. "For Duke Russell."

He scans his clipboard as if it holds vital information, finds what he wants, and nods to a plastic basket on a short conveyor belt. In it, I place my briefcase and cell phone, same as before.

"Watch and belt?" I ask like a real smart-ass.

"No," he grunts with an effort. I step through the detector, get cleared, and once again an innocence lawyer manages to properly enter death row without weaponry. I grab my briefcase and cell phone and follow the other guard down a sterile hallway to a wall of bars. He nods, switches click and clang, the bars slide open, and we hike down another hallway, trudging deeper into this miserable building. Around a corner, some men are waiting outside a windowless steel door. Four are in uniform, two in suits. One of the latter is the warden.

He looks gravely at me and steps over. "Got a minute?"

"Not many," I reply. We move away from the group for a private chat. He's not a bad guy, just doing his job, which he's

2

new at and thus he's never pulled off an execution. He's also the enemy, and whatever he wants he will not get from me.

We huddle up like pals and he whispers, "What's it look like?"

I glance around as if to evaluate the situation and say, "Gee, I don't know. Looks like an execution to me."

"Come on, Post. Our lawyers are saying it's a go."

"Your lawyers are idiots. We've already had this conversation."

"Come on, Post. What are the odds right now?"

"Fifty-fifty," I say, lying.

This puzzles him and he's not sure how to respond. "I'd like to see my client," I say.

"Sure," he says louder as if frustrated. He can't be viewed as cooperating with me, so he storms off. The guards step back as one of them opens the door.

Inside the Death Room, Duke is lying on a cot with his eyes closed. For the festivities, the rules allow him a small color television so he can watch whatever he wants. It's on mute with cable news giddy over wildfires out west. His countdown is not a big story on the national front.

At execution time, every death state has its own silly rituals, all designed to create as much drama as possible. Here, they allow full-contact visits with close family members in a large visitation room. At 10:00 p.m., they move the condemned man to the Death Room, which is next door to the Death Chamber where he'll be killed. A chaplain and a lawyer are permitted to sit with him, but no one else. His last meal is served around 10:30, and he can order whatever he wants, except for alcohol.

"How you doing?" I ask as he sits up and smiles.

"Never felt better. Any news?"

"Not yet, but I'm still optimistic. We should hear something soon."

Duke is thirty-eight and white, and before getting arrested for rape and murder his criminal record consisted of two DUIs and a bunch of speeding tickets. No violence whatsoever. He was a party boy and hell-raiser in his younger days, but after nine years in solitary he has settled down considerably. My job is to set him free, which, at the moment, seems like a crazy dream.

I take the remote and change channels to one from Birmingham, but I leave it on mute.

"You seem awfully confident," he says.

"I can afford to. I'm not getting the needle."

"You're a funny man, Post."

"Relax, Duke."

"Relax?" He swings his feet to the floor and smiles again. He does indeed look rather relaxed, given the circumstances. He laughs and says, "Do you remember Lucky Skelton?"

"No."

"They finally got him, about five years ago, but not before serving him three last meals. Three times he walked the gangplank before getting the shove. Sausage pizza and a cherry Coke."

"And what did you order?"

"Steak and fries, with a six-pack of beer."

"I wouldn't count on the beer."

"Are you gonna get me outta here, Post?"

"Not tonight, but I'm working on it."

"If I get out I'm going straight to a bar and drinking cold beer until I pass out."

4

"I'll go with you. Here's the Governor." He appears on-screen and I hit the volume.

He's standing in front of a bank of microphones with camera lights glaring at him. Dark suit, paisley tie, white shirt, every tinted hair gelled with precision. A walking campaign ad. Sufficiently burdened, he says, "I have thoroughly reviewed Mr. Russell's case and discussed it at length with my investigators. I've also met with the family of Emily Broone, the victim of Mr. Russell's crimes, and the family is very much opposed to the idea of clemency. After considering all aspects of this case, I have decided to allow his conviction to stand. The court order will remain in place, and the execution will go forward. The people have spoken. Clemency for Mr. Russell is therefore denied." He announces this with as much drama as he can muster, then bows and slowly backs away from the cameras, his grand performance complete. Elvis has left the building. Three days ago, he found the time to grant me an audience for fifteen minutes, after which he discussed our "private" meeting with his favorite reporters.

If his review had been so thorough, he would know that Duke Russell had nothing to do with the rape and murder of Emily Broone eleven years ago. I hit the mute again and say, "No surprise there."

"Has he ever granted clemency?" Duke asks.

"Of course not."

There is a loud knock on the door and it swings open. Two guards enter and one is pushing a cart with the last meal. They leave it and disappear. Duke stares at the steak and fries and a rather slim slice of chocolate cake, and says, "No beer."

"Enjoy your iced tea."

He sits on the cot and begins to eat. The food smells delicious and it hits me that I have not eaten in at least twenty-four hours. "Want some fries?" he asks.

"No thanks."

"I can't eat all this. For some reason I don't have much of an appetite."

"How was your mom?"

He stuffs in a large chunk of steak and chews slowly. "Not too good, as you might expect. A lot of tears. It was pretty awful."

The cell phone in my pocket vibrates and I grab it. I look at the caller ID and say, "Here it is." I smile at Duke and say hello. It's the law clerk at the Eleventh Circuit, a guy I know pretty well, and he informs me that his boss has just signed an order staying the execution on the grounds that more time is needed to determine whether Duke Russell received a fair trial. I ask him when the stay will be announced and he says immediately.

I look at my client and say, "You got a stay. No needle tonight. How long will it take to finish that steak?"

"Five minutes," he says with a wide smile as he carves more beef.

"Can you give me ten minutes?" I ask the clerk. "My client would like to finish his last meal." We go back and forth and finally agree on seven minutes. I thank him, end the call, and punch another number. "Eat fast," I say. He has suddenly found his appetite and is as happy as a pig at the trough.

The architect of Duke's wrongful conviction is a small-town prosecutor named Chad Falwright. Right now he's waiting in the prison's administration building half a mile away, poised for the proudest moment of his career. He thinks that at 11:30 he'll be escorted to a prison van, along with the Broone family and the local sheriff, and driven here to death row where they'll be led to a small room with a large glass window that's covered with a curtain. Once situated there, Chad thinks, they'll wait for the moment when Duke is strapped to the gurney with needles in his arms and the curtain will be pulled back in dramatic fashion.

For a prosecutor, there is no greater sense of accomplishment than to witness an execution for which he is responsible.

Chad, though, will be denied the thrill. I punch his number and he answers quickly. "It's Post," I say. "Over here on death row with some bad news. The Eleventh Circuit just issued a stay. Looks like you'll crawl back to Verona with your tail between your legs."

He stutters and manages to say, "What the hell?"

"You heard me, Chad. Your bogus conviction is unraveling and this is as close as you'll ever get to Duke's scalp, which, I must say, is pretty damned close. The Eleventh Circuit has doubts about the trivial notion of a fair trial, so they're sending it back. It's over, Chad. Sorry to ruin your big moment."

"Is this a joke, Post?"

"Oh sure. Nothing but laughs over here on death row. You've had fun talking to the reporters all day, now have some fun with this." To say I loathe this guy would be a tremendous understatement.

I end the call and look at Duke, who's feasting away. With his mouth full he asks, "Can you call my mother?"

"No. Only lawyers can use cell phones in here, but she'll know soon enough. Hurry up." He washes it down with tea and attacks the chocolate cake. I take the remote and turn up the volume. As he scrapes his plate, a breathless reporter

7

appears somewhere on the prison grounds and, stuttering, tells us that a stay has been granted. He looks bewildered and confused, and there is confusion all around him.

Within seconds there is a knock on the door and the warden enters. He sees the television and says, "So I guess you've heard?"

"Right, Warden, sorry to ruin the party. Tell your boys to stand down and please call the van for me."

Duke wipes his mouth with a sleeve, starts laughing and says, "Don't look so disappointed, Warden."

"No, actually I'm relieved," he says, but the truth is obvious. He, too, has spent the day talking to reporters and savoring the spotlight. Suddenly, though, his exciting broken-field run has ended with a fumble at the goal line.

"I'm out of here," I say as I shake Duke's hand.

"Thanks Post," he says.

"I'll be in touch." I head for the door and say to the warden, "Please give my regards to the Governor."

I'm escorted outside the building where the cool air hits hard and feels exhilarating. A guard leads me to an unmarked prison van a few feet away. I get in and he closes the door. "The front gate," I say to the driver.

As I ride through the sprawl of Holman Correctional Facility, I am hit with fatigue and hunger. And relief. I close my eyes, breathe deeply, and absorb the miracle that Duke will live to see another day. I've saved his life for now. Securing his freedom will take another miracle.

For reasons known only to the people who run this place, it has been on lockdown for the past five hours, as if angry inmates might organize into a Bastille-like mob and storm death row to rescue Duke. Now the lockdown is subsiding;

the excitement is over. The extra manpower brought in to maintain order is withdrawing, and all I want is to get out of here. I'm parked in a small lot near the front gate, where the TV crews are unplugging and going home. I thank the driver, get in my little Ford SUV, and leave in a hurry. Two miles down the highway I stop at a closed country store to make a call.

His name is Mark Carter. White male, age thirty-three, lives in a small rental house in the town of Bayliss, ten miles from Verona. In my files I have photos of his house and truck and current live-in girlfriend. Eleven years ago, Carter raped and murdered Emily Broone, and now all I have to do is prove it.

Using a burner, I call the number of his cell phone, a number I'm not supposed to have. After five rings he says, "Hello."

"Is this Mark Carter?"

"Who wants to know?"

"You don't know me, Carter, but I'm calling from the prison. Duke Russell just got a stay, so I'm sorry to inform you that the case is still alive. Are you watching television?"

"Who is this?"

"I'm sure you're watching the TV, Carter, sitting there on your fat ass with your fat girlfriend hoping and praying that the State finally kills Duke for your crime. You're a scumbag Carter, willing to watch him die for something you did. What a coward."

"Say it to my face."

"Oh, I will Carter, one day in a courtroom. I'll find the evidence and before long Duke will get out. You'll take his place. I'm coming your way, Carter."

I end the call before he can say anything else.

2

Since gas is slightly cheaper than cheap motels, I spend a lot of time driving lonely roads at dark hours. As always, I tell myself that I will sleep later, as if a long hibernation is waiting just around the corner. The truth is that I nap a lot but rarely sleep and this is unlikely to change. I have saddled myself with the burdens of innocent people rotting away in prison while rapists and murderers roam free.

Duke Russell was convicted in a backwater redneck town where half the jurors struggle to read and all were easily misled by two pompous and bogus experts put on the stand by Chad Falwright. The first was a retired small-town dentist from Wyoming, and how he found his way to Verona, Alabama, is another story. With grave authority, a nice suit, and an impressive vocabulary, he testified that three nicks on the arms of Emily Broone were inflicted by Duke's teeth. This clown makes a living testifying across the country, always for the prosecution and always for nice fees, and in his twisted mind a rape is not violent enough unless the rapist somehow manages to bite the victim hard enough to leave imprints.

Such an unfounded and ridiculous theory should have been exposed on cross-examination, but Duke's lawyer was either drunk or napping.

The second expert was from the state crime lab. His area of expertise was, and still is, hair analysis. Seven pubic hairs were found on Emily's body, and this guy convinced the jury that they came from Duke. They did not. They probably came from Mark Carter but we don't know that. Yet. The local yokels in charge of the investigation had only a passing interest in Carter as a suspect, though he was the last person seen with Emily the night she disappeared.

Bite mark and hair analysis have been discredited in most advanced jurisdictions. Both belong to that pathetic and ever-shifting field of knowledge derisively known among defense and innocence lawyers as "junk science." God only knows how many innocent people are serving long sentences because of unqualified experts and their unfounded theories of guilt.

Any defense lawyer worth his salt would have had a fine time with those two experts on cross-examination, but Duke's lawyer was not worth the $3,000 the State paid him. Indeed, he was worth nothing. He had little criminal experience, reeked of alcohol during the trial, was woefully unprepared, believed his client was guilty, got three DUIs the year after the trial, got disbarred, and eventually died of cirrhosis.

And I'm supposed to pick up the pieces and find justice.

But no one drafted me into this case. As always, I'm a volunteer.

I'm on the interstate headed toward Montgomery, two and a half hours away, and I have time to plot and scheme. If I stopped at a motel I wouldn't be able to sleep anyway. I'm too pumped over the last-minute miracle that I just pulled out of thin air. I send a text to the law clerk in Atlanta and say thanks. I send a text to my boss who, hopefully, is asleep by now.

Her name is Vicki Gourley and she works in our little foundation's office in the old section of Savannah. She founded Guardian Ministries twelve years ago with her own money. Vicki is a devout Christian who considers her work to be derived straight from the Gospels. Jesus said to remember the prisoners. She doesn't spend much time hanging around jails but she works fifteen hours a day trying to free the innocent. Years ago she was on a jury that convicted a young man of murder and sentenced him to die. Two years later the bad conviction was exposed. The prosecutor had concealed exculpatory evidence and solicited perjured testimony from a jailhouse snitch. The police had planted evidence and lied to the jury. When the real killer was identified by DNA, Vicki sold her flooring business to her nephews, took the money and started Guardian Ministries.

I was her first employee. Now we have one more.

We also have a freelancer named Francois Tatum. He's a forty-five-year-old black guy who realized as a teenager that life in rural Georgia might be easier if he called himself Frankie and not Francois. Seems his mother had some Haitian blood and gave her kids French names, none of which were common in her remote corner of the English-speaking world.

Frankie was my first exoneree. He was serving life in Georgia for someone else's murder when I met him. At the time, I was working as an Episcopal priest at a small church in Savannah. We ran a prison ministry and that's how I met

Frankie. He was obsessed with his innocence and talked of nothing else. He was bright and extremely well-read, and had taught himself the law inside and out. After two visits he had me convinced.

During the first phase of my legal career I defended people who could not afford a lawyer. I had hundreds of clients and before long I reached the point where I assumed they were all guilty. I had never stopped for a moment to consider the plight of the wrongfully convicted. Frankie changed all that. I plunged into an investigation of his case and soon realized I might be able to prove his innocence. Then I met Vicki and she offered me a job that paid even less than my pastoral work. Still does.

So Francois Tatum became the first client signed up by Guardian Ministries. After fourteen years in prison he had been completely abandoned by his family. All his friends were gone. The aforementioned mother had dumped him and his siblings at the doorstep of an aunt and was never seen again. He's never known his father. When I met him in prison I was his first visitor in twelve years. All of this neglect sounds terrible, but there was a silver lining. Once freed and fully exonerated, Frankie got a lot of money from the State of Georgia and the locals who had put him away. And with no family or friends to hound him for cash, he managed to ease into freedom like a ghost with no trail. He keeps a small apartment in Atlanta, a post office box in Chattanooga, and spends most of his time on the road savoring the open spaces. His money is buried in various banks throughout the South so no one can find it. He avoids relationships because he has been scarred by all of them. That, and he's always fearful that someone will try to get in his pockets.

Frankie trusts me and no one else. When his lawsuits were settled, he offered me a generous fee. I said no. He'd earned every dime of that money surviving prison. When I signed on with Guardian I took a vow of poverty. If my clients can survive on two bucks a day for food, the least I can do is cut every corner.

East of Montgomery, I pull into a truck stop near Tuskegee. It's still dark, not yet 6:00 a.m., and the sprawling gravel lot is packed with big rigs purring away while their drivers either nap or get breakfast. The café is busy and the thick aroma of bacon and sausage hits me hard as I enter. Someone waves from the rear. Frankie has secured a booth.

Since we are in rural Alabama, we greet each other with a proper handshake, as opposed to a man hug we might otherwise consider. Two men, one black and the other white, hugging in a crowded truck stop might attract a look or two, not that we really care. Frankie has more money than all these guys combined, and he's still lean and quick from his prison days. He doesn't start fights. He simply has the air and confidence to discourage them.

"Congrats," he says. "That was pretty close."

"Duke had just started his last meal when the call came. Had to eat in a hurry."

"But you seemed confident."

"I was faking, the old tough lawyer routine. Inside, my guts were boiling."

"Speaking of which. I'm sure you're starving."

"Yes, I am. I called Carter as I left the prison. Couldn't help myself."

He frowns slightly and says, "Okay. I'm sure there was a reason."

"Not a good one. I was just too pissed not to. The guy was sitting there counting the minutes until Duke got the needle. Can you imagine what that's like, being the real killer and silently cheering from the sideline as somebody else is executed? We gotta nail him, Frankie."

"We will."

A waitress appears and I order eggs and coffee. Frankie wants pancakes and sausage.

He knows as much about my cases as I do. He reads every file, memo, report, and trial transcript. Fun for Frankie is easing into a place like Verona, Alabama, where no one has ever seen him, and digging for information. He's fearless but he never takes chances because he is not going to get caught. His new life is too good, his freedom especially valuable because he suffered so long without it.

"We have to get Carter's DNA," I say. "One way or the other."

"I know, I know. I'm working on it. You need some rest, boss."

"Don't I always? And, as we well know, being the lawyer I can't obtain his DNA by illegal means."

"But *I* can, right?" He smiles and sips his coffee. The waitress delivers mine and fills the cup.

"Maybe. Let's discuss it later. For the next few weeks, he'll be spooked because of my call. Good for him. He'll make a mistake at some point and we'll be there."

"Where are you headed now?"

"Savannah. I'll be there for a couple of days, then head to Florida."

"Florida. Seabrook?"

"Yes, Seabrook. I've decided to take the case."

15

Frankie's face never reveals much. His eyes seldom blink, his voice is steady and flat as if he's measuring every word. Survival in prison required a poker face. Long stretches of solitude were common. "Are you sure?" he asks. It's obvious he has doubts about Seabrook.

"The guy is innocent, Frankie. And he has no lawyer."

The platters arrive and we busy ourselves with butter, syrup, and hot sauce. The Seabrook case has been in our office for almost three years as we, the staff, have debated whether or not to get involved. That's not unusual in our business. Not surprisingly, Guardian is inundated with mail from inmates in fifty states, all claiming to be innocent. The vast majority are not, so we screen and screen and pick and choose with care, and take only those with the strongest claims of innocence. And we still make mistakes.

Frankie says, "That could be a pretty dangerous situation down there."

"I know. We've kicked this around for a long time. Meanwhile he's counting his days, serving someone else's time."

He chews on pancakes and nods slightly, still unconvinced.

I ask, "When have we ever run from a good fight, Frankie?"

"Maybe this is the time to take a pass. You decline cases every day, right? Maybe this is more dangerous than all the others. God knows you have enough potential clients out there."

"Are you getting soft?"

"No. I just don't want to see you hurt. No one ever sees me, Cullen. I live and work in the shadows. But your name is on the pleadings. You start digging around in an awful place like Seabrook and you could upset some nasty characters."

I smile and say, "All the more reason to do it."

THE SUN IS up when we leave the café. In the parking lot we do a proper man hug and say farewell. I have no idea which direction he is headed, and that's the beautiful thing about Frankie. He wakes up free every morning, thanks God for his good fortune, gets in his late-model pickup truck with a club cab, and follows the sun.

His freedom invigorates me and keeps me going. If not for Guardian Ministries, he would still be rotting away.

3

There is no direct route between Opelika, Alabama, and Savannah. I leave the interstate and begin meandering through central Georgia on two-lane roads that get busier with the morning. I've been here before. In the past ten years I've roamed virtually every highway throughout the Death Belt, from North Carolina to Texas. Once I almost took a case in California, but Vicki nixed it. I don't like airports and Guardian couldn't afford to fly me back and forth. So I drive for long stretches of time, with lots of black coffee and books on tape. And I alternate between periods of deep, quiet thought and frantic bouts with the phone.

In a small town, I pass the county courthouse and watch three young lawyers in their best suits hustle into the building, no doubt headed for an important matter. That could have been me, not too long ago.

I was thirty years old when I quit the law for the first time, and for a good reason.

THAT MORNING BEGAN with the sickening news that two sixteen-year-old white kids had been found dead with their

18

throats cut. Both had been sexually mutilated. Evidently they were parked in a remote section of the county when they were jumped by a group of black teenagers who took their car. Hours later the car was found. Someone inside the gang was talking. Arrests were being made. Details were being reported.

Such was the standard fare for early morning news in Memphis. Last night's violence was reported to a jaded audience who lived with the great question: "How much more can we take?" However, even for Memphis this news was shocking.

Brooke and I watched it in bed with our first cups of coffee, as usual. After the first report, I mumbled, "This could be awful."

"It *is* awful," she corrected me.

"You know what I mean."

"Will you get one of them?"

"Start praying now," I said. By the time I stepped into the shower I was feeling ill and scheming of ways to avoid the office. I had no appetite and skipped breakfast. On the way out, the phone rang. My supervisor told me to hurry. I kissed Brooke goodbye and said, "Wish me luck. This will be a long day."

The office of the public defender is downtown in the Criminal Justice Complex. When I walked in at eight o'clock the place was like a morgue. Everyone seemed to be cowering in their offices and trying to avoid eye contact. Minutes later, our supervisor called us into a conference room. There were six of us in Major Crimes, and since we worked in Memphis we had plenty of clients. At thirty, I was the youngest, and as I looked around the room I knew my number was about to be called.

Our boss said, "There appear to be five of them, all now locked up. Ages fifteen to seventeen. Two agreed to talk. Seems they found the kids in the back seat of the boy's car, having a go at it. Four of the five defendants are aspiring gang members, Ravens, and to be properly inducted one has to rape a white girl. One with blond hair. Crissy Spangler was a blonde. The leader, one Lamar Robinson, gave the orders. The boy, Will Foster, was tied to a tree and made to watch as they took turns with Crissy. When he wouldn't shut up, they mutilated him and cut his throat. Photos are on the way over from Memphis Police."

The six of us stood in muted horror as reality set in. I glanced at a window with a latch. Jumping headfirst onto the parking lot seemed like a reasonable thing to do.

He continued, "They took Will's car, ran a red light on South Third, smart boys. The police stopped three of them, noticed blood, and brought them in. Two started talking and gave the details. They claimed the others did it but their confessions implicate all five. Autopsies are underway this morning. Needless to say, we are involved up to our ears. Initial appearances are set for two this afternoon and it is going to be a circus. Reporters are everywhere and details are leaking out like crazy."

I inched closer to the window. I heard him say, "Post, you've got a fifteen-year-old named Terrence Lattimore. As far as we know, he hasn't said anything."

When the other assignments were made, the supervisor said, "Get to the jail right now and meet your new clients. Inform the police that they are not to be interrogated outside your presence. These are gang members and they will probably not cooperate, not this early anyway."

When he finished, he looked at each of us, the unlucky ones, and said, "I'm sorry."

An hour later I was walking through the entrance to the city jail when someone, probably a reporter, yelled, "Do you represent one of these murderers?"

I pretended to ignore her and kept walking.

When I entered the small holding room, Terrence Lattimore was cuffed at the wrists and ankles and chained to a metal chair. When we were alone I explained that I had been assigned his case and needed to ask some questions, just basic stuff for starters. I got nothing but a smirk and a glare. He may have been only fifteen years old, but he was a tough kid who had seen it all. Battle-hardened in the ways of gangs, drugs, and violence. He hated me and everyone else with white skin. He said he didn't have an address and told me to stay away from his family. His rap sheet included two school expulsions and four charges in juvenile court, all involving violence.

By noon I was ready to resign and go look for another job. When I joined the PD's office three years earlier I did so only when I couldn't find work with a firm. And after three years of toiling in the gutter of our criminal justice system, I was asking myself serious questions about why I had chosen law school. I really couldn't remember. My career brought me into daily contact with people I wouldn't get near outside of court.

Lunch was out of the question because no one could possibly choke down food. The five of us who had been chosen met with the supervisor and looked at the crime scene photos and autopsy reports. Any food in my stomach would have gone to the floor.

What the hell was I doing with my life? As a criminal defense lawyer, I was already sick of the question "How can you represent a person you know to be guilty?" I had always offered the standard law school response of, "Well, everyone has the right to a proper defense. The Constitution says so."

But I no longer believed that. The truth is that there are some crimes that are so heinous and cruel that the killer should either be (1) put to death, if one believes in the death penalty, or (2) put away for life, if one does not believe in the death penalty. As I left that awful meeting, I wasn't sure what I believed anymore.

I went to my cubbyhole of an office, which at least had a door that could be locked. From my window I looked at the pavement below and envisioned myself jumping and floating safely away to some exotic beach where life was splendid and all I worried about was the next cold drink. Oddly, Brooke wasn't with me in the dream. My desk phone snapped me out of it.

I had been hallucinating, not dreaming. Everything was suddenly in slow motion and I had trouble saying, "Hello." The voice identified itself as a reporter and she just had a few questions about the murders. As if I'm going to discuss the case with her. I hung up. An hour passed and I don't remember doing anything. I was numb and sick and just wanted to run from the building. I remembered to call Brooke and pass along the terrible news that I had one of the five.

The first appearance at 2:00 p.m. was moved from a small courtroom to a larger one, and it still wasn't big enough. Because of its crime rate, Memphis had a lot of cops, and most of them were in the building that afternoon. They blocked the doors and searched every reporter and spectator. In the courtroom, they stood two abreast down the center aisle and lined the three walls.

Will Foster's cousin was a Memphis city fireman. He arrived with a group of colleagues and they seemed ready to attack at any moment. A few blacks drifted to a rear corner of the other side, as far away from the victims' families as possible. Reporters were everywhere, but without cameras. Lawyers who had no business being there milled about, curious.

I entered the jury room through a service entrance and eased through a door for a look at the throng. The place was packed. The tension was thick, palpable.

The judge took the bench and called for order. The five defendants were brought in, all in matching orange jumpsuits, all chained together. The spectators gawked at this first sighting. The artists scribbled away. More cops formed a line behind the five as a shield. The defendants stood before the bench, all studying their feet. A loud, strong voice from the rear yelled, "Turn 'em loose, dammit! Turn 'em loose!" Cops scrambled to silence him.

A woman shrieked, in tears.

I moved to a position behind Terrence Lattimore, along with my four colleagues. As I did so, I glanced at the people sitting together on the two front rows. They were obviously close to the victims, and they looked at me with sheer hatred.

Hated by my client. Hated by his victims. What the hell was I doing in that courtroom?

The judge rapped his gavel and said, "I am going to maintain order in this courtroom. This is a first appearance, the purpose of which is to determine the identity of the defendants and make sure they are represented by counsel. Nothing more. Now, who is Mr. Lamar Robinson?"

Robinson looked up and mumbled something.

"How old are you, Mr. Robinson?"

"Seventeen."

"Ms. Julie Showalter from the office of the public defender has been appointed to represent you. Have you met with her?"

My colleague Julie took a step closer and stood between Robinson and the next one. Since the defendants were chained together, the lawyers could only get so close. The cuffs and chains were always removed in court, and the fact that they were not in this case said a lot about the mood of the judge.

Robinson glanced at Julie at his right shoulder and shrugged.

"Do you want her to represent you, Mr. Robinson?"

"Can I have a black lawyer?" he asked.

"You can hire anybody you want. Do you have money for a private lawyer?"

"Maybe."

"Okay, we'll discuss it later. Next is Mr. Terrence Lattimore." Terrence looked at the judge as if he would like to slit his throat too.

"How old are you, Mr. Lattimore?"

"Fifteen."

"Do you have money for a private lawyer?"

He shook his head, no.

"Do you want Mr. Cullen Post of the PD's office to represent you?"

He shrugged as if he didn't care.

The judge looked at me and asked, "Mr. Post, have you met with your client?"

Mr. Post couldn't answer. I opened my mouth but nothing came out. I took a step back and kept staring up at the bench where His Honor looked at me blankly. "Mr. Post?"

The courtroom was still and silent, but my ears were ringing with a shrill piercing sound that made no sense. My knees were rubbery, my breathing labored. I took another step back, then turned around and wedged myself through the wall of cops. I made it to the bar, opened the swinging gate at my knees, and headed down the center aisle. I brushed by cop after cop and none of them tried to stop me. His Honor said something like, "Mr. Post, where are you going?" Mr. Post had no idea.

I made it through the main door, left the courtroom behind, and went straight to the men's room where I locked myself in a stall and vomited. I retched and gagged until there was nothing left, then I walked to a sink and splashed water in my face. I was vaguely aware that I was on an escalator, but I had no sense of time, space, sound, or movement. I do not remember leaving the building.

I was in my car, driving east on Poplar Avenue, away from downtown. Without intending to, I ran a red light and narrowly avoided what would have been a nasty collision. I heard angry horns behind me. At some point I realized that I had left my briefcase in the courtroom, and this made me smile. I would never see it again.

My mother's parents lived on a small farm ten miles west of Dyersburg, Tennessee, my hometown. I arrived there at some point that afternoon. I had lost complete track of time and do not remember making the decision to go home. My grandparents were surprised to see me, they later said, but soon realized I needed help. They quizzed me, but all questions were met with a blank, hollow stare. They put me to bed and called Brooke.

Late that night, the medics loaded me into an ambulance. With Brooke at my side, we rode three hours to a psychiatric hospital near Nashville. There were no available beds in Memphis, and I didn't want to go back there anyway. In the following days I started therapy and drugs and long sessions with shrinks and slowly began to come to grips with my crack-up. After a month, we were notified that the insurance company was pulling the plug. It was time to leave and I was ready to get out of the place.

I refused to return to our apartment in Memphis, so I lived with my grandparents. It was during this time that Brooke and I decided to call it quits. About halfway through our three-year marriage, both of us realized that we could not spend the rest of our lives together, and that trying to do so would only lead to a lot of misery. This was not discussed at the time, and we rarely fought and quarreled. Somehow, during those dark days on the farm, we found the courage to talk honestly. We still loved each other, but we were already growing apart. At first we agreed on a one-year trial separation, but even that was abandoned. I have never blamed her for leaving me because of my nervous breakdown. I wanted out, as did she. We parted with broken hearts, but vowed to remain friends, or at least try to. That didn't work either.

As Brooke was leaving my life, God was knocking on the door. He came in the person of Father Bennie Drake, the Episcopal priest of my home church in Dyersburg. Bennie was about forty, cool and hip with a salty tongue. He wore faded jeans most of the time, always with his collar and black jacket, and he quickly became the bright spot in my recovery. His weekly visits soon became almost daily, and I lived for our long conversations on the front porch. I trusted him immediately and confessed that I had no desire to return to the law. I was only thirty and I wanted a new career helping others. I did not want to spend the rest of my life suing people or defending the guilty or working in a pressure-packed law firm. The closer I got to Bennie, the more I wanted to be like him. He saw something in me and suggested I at least think about the ministry. We shared long prayers and even longer conversations, and I gradually began to feel God's call.

Eight months after my last court appearance, I moved to Alexandria, Virginia, and entered the seminary where I spent the next three years studying diligently. To support myself, I worked twenty hours a week as research assistant in a mammoth D.C. law firm. I hated the work but managed to mask my contempt for it. I was reminded weekly of why I had left the profession.

I was ordained at the age of thirty-five and landed a position of associate priest at the Peace Episcopal Church on Drayton Street in Savannah's historic district. The vicar was a wonderful man named Luther Hodges, and for years he had a prison ministry. His uncle had died behind bars and he was determined to help those who were forgotten. Three months after moving to Savannah I met Mr. Francois Tatum, a truly forgotten soul.

Walking Frankie out of prison two years later was the greatest thrill of my life. I found my calling. Through divine intervention I had met Vicki Gourley, a woman with a mission of her own.

4

Guardian Ministries is housed in a small corner of an old warehouse on Broad Street in Savannah. The rest of the huge building is used by the flooring company Vicki sold years ago. She still owns the warehouse and leases it to her nephews, who run the business. Most of her rental income is absorbed by Guardian.

It's almost noon when I park and walk into our offices. I'm not expecting a hero's welcome and I certainly don't get one. There is no receptionist and no reception area, no pleasant place to greet our clients. They're all in prison. We don't use secretaries because we can't afford them. We do our own typing, filing, scheduling, phone answering, coffee making, and trash removing.

For lunch most days Vicki has a quick meal with her mother at a nursing home down the street. Her pristine office is empty. I glance at her desk, not a single sheet of paper is out of order. Behind it, on a credenza, is a color photo of Vicki and Boyd, her deceased husband. He built the business, and when he died young she took over and ran it like a tyrant until the judicial system pissed her off and she founded Guardian.

Across the hall is the office of Mazy Ruffin, our director of litigation and the outfit's brain trust. She too is away from her desk, probably hauling kids here and there. She has four of them and they can usually be found underfoot somewhere at Guardian in the afternoons. Once the day care starts, Vicki quietly closes her door. So do I, if I'm at the office, which is rare. When we hired Mazy four years ago, she had two nonnegotiable conditions. The first was permission to keep her kids in her office when necessary. She couldn't afford much babysitting. The second was her salary. She needed $65,000 a year to survive, not a penny less. Combined, Vicki and I were not at that level, but then we're not raising children, nor do we worry about our salaries. We agreed to both requests, and Mazy is still the highest-paid member of the team.

And she's a bargain. She grew up in the tough projects of south Atlanta. At times she was homeless, though she doesn't say much about those days. Because of her brains, a high school teacher took notice and showed some love. She blitzed through Morehouse College and Emory Law School with full rides and near perfect grades. She turned down the big firms and chose instead to work for her people at the NAACP Legal Defense Fund. That career flamed out when her marriage unraveled. A friend of mine mentioned her when we were looking for another lawyer.

The downstairs is the domain of these two alpha females. When I'm here I spend my time on the second floor, where I hole up in a cluttered room I call my office. Across the hall is the conference room, though there aren't many conferences at Guardian. Occasionally we'll use it for depositions or meetings with an exoneree and his family.

I step inside the conference room and turn on the lights. In the center is a long, oval-shaped dining table I bought at a flea market for $100. Around it is a collection of ten mismatched chairs that we've added over the years. What the room lacks in style and taste it more than makes up for in character. On one wall, our Wall of Fame, is a row of eight enlarged and framed color portraits of our exonerees, beginning with Frankie. Their smiling faces are the heart and soul of our operation. They inspire us to keep plugging along, fighting the system, fighting for freedom and justice.

Only eight. With thousands more waiting. Our work will never end, and while this reality might seem discouraging it is also highly motivational.

On another wall there are five smaller photos of our current clients, all in prison garb. Duke Russell in Alabama. Shasta Briley in North Carolina. Billy Rayburn in Tennessee. Curtis Wallace in Mississippi. Little Jimmy Flagler in Georgia. Three blacks, two whites, one female. Skin color and gender mean nothing in our work. Around the room there is a hodgepodge collection of framed newspaper photos capturing those glorious moments when we walked our innocent clients out of prison. I'm in most of them, along with other lawyers who helped. Mazy and Vicki are in a few. The smiles are utterly contagious.

I climb the stairs again to my penthouse. I live rent-free in a three-room apartment on the top floor. I won't describe the furnishings. It's fair to say that the two women in my life, Vicki and Mazy, won't go near the place. I average ten nights a month here and the neglect is evident. The truth is that my apartment would be even messier if I were a full-time resident.

I shower in my cramped bathroom, then fall across my bed.

AFTER TWO HOURS in a coma, I am awakened by noises downstairs. I get dressed and stumble forth. Mazy greets me with an enormous smile and a bear hug. "Congratulations," she says over and over.

"It was close, girl, damned close. Duke was eating his steak when we got the call."

"Did he finish it?"

"Of course."

Daniel, her four-year-old, runs over for a hug. He has no idea where I was last night or what I was doing, but he's always ready for a hug. Vicki hears voices and charges over. More hugs, more congratulations.

When we lost Albert Hoover in North Carolina we sat in Vicki's office and had a good cry. This is far better.

"I'll make some coffee," Vicki says.

Her office is slightly larger, and not cluttered with toys and folding tables stacked with games and coloring books, so we retire there for the debriefing. Since I was on the phone with both of them throughout last night's countdown, they know most of the details. I replay my meeting with Frankie, and we discuss the next step in Duke's case. Suddenly we have no deadlines there, no execution date, no dreaded countdown on the horizon, and the pressure is off. Death cases drag on for years at a glacial pace until there is an appointment with the needle. Then things get frantic, we work around the clock, and when a stay is issued we know that months and years will pass before the next scare. We never relax, though,

31

because our clients are innocent and struggling to survive the nightmare of prison.

We discuss the other four cases, none of which are facing a serious deadline.

I broach our most unpleasant issue when I ask Vicki, "What about the budget?"

She smiles as always and says, "Oh, we're broke."

Mazy says, "I need to make a phone call." She stands, pecks me on the forehead and says, "Nice work, Post."

The budget is something she prefers to avoid, and Vicki and I don't burden her with it. She steps out and returns to her office.

Vicki says, "We got the check from the Cayhill Foundation, fifty grand, so we can pay the bills for a few months." It takes about a half a million dollars a year to fund our operations and we get this by soliciting and begging small nonprofits and a few individuals. If I had the stomach for fund-raising I would spend half my days on the phone, and writing letters, and making speeches. There is a direct correlation between the amount of money we can spend and the number of innocent people we can exonerate, but I simply don't have the time or desire to beg. Vicki and I decided long ago that we could not handle the headaches of a large staff and constant pressure to raise money. We prefer a small, lean operation, and lean we are.

A successful exoneration can take many years and consume at least $200,000 in cash. When we need the extra money, we always find it.

"We're okay," she says, as always. "I'm working on grants and hounding a few donors. We'll survive. We always do."

"I'll make some calls tomorrow," I say. As distasteful as it is, I force myself to spend a few hours each week cold-calling sympathetic lawyers and asking for money. I also have a small network of churches I hit up for checks. We're not really a ministry as such, but calling ourselves one does not hurt our efforts.

Vicki says, "I assume you're going to Seabrook."

"I am. I've made my decision. We've kicked it around for three years and I'm sort of tired of the discussion. We're convinced he's innocent. He's been in prison for twenty-two years and has no lawyer. No one is working his case and I say we go in."

"Mazy and I are on board."

"Thanks." The truth is that I make the final decision about whether to take a case or pass. We evaluate a case for a long time and know the facts as intimately as possible, and if one of the three becomes adamantly opposed to our representation, then we back off. Seabrook has tormented us for a long time, primarily because we're certain our next client was framed.

Vicki says, "I'm roasting Cornish hens tonight."

"Bless you. I was waiting on an invitation." She lives alone and loves to cook, and when I'm in town we usually gather at her cozy little bungalow four blocks away and partake of a long meal. She worries about my health and eating habits. Mazy worries about my love life, which is nonexistent and therefore doesn't bother me at all.

5

The town of Seabrook is in the rural backwaters of north Florida, far away from the sprawling developments and retirement villages. Tampa is two hours to the south, Gainesville an hour to the east. Though the Gulf is only forty-five minutes away, on a two-lane road, the coastline there has never attracted the attention of the state's manic developers. With 11,000 people, Seabrook is the seat of Ruiz County and the center for most of the commercial activity in a neglected area. The population drain has been stymied somewhat by a few retirees attracted to cheap living in mobile home parks. Main Street hangs on, with few empty buildings, and there are even some large discount houses on the edge of town. The handsome, Spanish-style courthouse is well preserved and busy, and two dozen or so lawyers tend to the mundane legal business of the county.

Twenty-two years ago, one of them was found murdered in his office, and for a few months Seabrook made the only headlines in its history. His name was Keith Russo, age thirty-seven at the time of his death. His body was found on the floor behind his desk with blood everywhere. He had been shot twice in the head with a 12-gauge shotgun, and there wasn't much left of his face. The crime scene photos were grisly, even sickening, at least for some of the jurors. He was alone in his office working late that fateful December evening. Shortly before he died, the electricity to his office was cut off.

Keith had practiced law in Seabrook for eleven years with his partner and wife, Diana Russo. They had no children. In the early years of their firm, they had worked hard as general practitioners, but both wanted to step up their game and escape the dreariness of writing wills and deeds and filing no-fault divorces. They aspired to be trial lawyers and tap into the state's lucrative tort system. At that level, though, competition proved fierce and they struggled to land the big cases.

Diana was at the hair salon when her husband was murdered. She found his body three hours later when he didn't come home and wouldn't answer the phone. After his funeral, she became reclusive and mourned for months. She closed the office, sold the building, and eventually sold their home and returned to Sarasota, where she was from. She collected $2 million in life insurance and inherited Keith's interest in their joint assets. The life insurance policy was discussed by investigators but not pursued. Since the early days of their marriage the couple had believed strongly in life insurance protection. There was an identical policy on her life.

Initially there were no suspects, until Diana suggested the name of one Quincy Miller, a former client of the firm, and a very disgruntled one at that. Four years before the murder, Keith had handled a divorce for Quincy, and the client was less than satisfied with the result. The judge hit him for more alimony and child support than he could possibly afford, and it wrecked his life. When he was unable to pay more attorney's fees for an appeal, Keith dropped the matter, terminated his representation, and the deadline for the appeal expired. Quincy earned a good salary as a truck driver for a regional company but lost his job when his ex-wife garnished his paychecks for delinquent obligations. Unable to pay, he filed for bankruptcy and eventually fled the area. He was caught, returned to Seabrook, thrown in jail for nonpayment and served three months before the judge turned him loose. He fled again and was arrested for selling drugs in Tampa. He served a year before being paroled.

Not surprisingly, he blamed all of his problems on Keith Russo. Most of the town's lawyers quietly agreed that Keith could have been more assertive in his representation. Keith hated divorce work and considered it demeaning for an aspiring big-time trial lawyer. According to Diana, Quincy stopped by the office on at least two occasions, threatened the staff, and demanded to see his ex-lawyer. There was no record of anyone calling the police. She also claimed that Quincy called their home phone with threats, but they were never concerned enough to change numbers.

A murder weapon was never found. Quincy swore he had never owned a shotgun, but his ex-wife told the police that she believed he had one. The break in the case came two weeks after the murder when the police confiscated his car with a search warrant. In the trunk they found a flashlight with tiny specks of a substance splattered across the lens. They assumed it was blood. Quincy maintained that he had never seen the flashlight, but his ex-wife said she believed it belonged to him.

A theory was quickly adopted and the murder was solved. The police believed that Quincy carefully planned the attack and waited until Keith was working late and alone. He cut off the electricity at a meter box behind the office, entered through the unlocked rear door, and, since he had been in the office several times, knew exactly where to find Keith. Using a flashlight in the darkness, he burst into Keith's office, fired two shotgun blasts, and fled the scene. Given the amount of blood at the scene, it seemed reasonable that many items in the office got splattered.

Two blocks away on a side street, a drug addict named Carrie Holland saw a black man running away from the area. He appeared to be carrying a stick or something, she wasn't sure. Quincy is black. Seabrook is 80 percent white, 10 percent black, 10 percent Hispanic. Carrie could not identify Quincy but swore he was of the same height and build as the man she saw.

Quincy's court-appointed lawyer succeeded in getting a change of venue, and the trial took place in the county next door. It was 83 percent white. There was one black person on the jury.

The case revolved around the flashlight found in Quincy's trunk. A bloodstain-analysis expert from Denver testified that given the location of the body, and the probable line of fire from the shotgun, and the height of both the deceased and the assailant, and the sheer volume of blood found on the walls, floor, bookshelves, and credenza, he was certain that the flashlight was present at the shooting. The mysterious specks on its lens were described as "back spatter." They were too small to be tested, so there was no match with Keith's blood. Undaunted by this, the expert told the jury that the specks were definitely blood. Remarkably, the expert admitted that he had never actually seen the flashlight but had examined it "thoroughly" by studying a series of color photos taken by the investigators. The flashlight disappeared months before the trial.

Diana testified with certainty that her husband knew his ex-client well and was terrified of him. Many times he confided to her that he was afraid of Quincy, and even carried a handgun at times.

Carrie Holland testified and did everything but point a finger at Quincy. She denied she was being coerced into testifying for the prosecution, and denied she had been offered leniency on a pending drug charge.

While Quincy was awaiting trial, he was moved to a regional jail in Gainesville. No explanation was given for the transfer. He spent a week there and was returned to Seabrook. However, while away, he was put in a cell with a jailhouse snitch named Zeke Huffey who testified that Quincy had boasted of the killing and was quite proud of himself. Huffey knew the details of the murder, including the number of shots fired and the gauge of the shotgun. To spice up his testimony, he told the jury that Quincy laughed about driving to the coast the following day and tossing the shotgun into the Gulf. On cross-examination, Huffey denied cutting a deal with the prosecutor for leniency.

The investigator from the state police testified that none of Quincy's fingerprints were found at the scene, or on the meter box behind the office, and was allowed to speculate that "the assailant was probably wearing gloves."

A pathologist testified and presented large color photographs of the crime scene. The defense lawyer objected strenuously, claiming the photos were highly prejudicial, even inflammatory, but the judge allowed them anyway. Several of the jurors appeared to be shocked by the vivid images of Keith covered in blood with most of his face missing. The cause of death was obvious.

Because of his criminal record and other legal problems, Quincy did not take the stand. His lawyer was a rookie named Tyler Townsend, court-appointed and not yet thirty years old. The fact that he had never defended a capital murder client would have normally raised issues on appeal, but not in Quincy's case. His defense was tenacious. Townsend attacked every witness for the State and every piece of evidence. He challenged the experts and their conclusions, pointed out the flaws in their theories, and mocked the sheriff's department for losing the flashlight, the most important piece of evidence. He waved its color photos in front of the jury and questioned whether the specks on the lens were actually blood. He sneered at Carrie Holland and Zeke Huffey and called them liars. He suggested to Diana that she was not the innocent widow and made her cry on cross-examination, which didn't require much effort. He was repeatedly cautioned by the judge but remained unfazed. So zealous was his defense that the jurors often could not mask their contempt for him. The trial became a brawl as young Tyler rebuked the prosecutors, disrespected the judge, and harangued the State's witnesses.

The defense offered an alibi. According to a woman named Valerie Cooper, Quincy was with her at the time of the killing. She was a single mother who lived in Hernando, an hour south of Seabrook. She had met Quincy in a bar and their romance had been on and off. She claimed to be certain that Quincy had been with her, but on the stand she was intimidated and not credible. When the prosecutor brought up a drug conviction, she broke down.

In his passionate closing argument, Tyler Townsend used two props—a 12-gauge shotgun and a flashlight—and argued that it would have been almost impossible to fire two shots at the target while holding both. The jurors, mostly from rural areas, seemed to understand this, but it made little difference. Tyler was in tears as he begged for a not-guilty verdict.

He didn't get one. The jury wasted little time convicting Quincy of the murder. His punishment proved more complicated, as the jury got hung. Finally, after two days of intense and heated debate, the lone black held out for life with no parole. The eleven whites were disappointed that they could not return a death verdict.

Quincy's appeals ran their course and his conviction was unanimously affirmed at every level. For twenty-two years he has maintained his innocence, but no one is listening.

Young Tyler Townsend was devastated by the loss and never recovered. The town of Seabrook turned against him and his fledgling law practice dried up. Not long after the appeals were extinguished he finally gave up and moved to Jacksonville, where he worked as a part-time public defender before pursuing another career.

Frankie found him in Fort Lauderdale, where he seems to be living a pleasant life with a family and a good business developing shopping centers with his father-in-law. Approaching him will require care and forethought, something we do well.

Diana Russo never returned to Seabrook, and, as far as we know, never remarried. But we are not certain. Working with a private security group that we hire occasionally, Vicki found her a year ago living on the island of Martinique. For another chunk of money, our spies can dig deeper and give us more. For the moment, though, we can't justify the money. Trying to have a chat with her would be a waste of time.

Exonerating Quincy Miller is our goal. Finding the real killer is not a priority. To succeed at the former, we must unravel the State's case. Solving the crime is someone else's business, and after twenty-two years you can bet no one is working on it. This is not a cold case. The State of Florida got a conviction. The truth is irrelevant.

6

Quincy has spent the last eight years at a prison called Garvin Correctional Institute near the rural town of Peckham, about an hour north of the sprawl of Orlando. My first visit here was four months ago when I came as a priest doing prison ministry work. I wore my old black shirt and collar then. It's amazing how much more respect I get as a priest than as a lawyer, at least around prisons.

I'm wearing the collar again today, just to screw with them. Vicki has done the paperwork and I'm officially on record as Quincy's lawyer. The guard at the front desk studies the paperwork, studies my collar, has questions but is too confused to ask them. I surrender my cell phone, get cleared through the scanners, and then wait an hour in a dingy holding room where I flip through tabloid magazines and wonder once again what the world is coming to. They finally fetch me and I follow a guard out of the first building and along a sidewalk lined with fencing and razor wire. I've seen the inside of so many prisons I'm no longer shocked by their harshness. In so many awful ways they're all the same: squat concrete buildings with no windows, rec yards filled with men in matching uniforms killing time, scowling guards reeking of contempt because I'm a trespasser there to help the lowlifes. We enter another building and walk into a long room with a row of cubicles. The guard opens a door to one and I step inside.

Quincy is already there, on the other side of a thick plastic window. The door closes and we are alone. To make the visits as difficult as possible, there are no openings in the partition and we are forced to talk with bulky phones that date back at least three decades. If I want to pass a document to my client, I have to call a guard who first examines it and then walks it around to the other side.

Quincy smiles and taps his fist on the window. I return the salute and we have officially shaken hands. He's fifty-one now, and except for the graying hair he could pass for forty. He lifts weights every day, does karate, tries to avoid the slop they serve him, stays lean and meditates. He takes his phone and says, "First, Mr. Post, I want to thank you for taking my case." His eyes water immediately and he's overcome.

For at least the last fifteen years Quincy has not had a lawyer or any type of legal representative, not a soul out there in the free world working to prove his innocence. I know from my vast experience that this is a burden that is almost unbearable. A corrupt system locked him away, and there's no one fighting the system. His burdens are heavy enough as an innocent man, but with no voice he feels truly helpless.

I say, "You are indeed welcome. I'm honored to be here. Most of my clients just call me Post, so let's drop the 'mister' stuff."

Another smile. "Deal. And I'm just Quincy."

"The paperwork has been filed so I'm officially on board. Any questions about that?"

"Yeah, you look more like a preacher or something. Why are you wearing that collar?"

"Because I'm an Episcopal priest, and this collar has a way of getting more respect, at times."

"We had a preacher once who wore one of those. Never could understand why."

He was raised in the African Methodist Episcopal Church, and their ministers and bishops do indeed wear collars. He dropped out as a teenager. At eighteen he married his girlfriend because she was pregnant, and the marriage was never stable. Two other children followed. I know their names and addresses and places of employment, and I know that they haven't spoken to him since his trial. His ex-wife testified against him. His only brother is Marvis, a saint who visits him every month and sends him a small check occasionally.

Quincy is lucky to be alive. One black juror saved his life. Otherwise, he would have gone to death row at a time when Florida was enthusiastically killing folks.

As always, Guardian's file on him is thick and we know as much about him as possible.

"So what do we do now, Post?" he asks with a smile.

"Oh, we have a lot of work to do. We start with the scene of the crime and investigate everything."

"That was a long time ago."

"True, but Keith Russo is still dead, and the people who testified against you are still alive. We'll find them, try to gain their trust, and see what they're saying now."

"What about that snitch?"

"Well, surprisingly, the drugs haven't killed him. Huffey's back in prison, this time in Arkansas. He's spent nineteen of his forty years behind bars, all due to drugs. I'll go see him."

"You don't expect him to say he lied, do you?"

"Maybe. You never know with snitches. Professional liars have a way of laughing about their lies. Over his miserable career he's snitched in at least five other cases, all for sweetheart deals with the cops. He has nothing to gain by sticking to the lies he told your jury."

"I'll never forget when they brought that boy in, all cleaned up with a white shirt and tie. At first I didn't recognize him. It had been months since we were in the same cell. And when he started talking about my confession I wanted to scream at him. It was obvious the cops had fed him details of the crime—cutting off the electricity, using the flashlight—all that stuff. I knew right then that my ass was cooked. I looked at the jurors and you could tell they were eating it up. All of it. Every last lie he told. And you know what, Post? I sat there listening to Huffey and I thought to myself, 'Man, that guy swore to tell the truth. And the judge is supposed to make sure all witnesses tell the truth. And the prosecutor, he knows his witness is lying. He knows the guy cut a deal with the cops to save his ass. Everybody knew, everybody but those morons on the jury.'"

"I'm ashamed to say it happens all the time, Quincy. Jailhouse snitches testify every day in this country. Other civilized countries prohibit them, but not here."

Quincy closes his eyes and shakes his head. He says, "Well, when you see that sack-a-shit tell him I'm still thinking about him."

"Thinking about revenge is not helpful here, Quincy. It's wasted energy."

"Maybe so, but I have plenty of time to think about everything. You gonna talk to June?"

45

"If she'll talk."

"I bet she won't."

His ex-wife remarried three years after his trial, then divorced, then remarried again. Frankie found her in Tallahassee living as June Walker. Evidently, she eventually found some stability and is the second wife of Otis Walker, an electrician on the campus at Florida State. They live in a middle-class neighborhood that is predominantly black and have one child together. She has five grandchildren from her first marriage, grandchildren that Quincy has never seen even in a photo. Nor has he seen their three children since his trial. For him, they exist only as toddlers, frozen in time.

"Why shouldn't she talk to me?" I ask.

"Because she lied too. Come on, Post, they all lied, right? Even the experts."

"I'm not sure the experts thought they were lying. They just didn't understand the science and they gave bad opinions."

"Whatever. You figure that out. I know damned well June lied. She lied about the shotgun and the flashlight, and she lied when she told the jury I was somewhere around town the night of the murder."

"And why did she lie, Quincy?"

He shakes his head as if my question is foolish. He puts the phone down, rubs his eyes, then picks it up again. "We were at war, Post. Should've never got married and damned sure needed a divorce. Russo screwed me big-time in the divorce and suddenly I couldn't pay all that child support and alimony. She was out of work and in a bad way. When I got behind, she sued me again and again. The divorce was bad but not nearly as bad as what came after. We grew to thoroughly hate each other. When they arrested me for murder

I owed something like forty thousand bucks in payments. Guess I still do. Hell, sue me again."

"So it was revenge?"

"More like hatred. I ain't never owned a shotgun, Post. Check the records."

"We have. Nothing."

"See."

"But records mean little, especially in this state. There are a hundred ways to get a gun."

"Who you believe, Post, me or that lying woman?"

"If I didn't believe you, Quincy, I wouldn't be here."

"I know, I know. I can almost understand the shotgun, but why would she lie about that flashlight? I never saw it before. Hell, they couldn't even produce it at trial."

"Well, if we are assuming that your arrest, prosecution, and conviction were carefully planned to frame an innocent man, then we must assume the police leaned on June to say the flashlight belonged to you. And hatred was her motive."

"But how was I supposed to pay all that money from death row?"

"Great question, and you're asking me to get inside her mind."

"Oh, please don't go there. She's crazy as hell."

We both have a good laugh. He stands and stretches and asks, "How long you staying today, Post?"

"Three hours."

"Hallelujah. You know something, Post? My cell is six feet by ten, just about the same size as this little shithole we're in now. My cellie is a white boy from downstate. Drugs. Not a bad kid, not a bad cellie, but can you imagine spending ten hours a day living with another human in a cage?"

"No."

"'Course, we ain't said a word to each other in over a year."

"Why not?"

"Can't stand each other. Nothing against white folks, Post, but there are a lot of differences, you know? I listen to Motown, he likes that country crap. My bunk is neat as a pin. He's a slob. I don't touch drugs. He's stoned half the time. Enough of this, Post. Sorry to bring it up. I hate whiners. I'm so glad you're here, Post. You have no idea."

"I'm honored to be your lawyer, Quincy."

"But why? You don't make much money, do you? I mean, you can't make much representing people like me."

"We haven't really discussed fees, have we?"

"Send me a bill. Then you can sue me."

We laugh and he sits down, the phone cradled in his neck. "Seriously, who pays you?"

"I work for a nonprofit and, no, I don't make much. But I'm not in it for the money."

"God bless you, Post."

"Diana Russo testified that on at least two occasions you went to their office and threatened Keith. True?"

"No. I was in his office several times during my divorce but stopped going when the case was over. When he wouldn't talk to me on the phone, I went to the office one time, and, hell yes, I was thinking about taking a baseball bat and beating his brains out. But the little receptionist out front said he wasn't in, said he was in court. It was a lie because his car, a fancy black Jaguar, was parked behind the office. I knew she was lying and I started to make a scene, but didn't. I bit my tongue and left, never went back. I swear that's the truth, Post. I swear. Diana lied, like everybody else."

"She testified that you called their home several times and threatened him."

"More lies. Phone calls leave a trail, Post. I ain't that stupid. My lawyer, Tyler Townsend, tried to get the records from the phone company, but Diana blocked him. He tried to get a subpoena but we ran out of time during the trial. After I was convicted, the judge wouldn't approve a subpoena. We never got those records. By the way, have you talked to Tyler?"

"No, but he's on the list. We know where he is."

"Good dude, Post, a real good dude. That young man believed me and fought like hell, a real bulldog. I know you lawyers get a bad rap, but he was a good one."

"Any contact with him?"

"Not anymore, it's been too long. We wrote letters for years, even after he quit the law. He told me once in a letter that my case broke his spirit. He knew I was innocent, and when he lost my case he lost faith in the system. Said he couldn't be a part of it. He stopped by about ten years ago and it was a blessing to see him, but it also brought back bad memories. He actually cried when he saw me, Post."

"Did he have a theory about the real killer?"

He lowers the phone and looks at the ceiling, as if the question is too involved. He raises it again and asks, "You trust these phones, Post?"

It's against the law for the prison to eavesdrop on confidential talks between a lawyer and his client, but it happens. I shake my head. No.

"Neither do I," he says. "But my letters to you are safe, right?"

"Right." A prison cannot open mail related to legal matters, and it has been my experience that they don't try. It's too easy to notice if mail has been tampered with.

Quincy uses sign language to indicate he will put it in writing. I nod.

The fact that he has spent twenty-two years inside a prison where he is presumably safe from the outside, and is still worried, is revealing. Keith Russo was murdered for a reason. Someone other than Quincy Miller planned the killing, pulled it off with precision, then got away. What followed was a thorough framing that involved several conspirators. Smart guys, whoever they were, and are. Finding them may be impossible, but if I didn't think we could prove Quincy's innocence I wouldn't be sitting here.

They're still out there, and Quincy is still thinking about them.

The three hours pass quickly as we cover many topics: books—he reads two or three a week; my exonerees—he's fascinated by the ones we've freed; politics—he stays abreast with newspapers and magazines; music—he loves the 1960s stuff from Detroit; corrections—he rails against a system that does so little to rehabilitate; sports—he has a small color television and lives for the games, even hockey. When the guard taps on my door I say goodbye and promise to be back. We touch fists at the window and he thanks me again.

7

The Chevrolet Impala owned by Otis Walker is parked in an employees' lot behind a physical plant at the edge of campus. Frankie is parked nearby, waiting. It's a 2006 model, purchased used by Otis and financed through a credit union. Vicki has the records. His second wife, June, drives a Toyota sedan with no liens. Their sixteen-year-old son doesn't have his license yet.

At five minutes after 5:00 p.m., Otis emerges from the building with two coworkers and heads for the parking lot. Frankie gets out and checks a tire. The coworkers scatter and yell goodbye. As Otis is about to open his driver's door, Frankie materializes from nowhere and says, "Say, Mr. Walker, you got a second?"

Otis is immediately suspicious, but Frankie is a black guy with a pleasant smile and Otis is not the first stranger he's approached. "Maybe," he says.

Frankie offers his hand and says, "My name's Frankie Tatum and I'm an investigator for a lawyer out of Savannah."

Now Otis is even more suspicious. He opens the door, tosses in his lunch pail, closes the door and says, "Okay."

51

Frankie raises both hands in mock surrender and says, "I come in peace. I'm just looking for information about an old case."

At this point a white man would have been rebuffed, but Frankie appears harmless. "I'm listening," Otis says.

"I'm sure your wife has talked about her first husband, Quincy Miller."

The name causes a slight sag of the shoulders, but Otis is curious enough to continue for a moment. "Not much," he says. "A long time ago. Why are you involved with Quincy?"

"The lawyer I work for represents him. We're convinced Quincy got framed for that murder and we're trying to prove it."

"Good luck with that one. Quincy got what he deserved."

"Not really, Mr. Walker. Quincy is an innocent man who's served twenty-two years for somebody else's crime."

"You really believe that?"

"I do. So does the lawyer I work for."

Otis considers this for a moment. He has no record, has never been to prison, but his cousin is doing hard time for assaulting a police officer. In white America, prisons are good places where bad men pay for their crimes. In black America, they are too often used as warehouses to keep minorities off the streets.

Otis asks, "So who killed that lawyer?"

"We don't know, and may never know. But we're just trying to find the truth and get Quincy out."

"I'm not sure I can help you."

"But your wife can. She testified against him. I'm sure she's told you all about it."

Otis shrugs and glances around. "Maybe, but it was a long time ago. She hasn't mentioned Quincy's name in years."

"Can I talk to her?"

"Talk about what?"

"Her testimony. She didn't tell the truth, Mr. Walker. She told the jury that Quincy owned a 12-gauge shotgun. That was the murder weapon, and it was owned by somebody else."

"Look, I met June years after the murder. In fact, she had another husband before she met me. I'm number three, you understand? I know she had a rough time when she was younger but our life is pretty good right now. The last thing she wants is any trouble related to Quincy Miller."

"I'm asking for help, Otis. That's all. We got a brother wasting away in prison not two hours from here. The white cops and white prosecutor and white jury said he killed a white lawyer. Didn't happen that way."

Otis spits, leans on his door, and crosses his arms over his chest.

Frankie gently presses on. "Look, I served fourteen years in Georgia for somebody else's murder. I know what it's like, okay? I got lucky and got out, but I left some innocent guys behind. Guys like me and you. There's a lot of us in prison. The system's rigged against us, Otis. We're only trying to help Quincy."

"So what's June got to do with this?"

"Has she ever told you about the flashlight?"

Otis thinks for a second and shakes his head. Frankie doesn't want a gap in the conversation. "There was a flashlight with some blood on it. Cops said it came from the crime scene. Quincy never saw it, never touched it. June told the

jury he had one very similar to it. Not true, Otis. Not true.
She also told the jury that Quincy was somewhere around
Seabrook the night of the killing. Not true. He was with a
girlfriend an hour away."

Otis has been married to June for seventeen years. Frankie
is assuming he is quite aware of her struggles with the truth,
so why beat around the bush?

"You're calling her a liar?" Otis said.

"No, not now. But you said yourself she was a different
woman back then. She and Quincy were at war. He owed her
a bunch of money that he couldn't pay. The cops leaned on
her to take the stand and point the finger."

"A long time ago, man."

"Damned right. Ask Quincy about it. He's spent twenty-
two years in prison."

"Well, let's say she didn't tell the truth back then. You
expect her to admit it now? Come on."

"I just want to talk to her. I know where she works. I
could've gone there, but we don't operate that way. This is
not an ambush, Otis. I respect your privacy and I'm asking
you to run it by June. That's all."

"Feels like an ambush."

"What else could I do? Send an e-mail? Look, I'm leaving
town. You talk to her and see what she says."

"I know what she'll say. She ain't got nothing to do with
Quincy Miller."

"I'm afraid she does." Frankie hands him a Guardian Ministries business card. "Here's my phone number. I'm just asking for a favor, Otis."

Otis takes it and reads the front and back. "You with some
kinda church?"

"No. The guy who runs it is the lawyer who got me out of prison. He's a preacher too. Good guy. This is all he does, gets innocent folk out."

"White guy?"

"Yep."

"Must be a bad dude."

"You'd like him. So would June. Give us a chance, Otis."

"Don't bet on it."

"Thanks for your time."

"Don't mention it."

8

At Guardian, we have a collection of brochures we use for a variety of purposes. If our target is a white guy, I use the one with my smiling face front and center. With the collar. If we need to approach a white woman, we'll use Vicki's. Blacks get the one with Mazy arm-in-arm with a black exoneree. We like to say that skin color doesn't matter, but that's not always true. We often use it to open doors.

Since Zeke Huffey is white, I sent him my brochure with a chatty letter informing him that his plight has come to the attention of our little foundation and we're reaching out. Two weeks later, I received a handwritten letter on ruled notebook paper thanking me for my interest. I responded with my usual follow-up and asked if he needed anything. Not surprisingly, his next letter asked for money. I sent him a $200 MoneyGram with another letter asking if it's okay to visit him. Of course it's okay.

Zeke is a career criminal who has done time in three states. He is originally from the Tampa area but we have found no trace of his family. When he was twenty-five he married a woman who quickly divorced him when he was convicted of drug trafficking. As far as we know, he has no children, and we're assuming his visitors are scarce. Three years ago he got busted in Little Rock, Arkansas, and is currently doing five years in the Land of Opportunity.

His career as a snitch began with the trial of Quincy Miller. He was eighteen when he testified, and a month after the trial his drug charges were reduced and he walked. That deal worked so beautifully that he did it again and again. Every jail has a druggie facing more time and eager to avoid it. With the proper coaching from cops and prosecutors, a snitch can be quite effective with his perjury. Jurors simply cannot believe that a witness, any witness, will take the oath, swear to tell the truth, then tell them an outlandish story of pure fiction.

These days Zeke is doing time at a satellite prison in the middle of the cotton fields of northeastern Arkansas. I'm not sure why it is referred to as a satellite. It's a prison, with all the usual dreary architecture and fencing. Unfortunately, the facility is operated for profit by an out-of-state corporation, which means the guards earn even less and there are fewer of them, the terrible food is even worse, the commissary gouges the men on everything from peanut butter to toilet paper, and the medical care is almost nonexistent. I suppose that in America everything, including education and corrections, is fair game for profiteers.

I am led to a room with a row of enclosed booths for AT-TORNEY VISITS. A guard locks me inside. I take a seat and stare at a thick plastic divider. Minutes pass, then half an hour, but I'm in no hurry. The door on the other side opens and Zeke Huffey steps in. He offers me a smile as the guard removes the handcuffs. When we're alone he says, "Why are we in a lawyer's room?" He's looking at my collar.

"Nice to meet you, Zeke. Thanks for taking the time."

"Oh, I got plenty of time. Didn't know you were a lawyer."

"I'm a lawyer and a priest. How are they treating you here?"

He laughs and lights a cigarette. Of course the room has no ventilation. "I've seen my share of prisons and this has to be the worst," he says. "Owned by the state but leased to an outfit called Atlantic Corrections Corporation. Ever heard of them?"

"Yes. I've been a guest in several of their units. Seriously bad stuff, right?"

"Four bucks for a roll of toilet paper. Should be a dollar. They give us one roll per week, sandpaper that makes you limp when you walk. I guess I'm lucky you sent me that money. Thank you, Mr. Post. Some of my buddies never see a dime from the outside."

Hideous prison tattoos are crawling up his neck. His eyes and cheeks are sunken, the look of a street addict who's been stoned on cheap drugs for most of his life.

I say, "I'll send some more money when I can, but we operate on a pretty lean budget."

"Who is 'we' and why are you really here? A lawyer ain't gonna help me."

"I work for a nonprofit foundation dedicated to saving innocent men. One of our clients is Quincy Miller. Remember him?"

He chuckles and releases a cloud of smoke. "So you're here under false pretenses, huh?"

"You want me to leave?"

"Depends on what you want." As a career criminal, Zeke knows that the game has suddenly changed. I want something that only he possesses, and he's already thinking about how to capitalize. He has played this game before.

I say, "Let's start with the truth."

He laughs and says, "Truth, justice, and the American way. You must be a fool, Mr. Post, searching for the truth in a place like this."

"It's my job, Zeke. It's the only way I can get Quincy out of prison. You and I both know that you're an experienced snitch who lied to the jury at Quincy's trial. He never confessed to you. The details of the crime were fed to you by the cops and prosecutor who rehearsed your story with you. The jury bought it and Quincy has been locked up for twenty-two years. It's time to get him out."

He smiles as if he's only humoring me. "I'm hungry. Can you fetch me a Coke and some peanuts?"

"Sure." It's not unusual, even in a place like this, for visitors to buy snacks. I tap on my door and a guard eventually opens it. He and I walk to a wall of vending machines where I start shoving in quarters. Two bucks for a twelve-ounce soda, a dollar each for two small packs of peanuts. The guard takes me back to our room and a few minutes later reappears on Zeke's side and hands him the goodies. "Thanks," he says and takes a drink.

It's important to keep the conversation flowing, so I ask, "How did the cops convince you to testify against Quincy?"

"You know how they operate, Mr. Post. They're always looking for witnesses, especially when they got no proof. I don't remember all the details. It was a long time ago."

"Yes. It's certainly been a long time for Quincy. Do you ever think about him, Zeke? You know how bad prison is.

You ever stop and think that you helped put an innocent man behind bars for the rest of his life?"

"Not really. Been too busy doing other things, you know?"

"Don't know. Quincy has a chance of getting out. It's a long shot but then all of them are. This is my work, Zeke, and I know what I'm doing. We need your help."

"Help? What am I supposed to do?"

"Tell the truth. Sign an affidavit saying that you lied at trial and you did so because the cops and prosecutors offered you a sweet deal."

He crunches on a mouthful of peanuts and studies the floor. I press on. "I know what you're thinking, Zeke. You're thinking that Florida is far away and you have no desire to get involved in a case this old. You're thinking that if you come clean now with the truth then the cops and prosecutor will charge you with perjury and lock you up again. But that's not going to happen. The statute of limitations on perjury ran out a long time ago. Plus, they're all gone. The sheriff retired. The prosecutor did too. The judge is dead. The system back there has no interest in you whatsoever. You have nothing to gain and nothing to lose by helping Quincy get out. It's really a no-brainer, Zeke. Do the right thing, tell the truth, and your life goes on."

"Look, Mr. Post, I get out in seventeen months, and I'm not doing anything to screw that up."

"Arkansas doesn't care what you did in a Florida court-room twenty-two years ago. You didn't perjure yourself here. These guys couldn't care less. Once you're paroled, their only concern is filling your cell with the next man. You know how it all works, Zeke. You're a pro at this game."

He's stupid enough to smile at this compliment. He likes the idea of being in control. He sips his Coke, lights another cigarette, finally says, "I don't know, Mr. Post, it sounds awfully risky to me. Why should I get involved?"

"Why not? You have no loyalty to the cops and prosecutors. They don't care what happens to you, Zeke. You're on the other side of the street. Do something good for one of your own."

There is a long gap in the conversation. Time means nothing. He finishes one pack of peanuts and opens the second. He says, "Never knew of lawyers who do what you do. How many innocent people have you sprung?"

"Eight, in the past ten years. All innocent. We have six clients now, including Quincy."

"Can you get me out?" he says, and it strikes both of us as funny.

"Well, Zeke, if I thought you were innocent I might give it a shot."

"Probably a waste of your time."

"Probably so. Can you help us, Zeke?"

"When's all this going down?"

"Well, we're hard at work now. We investigate everything and build a case for innocence. But it's slow work, as you might guess. There's no real rush on your part, but I would like to keep in touch."

"You do that, Mr. Post, and if you find a few extra bucks pass them along. Peanuts and a Coke mean fine dining in this dump."

"I'll send some money, Zeke. And if you find a few extra minutes of time, think about Quincy. You owe him one."

"That I do."

9

Carrie Holland was nineteen years old when she told Quincy's jury that she saw a black man running down a dark street at the time of the murder. He was of the same height and build as Quincy and was carrying what appeared to be a stick, or something. She said she had just parked her car in front of an apartment building, heard two loud noises coming from the direction of the Russos' law office three blocks away, and saw a man running. On cross-examination, Tyler Townsend attacked. She didn't live in the apartment building but said she was there to visit a friend. The friend's name? When she hesitated, Tyler reacted with disbelief and mocked her. When he said, "Give me the friend's name and I'll call her as a witness," the prosecutor objected and the judge sustained. From the transcript, it appeared as though she couldn't remember a name.

Tyler zeroed in on the dark street, one without lighting. Using a map, he pinpointed the buildings and the distance from her car to the Russos' office and raised questions about her ability to see what she claimed she saw. He argued with her until the judge intervened and made him stop.

She had a drug charge from the year before and Tyler assaulted her with it. He asked her if she was under the influence on the witness stand and suggested that she was still struggling with addiction. He demanded to know if it was true that she had been dating a deputy on the Ruiz County police force. She denied this. When his cross-examination dragged on, the judge asked him to speed things along. When he protested that the prosecutor seemed to be taking his time, the judge threatened him with contempt, and not for the first time. When Tyler was finished with Carrie Holland he had raised doubts about her credibility, but he had also verbally abused her to the point of making her sympathetic to the jury.

Not long after the trial, Carrie left the area. She lived for a while near Columbus, Georgia, married a man there, had two kids, got a divorce and dropped out of sight. It took Vicki a year in one of her many desktop investigations to find the witness living as Carrie Pruitt in a remote part of western Tennessee. She works in a furniture factory near Kingsport, and lives off a county road in a mobile home she shares with a man called Buck.

To her credit, she has managed to stay out of trouble. Her rap sheet has only the drug conviction from Seabrook, one that was never expunged. We're assuming that Carrie is clean and sober, and in our business that's always a plus.

A month ago, Frankie eased into the area and did his usual reconnaissance. He has photos of her mobile home and the acreage around it, and of the factory where she is employed. Working with an investigator from Kingsport, he has learned that she has one son in the army and another living in Knoxville. Buck drives a truck and has no criminal record. Oddly

63

enough, his father once pastored a small rural church twenty miles from where they live. There could be an element of stability in the family.

There is also an excellent chance that neither Buck nor anyone else within five hundred miles knows much about her past. This complicates matters. Why should she revisit her brief encounter with Quincy Miller two decades earlier and upset her life now?

I meet Frankie at a pancake house in Kingsport, and over waffles we discuss the photos. The mobile home is remote with a fenced dog-run out back where Buck keeps some hounds. He drives the obligatory pickup. She has a Honda. Vicki has run the tag numbers and verified ownership. Neither is registered to vote. A nice bass boat sits under a shelter beside the trailer. Buck is obviously serious about his hunting and fishing.

"I don't like the looks of this place," Frankie says, shuffling the photos.

"I've seen worse," I say, and I certainly have. I've knocked on a lot of doors where I expected to be met by either a Doberman or a rifle. "But let's assume Buck doesn't know about her past, never heard of Quincy. If we assume that, then we can also assume she really would like to keep it quiet."

"Agreed. So stay away from the house."

"What time does she leave for work?"

"I don't know, but she punches in at eight, out at five, doesn't leave for lunch. Makes about nine bucks an hour. She's on an assembly line, not in an office, so you can't call her at work."

"And she won't talk around her coworkers. What's the weather forecast for Saturday?"

"Clear and sunny. Perfect day for fishing."

"Let's hope so."

AT DAYBREAK SATURDAY, Frankie is pumping gas at a convenience store a mile from the trailer. It's our lucky day, or so we think for a moment. Buck and a friend roll past towing the bass rig, headed for a lake or a river. Frankie calls me, and I immediately call the listed number of their land line.

A sleepy woman answers the phone. In a friendly voice I say, "Ms. Pruitt, my name is Cullen Post, and I'm a lawyer from Savannah, Georgia. Got a minute?"

"Who? What do you want?" The sleepiness vanishes.

"Cullen Post is my name. I'd like to talk to you about a trial you were involved in a long time ago."

"You got the wrong number."

"You were Carrie Holland back then and you lived in Seabrook, Florida. I have all the records, Carrie, and I'm not here to cause you any trouble."

"Wrong number, mister."

"I represent Quincy Miller. He's been in prison for twenty-two years because of you, Carrie. The least you can do is give me thirty minutes."

The line goes dead. Ten minutes later, I park in front of the trailer. Frankie is not far away, just in case I get shot.

Carrie finally comes to the door, opens it slowly, and steps onto the narrow wooden porch. She is slim and wearing tight jeans. Her blond hair is pulled back. Even with no makeup, she is not a bad-looking woman, but the years of nicotine have bunched lines of wrinkles around her eyes and mouth. She holds a cigarette and glares at me.

John Grisham

I'm wearing my collar but she is not impressed by it. I smile and say, "Sorry to barge in like this, but I just happened to be in the area."

"What do you want?" she asks and takes a puff.

"I want my client out of prison, Carrie, and that's where you come in. Look, I'm not here to embarrass or harass you. I'll bet Buck has never heard of Quincy Miller, right? Can't blame you for that. I wouldn't talk about it either. But Quincy is still serving hard time for a murder committed by someone else. He didn't kill anyone. You didn't see a black man running from the scene. You testified because the cops leaned on you, right? You had been dating one of them and so they knew you. They needed a witness and you had that little drug problem, right Carrie?"

"How'd you find me?"

"You're not exactly hiding."

"Get outta here before I call the law."

I raise my hands in mock surrender. "No problem. It's your property. I'm leaving." I toss a business card on the grass and say, "Here's my number. My job will not allow me to forget about you, so I'll be back. And I promise I will not blow your cover. I just want to talk, that's all, Carrie. You did a terrible thing twenty-two years ago and it's time to make it right."

She doesn't move, and watches me drive away.

THE LETTER FROM Quincy is handwritten in neat block letters. It must have taken him hours. It reads:

DEAR POST:

THANK YOU SIR ONCE AGAIN FOR TAKING MY CASE.
YOU CANNOT KNOW WHAT IT MEANS TO BE LOCKED UP

66

LIKE THIS WITH NO ONE OUT THERE BELIEVING IN YOU. I'M A DIFFERENT PERSON THESE DAYS, POST, AND IT'S ALL BECAUSE OF YOU. NOW GET TO WORK AND GET ME OUT OF HERE.

YOU ASKED ME IF MY WONDERFUL YOUNG LAWYER TYLER TOWNSEND HAD A THEORY ABOUT THE REAL MURDERER. HE DID. HE TOLD ME MANY TIMES THAT IT WAS WELL-KNOWN AROUND THAT PART OF FLORIDA THAT KEITH RUSSO AND HIS WIFE WERE INVOLVED WITH THE WRONG PEOPLE. THEY WERE LAWYERS FOR SOME DRUG DEALERS. THEY STARTED MAKING A LOT OF MONEY AND THIS GOT NOTICED. THERE AIN'T MUCH MONEY IN SEABROOK, NOT EVEN FOR LAWYERS, AND FOLKS BECAME SUSPICIOUS. THE HIGH SHERIFF, PFITZNER, WAS A CROOK HIMSELF AND TYLER SAID HE WAS IN ON THE DRUGS. PROBABLY IN ON THE KILLING TOO.

I KNOW THIS FOR A FACT, POST. SOMEBODY PUT THAT DAMNED FLASHLIGHT IN THE TRUNK OF MY CAR, AND I JUST KNOW IT WAS PFITZNER. THE WHOLE DEAL WAS ONE BIG FRAME JOB. THEY KNEW IT WOULD BE EASIER TO CONVICT A BLACK GUY IN SEABROOK THAN A WHITE ONE AND MAN THEY GOT THAT RIGHT.

A FRIEND SAID I SHOULD HIRE RUSSO FOR MY DIVORCE. BAD, BAD ADVICE. HE CHARGED ME TOO MUCH MONEY AND DID A TERRIBLE JOB. ABOUT HALFWAY THROUGH I COULD TELL HE DIDN'T WANT TO BE NO DIVORCE LAWYER. WHEN THE JUDGE HIT ME WITH ALL THAT ALIMONY AND CHILD SUPPORT I SAID TO RUSSO, MAN YOU GOTTA BE KIDDIN ME. NO WAY I CAN PAY ALL THAT. YOU KNOW WHAT HE SAID? SAID, YOU'RE LUCKY IT WASN'T MORE. THE JUDGE WAS A BIG CHURCH MAN

AND REALLY DISLIKED MEN WHO CHASED SKIRTS. MY
EX SAID I WAS SCREWING AROUND. RUSSO ACTED LIKE I
GOT WHAT I DESERVED.

RUSSO HIMSELF WAS A LADIES' MAN. ANYWAY,
ENOUGH OF THAT. HE'S DEAD.

TYLER DIDN'T KNOW WHY THEY KILLED RUSSO, BUT,
WHEN YOU'RE DEALING WITH A DRUG GANG YOU HAVE
TO FIGURE HE DOUBLE-CROSSED THEM IN SOME WAY.
MAYBE HE KEPT TOO MUCH OF THE MONEY. MAYBE HE
WAS SNITCHING. MAYBE HIS WIFE DIDN'T WANT TO LOSE
EVERYTHING THEY HAD. I MET HER A FEW TIMES WHEN
I WAS IN THE OFFICE AND DIDN'T LIKE HER. ONE TOUGH
GAL.

AFTER MY TRIAL, TYLER GOT THREATS AND HE
WAS REALLY SCARED. THEY FINALLY RAN HIM OUT OF
TOWN. HE SAID THERE WERE SOME BAD PEOPLE BACK
THERE AND HE WAS MOVING ON. YEARS LATER, AFTER
MY APPEALS WERE OVER, AND HE WASN'T MY LAWYER
ANYMORE, HE TOLD ME THAT A DEPUTY SHERIFF
GOT KILLED IN SEABROOK. SAID HE THOUGHT IT WAS
RELATED TO THE RUSSO MURDER AND THE DRUG GANGS.
BUT HE WAS ONLY SPECULATING BY THEN.

SO THERE IT IS, POST. TYLER'S THEORY OF WHO
REALLY KILLED RUSSO. AND HE ALSO THOUGHT THAT
RUSSO'S WIFE WAS PROBABLY INVOLVED TOO. BUT IT'S
TOO LATE TO PROVE ANY OF THAT.

THANKS AGAIN, POST. HOPE THIS IS HELPFUL AND I
HOPE TO SEE YOU SOON. GET BUSY.

YOUR CLIENT AND FRIEND, QUINCY MILLER.

10

The bloodstain expert who testified against Quincy was a former Denver homicide detective named Paul Norwood. After working crime scenes for a few years, he had decided to hand in his badge, buy a couple of nice suits, and become an expert witness. He had dropped out of college and did not have the time to pursue a degree in criminology or anything related to actual science, so he attended seminars and workshops on forensics, and he read books and magazine articles written by other experts. He was a smooth talker with a good vocabulary, and he found it easy to convince judges that he knew his stuff. Once qualified as a forensics expert, he found it even easier to convince unsophisticated jurors that his opinions were based on solid science.

Norwood was far from alone. In the 1980s and 1990s, expert testimony proliferated in the criminal courts as all manner of self-anointed authorities roamed the country impressing juries with their freewheeling opinions. To make matters worse, popular television crime shows portrayed forensic investigators as brilliant sleuths able to solve complex crimes with infallible science. The famous ones could practically look at a bloodied corpse and, within an hour or two, name the killer. In real life, thousands of criminal defendants were convicted and put away by shaky theories about bloodstains, blood spatter, arson, bite marks, fabrics, glass breakage, scalp and pubic hair, boot prints, ballistics, and even fingerprints.

Good defense lawyers challenged the credibility of these experts, but were rarely successful. Judges were often overwhelmed by the science and had little or no time to educate themselves. If a proffered witness had some training and seemed to know what he was talking about, he was allowed to testify. Over time, judges adopted the rationale that since a witness had been qualified as an expert in other trials in other states, then certainly he must be a genuine authority. Appellate courts got into the act by affirming convictions without seriously questioning the science behind the forensics, and thus bolstering the reputations of the experts. As résumés grew thicker, the opinions grew to encompass even more theories of guilt.

The more Paul Norwood testified, the smarter he became. One year before Quincy's trial in 1988, Norwood spent twenty-four hours in a bloodstain analysis seminar put on by a private company in Kentucky. He passed the course, was given a certificate to prove his knowledge, and added another field of expertise to his growing repertoire. He was soon impressing juries with his scientific knowledge of the many intricate ways blood is dispersed in a grisly crime. He specialized in blood, crime scene reconstruction, ballistics, and hair analysis. He advertised his services, networked with law enforcement and prosecutors, and even wrote a book on forensics. His reputation grew and he was in demand.

Over a twenty-five-year career, Norwood testified in hundreds of criminal trials, always for the prosecution and always implicating the defendant. And always for a nice fee.

Then DNA testing arrived and put a serious dent in his business. DNA testing not only changed the future of criminal investigations, it brought a fresh and devastating scrutiny to the junk science Norwood and his ilk had been peddling. In at least half of the DNA exonerations of innocent men and women, bad forensics have been the cornerstone of the prosecution's evidence.

In one year, 2005, three of Norwood's convictions were invalidated when DNA testing exposed his faulty methods and testimony. His three victims had spent a combined fifty-nine years in prison, one on death row. He retired under pressure after a single trial in 2006. On cross-examination, after giving his standard bloodstain analysis, he was discredited like never before. The defense lawyer painfully walked him through each of the prior year's three exonerations. The questioning was brilliant, brutal, and revealing. The defendant was found not guilty. The real killer was later identified. And Norwood called it quits.

However, the damage was done. Quincy Miller had long since been convicted because of Norwood's analysis of the bloody flashlight, which, of course, he had never seen. His razor-sharp analysis of the case consisted of reviewing large color photos of the crime scene and the flashlight. He never touched the most crucial piece of evidence, but rather relied on photos of it. Undaunted by this, he testified with certainty that the specks of blood on the lens were back spatter from the shotgun blasts that killed Keith Russo.

The flashlight disappeared before the trial.

*　　*　　*

NORWOOD REFUSES TO discuss the case with me. I've written him twice. He responded once and said he would not talk about it, not even on the phone. He claims he's in bad health; the case was a long time ago; his memory is failing; and so on. Not that a conversation would be that productive. As of now, at least seven of his convictions have been exposed as frauds and he is regularly used as the poster boy for junk science gone awry. Death penalty lawyers attack regularly. He's even been sued. Bloggers excoriate him for the misery he created. Appellate judges detail his wretched career. An innocence group is trying to raise a fortune in funds to review all of his cases, but that kind of money is hard to find. If given an audience, I would ask him to repudiate his work and try to help Quincy, but so far he has shown no sign of remorse.

With or without Norwood, we have no choice but to hire our own forensic scientists, and the best ones are expensive.

I'm in Savannah for a couple of days putting out fires. Vicki, Mazy, and I are in the conference room discussing forensics. On the table in front of us are four résumés, our final four. All are top criminologists with impeccable credentials. We'll start with two and send them the case. The cheapest wants $15,000 for a review and consultation. The most expensive gets $30,000 and there's no negotiating. As innocence work has intensified over the past decade, these guys have become highly sought-after by groups advocating for the wrongfully convicted.

Our top man is Dr. Kyle Benderschmidt at Virginia Commonwealth University in Richmond. He has taught for decades and has built one of the leading forensic science departments in the country. I've talked to other lawyers and they rave about him.

We try to keep $75,000 in a war chest to pay experts, private investigators, and lawyers when necessary. We don't like to pay lawyers, and over the years we have become quite convincing at begging sympathetic litigators to go pro bono. We have a loose network of them around the country. And some scientists will reduce their fees to help an innocent person, but that's rare.

Benderschmidt's standard rate is $30,000. "Do we have it?" I ask Vicki.

"Of course," she says with a smile, always the optimist. If we don't have it, she'll get on the phone and fire up some donors.

"Then let's hire him," I say. Mazy agrees. We move on to the second expert.

Mazy says, "Looks like you're off to another slow start on this one, Post. I mean, you've struck out with June Walker, Zeke Huffey, and Carrie Holland. So far nobody wants to talk to you."

As with any office, there is a fair amount of good-natured ribbing within Guardian. Vicki and Mazy get along well enough, though each gives the other a wide berth. When I'm in town I become an easy target. If we didn't love each other we would be throwing rocks.

I laugh and say, "No kidding. And please remind me of the last case where we got off to a fast start."

"We're a tortoise not a rabbit," Vicki says, offering one of her favorites.

I say, "Yep. It took us three years before we signed on. You want an exoneration in a month?"

"Just show us some progress," Mazy says.

"I haven't hit the charm button yet," I say.

Mazy smiles along. "When are you going to Seabrook?"

"Don't know. I'm putting it off as long as I can. No one there knows we're involved and I'd like to stay in the shadows."

"What's the level of fear?" Vicki asks.

"Hard to say but it's definitely a factor. If Russo got himself rubbed out by a drug gang, then those guys are still around. The killer is among them. When I show up, they'll probably know it."

"It sounds awfully risky, Post," Mazy says.

"It is, but there's risk in most of our cases, right? Our clients are in prison because someone else pulled the trigger. They're still out there, laughing because the cops nailed the wrong guy. The last thing they want is an innocence lawyer digging through the old case."

"Just be careful," Vicki says. It's obvious these two have worried at length behind my back.

"I'm always careful. Are you cooking tonight?"

"Sorry. Bridge."

"We're having frozen pizza," Mazy says. She dislikes cooking, and with four kids at home she relies heavily on the frozen food section.

"Is James around?" I ask. Mazy and her husband separated a few years back and attempted a divorce. It didn't work, but living together is not working either. She knows I truly care and I'm not being nosy.

"He comes and goes, spends some time with the kids."

"I pray for you guys."

"I know you do, Post. And we pray for you."

★   ★   ★

I DON'T KEEP food in my penthouse because it tends to rot from neglect. Since I can't squeeze a meal out of either of my colleagues, I work until after dark then go for a long walk through the old section of town. Christmas is two weeks away and the air is cool. I've been in Savannah for a dozen years but don't really know the city. I'm away too much to enjoy its charm and history, and it's difficult to foster friendships with a nomadic lifestyle. But my first friend is at home and looking for company.

Luther Hodges hired me out of seminary and enticed me to Savannah. He's retired now and his wife died a few years ago. He lives in a small cottage owned by the diocese, two blocks from Chippewa Square. He's waiting on the porch, eager to get out of the house.

"Hello Padre," I say as we embrace.

"Hello, my son," he says piously. Our standard greetings.

"You look thin," he says. He worries about my lifestyle— bad diet, little sleep, stress.

"Well, you certainly don't," I reply. He pats his stomach and says, "I can't stay away from the ice cream."

"I'm starving. Let's go."

We're on the sidewalk, arm in arm, strolling Whitaker Street. Luther is almost eighty now, and with each visit I notice he's moving a bit slower. He has a slight limp and needs a new knee but says replacement parts are for geezers. "You just can't let the old man in," is one of his favorite lines.

"Where have you been?" he asks.

"The usual. Here and there."

"Tell me about the case," he says. He is fascinated by my work and wants updates. He knows the names of Guardian's clients and follows any developments online.

I talk about Quincy Miller and our typical slow start. He listens carefully, and, as always, says little. How many of us have a true friend who loves what we do and is willing to listen for hours? I am blessed to have Luther Hodges.

I hit the high points without revealing anything confidential, and ask about his work. He spends hours each day writing letters to men and women behind bars. This is his ministry and he's committed to it. He keeps meticulous records and copies of all correspondence. If you're on Luther's list, you get letters along with birthday and Christmas cards. If he had money, he would send it all to prisoners.

There are sixty on his list at the moment. One died last week. A young man in Missouri hung himself, and Luther's voice breaks as he talks about it. The guy had mentioned suicide in a couple of letters and Luther was concerned. He called the prison numerous times looking for help but got nowhere.

We descend to the Savannah River and walk the cobblestone street near the water. Our favorite little bistro is a seafood joint that's been here for decades. Luther took me to lunch there on my first visit. At the door, he says, "My treat."

He knows my financial situation. "If you insist," I say.

11

VCU is a city campus and seems to occupy most of downtown Richmond. On a raw January afternoon, I make my way to the Department of Forensic Science on West Main Street. Kyle Benderschmidt has chaired the department for two decades and rules the place. His suite occupies an entire corner of the floor. A secretary offers coffee and I never decline. Students come and go. At exactly 3:00 p.m., the renowned criminologist appears and welcomes me with a smile.

Dr. Benderschmidt is in his early seventies, lean and energetic, and still dresses like the old frat boy he was back in the day. Starched khakis, penny loafers, a button-down shirt. Though he is in demand as an expert, he still loves the classroom and teaches two courses each semester. He does not like courtrooms and tries to avoid testifying. He and I both know that if we get as far as a retrial in Quincy's case, it will be years away. Typically, he reviews a case, prepares his findings, offers his opinions, and moves on to the next one as the lawyers go about their business.

I follow him into a small conference room. On the table is the stack of materials I sent him three weeks ago: photos and diagrams of the crime scene, photos of the flashlight, the autopsy report, and the entire trial transcript, almost 1,200 pages.

I wave at the paperwork and ask, "So what do you think?"

He smiles and shakes his head. "I've read everything and I'm not sure how Mr. Miller got convicted. But then this is not unusual. What really happened to the flashlight?"

"There was a fire in the storage unit where the cops stored evidence. It was never found."

"I know, I read that part too. But what really happened?"

"Don't know yet. We haven't investigated the fire and probably won't be able to."

"So, let's assume the fire was deliberate and somebody wanted the flashlight to disappear. There is no link to Miller without it. What do the police gain by destroying it and keeping it away from the jury?"

I feel like I'm a witness getting peppered on cross-examination. "Good question," I say and sip my coffee. "Since we're working with assumptions, then let's assume the police did not want a defense expert taking a close look at it."

"But there was no defense expert," he says.

"Of course not. It was an indigent defense case with a court-appointed lawyer. The judge refused to provide funds for an opposing expert. The cops probably anticipated this, but decided not to take a chance. They figured they could find a guy like Norwood who would be happy to analyze and speculate using only the photos."

"I suppose that makes sense."

"We're just guessing here, Dr. Benderschmidt. It's all we can do at this point. And maybe those little specks of blood belong to someone else."

"Precisely," he says with a smile, as if he's already figured out something. He takes an enlarged color photo of the two-inch flashlight lens. "We've examined this with all sorts of image enhancers. Me and some of my colleagues. I'm not even sure these specks are human blood, or blood at all."

"If they're not blood, then what are they?"

"It's impossible to tell. What is so troubling about this is that the flashlight was not recovered from the crime scene. We don't know where it came from or how the blood, if it's blood, made it to the surface of the lens. There is such a small sample to work with, it's impossible to determine anything."

"If it's back spatter, wouldn't the shotgun and even the killer be covered as well?"

"More than likely but we'll never know. Neither the shotgun nor the killer's clothing were recovered. But, we know it was a shotgun because of the buckshot. Two blasts in such a confined area will produce an enormous amount of blood. I guess the photos prove that. What is surprising is that there were no bloody footprints made by the killer as he left."

"There is no record of any."

"Then I'd say the killer went to great lengths to avoid detection. No fingerprints, so he probably wore gloves. No shoe or boot prints, so he probably had some type of covering on the soles of his feet. Sounds like a pretty sophisticated killer."

"It could've been a gang killing, by a professional."

"Well, that's your business. I can't go there."

"Is it possible to fire a shotgun with one hand while holding the flashlight with the other?" I ask, though the answer is fairly obvious.

"Highly unlikely. But it's a small flashlight with a two-inch lens. It would be possible to hold the flashlight in one hand and use that same hand to steady the forestock of the shotgun. That's assuming you buy into the prosecution's theory. But I doubt seriously that the flashlight was at the scene."

"But Norwood testified that this is blood on the flashlight and it is back spatter."

"Norwood was wrong again. He should be locked up himself."

"So your paths have crossed?"

"Oh yes. Twice. I've debunked two of his convictions, though both men are still in prison. Norwood was well-known in the business back in his heyday, just one of many. Mercifully he quit, but there are plenty of these guys still out there, still at it. It makes me sick."

Benderschmidt has been vociferous in his criticism of the one-week seminars in which police officers, investigators, anyone, really, with enough money for the tuition, can be trained quickly, get a graduation certificate, and declare themselves experts.

He continues, "It was grossly irresponsible for him to tell the jury that these specks are blood that came from Russo's body." He shakes his head in disbelief and disgust. "There is simply no scientific way to prove it."

Norwood told the jury that back spatter cannot travel more than forty-eight inches through the air, a common belief back then. Therefore, the barrel was close to the victim. Not so, says Benderschmidt. The distance blood travels varies greatly with each shooting, and for Norwood to be so precise was flat out wrong. "There are just far too many variables involved here to give opinions."

"So what's your opinion?"

"That there is no scientific basis for what Norwood told the jury. That there is no way to know if the flashlight was even at the scene. That there is an even chance that these specks of blood are not even blood. Lots of opinions, Mr. Post. I'll dress 'em all up in beautiful language that leaves no doubt."

He looks at his watch and says he needs to take a call. He asks if I mind. Of course not. While he's gone, I pull out some notes, some questions that I cannot answer. Neither can he, but I value his thoughts. I'm certainly paying for them. He returns in fifteen minutes with a cup of coffee.

"So what's bugging you?" I ask. "Forget the science and let's do some speculating."

"That's almost as much fun as the science," he says with a grin. "Question one: If the police planted the flashlight in the trunk of Miller's car, why didn't they go ahead and plant the shotgun too?"

I've asked myself the same question a hundred times. "Maybe they were worried about proving he owned it. I'm sure it was not registered. Or maybe it would have been harder to plant in his trunk. The flashlight is much smaller and easier to simply place there. Pfitzner, the sheriff, testified that he found it when he was searching the trunk. There were other cops at the scene."

He listens intently and nods along. "That's plausible."

"It would have been easy to simply pull the flashlight out of a pocket and drop in the trunk. Not so with a shotgun."

He keeps nodding. "I can buy that. Next question: According to the snitch, Miller said he drove to the Gulf the next day and tossed the shotgun into the ocean. Why wouldn't he have tossed the flashlight too? Both were at the

81

crime scene. Both had blood on them. It makes no sense not to dispose of both."

I respond, "I have no answer to that and it's a huge gap in the fiction the cops fed to the snitch."

"And why the ocean where the water is shallow and the tides rise and fall?"

"It makes no sense," I say.

"It does not. Next question: Why use a shotgun? They make too much noise. The killer got lucky when no one heard the blasts."

"Well, Carrie Holland said she heard something, but she's not credible. They used a shotgun because that's what a guy like Miller would have used, maybe. A pro would have used a pistol with a silencer, but they weren't framing a pro. They wanted Miller."

"Agreed. Did Miller have a history of hunting?"

"None whatsoever. Says he never hunted in his life."

"Did he own guns?"

"He says he kept two pistols in the house for protection. His wife testified that he owned a shotgun, but she's not credible either."

"You're pretty good, Post."

"Thanks. I've had some experience on the streets. So have you, Dr. Benderschmidt. Now that you know the case, I'd like to hear your version of educated guessing. Put the science aside and tell me how this murder happened."

He gets to his feet and steps to a window for a long gaze. "There's a brain at work here, Mr. Post, and that's why you're not likely to solve this crime, short of a miracle. Diana Russo told a convincing story of the conflict between Miller and her husband. I suspect she exaggerated, but the jury believed her. She pointed to a black guy in a white town. And one with a motive, at that. They, the conspirators, knew enough about crime scene evidence to use the flashlight as the link to Miller. The real killer left behind no traceable clues, which is remarkable and says a lot about his high level of planning. If he did make a mistake, the cops missed it or perhaps covered it up. After twenty-two years, it is indeed a cold case, and one that looks impossible to solve. You won't find the killer, Mr. Post, but you might succeed in proving your client innocent."

"Is there a chance he's guilty?"

"So you have doubts?"

"Always. The doubts keep me awake at night."

He returns to his chair and takes a sip of coffee. "I don't see it. Motive is weak. Sure, he may have hated his former lawyer, but blowing his head off is a sure ticket to death row. Miller had an alibi. There is nothing that links him to the crime scene. My best educated guess is that he didn't do it."

"That's good to hear," I reply with a smile. He is no bleeding-heart and has testified for the prosecution more than the defense. He shoots straight and is not afraid to criticize another expert, even a colleague, when he disagrees. We spend a few minutes talking about other famous bloodspatter cases, and it's soon time to leave.

"Thanks, Doctor," I say as I gather my things. "I know your time is valuable."

"You're paying for it," he says with a smile. Yep, $30,000.

As I open the door, he says, "One last thing, Mr. Post, and this is even farther from my expertise, but that situation down there could get sticky. None of my business, you know, but you'd better be careful."

"Thanks."

12

My travels take me to the next prison on my little check-list. It's called Tully Run and it's hidden at the foot of the Blue Ridge Mountains in the western part of Virginia. This is my second visit here. Because of the Internet, there are now hundreds of thousands of convicted sex offenders. For many reasons, they do not fare well in general prison populations. Most states are trying to segregate them into separate facilities. Virginia sends most of its to Tully Run.

The man's name is Gerald Cook. White male, age forty-three, serving twenty years for molesting his two stepdaughters. Because I have so many other clients to choose from, I have always tried to avoid sex offenders. However, in this line of work I've learned that some of them are actually innocent.

In his younger days, Cook was a wild man, a hard-drinking redneck prone to brawling and chasing women. Nine years ago he caught the wrong one and married her. They spent a few rough years together taking turns moving in and out. Both had trouble keeping jobs and money was always an issue. A week after his wife filed for divorce, Gerald won $100,000 in the Virginia State Lottery and tried to keep it quiet. She heard about it almost immediately and her lawyers got excited. Gerald fled the area with his loot and the divorce dragged on. To get his attention, and at least some of the money, she conspired with her daughters, then ages eleven and fourteen, to accuse him of sexual abuse, crimes that had never been mentioned. The girls signed sworn written statements detailing a pattern of rape and molestation. Gerald was arrested, thrown in jail with an exorbitant bond, and has never stopped claiming he is innocent.

In Virginia, it is difficult to defend such charges. At his trial, both girls took the stand, and in wrenching testimony described the horrible things their stepfather had allegedly done. Gerald countered with his own testimony but, being a hothead, made a poor witness. He was sentenced to twenty years. By the time he left for prison, his lottery winnings were long gone.

Neither stepdaughter finished high school. The older has led a life of astonishing promiscuity, and, at the age of twenty-one, is in her second marriage. The younger has a child and works for minimum wage at a fast-food restaurant. Their mother owns a beauty salon on the outskirts of Lynchburg, and has a big mouth. Our investigator there has affidavits from two former clients who describe the woman constantly telling hilarious stories of framing Gerald with the bogus charges. We also have an affidavit from a former boyfriend with similar stories. She frightened him so bad he moved out.

Cook came to our attention two years ago with a letter from prison. We receive about twenty per week, and the backlog is frustrating. Vicki, Mazy, and I spend as much time as possible reading them and trying to weed out the ones we cannot help. The vast majority are from guilty inmates who have plenty of time to work on their claims of innocence and write long letters. I travel with a stack that I read when I should be sleeping. At Guardian, we have a policy of answering every letter.

Cook's story sounded plausible and I wrote back. We swapped a few letters and he sent his trial transcript and file. We did a preliminary investigation and became convinced that he was probably telling the truth. I visited him a year ago and disliked him immediately. He confirmed what I had learned through our correspondence: he is obsessed with thoughts of revenge. His goal is to get out and either do bodily harm to his ex-wife and her daughters, or, more likely, to frame them on drug charges and see them locked up. He dreams of one day visiting them in prison. I have tried to temper this by explaining that we have expectations of our clients once they are free, and that we will not be involved with anyone plotting retribution.

Most of the inmates I visit in prison are subdued and thankful for the face time. But, again, Cook is belligerent. He sneers at me through the Plexiglas, grabs the phone and says, "What's taking so long, Post? You know I'm innocent, now get me out of here."

I smile and say, "Nice to see you, Gerald. How are you doing?"

"Don't give me that happy horseshit, Post. I want to know what you're doing out there while I'm stuck in here with a bunch of perverts. I've been fighting these fairies off for seven years now and I'm damned tired of it."

Calmly I say, "Gerald, perhaps we should start over with this session. You're already yelling at me and I don't appreciate it. You're not paying me. I'm a volunteer. If you can't keep things pleasant then I'll leave."

He lowers his head and starts crying. I wait patiently as he tries to collect himself. He wipes both cheeks on his sleeves and doesn't make eye contact.

"I am so innocent, Post," he says, his voice cracking.

"I believe that or I wouldn't be here."

"That bitch put those girls up to lying and all three are still laughing about it."

"I believe that, Gerald. I really do, but getting you out will take a long time. There is simply no way to speed things along. As I told you before, it's fairly easy to convict an innocent man and virtually impossible to exonerate one."

"This is so wrong, Post."

"I know, I know. Here's my problem right now, Gerald. If you walked out tomorrow, I'm afraid you would do something really stupid. I've cautioned you many times about harboring thoughts of revenge, and if that's still on your mind, then I'm not getting involved."

"I won't kill her, Post. I promise. I won't do something stupid enough to get my ass thrown back into a place like this."

"But?"

"But what?"

"But what might you do, Gerald?"

"I'll think of something. She deserves to do some time after what she's done to me, Post. I can't just let it go."

"You have to let it go, Gerald. You have to go somewhere far away and forget about her."

"I can't do it, Post. I can't keep my mind off that lying bitch. And her two daughters. I hate them with every bone in my body. Here I sit, an innocent man, and they're going about their lives laughing at me. Where is the justice?"

Because I am cautious out of necessity, I am not yet his attorney. Though Guardian has spent almost $20,000 and two years investigating, we are not officially involved. He worried me from the beginning and I've kept the escape hatch open.

"You still want revenge, don't you, Gerald?"

His lip quivers and his eyes water again. He glares at me and nods yes.

"I'm sorry, Gerald, but I'm saying no. I will not represent you."

He suddenly erupts in a fit of rage. "You can't do that, Post!" he screams into the phone, then flings it and lunges at the Plexiglas partition. "No! No! You can't do that, dammit! I'll die in here!" He begins slapping the Plexiglas.

I am startled and move back.

"You gotta help me, Post! You know I'm innocent! You can't just walk out of here and leave me to die. I'm innocent! I'm innocent and you damned well know I'm innocent!"

The door behind me jerks open and a guard steps in. "Sit down," he yells at Gerald who is pounding the Plexiglas with his fists on the other side. The guard yells at him as the door behind him opens and another guard appears. He grabs Gerald and pushes him away from the partition. As I ease through the door to escape he's screaming, "I'm innocent, Post! I'm innocent."

I can almost hear him as I drive away from Tully Run.

FOUR HOURS LATER I enter the grounds of the North Carolina Correctional Institute for Women (NCCIW) in Raleigh. The parking lot is full and, as always, I grumble about the money spent on corrections in this country. It's a huge business, quite literally a profit-maker in some states, but certainly a big employer for any community lucky enough to get itself a prison. In the U.S. there are over two million people locked up, and it takes one million employees and $80 billion in tax dollars to take care of them.

NCCIW should be closed, like all women's prisons. Very few women are criminals. Their mistakes are picking bad boyfriends.

North Carolina sends its female death row inmates to NCCIW. There are seven of them now, including our client, Shasta Briley. She was convicted of murdering her three children about twenty miles from where she is now incarcerated.

Hers is another sad story of a kid who never had a chance. She was a crack baby who was bounced from foster homes to orphanages to in-laws in the projects. She dropped out of school, had a baby, lived with an aunt, worked here and there for minimum wages, had another baby, became an addict. After her third child was born, she got a break and found a room in a homeless shelter where a counselor helped her get clean. A man from a church gave her a job and sort of adopted her and the kids, and she moved into a small rental duplex. Every day was a struggle, though, and she was arrested for bad checks. She sold her body for cash, and then began selling drugs.

Her life was a nightmare; thus, she was easy to convict.

Eight years ago her duplex caught on fire in the middle of the night. She escaped through a window, with cuts and burns, and ran around the outside of the house screaming as neighbors rushed to help. Her three daughters perished in the fire. The community rallied around her after the tragedy. The funeral was gut-wrenching and made the local news. Then the state arson investigator came to town. When he mentioned the word "arson," all sympathy for Shasta vanished.

At her trial, the State proved that she had been busy buying insurance in the months before the fire: three policies of $10,000 for the life of each child, and a $10,000 policy on the contents of her duplex. A relative testified that Shasta had offered to sell her the children for $1,000 each. The arson expert was clear with his opinions. Shasta had plenty of baggage: a criminal record, three children by three different men, and a history of drug use and prostitution. At the scene, her neighbors had told the police that she tried to enter the burning duplex but the flames were too much. She was covered in blood, had burns on her hands, and was frantic out of her mind. However, once the arson theory was circulated, most of the neighbors backed off. At trial, three of them told the jury that she had seemed unconcerned as the fire raged. One was allowed to speculate that she was probably stoned.

Seven years later, she spends her days alone in a cell with little human contact. Sex is the currency in a women's prison, but so far the guards have left her alone. She is frail, eats little, reads the Bible and old paperbacks for hours, and speaks in a soft voice. We talk through a screen, so phones are not necessary. She thanks me for coming and asks about Mazy.

With four kids, Mazy seldom leaves Savannah, but she has visited here twice and has bonded with Shasta. They swap letters weekly and talk by phone once a month. By now, Mazy knows more about arson than most experts.

"Got a letter from Mazy yesterday," she says with a smile. "Sounds like her kids are doing well."

"Her kids are doing great."

"I miss my kids, Mr. Post. That's the worst thing of all. I miss my babies."

Today time is not important. Here they allow the lawyers to stay as long as we want, and Shasta enjoys being out of her cell. We talk about her case, Mazy's children, the weather, the Bible, books, anything that interests her. After an hour I ask, "Have you read the report?"

"Every word, twice. Sounds like Dr. Muscrove knows his stuff."

"Let's hope so." Muscrove is our arson expert, a genuine scientist who has thoroughly debunked the State's investigation. He is of the firm opinion that the fire was not deliberate. In other words, there was no crime at all. But getting his report in the hands of a sympathetic judge will be difficult. Our best shot will be an eleventh-hour pardon from the Governor, another unlikely scenario.

As we talk, I remind myself that this is a case we will probably lose. Of our six current clients, Shasta Briley has the worst chance of survival.

We try to talk about Muscrove's report, but the science is often overwhelming, even for me. She drifts back to the latest romance novel she's read, and I happily go along. I am often amazed at how literate some of these inmates become during their incarcerations.

A guard reminds me that it's late. We've been chatting for three hours. We touch hands at the screen and say goodbye. As always, she thanks me for my time.

13

At the time of the Russo murder, Seabrook's police chief was Bruno McKnatt, who, according to our research, apparently had little to do with the investigation. In Florida, the county sheriff is the principal law enforcement official and can assume jurisdiction over any crime, even those within municipalities, though in the larger cities the police departments run things. Russo was murdered inside the city limits of Seabrook, but McKnatt was shoved aside by Bradley Pfitzner, the longtime sheriff.

McKnatt was police chief from 1984 through 1990, then moved on to police work in Gainesville. There his career sputtered and he tried selling real estate. Vicki found him in a low-end retirement village called Sunset Village near Winter Haven. He is sixty-six and drawing two pensions, one from Social Security, the other from the State. He is married with three adult children scattered around south Florida. Our file on McKnatt is thin because he had little to do with the investigation. He did not testify at trial and his name is barely mentioned.

Contacting McKnatt is my first real foray into Seabrook. He is not from the town and spent only a few years there. I am assuming he left behind few contacts and had little interest in the murder. I called him the day before I arrived and he seemed willing to talk.

Sunset Village is a series of neat circles of tidy mobile homes around a central community center. Each home has a shade tree beside a concrete driveway, and each vehicle is at least ten years old. The residents seem eager to escape the confines of their cramped quarters and there is a lot of porch sitting and socializing. Many of the trailers have jerry-rigged ramps for wheelchairs. As I loop around the first circle, I am carefully observed. A few of the old folks offer friendly waves but most stare at my Ford SUV with Georgia plates as if noting the intrusion of a trespasser. I park near the community center and watch for a moment as some elderly men slowly go about a game of shuffleboard under a large pavilion. Others are playing checkers, chess, and dominoes.

At sixty-six, McKnatt is definitely on the younger side of this population. I spot him wearing a blue Braves baseball cap and walk over. We sit at a picnic table near a wall with dozens of posters and bulletins. He's overweight but seems to be in decent shape. At least he's not on oxygen.

He says, somewhat defensively, "I like it here, lots of good people who take care of each other. No one has any money so there's no pretense. We try to stay active and there's plenty to do."

I offer something banal, like it seems to be a nice place. If he's suspicious he doesn't appear so. He wants to talk and seems proud to have a visitor. I walk him through his career in law enforcement for a few minutes, and he finally gets to the point.

"So why are you interested in Quincy Miller?"

"He's my client and I'm trying to get him out of prison."

"Been a long time, hasn't it?"

"Twenty-two years. Did you know him?"

"No, not till the murder."

"Were you at the crime scene?"

"Of course I was. Pfitzner was already there, got there pretty fast, and he asked me to take Ms. Russo home. She'd found the body, you know, and called 911. Poor lady was a mess, as you might guess. I drove her home and sat with her until some friends came over, it was awful, then I went back to the scene. Pfitzner was in charge, as always, and he was barking orders. I said I thought we should call the state police, which is what we were supposed to do, but Pfitzner said he would do it later."

"Did he?"

"The next day. He took his time. He didn't want anybody else working the case."

"What was your relationship with Pfitzner?" I ask.

He smiles but not in a pleasant way. "I'll be honest with you," he says, as if he has been dishonest so far. "Pfitzner got me fired, so I have no use for the man. He'd been the sheriff for twenty years when the town hired me as chief, and he never respected me or any officer in my department. He had an iron grip on the county and didn't want anybody else with a badge trespassing on his turf. That's just the way it was."

"Why did he get you fired?"

McKnatt grunts and watches the old men play shuffleboard. He finally shrugs and says, "You gotta understand small-town politics. I had about a dozen men, Pfitzner had twice that. He had a big budget, whatever he wanted, and I got the leftovers. We never got along because he saw me as a threat. He fired a deputy, and when I hired the guy Pfitzner got pissed. All the politicians were afraid of him and he pulled some strings, got me sacked. I couldn't leave town fast enough. You been to Seabrook?"

"Not yet."

"You won't find much. Pfitzner's been gone for a long time and I'm sure all his tracks are covered."

It is a loaded statement, as if he wants me to jump in, but I let it slide. This is the first meeting, and I don't want to seem too eager. I have to build trust and that takes time. Enough of Sheriff Pfitzner. I'll circle back in due course.

"Did you know Keith Russo?" I ask.

"Sure. I knew all the lawyers. It's a small town."

"What was your opinion of him?"

"Smart, cocky, not one of my favorites. He roughed up a couple of my men once in a trial and I didn't like it. Guess he was just doing his job. He wanted to be a big-shot lawyer and I guess he was on his way. One day we looked up and he was driving a sleek new black Jaguar, probably the only one in town. Rumor was he settled a big case down in Sarasota and made a killing. He was flashy like that."

"And his wife, Diana?"

He shakes his head as if in pain. "Poor lady. I guess I'll always have a soft spot for her. Can you imagine what she went through finding his body like that? She was a mess."

"I cannot. Was she a good lawyer?"

"Well regarded, I guess. I never had dealings with her. A knockout, though, a real beauty."

"Did you watch the trial?"

"No. They moved it next door to Butler County, and I couldn't justify taking time off to sit through a trial."

"At the time, did you think Quincy Miller committed the murder?"

He shrugs, says, "Sure. I never had any reason to doubt it. As I recall, there was a pretty strong motive for the killing, some bad blood. Wasn't there a witness who saw him running away from the scene?"

"Yes, but she didn't make a positive ID."

"Didn't they find the murder weapon in Miller's car?"

"Not exactly. They found a flashlight with some blood on it."

"And the DNA matched, right?"

"No, there was no DNA testing in 1988. And the flashlight disappeared."

He thinks about this for a moment and it's obvious he doesn't remember the important details. He left Seabrook two years after the murder and has tried to forget the place. He says, "I always thought it was an open-and-shut case. I suppose you think otherwise, right?"

"I do, or else I wouldn't be here."

"So what makes you think Miller's innocent after all these years?"

I'm not about to share my theories, not at this point anyway. Maybe later. I reply, "The State's case doesn't hold up," I say vaguely, then move on with "Did you maintain any contacts in Seabrook after you left?"

He shakes his head. "Not really. I wasn't there very long and, as I said, sort of left in a hurry. It was not the highlight of my career."

"Did you know a deputy named Kenny Taft?"

"Sure, knew 'em all, some better than others. When he got killed I read about it in the newspapers. I was in Gainesville doing narcotics. I remember his photo. Good guy. Why are you curious about him?"

"Right now, Mr. McKnatt, I'm curious about everything. Kenny Taft was the only black deputy working for Pfitzner."

"Drug thugs don't care if you're black or white, especially in a gun battle."

"You're right about that. Just curious if you knew him."

An elderly gent in shorts, black socks, and red sneakers approaches and sets two paper cups of lemonade on our table. McKnatt says, "Well, thank you, Herbie. It's about time."

Herbie snaps, "I'll send you the bill," and moves on. We sip our drinks and watch the slow-motion shuffleboard.

McKnatt asks, "So, if your boy Miller didn't kill Russo, who did?"

"I have no idea, and we'll probably never know. My job is to prove Miller didn't do it."

He shakes his head and smiles. "Good luck. If somebody else did it, then he's had twenty-plus years to run away and hide. Talk about a cold case."

"Ice cold," I agree with a smile. "But then all of my cases are like this."

"And this is all you do? Solve old cases and get people out of prison?"

"That's it."

"How many?"

"Eight, in the past ten years."

"And all eight were innocent?"

"Yes, as innocent as you and me."

"How many times have you found the real killer?"

"Not all were murders, but in four of the cases we identified the guilty parties."

"Well, good luck with this one."

"Thanks. I'll need it." I move the conversation to sports. He's a real Gators fan and proud that his basketball team is winning. We touch on the weather, retirement, a bit of politics. McKnatt is not the sharpest guy I've met and seems to have little interest in Russo's murder.

After an hour, I thank him for his time and ask if I can come back. Certainly, he says, eager to have a visitor.

Driving away, I'm struck by the fact that he offered no warning about Seabrook and its shady history. Though he clearly has no affection for Sheriff Pfitzner, he did not offer the slightest hint of corruption.

There is more to his story.

14

Two months into a slow start, we get our first break. It comes with a phone call from Carrie Holland Pruitt, and she wants to talk. I leave before dawn on a Sunday morning and drive six hours to Dalton, Georgia, about halfway between Savannah and Kingsport, Tennessee. The truck stop is just off Interstate 75 and it's one I've been to before. I park with a view of the entrance and wait on Frankie Tatum. We chat on the phone and twenty minutes later he parks near me. I watch as he enters the restaurant.

Inside he selects a booth near the rear and orders coffee and a sandwich and opens a newspaper. On the table next to the wall is the usual assortment of condiments and a dispenser with paper napkins. With the newspaper as a shield, he removes the salt and pepper shakers and replaces them with our own versions, cheap stuff from any grocery store. At the bottom of our salt shaker is a recording device. When his sandwich arrives, he sprinkles some salt to make sure there is nothing suspicious. He texts me and says all is well, the place is not that crowded.

At 1:00 p.m., our agreed-upon meeting time, I text Frankie and tell him to eat slow. There is no sign of either

Buck's pickup or Carrie Pruitt's Honda. I have their color photos in my file and I've memorized their Tennessee license plate numbers. At 1:15, I watch the truck slow on the exit ramp and text Frankie. I get out of my SUV, walk into the restaurant, and see Frankie at the counter paying his bill. A waitress is clearing his table and I ask if it's okay to sit there.

Carrie has brought Buck with her, which is a good sign. She's obviously told him her backstory and needs his support. He's a burly guy with thick arms and a graying beard and, I assume wrongly, a short fuse. As soon as they walk in the door, I jump up and wave them over. We make awkward introductions and I motion to the table. I thank her for the meeting and insist that they order lunch. I'm starving myself and ask for eggs and coffee. They order burgers and fries.

Buck stares at me with many doubts. Before I can get to the point he says, "We checked you out online. Guardian Ministries. You a preacher or a lawyer?"

"Both," I say with a winning smile and then ramble a bit about my background.

He says proudly, "My daddy was a preacher, you know?"

Oh, we know. Four years ago, his daddy retired after thirty years at a small country church far outside of Blountville. I feign interest and we tiptoe around theology lite. I suspect Buck strayed from the faith a long time ago. In spite of his rustic appearance, he has a soft voice and a pleasant manner.

Carrie says, "For a lot of reasons, Mr. Post, I've never told Buck much about my past."

"Please, it's just Post," I say. She smiles and I'm once again struck by her pretty eyes and strong features. She's wearing makeup and has pulled back her blond hair, and in a different life her looks could have opened more promising doors.

Buck says, "Okay, first things first. How do we know that we can trust you?" He is asking this of a man who's secretly recording them.

Before I can respond, he says, "I mean, Carrie told me what happened back then, what she did, and obviously we're concerned or we wouldn't be here. But this looks like trouble to me."

She asks, "What do you really want?"

"The truth," I say.

"You ain't wearing no wire or anything like that, are you?" Buck asks.

I snort at this and raise my hands as if I have nothing to hide. "Come on, I'm not a cop. You want to pat me down, go ahead."

The waitress arrives with more coffee and we clam up. When she's gone I take the initiative. "No, I'm not wearing a wire. I don't operate like that. What I want is simple. Ideally, you tell me the truth, then sign an affidavit that I may one day use to help Quincy Miller. I'm also talking to the other witnesses and trying to get the same thing—the truth. I know that much of the testimony at trial was fabricated by the cops and prosecutor, and I'm just trying to piece it all together. Your statement will certainly help, but it's just one part of the big picture."

"What's an affidavit?" Buck asks.

"Just a sworn statement, under oath. I'll prepare it and you guys review it. Then I'll keep it under wraps until it's needed. No one around Kingsport will ever know. Seabrook is too far away."

"Do I have to go to a courtroom?" she asks.

"Unlikely. Let's assume I can convince a judge that Quincy

did not get a fair trial. That, frankly, is a long shot. But if it happens, then there is the remote possibility that the prosecutor will decide to try him again for the murder. That could be years down the road. If so, you could be called as a witness, which is quite unlikely because you did not see a black man running from the scene, right?"

She doesn't nod or say anything for a moment. Our plates arrive and we prepare our food. Buck likes ketchup. Neither wants salt or pepper. I sprinkle salt on my eggs and place the shaker in the center of the table.

Carrie nibbles on a French fry and avoids eye contact. Buck chomps on his burger. They've obviously talked about the situation at length without making a decision. She needs prodding and I ask, "Who convinced you to testify? Sheriff Pfitzner?"

She says, "Look, Mr. Post, I'll talk to you and tell you what happened, but I'm not sold on the idea of getting involved. I'm gonna think long and hard before I sign any affidavit."

"You can't repeat what she says, can you?" Buck asks as he wipes his mouth with a paper napkin.

"I can't repeat it in court, if that's what you're asking. I can talk to my staff about it, but that's as far as I can go. Any judge will require an affidavit from a witness."

"I'm worried about my boys," she says. "They don't know. I'd be ashamed if they found out their mother lied in court and sent a man to prison."

I reply, "I understand that, Carrie, and you should be concerned. But there's also the likelihood that they will be proud of the fact that you came forward to help free an innocent man. We all did bad things when we were twenty, but some mistakes can be corrected. You're worried about your boys.

Think about Quincy Miller. He has three kids he hasn't seen in twenty-two years. And five grandchildren he's never seen, not even in a photograph."

They absorb this and stop eating for a moment. They are overwhelmed and frightened, but the wheels are turning. I say, "We have the records and they tell us that your drug charge was dismissed a few months after the trial. Pfitzner convinced you to take the stand, tell your story, and the prosecutor promised to lose the drug charge, right?"

She breathes deeply and looks at Buck, who shrugs and says, "Go ahead. We didn't drive five hours for cheeseburgers."

She tries to drink from her coffee cup but her hands are shaking. She puts it down and shoves her plate a few inches away. Staring straight ahead, she says, "I was dating a deputy named Lonnie. We were doing drugs, lots of drugs. I got caught but he kept me out of jail. Then the lawyer got murdered and a few weeks later Lonnie told me he had things worked out. If I would claim that I saw a black man running away from the lawyer's office, then the drug charge would get dismissed. Just like that. So he took me down to Pfitzner's office and I told my story. The next day, Lonnie and Pfitzner took me to see the prosecutor, can't remember his name."

"Burkhead, Forrest Burkhead."

"That's him. And I told the story again. He recorded me, but didn't say a thing about the drug charge. When I asked Lonnie about it later, he said the deal had been worked out between Pfitzner and Burkhead, not to worry. Lonnie and I were fighting, mainly about the drugs. I've been clean and sober for fourteen years now, Mr. Post."

"That's wonderful. Congratulations."

"Buck got me through it."

Buck said, "I like my beer but always stayed away from drugs. I knew my daddy would shoot me."

"Anyway, they took me to Butler County for the trial and I testified. I felt rotten about it but I really didn't want to spend a lot of time in jail. I figured it was either me or Quincy Miller and I've always been loyal to me. Every dog for himself, you know? Over the years I've tried to forget about the trial. That young lawyer made a fool out of me."

"Tyler Townsend."

"That's him. I'll never forget him."

"And then you left town?"

"Yes sir. As soon as the trial was over, Pfitzner called me to his office, thanked me, gave me a thousand dollars in cash and told me to get lost. Said if I came back to Florida within five years he'd have me arrested for lying to the jury. Can you believe that? A deputy drove me to Gainesville and put me on the bus to Atlanta. Never been back and don't want to go. I didn't even tell my friends where I was. Didn't have many. It was an easy place to leave."

Buck wants some credit and says, "When she first told me about this a few weeks ago, I said, 'You gotta tell the truth, babe. That man's been locked up because of you.'"

"There's still a drug charge on your record," I say.

"That was the first one, a year before."

"You should get it expunged."

"I know, but it was a long time ago. Buck and I are doing okay these days. We both work hard and pay our bills. I don't really want to be bothered with the past, Mr. Post."

"If she signs the affidavit, can they get her for perjury in Florida?" Buck asks.

"No, the statute of limitations has run out. Besides, no one

104

really cares anymore. There's a new sheriff, new prosecutor, new judge."

"When will all this happen?" she asks, obviously relieved now that she's told the truth.

"It's a slow process, could take months or years, if it happens at all. First you have to sign the affidavit."

"She'll sign it," Buck says, then takes another bite. With his mouth full, he adds, "Won't you, babe?"

"I gotta think about it," she says.

Buck says, "Look, if we have to go to Florida, then I'll drive you down there and punch anybody who causes trouble."

"There will be no trouble, I can assure you. The only downside for you, Carrie, is telling your sons. The rest of your family and your friends will probably never know. If Quincy Miller walked out of prison tomorrow, who in Kingsport, Tennessee, would hear about it?"

Buck nods in agreement and takes another bite. Carrie picks up another fry. Buck says, "They're good boys, her two. I got a couple of wild ones, but Carrie's are fine boys. Hell, like you say, I'll bet they'll be proud of you, babe."

She smiles but I'm not sure she's convinced. Buck, my new ally, is confident.

I finish my eggs and begin prodding her about the drug scene in Seabrook back then. Cocaine and pot were the preferred choices, and Lonnie always had a supply. Their romance was on and off and she did not spend time with the other deputies, though some were known to deal in small quantities. She claims she knew nothing about Pfitzner's alleged role in the trade.

When the table is cleared I ask for the check. I graciously thank them and offer my admiration for her courage in coming forward. I promise not to prepare the affidavit until she makes up her mind. We say goodbye in the parking lot and I watch them drive away. I return to the restaurant and walk to our table to fetch a baseball cap I deliberately left behind. When no one is looking I swap the salt and pepper shakers with two from my pocket.

Three miles down the road, I exit the interstate and pull into the parking lot of a shopping center. Seconds later, Frankie wheels in, parks next to me, and gets into the front seat, all smiles. He holds a small recorder and says, "Clear as a bell."

This can be a dirty business. We are forced to deal with witnesses who have lied, police who have fabricated evidence, experts who have misled juries, and prosecutors who have suborned perjury. We, the good guys, often find that getting our hands dirty is the only way to save our clients.

If Carrie Holland Pruitt refuses to cooperate and sign an affidavit, then I'll find a way to get her statements into the court record. I've done it before.

15

Our hands get even dirtier. Frankie has hired an investigator out of Birmingham to stalk Mark Carter, the man who raped and murdered Emily Broone. He lives in the small town of Bayliss, ten miles from Verona, where Duke Russell was convicted. Carter sells tractors for a dealer in Verona, and he ends most workdays at a dive where he meets some buddies for a few beers and pool.

He is at a table drinking Bud Light from a bottle when a man stumbles and crashes into the little party. Bottles fly as beer is spilled. The man gets to his feet, apologizing profusely, and the situation is tense for a moment. He scoops up the half-empty bottles, buys another round, and keeps apologizing. He sets four fresh bottles on the table and cracks a joke. Carter and his pals finally laugh. All is well as the man, our investigator, retreats to a corner and pulls out his cell phone. In a coat pocket he has the beer bottle Carter was working on.

The next day, Frankie drives it to a lab in Durham and hands it over, along with a single pubic hair we filched from the police evidence file. Guardian pays $6,000 for an expedited test. The results are beautiful. We now have DNA proof linking Carter to the rape and murder.

At Duke's trial, seven pubic hairs were entered into evidence by the State of Alabama. They were supposedly collected from the crime scene, from Emily's body. Duke submitted samples of his own. With great certainty, the State's expert testified that they matched those found on the corpse, overwhelming proof that Duke raped Emily before he strangled her. Another expert testified that he also bit her several times during the assault.

There was no semen found in or around her body. Undaunted by this, the prosecutor, Chad Falwright, simply told the jury that Duke "had probably just used a condom." There was no proof of this, one was never found, but this made perfect sense to the jury. To get a death verdict, Falwright had to prove murder plus rape. The victim was naked and had probably been sexually assaulted, but the proof was weak. The pubic hairs became crucial evidence.

In a sober moment, Duke's lawyer asked the court for money to hire his own expert hair analyst. The court said no. The lawyer either knew nothing about DNA testing or didn't want to bother with it. He may have assumed the court would not authorize it. Thus, the seven pubic hairs were never tested.

But they were certainly analyzed. The expert testimony sent Duke to death row, and three months ago came within two hours of getting him killed.

Now we have the truth.

VERONA SITS IN the center of the state, in a desolate, sparsely populated flatland packed with piney woods. For its 5,000 inhabitants, a good job is driving a pulpwood truck, a bad one is sacking groceries. One in five has no job at all. It's a depressing place, but then most of my stops are in towns that time has passed by.

Chad Falwright's office is in the courthouse, just down the dusty hallway from where Duke was convicted nine years ago. I've been here once before and would prefer to avoid it in the future. This meeting will not be pleasant, but I'm accustomed to that. Most prosecutors despise me and the sentiments are mutual.

As agreed upon, I arrive at 1:58 p.m. and give a nice smile to Chad's secretary. It's obvious she does not like me either. He's busy, of course, and she invites me to have a seat under a dreadful portrait of a scowling and, hopefully, dead judge. Ten minutes pass as she pecks away at a keyboard. There are no sounds coming from his office. Fifteen minutes. After twenty minutes, I say rudely, "Look, we made an appointment for two p.m. I drove a long way to get here, now what the hell is going on?"

She glances at an old desk phone and says, "He's still talking to a judge."

"Does he know I'm out here?" I demand, loud enough for him to hear.

"Yes. Now please."

I sit down, wait ten more minutes, then walk to his door and knock loudly. Before he or she can say anything, I barge in and find Chad not on the phone but at his window, as if enthralled by the vibrant city below.

"We agreed on two o'clock, Chad. What the hell?"

"Sorry, Post. I was on the phone with a judge. Come on in."

"Don't mind if I do. I drove five hours to get here. A little courtesy would be nice."

"My apologies," he says sarcastically and falls into his large leather swivel. He's about my age and has spent the last fifteen years prosecuting criminals, primarily cookers and peddlers of meth. By far his most thrilling case was Emily's murder. Three months ago, as the clock ticked, he chased every TV reporter within sight and chatted about the burdens of his job.

"No problem," I say and take a seat.

"What's on your mind?" he asks and glances at his watch.

"We've done some DNA testing," I say and manage to maintain my sour expression. What I want to do is get in his face with some serious smack. "We know who the real killer is, Chad, and it ain't Duke Russell."

He takes it well. "Do tell."

"Do tell. We obtained a sample from the killer and matched it with one of the State's pubic hairs. Bad news, Chad. You got the wrong man."

"You tampered with our evidence?"

"Brilliant. You're more concerned with my sins than with your own. You almost executed an innocent man, Chad. Don't worry about me. I'm just the guy who's found the truth."

"How did you steal a pubic hair?"

"It was easy. You gave me the file, remember? A year ago, down the hall. For two days I sweated in that cramped little room and went through the evidence. One pubic hair stuck to my finger. A year has passed and no one here has even realized it."

"You stole a pubic hair. Unbelievable."

"Didn't steal it, Chad. I just borrowed it. You refused DNA testing, so somebody had to do it. Indict me, I don't care. You have bigger problems right now."

He exhales as his shoulders sag. A minute passes as he collects his thoughts. Finally, "Okay, who killed her?"

"The last man seen with her before she was murdered. Mark Carter. They had a history from high school. The cops should have pursued him, but didn't for some reason."

"How do you know it's him?"

"Got a sample."

"How?"

"A beer bottle. He likes beer, leaves behind a lot of bottles. We ran to the lab and I've brought you a copy of the test results."

"You stole a beer bottle too?"

"Indict me again, Chad, and keep playing games. Look in the mirror, man, and give it up. Your bogus prosecution is going down the drain and you're about to be humiliated."

He offers a goofy grin and gives me a prosecutor's favorite line: "No way, Post, I still believe in my case."

"Then you're an idiot, Chad. But we knew that a long time ago." I toss a copy of the report on his desk and head for the door.

"Wait a minute, Post," he says. "Let's finish the conversation. Assuming you're telling the truth here, what, uh, what's next?"

I sit down calmly and crack my knuckles. Duke will get out earlier if I can persuade Chad to cooperate. If he fights me, which prosecutors usually do, then the exoneration will take months instead of weeks.

"Here's the best way out of this, Chad, and I'm not going to argue strategy here. For a change, I'm holding all the cards. There are six other pubic hairs. Let's get them tested too, so we'll know a lot more. If all seven exclude Duke, then he

111

walks. If all seven nail Carter, then you have a new case on your hands. If you agree to the additional testing, then things will go smooth. If you block it, then I'll file in state court, probably lose, then go to federal court. Eventually, I'll get the testing done and you know it."

Reality sets in and he is angry. He pushes his chair back and walks to the window, deep in thought. He breathes heavily, rolls his head around as his neck crackles, strokes his chin. What all of this produces should surprise me, but it doesn't. Not anymore. He says, "You know, Post, I can see both of them there with Emily, taking turns."

"You can't see the sky, Chad, because you don't want to." I stand and walk to the door.

"I believe in my case, Post."

"Here's the plan, Chad. You have two weeks. If you're still delusional in two weeks, I'll file my motion for testing and I'll also sit down with Jim Bizko at *The Birmingham News*. As you know, he's covered the case and we're acquaintances. When I tell him about the DNA, you'll be front-page news and it won't be the headlines you dream about. Between Bizko and myself, we can paint you as one enormous fool, Chad. Won't be that hard."

I open the door and leave. My last image of Chad is him standing at the window, gawking at me, stunned, mouth-breathing, thoroughly defeated. I wish I could have taken a photo.

I leave Verona in a hurry and settle in for the long drive to death row. Duke doesn't know about the DNA results. I want to tell him in person. Our meeting will be a wonderful occasion.

16

There is no urgent need for me to visit Seabrook. All of the players in Quincy's trial have either died, retired, fled, or disappeared under mysterious circumstances. I have no idea who I'm supposed to be afraid of, but there is a palpable sense of fear.

So I send Frankie on reconnaissance. He spends two days and two nights there moving through the shadows as only he can do. His verbal report is typically blunt: "Ain't much to it, boss."

He leaves and drives several hours to Deerfield Beach, near Boca Raton. He roams the streets, works the Internet, scopes out locations, and in short order puts on a handsome suit and makes the call. Tyler Townsend agrees to meet him at a new shopping center his company is finishing. Big signs announce plenty of space to lease. Frankie claims he and a partner are looking at prime spots for a sporting goods store. It's a new company, one with no presence online.

Tyler seems friendly enough, but a bit wary. He's fifty now, and he left the law a long time ago, a good move. He's prospered in south Florida real estate and knows his business. He and his wife have three teenagers in their spacious home.

Property taxes on it were $58,000 last year. He drives a fancy import and dresses and looks like money.

Frankie's ruse doesn't last long. They step into a 4,000-square-foot space with drying plaster and Tyler asks, "Now what was the name of your company?"

"No name, no company. I'm here under false pretenses but it's still important."

"Are you a cop?"

"Anything but. I'm an ex-con who spent fourteen years in a Georgia prison for somebody else's murder. A young lawyer took my case and proved I was innocent, got me exonerated, and dear old Georgia forked over some cash. My record is clean. From time to time I work for the lawyer. Figure it's the least I can do."

"Is this by chance related to Quincy Miller?"

"It is. The lawyer now represents him. We know he's innocent, as do you."

He gives a deep breath and actually smiles, but only for a moment. He walks to a large front window and Frankie follows him. They watch an asphalt crew pave the parking lot.

Tyler asks, "And your name?"

"Frankie Tatum." He hands over a Guardian business card and Tyler examines both sides. He asks, "So how is Quincy doing?"

"It's been twenty-two years. I did only fourteen as an innocent man, somehow managed to keep my sanity. But every day is another nightmare."

Tyler hands the card back as if he's removing the evidence. "Look, I really don't have time for any of this. I don't know what you want, but I'm not getting involved, okay? Sorry and all that, but Quincy is a closed chapter in my book."

"You were a helluva lawyer, Tyler. You were just a rookie, but you fought for Quincy."

He smiles, shrugs, says, "And I lost. I'll ask you to leave now."

"Sure. Your property and all. My boss is a lawyer named Cullen Post, check him out. He's exonerated eight people and he didn't do that by taking no for an answer. He wants to talk to you, Tyler, somewhere private. Very private. Believe me, Tyler, Post knows the game, and he ain't going away. You can save a lot of time and trouble if you'll just meet with him for fifteen minutes."

"And he's in Savannah?"

"No. He's across the street." Frankie points in my direction.

The three of us walk around the corner to a family-style restaurant that Tyler's company is building. It's unfinished and workers are taking chairs out of boxes. The avenue beyond is choked with new buildings: car dealerships, fast-food huts and drive-throughs, strip malls, a car wash, gas stations, a couple of branch banks. Florida sprawl at its finest. We stand in a corner, away from the workers, and Tyler says, "Okay, let's have it."

I get the impression that this conversation may end abruptly, so I ditch the small talk with "Is it possible to prove Quincy is innocent?"

He considers this and shakes his head. "Look, I'm not getting involved in this. Years ago I tried my best to prove his innocence and I failed. That was another life. Now I have three kids, a beautiful wife, money, no worries. I'm not going back there. Sorry."

"Where's the danger, Tyler?"

"Oh, you'll find out. I mean, I hope not, for your sake anyway, but you're walking into a bad situation, Mr. Post."

"All of my cases are bad situations."

He grunts as if I have no idea. "Nothing like this."

"We're about the same age, Tyler, and we quit the law at the same time because we were disillusioned. My second career didn't exactly work and then I found a new calling. I spend my time pounding the streets looking for a break, looking for help. Right now, Tyler, Quincy needs your help."

He takes a deep breath and has had enough. "I suppose you have to be pushy in your line of work, but I'm not getting pushed, Mr. Post. Good day. Leave me alone and don't come back." He turns around and walks out the door.

NOT SURPRISINGLY, Chad Falwright digs in. He will not agree to DNA testing of the other six pubic hairs. He now has them under lock and key, along with the other evidence. And, to show what a tough prosecutor he really is, he's threatening to have me indicted for tampering. Alabama prohibits it, as do all states, though with varying penalties, and he gleefully writes that I could face up to a year in jail.

Locked up over one lousy pubic hair.

In addition, he says he plans to file ethics complaints against me with the Alabama and Georgia bar associations. I laugh at this. I've been threatened before, and by far more creative prosecutors.

Mazy prepares a thick petition for post-conviction relief. Procedurally, it has to be filed first in state court, in Verona. The day before we file it, I drive to Birmingham and meet with Jim Bizko, a veteran reporter who covered Duke's trial. He followed the case as the appeals dragged on and expressed doubts about the fairness of the trial. He was especially harsh with his criticism of Duke's defense lawyer. When the poor guy died of cirrhosis, Jim covered it and suggested that another investigation into the murder would be appropriate. He is delighted by the news that DNA testing has cleared Duke. I'm careful not to name Mark Carter as the killer. That will come later.

The day after we file the petition, Bizko runs a lengthy article that lands on the front page of the Metro section. Chad Falwright is quoted as saying: "I remain confident that we got the right man and I'm working diligently to bring about the execution of Duke Russell, a ruthless killer. DNA testing means nothing in this case."

AFTER TWO MORE conversations with Otis Walker, both by phone, Frankie is convinced that June Walker wants nothing to do with Quincy Miller. Obviously, their chaotic divorce left permanent scars and she is adamant in her determination not to get involved. There's nothing in it for her except bad memories and the embarrassment of confronting old lies.

Otis warns Frankie to leave them alone.

He promises to do so. For now.

17

There are twenty-three lawyers working in Seabrook these days and we have a thin file on each of them. About half were in town when Russo was murdered. The senior barrister is a ninety-one-year-old gentleman who still drives himself to the office every day. Two rookies showed up last year and hung out a shingle. All are white, six are female. The most prosperous appear to be a couple of brothers who've spent twenty years doing bankruptcies. Most of the local bar seems to be barely hanging on, same as in most small towns.

Glenn Colacurci once served in the Florida Senate. His district covered Ruiz County and two others, and he was in his third term at the time of the murder. Keith Russo was a distant relative. Both came from the same Italian neighborhood in Tampa. In his younger years Colacurci ran the biggest law firm in town and hired Keith out of law school. When he showed up in Seabrook he brought a wife with him, but Colacurci had no position for her. Keith didn't last long, and a year later the Russo firm was founded in a two-room walk-up above a bakery on Main Street.

I select Colacurci because his file is slightly thicker, and because he'll probably know more about Keith. Of all the active lawyers in town, he'll have a better recollection of history. On the phone he says he can spare half an hour.

Driving through Seabrook for the first time, I feel as though I know the place. There are not that many points of interest: the office building once owned by Keith and Diana and the place where the crime occurred; the street behind it where Carrie Holland claimed to have seen a black man making his escape; the courthouse. I park across from it on Main Street and sit and watch the languid foot traffic. I wonder how many of these people remember the murder. How many knew Keith Russo? Quincy Miller? Do they know the town got it wrong and sent an innocent man to prison? Of course not.

When it's time, I join them on the sidewalk and go half a block to the office. In thick black letters of peeling paint, the sign on the windows says: COLACURCI LAW FIRM. An old bell jingles on the door as I step inside. An ancient tabby cat slides off a sofa and disturbs a layer of dust. To my right is a rolltop desk with a manual Underwood typewriter, as if just waiting for a gray-haired secretary to return and resume pecking away. The smell is of old leather and stale tobacco, not altogether unpleasant but begging for a good cleaning.

Remarkably, though, in the midst of an earlier century, a stunning young Asian woman in a short skirt appears with a smile and says, "Good morning. May I help you?"

I return the smile and say, "Yes, I'm Cullen Post. I talked to Mr. Colacurci yesterday and we agreed to meet this morning."

She manages to grin and frown at the same time as she steps to a slightly more modern desk. Quietly, she says, "He didn't tell me. Sorry. My name is Bea."

"Is he here?" I ask.

"Sure. I'll get him. He's not that busy." She smiles again and glides away. A moment later she waves me back and I enter the big office where Glenn has held court for decades. He is standing by his desk as if pleased to have a visitor, and we go through quick introductions. He motions to a leather sofa and says to Bea, "Fetch us some coffee, please." He hobbles on a cane to a chair that would hold two people. He's almost eighty and certainly looks it, with extra weight and white beard and a mass of unkempt white hair in bad need of a trimming. At the same time, he looks sort of dapper with a pink bow tie and red suspenders.

"Are you a priest or something?" he asks, staring at my collar.

"Yes. Episcopal." I give him the quick version of Guardian Ministries. As I talk he rests his fuzzy chin on the grip of his cane and absorbs every word with piercing green, though apparently bloodshot, eyes. Bea brings the coffee and I take a sip. Lukewarm, probably instant.

When she leaves and closes the door, he asks, "What exactly is a priest doing sticking his nose into an old case like Quincy Miller?"

"Great question. I wouldn't be here if I didn't think he is innocent."

This amuses him. "Interesting," he mumbles. "I've never had a problem with Miller's conviction. There was an eyewitness, as I remember."

"There were no witnesses. A young woman named Carrie Holland testified she saw a black man running away from the scene carrying what was implied to have been a shotgun. She lied. She was a druggie who cut a deal with the authorities to avoid jail. She has now admitted she lied. And she wasn't the only liar at trial."

He takes his fingers and sweeps back his long hair. It's oily and appears to be unwashed. "Interesting."

"Were you close to Keith?"

A grunt in frustration and half a smile. "What do you want from me?"

"Just background. Did you watch the trial?"

"Naw. Wanted to, but they moved it next door to Butler County. I was in the senate back then and pretty busy. Had seven lawyers working around here, biggest firm in these parts, and I couldn't exactly spend my time sitting in a court-room watching other lawyers."

"Keith was a relative, right?"

"Sort of. Quite distant. I knew his people down in Tampa. He pestered me for a job and I gave him one, but he never fit. He wanted me to hire his wife too, but I didn't want to. He hung around here for a year or so, then struck out on his own. I didn't like that. Italians place a premium on loyalty."

"Was he a good lawyer?"

"Why is that important now?"

"Just curious. Quincy says that Keith did a terrible job handling his divorce, and the court file tends to support this. The prosecutor played up their conflict to prove motive, which is kind of a stretch. I mean, a client is so disgruntled he blows off his lawyer's face?"

"Never happened to me," he says and roars with laughter. I gamely laugh along. "But I've had my share of crazy clients. Had a guy show up one time with a gun, years ago. Pissed off over a divorce. At least he said he had a gun. Every lawyer in the building had a weapon and it could've been ugly, but a cute little secretary calmed him down. I've always believed in cute secretaries."

Old lawyers would rather tell war stories than eat lunch, and I would like nothing better than to get him cranked up. I say, "You had a big firm back then."

"Big for this part of the state. Seven, eight, sometimes ten lawyers, a dozen secretaries, offices upstairs, clients lined up out the front door. It was pretty crazy back in those days, but I got tired of all the drama. I spent half my time refereeing my employees. You ever practiced?"

"I'm practicing now, just a different specialty. Years ago I worked as a public defender but burned out. I found God and he led me to the seminary. I became a minister and through an outreach program met an innocent man in prison. That changed my life."

"You get him out?"

"I did. Then seven more. I'm working on six cases now, including Quincy's."

"I read somewhere that maybe ten percent of all people locked up are innocent. You believe that?"

"Ten percent might be on the high side, but there are thousands of innocent people in prison."

"I'm not sure I believe that."

"Most white folks don't, but go to the black community and you'll find plenty of believers."

In his eighteen years in the state senate, Colacurci voted consistently on the side of law and order. Pro death penalty, pro gun rights, a real drug warrior and big spender for whatever the state police and prosecutors wanted.

He says, "I never had the stomach for criminal law. Can't make any money there."

"But Keith made money on the criminal side, didn't he?"

He glares at me with a frown, as if I've stepped out of bounds. Eventually he says, "Keith's been dead for over twenty years. Why are you so interested in his law practice?"

"Because my client didn't kill him. Someone else did, someone with a different motive. We know Keith and Diana were representing drug dealers in the late eighties, had some clients in the Tampa area. Those guys make good suspects."

"Maybe, but I doubt if they'll do much talking after all these years."

"Were you close to Sheriff Pfitzner?"

He glares at me again. In a not so subtle way, I've just linked Pfitzner to the drug dealers, and Colacurci knows where I'm fishing. He takes a deep breath, exhales loudly, says, "Bradley and I were never close. He ran his show, I ran mine. We were both after the same votes but we dodged each other. I didn't mess with the criminal side so our paths seldom crossed."

"Where is he now?" I ask.

"Dead, I presume. He left here years back."

He's not dead but living a good life in the Florida Keys. He retired after thirty-two years as sheriff and moved away. His three-bedroom condo in Marathon is assessed at $1.6 million. Not a bad retirement for a public servant who never earned more than $60,000 a year.

"You're thinking Pfitzner was somehow involved with Keith?" he asks.

"Oh no. Didn't mean to imply that."

Oh yes. But Colacurci is not taking the bait. He narrows his eyes and says, "This eyewitness, she says Pfitzner convinced her to lie on the stand?"

If and when Carrie Holland recants her false testimony, it will be included in a court filing for everyone to see. However, I'm not ready to reveal anything to this guy. I say, "Look, Mr. Colacurci, this is all confidential, right?"

"Of course, of course," he readily agrees. He was a stranger until about fifteen minutes ago and he'll probably be on the phone before I get to my vehicle.

"She didn't name Pfitzner, just said it was the cops and prosecutor. I have no reason to suspect Pfitzner of anything."

"That's good. This murder was solved twenty years ago. You're spinning your wheels, Mr. Post."

"Maybe. How well did you know Diana Russo?"

He rolls his eyes as if she is the last subject he wants to discuss. "Not well at all. I kept my distance from the beginning. She wanted a job but back then we didn't hire girls. She took it as an insult and never liked me. She soured Keith on me and we never got along. I was relieved when he left, though I wasn't finished with him. He became a real pain in the ass."

"In what way?"

He gazes at the ceiling as if debating whether or not to tell me a story. Being an old lawyer, he can't help himself. "Well, this is what happened," he begins as he shifts weight and settles in for the narrative. "Back in the day, I had all the tort business sewed up in Ruiz County. All the good car wrecks, bad products, med-mal, bad faith, everything. If a person got injured, they showed up here, or sometimes I went to see them in the hospital. Keith wanted some of the action because it's no secret that injuries are the only way to make money out there on the streets. Big-firm guys in Tampa do okay, but nothing like big tort lawyers. When Keith left my office he stole a case, took it with him, and we had one helluva fight. He was broke and needed the cash but the case belonged to my firm. I threatened to sue him and we fought for two years. He eventually agreed to give me half the fee, but there was bad blood. Diana was in the middle of it too."

Law firms blow up every week and it's always over money.

"Did you and Keith ever reconcile?"

"Sort of, I guess, but it took years. It's a small town and the lawyers generally get along. We had lunch the week before he was murdered and had a laugh or two. Keith was a good boy who worked hard. Maybe a bit too ambitious. I never warmed up to her, though. But you had to feel sorry for her. Poor girl found her husband with his face blown off. Handsome guy too. She took it hard, never recovered, sold the building and eventually left town."

"No contact since then?"

"None whatsoever." He glances at his watch as if he's facing another hectic day and the hint is clear. We wind down the conversation, and after thirty minutes I thank him and leave.

18

Bradley Pfitzner ruled the county for thirty-two years before retiring. During his career he avoided scandal and ran a tight operation. Every four years he was either unopposed or faced light opposition. He was succeeded by a deputy who served seven years before bad health forced him out.

The current sheriff is Wink Castle, and his office is in a modern metal building that houses all local law enforcement—sheriff, city police, and jail. A dozen brightly painted patrol cars are parked in front of the building at the edge of town. The lobby is busy with cops and clerks and sad relatives checking on inmates.

I'm led to Castle's office and he greets me with a smile and firm handshake. He's about forty and has the easy manner of a rural politician. He did not live in the county at the time of the Russo murder, so hopefully he carries no baggage from those days.

After a few minutes of weather talk, he says, "Quincy Miller, huh? I looked through the file last night to get up to speed. Are you a priest or something?"

"A lawyer and a minister," I say, and spend a moment

talking about Guardian. "I take old cases that involve the innocent."

"Good luck with this one."

I smile and say, "They're all difficult, Sheriff."

"Got it. So how do you plan to prove that your client did not kill Keith Russo?"

"Well, as always, I go back to the scene and start digging. I know that most of the State's witnesses lied at trial. The evidence is shaky at best."

"Zeke Huffey?"

"Typical jailhouse snitch. I found him in prison in Arkansas and I expect him to recant. He's made a career out of lying and recanting, not unusual for those guys. Carrie Holland has already told me the truth—she lied under pressure from Pfitzner and Burkhead, the prosecutor. They gave her a good deal on a pending drug charge. After the trial, Pfitzner gave her a thousand bucks and ran her out of town. She hasn't been back. June Walker, Quincy's ex-wife, lives in Tallahassee but so far has refused to cooperate. She testified against Quincy and lied because she was angry over their divorce. Lots of lies, Sheriff."

This is all new to him and he absorbs it with interest. Then he shakes his head and says, "Still a long way to go. There's no murder weapon."

"Right. Quincy never owned a shotgun. The key, obviously, is the blood-spattered flashlight that mysteriously disappeared not long after the murder."

"What happened to it?" he asks. He's the sheriff. I should be asking him.

"You tell me. The official version, according to Pfitzner, is that it was destroyed in a fire where they kept evidence."

"You doubt that?"

"I doubt everything, Sheriff. The expert for the State, a Mr. Norwood, never saw the flashlight. His testimony was pretty outrageous." I reach into my briefcase, pull out some papers, and place them on his desk. "This is our summary of the evidence. In there you'll see a report from a Dr. Kyle Benderschmidt, a renowned criminologist, that raises serious doubts about Norwood's testimony. Have you looked at the photographs of the flashlight?"

"Yes."

"Dr. Benderschmidt believes that the specks, or flecks, on the lens are probably not even human blood. And the flashlight was not found at the scene. We're not sure where it came from and Quincy swears he had never seen it."

He takes the report and takes his time flipping through it. When he gets bored he tosses it onto his desk and says, "I'll spend some time with it tonight. What, exactly, do you want me to do here?"

"Help me. I'll file a petition for post-conviction relief based on new evidence. It will have reports from our experts and statements from the witnesses who lied. I need for you to reopen the investigation into the murder. It will be a tremendous help if the court knows that the locals believe the wrong man was convicted."

"Come on, Mr. Post. This case was closed over twenty years ago, long before I came to town."

"They're all old cases, Sheriff, old and cold. That's the nature of our work. Most of the actors are gone—Pfitzner, Burkhead, even the judge is dead. You can look at the case with a fresh perspective and help get an innocent man out of prison."

He's shaking his head. "I don't think so. I can't see getting involved in this. Hell, I never thought about the case until you called yesterday."

"All the more reason to get involved. You can't be blamed for anything that went wrong twenty years ago. You'll be seen as the good guy trying to do the right thing."

"Do you have to find the real killer to get Miller out?"

"No. I have to prove him innocent, that's all. In about half of our cases we manage to nail the real criminal, but not always."

He keeps shaking his head. The smiles are gone. "I can't see it, Mr. Post. I mean, you expect me to pull one of my overworked detectives off his active cases and start digging through a twenty-year-old murder that folks around here have forgotten about. Come on, man."

"I'll do the heavy lifting, Sheriff. That's my job."

"So what's my job?"

"Cooperate. Don't get in the way."

He leans back in his chair and locks his hands behind his head. He stares at the ceiling as minutes pass. Finally, he asks, "In your cases, what do the locals normally do?"

"Cover up. Stonewall. Hide evidence. Fight me like hell. Contest everything I file in court. You see, Sheriff, in these cases the stakes are too high and the mistakes are too egregious for anyone to admit they were wrong. Innocent men and women serve decades while the real killers roam free, and often kill again. These are enormous injustices, and I've yet to find a cop or a prosecutor with the spine to admit they blew it. This case is a bit different because those responsible for Quincy's wrongful conviction are gone. You can be the hero."

"I'm not interested in being a hero. I just cannot justify spending the time. Believe me, I've got enough to worry about."

"Sure you do, but you can cooperate and make my job easier. I'm just searching for the truth here, Sheriff."

"I don't know. Let me think about it."

"That's all I ask, for now anyway."

He takes a deep breath, still unconvinced and definitely uncommitted to the cause. "Anything else?"

"Well there is one other matter, another possible piece of the puzzle. Are you familiar with the death of Kenny Taft? Happened about two years after the murder?"

"Sure. He was the last officer killed on duty. His photo is hanging on the wall out there."

"I'd like to see the case file without having to go through the Freedom of Information Act and all that crap."

"And you think it was somehow related to Quincy Miller?"

"I doubt it, but I'm just digging, Sheriff. That's what I do, and there are always surprises along the way."

"Let me think about it."

"Thanks."

THE FIRE CHIEF is a potbellied, grizzled old veteran who goes by Lieutenant Jordan and is not nearly as friendly as the sheriff. Things are slow around the firehouse two blocks off Main Street. Two of his men polish a shiny pumper in the driveway, and inside an ancient secretary fiddles with paperwork on her desk. Jordan eventually appears, and after a brief round of forced pleasantries leads me to a cramped room with banks of 1940s-style file cabinets. For a moment he searches through history and finds the drawer for 1988. He opens it, flips through a row of dingy files, finds what I'm after and pulls it out.

"Not much of a fire, as I recall," he says as he places it on the table. "Help yourself." He leaves the room.

Back then, the sheriff's office was several blocks away in an old building that has since been razed. In Ruiz County, as in hundreds of other places, it was not at all unusual to store crime scene evidence anywhere there happened to be an empty space or closet. I've crawled through courthouse attics and suffocating basements in search of old records.

To alleviate the shortage of storage space, Pfitzner used a portable shed behind his office. In the file there is a black-and-white photo of it before the fire, and a heavy padlock on the only door is visible. There were no windows. I estimate it was thirty feet long, twelve feet wide, eight feet in height. A photo taken after the fire shows nothing but charred rubble.

The first alarm came at 3:10 a.m. and the firemen found the shed fully engulfed. The fire was extinguished in a matter of minutes with nothing salvageable. Its cause is listed as "Unknown."

As Jordan said, it wasn't much of a fire. The flashlight found in Quincy's trunk was apparently destroyed. No trace was found. Conveniently, the autopsy reports, witness statements, diagrams, and photos were safely locked away inside Pfitzner's desk. He had what he needed to convict Quincy Miller.

For the moment, the fire is a dead end.

19

I call Carrie and Buck once a week to check on them. They realize I'm not going away and are slowly coming around. I repeatedly assure her that she runs no risks by cooperating with me, and we establish a level of trust.

We meet in a coffee shop near Kingsport and eat omelets. She reads the affidavit Mazy has prepared, then Buck goes through it slowly. I answer the same questions about what happens next and so on, and after an hour of gentle cajoling she signs it.

In the parking lot, I give her a hug and Buck wants one too. We're trusted pals now and I thank them for having the courage to help Quincy. Through tears, she asks me to ask him to forgive her. It's already done, I reply.

MY MOTHER INHERITED the family farm near Dyersburg, Tennessee, my hometown. Mom is seventy-three and has lived by herself since Dad died two years ago. I worry about her because of her age, though she is healthier than me and not at all lonely. She worries about me because of my no-madic lifestyle and absence of a serious romantic relationship.

She has grudgingly accepted the reality that starting a family is not one of my priorities and I am not likely to produce more grandchildren. My sister has given her three but they live far away.

She doesn't eat animals and is sustained by the land. Her garden is legendary and could feed hundreds, and in fact does. She hauls baskets of fresh fruits and vegetables to the local food bank. We dine on tomatoes stuffed with rice and mushrooms, thick butterbeans, and a squash casserole. In spite of the abundance, she eats like a bird and drinks nothing but tea and water. She is fit and spry and refuses to take pills, and as she pushes her vegetables around her plate she encourages me to eat more. She is concerned about my lack of weight, but I wave her off. I hear this from others.

Afterwards, we sit on the front porch and drink mint tea. Little has changed on the porch since my convalescence many years ago, and we talk about those dark days. We also talk about Brooke, my ex. They were fond of each other and kept in touch for years. Mom was angry with her at first for leaving me during my breakdown, but I finally convinced her that our split had been inevitable on our wedding day. Brooke married an entrepreneur who has done well. They have four children, beautiful teenagers, and Mom gets a bit wistful when she thinks about what might have been. As soon as I get an opening, I move the conversation in another direction.

In spite of my unconventional lifestyle, Mom is proud of what I do, though she understands little about the criminal justice system. She finds it depressing that there is so much crime, so many people imprisoned, so many broken families. It has taken me years to convince her that there are thousands of innocent people locked away. This is our first chance to talk about Quincy Miller and she loves getting the details. A murdered lawyer, a crooked sheriff, a drug cartel, an innocent man perfectly framed. She can't believe it at first and relishes the story. I don't worry about telling her too much. We are, after all, sitting on a dark porch in rural Tennessee, far away from Florida, and who would she tell anyway? I can trust my mom to keep secrets.

We go through each of my other clients: Shasta Briley on death row in North Carolina, convicted of arson that killed her three daughters; Billy Rayburn in Tennessee, convicted by the dubious science of what has become known as the Shaken Baby Syndrome after he tripped and fell while holding his girlfriend's baby; Duke Russell, still on death row in Alabama; Curtis Wallace, convicted in Mississippi of the abduction, rape, and murder of a young woman he never met; and Little Jimmy Flagler, who was seventeen and mentally retarded when Georgia locked him away for life.

These six cases are my life and career. I live with them every day and I often tire of thinking and talking about them. I ease the conversation back to Mom and ask how her poker game is going. She plays once a week with a group of lady friends, and though the stakes are small it's cutthroat competition. She's currently up $11.50. They settle their debts at Christmas with a party where they break bad and consume alcohol—cheap champagne. With another group she plays bridge twice a month, but she prefers poker. She is in two book clubs—one with church ladies and they stick to theology, and the other with looser friends who prefer popular fiction. Sometimes even trash. She teaches a Sunday School class, reads to seniors at a retirement home, and volunteers with more nonprofits than she can name. She just bought an electric car and explains in detail what makes it run.

Several times each year, Frankie Tatum stops by for dinner. They are close friends and she loves cooking for him. He was here last week and she talks about his visit. She is quite proud of the fact that he would still be locked away if not for me. This shifts the conversation back to my work. At one time she wanted me to get through this phase and move on to a more sustainable career, maybe in a real law firm, but those conversations are over. Her pensions provide a comfortable life, she does not do debt, and she sends Guardian a small check each month.

She goes to bed promptly at ten o'clock and sleeps for eight uninterrupted hours. She leaves me on the porch, with a kiss on the head, and I sit wide-eyed for hours on this cool, quiet night and think of my clients sleeping on cramped bunks and cots behind bars.

Innocent people.

20

Acting on a tip, the guards raided Zeke Huffey's cell a month ago and found a shank, a homemade knife. Drugs are routinely found in raids and are dealt with casually. But a weapon is a serious offense because it is such a threat to the guards. Zeke is spending time in the Cave, an underground unit used to punish offenders with solitary confinement. His dreams of being paroled early are gone. Instead, he'll serve additional time.

I'm met at a front office by a man in a suit, a deputy warden of some variety, and, along with a guard, I'm whisked through security and led to a building away from the prisoners' units. The deputy warden nods and frowns and doors open immediately. The right strings are being pulled. I walk down some concrete stairs and into a square, damp, windowless room. Zeke is waiting, in a metal chair with leg irons locked to the floor. There is no partition between us. His hands are free, and after a momentary shock of seeing me, he offers a limp handshake.

When the guard leaves and slams the door, Zeke asks, "What are you doing here?"

"I'm here for a visit, Zeke. I've missed you."

He grunts and can't think of a response. Residents of the Cave are not allowed visitors. I pull out a pack of cigarettes and ask, "Want a smoke?"

"Hell yes!" he says, suddenly the addict again. I hand him one and notice his shaking hands. I light it with a match. He closes his eyes and sucks hard in a mighty effort to consume it with one fierce pull. He blows a cloud at the ceiling and hits it again. After three, he flicks ashes on the floor and manages a smile.

"How'd you get in here, Post? This hole is off-limits."

"I know. Got a friend down in Little Rock."

He burns it down to the filter, thumps the butt against the wall, says, "How 'bout another one?"

I light another cigarette. He is pale and gaunt, even thinner than the last time I saw him, and he has a new tattoo across his throat. The nicotine calms him and most of the shaking stops. I say, "They plan to add a few months to your time here, Zeke. Pretty stupid, hiding a shank like that."

"Most of what I do can be classified as stupid, Post. You know that. Smart people don't live like this."

"True. Quincy Miller is a smart guy, Zeke, and he's been locked away for a long time because of you. It's time to set the boy free, don't you think?"

We've swapped a few letters since my last visit, and Guardian sent another small check. However, from the tone of his correspondence he is not ready to admit he lied. He considers himself to be in charge of our fragile relationship and will manipulate it from every angle.

"Oh, I don't know, Post. It was a long time ago. Not sure I remember all the details."

"I have the details here in an affidavit, Zeke. One I want you to sign. Remember an old pal named Shiner? Another junkie you served time with in Georgia?"

He smiles and replies, "Sure, I remember Shiner. What a loser."

"And he remembers you. We found him near Atlanta and he's doing okay. Much better than you. Got himself cleaned up and so far has stayed out of trouble. We have an affidavit signed by him in which he says the two of you often bragged about your careers as jailhouse informants. Says you laughed about Quincy Miller. And the Preston kid in Dothan, still serving time. And Shiner says you always got a kick out of your performance in a murder trial in Gulfport, Kelly Morris, now serving life because of you. We've verified these cases, Zeke, read the transcripts with your testimony. Shiner is telling the truth, for a change."

He glares at me, flicks more ashes. "So what?"

"So, it's time for you to come clean and help Quincy. It's no skin off your balls, Zeke. You're not going anywhere. As I've said before several times, the folks in Florida forgot about you a long time ago. They couldn't care less if you now admit you lied about Quincy."

He thumps the remainder of number two and asks for number three. I light it for him. He pulls hard, adds to the fog above our heads, says, sarcastically, "Gee, I don't know, Post, I'm worried about my reputation."

"Very funny, but I wouldn't waste much time worrying about that. I have a deal for you, Zeke, one that will last for fifteen minutes then disappear forever. As I said, I have a friend down in Little Rock, one with some clout, otherwise I wouldn't be sitting here right now. No one in the Cave gets visits, right? So the deal goes something like this. Arkansas plans to add an additional six months to your time, punishment for the shank. That adds up to another twenty-one months in this dump. My friend can make it go away, all but three months. A year and a half can vanish into thin air. All you have to do is sign the affidavit."

He puffs, flicks, stares at me in disbelief. "You gotta be kidding."

"And why would I be kidding? You do what you should do anyway, as a decent human being, something you're not and we both know it, and Quincy gets a break."

"Ain't no judge gonna let him out just because I come along twenty years later and say I lied, Post. Come on."

"Let me worry about that. Every piece of evidence helps in these cases, Zeke. You probably don't remember a witness named Carrie Holland. She lied too, but the difference is that she now has the guts to admit it. I have her affidavit if you'd like to see it. A woman with courage, Zeke. It's time to man up, big boy, and tell the truth for a change."

"You know, Post, I was just starting to like you."

"Don't bother. I'm not that likeable and really don't care. My mission is to untangle the web of lies that convicted Quincy. You want eighteen months knocked off or not?"

"How can I trust you?"

"The word 'trust' doesn't sound right coming from you, Zeke. I'm an honest man. I don't lie. I guess you'll just have to roll the dice."

"Give me another."

I light the fourth cigarette. He is calm now, calculating, says, "This deal. Can you put it in writing?"

"No, it doesn't work that way. Every prison in Arkansas is overcrowded and the state needs some relief. The county jails are backed up, some sleeping six to a cell, and the powers that be are looking for space. They don't care what happens to you."

"You got that right."

I glance at my watch. "They promised me thirty minutes, Zeke. Time's about up. Deal or no deal?"

He thinks and smokes. "How long do I stay in the Cave?"

"You'll get out tomorrow, I promise."

He nods and I hand him the affidavit. Assuming he doesn't read much, the wording is simple, nothing more than three syllables. With a cigarette screwed into the corner of his mouth, and smoke burning his eyes, he reads it carefully. Ashes fall onto his shirt and he swats them away. After the last page he tosses the butt and says, "I got no problem with this."

I hand him a pen.

"You promise me, Post?"

"I promise."

THE LEADING death penalty lawyer in Arkansas is a friend I worked with on another case. His wife's first cousin is a state senator, chairman of the Appropriations Committee, and thus in charge of funding all agencies, including Corrections. I don't like working the favor bank because I have so little to give in return, but in this business I'm forced to network. Occasionally, something clicks and a miracle happens.

Leaving the cotton fields of northeastern Arkansas, I call Vicki with the news. She is thrilled and runs to tell Mazy.

★ ★ ★

ONCE THE NIGHTMARE of Quincy was behind her, June married again. Her second effort, with a man named James Rhoad, was slightly less chaotic than her first but didn't last long. She was still a mess at that point, emotionally unstable and doing drugs. Frankie found Rhoad in Pensacola. He had nothing nice to say about his ex-wife, and over a few beers delivered the story we were hoping for.

They lived together before they married, and during that brief period of romance and bliss they drank too much and smoked crack, but always away from the kids. On several occasions June laughed about Quincy, a man she would loathe forever. She confided in Rhoad that she had lied to help put him away, and that the lies were encouraged by Sheriff Pfitzner and Forrest Burkhead, the prosecutor.

Rhoad was reluctant to get involved, but Frankie knows persistence. It's part of our culture. Ease in, get to know the witnesses, develop a level of trust, and always gently remind them that an innocent man has been wronged by the system. In this case, by white folks in a small backward town.

Frankie assured Rhoad that he had done nothing wrong and would face no trouble. June had lied and she was unwilling to acknowledge the damage she had done. He, Rhoad, could help immeasurably.

In another bar and over another round of beers, he agreed to sign an affidavit.

21

For the past three months, our work has been done as quietly as possible. If the men who killed Keith Russo know we're digging, we're not aware of it. This changes when we file our petition for post-conviction relief on behalf of Quincy Miller.

Mazy's brief is an inch thick, beautifully written and skillfully argued, as always. It begins with a thorough dismantling of Paul Norwood's expert testimony about bloodstain analysis. She attacks his credentials and says unkind things about him. In excruciating detail, she goes through the seven cases where he pointed the finger at innocent men who were later exonerated by DNA testing. She drives home the point that these seven men served a total of ninety-eight years in prison, but none as long as Quincy Miller.

Once Mazy's brief has Norwood drowning in his own blood, she charges in with the real science and Kyle Benderschmidt takes the stage. His impeccable credentials are presented and contrasted with the State's expert. His report begins with incredulity: The flashlight is the only link to Quincy, and it was not recovered from the crime scene.

There is no proof whatsoever that it was actually present during the shooting. There is no proof that the tiny flecks on the lens are actually human blood. It is impossible to determine from the photographs if the little orange dots are really blood samples. It is impossible to determine the angle of the gunshots. It is impossible to know how the killer held the flashlight as he was firing away, if indeed he held it at all. Lots of impossibilities. Norwood's testimony was factually wrong, scientifically unproven, contrary to reason, and legally irresponsible. Norwood assumed crucial facts that were not in evidence, and when confronted with unknowns he simply fabricated more testimony.

The summary of Benderschmidt's findings is compelling, convincing, and constitutes new evidence. But there's more.

Our second expert is Dr. Tobias Black, a renowned criminologist in San Francisco. Working independently of Dr. Benderschmidt, Dr. Black studied the photos and exhibits and read the trial transcript. His disdain for Norwood and his fellow pseudoscientists is hardly controlled. His conclusions are the same.

Mazy writes like a Nobel laureate, and when she's armed with the facts she is unassailable. I don't want her angry at me if I commit a crime.

She criticizes the investigation of Sheriff Pfitzner. Using the Freedom of Information Act, Vicki obtained records from the Florida state police. In a memo, an investigator complained of Pfitzner's heavy-handedness and his efforts to maintain sole and complete control of the case. He did not want outside interference and refused to cooperate.

With no physical evidence linking Quincy to the crime, it became imperative for Pfitzner to create his own. Without notifying the state police, he obtained a search warrant for Quincy's car, and, rather conveniently, found the flashlight in its trunk.

The brief then moves to the lying witnesses, and includes the affidavits from Carrie Holland Pruitt, Zeke Huffey, Tucker Shiner, and James Rhoad. Mazy is restrained but almost cruel in her treatment of the liars, and she rages on with a blistering commentary on the use of snitch testimony in American prosecutions.

Next, she analyzes the issue of motive and makes much of the fact that Quincy's alleged grudge against Keith Russo was more anecdotal than factual. She presents an affidavit from the law firm's former receptionist who says she remembers only one visit by the disgruntled client, who was "mildly perturbed." But he made no threats and left when she informed him that Keith was not in his office. She does not remember the second and more threatening visit that Diana Russo described to the jury. The police were never called. Indeed, there was no record of anyone at the firm complaining about Quincy's behavior. Regarding the phone threats, there was simply no proof. Diana blocked the defense's efforts to obtain the couple's phone records, and they have since been destroyed.

The last section of the brief covers Quincy's own testimony. Since he did not testify at trial, he is now able to tell his story with his own affidavit. He denies any involvement, denies ever owning, or firing, a 12-gauge shotgun, and denies knowing anything about the flashlight until photos of it were presented in court. He denies being in Seabrook on the night of the murder. His alibi was and remains his old girlfriend, Valerie Cooper, who has never budged from her testimony that he was with her that night. We attach an affidavit from Valerie.

The brief is fifty-four pages of clear, sound reasoning, and leaves little doubt, at least in the minds of the fine folks at Guardian Ministries, that Florida got the wrong man. It should be read by learned and fair-minded judges who should be appalled and move quickly to correct an injustice, but that never happens.

We file it quietly and wait. After three days, it becomes obvious that the press has no interest, and that's fine with us. After all, the case has been closed for twenty-two years.

Since I am not licensed to practice law in Florida, we associate Susan Ashley Gross, an old friend who runs the Central Florida Innocence Project. Her name is listed first on the pleadings, above mine and Mazy's. Our representation is now public record.

I send a copy of our petition and brief to Tyler Townsend and hope for a response.

OVER IN ALABAMA, Chad Falwright makes good on his promise to seek justice for me and not the real killer. He files an ethics complaint with the Alabama bar, of which I am not a member, and one in Georgia, where my license is registered. Chad wants me disbarred for tampering with the evidence. For borrowing a pubic hair.

I've been through this before. It's a hassle and can be intimidating, but I can't slow down. Duke Russell is still serving time for Mark Carter, and this keeps me awake at night. I call a lawyer friend in Birmingham and he's itch-

ing for a fight. Mazy will take care of the complaint in
Georgia.

I'M IN THE conference room upstairs working through a
pile of desperate letters from prison when Mazy yells. I bound
down the stairs and step into her office where she and Vicki
are staring at her desktop screen. The message is in a bold,
silly font that's almost difficult to read, but the message is
clear.

> your filing in Poinsett County makes for interesting reading but
> it never mentions Kenny Taft. maybe he wasn't shot by drug dealers;
> maybe he knew too much. (this message will evaporate five minutes
> after being opened. it cannot be traced. don't bother).

We gawk at it until it slowly fades away and the page goes
blank. Vicki and I back into chairs and stare at the walls.
Mazy is pecking away and finally says, "It's a site called From
Under Patty's Porch. For twenty dollars a month, with a
credit card, you get thirty days' access to a private chat room
where messages are confidential, temporary, and cannot be
traced."

I have no idea what she's talking about. She pecks some
more, says, "Looks legitimate and probably harmless. A lot of
these servers are in Eastern Europe where the privacy rules
are stricter."

"Can we reply?" Vicki asks.

"Do we want to?" I ask.

Mazy says, "Yes, we can reply, for twenty dollars."

"It's not in the budget," Vicki says.

"This person is using the address of cassius.clay.444. We could pay up and send him a note."

"Not now," I say. "He doesn't want to talk and he's not going to say anything. Let's think about this."

Anonymous tips are part of the game and they provide an excellent way to waste a lot of time.

KENNY TAFT WAS twenty-seven years old when he was killed in a remote part of Ruiz County in 1990. He was the only black deputy on Pfitzner's force and had worked there for three years. He and his partner, Gilmer, were dispatched by Pfitzner to a site believed to be used as a staging point by cocaine smugglers, none of whom were supposed to be in the area. Taft and Gilmer were not expecting trouble. Their mission was a scouting trip supposedly requested by the DEA office in Tampa. There was only a slight possibility that the site was in fact being used, and their job was to take a look and file a report.

According to Gilmer, who survived with minor injuries, they were ambushed as they drove slowly along a gravel road at 3:00 a.m. The woods were thick and they saw no one. The first shots hit the side of the unmarked car Gilmer was driving, then the rear windows were blown out. He stopped the car and lunged out and scrambled into a ditch. On the other side, Kenny Taft also bailed out but was immediately hit in the head and died at the scene. He did not have time to pull his service revolver. When the bullets stopped, Gilmer crawled to his car and called for help.

The gunmen vanished without a trace. DEA officials believed it was the work of traffickers. Months later, an informant allegedly said the killers did not realize they were dealing with cops. There was a lot of cocaine hidden at the site, just down the road, and they were forced to protect their inventory.

The informant allegedly said they were somewhere in South America. Good luck with the search.

22

I get an angry phone call from Otis Walker. Seems his wife, June, is upset because her second husband, James Rhoad, said something bad about her in court. I patiently explain that we have not been to court yet, but we did file an affidavit signed by Rhoad in which he claims that June laughed about lying in court to nail Quincy.

"He called her a liar?" Otis asks, as if surprised. "In front of a jury?"

"No, no, Mr. Walker, not in a courtroom, just in some papers."

"Why'd he do that?"

"Because we asked him to. We're trying to get Quincy out of prison because he didn't kill that lawyer."

"So, you're saying my wife June is a liar, right?"

"We're saying she lied in court way back then."

"Same difference. Don't know how y'all can drag up all this old shit after twenty years."

"Yes sir. It's been a long time. Just ask Quincy."

"I think I should talk to a lawyer."

"You do that. Give him my phone number and I'll be happy to have a chat. But you're wasting your money."

★　　★　　★

149

FROM UNDER Patty's Porch, Mazy gets the message:

the salty pelican is an old bar on the nassau waterfront,
bahamas; be there next Tuesday at noon; it is important;
(this message will burn itself five minutes after being opened;
don't even think about trying to track it).

I grab a credit card, go to Patty's, pay up, log in as joe. frazier.555 and send my message: *Should I bring a gun or a bodyguard?*

Ten minutes later, I get: *No, I come in peace. The bar is always crowded, plenty of people around.*

I reply: *Who is supposed to recognize the other person?*

It'll work. Don't get yourself followed.

See ya.

THE DEBATE ALMOST becomes an argument. Mazy is adamant in her belief that I would be foolish to walk into such a meeting with a stranger. Vicki doesn't like it either. I maintain that it's a risk we have to take for reasons that are obvious. The person knows a lot about the case and wants to help. He or she is also frightened enough to meet out of the country, which, at least to me, indicates some really rich dirt could be collected.

Outnumbered two to one, I leave anyway and drive to Atlanta. Vicki is masterful at finding the absolute rock-bottom prices for flights, hotels, and rent-a-wrecks, and she books me on a Bahamian turbo-prop that stops twice before I leave America. It has only one flight attendant, who cannot smile and has no interest in getting out of her jump seat.

With no luggage I'm waved through customs and pick a cab from a long line. It's a vintage 1970s Cadillac with a loud radio blaring Bob Marley for us tourists. The driver smokes a joint to add to the local color. Traffic barely moves so there is little chance of a deadly crash. We stall in an impressive jam and I've had enough. I get out, pay him as he points this way and that.

The Salty Pelican is an old bar with sagging rafters and a thatched roof. Large creaky fans drop from the ceiling and offer the slightest of breezes. Genuine Bahamians play a rowdy game of dominoes at a crowded table. They appear to be gambling. Others are tossing darts in a corner. White people outnumber the natives and it's obviously a popular place for tourists. I get a beer from the bar and sit at a table under an umbrella, ten feet from the water. I'm wearing sunglasses and a baseball cap, and I'm trying to casually notice things around me. Over the years I've become a pretty good investigator, but I'm still a lousy spy. If someone is following me, I'll never know.

Noon comes and goes as I gaze at the water.

A voice behind me says, "Hello, Post." Tyler Townsend eases into the chair beside me. His was the first name on my list of prospects. "Hello," I say without calling his name, and we shake hands. He sits down with a bottle of beer.

He is also wearing sunglasses and a cap, and he's dressed like he's ready for tennis. Tanned and handsome with only a few streaks of gray. We're about the same age but he looks younger. "Come here often?" I ask.

"Yes, we own two shopping centers in Nassau, so my wife thinks I'm here on business."

"Why are we really here?"

"Let's take a walk," he says, standing. We stroll along the harbor, saying nothing, until we enter a large dock with a hundred boats. He says, "Follow me." We step down to a lower platform and he points to a beauty. It's about fifty feet long and designed to venture far into the ocean and catch those sailfish you see stuffed and hanging on walls. He jumps on board and reaches to steady me.

"This is yours?" I ask.

"I own it with my father-in-law. Let's take it for a spin." He gets two beers from a cooler, settles into the captain's chair, and starts the engines. I recline on a padded sofa and breathe in the salty air as we putter through the harbor. Before long a fine mist is spraying my face.

TYLER GREW UP in Palm Beach, the son of a prominent trial lawyer. He spent eight years at the University of Florida pursuing degrees in political science and law, with plans to go home and join the family firm. His life was derailed when his father was killed by a drunk driver a week before he was scheduled to take the bar exam. Tyler waited a year, managed to pull things together, passed the bar exam, and found a job in Seabrook.

With his future employment always secure, he had not troubled himself with diligent studying. His undergraduate résumé was quite thin. It took him five riotous years to get a bachelor's degree. He finished in the bottom third of his law class and liked it down there. He had the reputation of a quick-talking party boy, often cocky because his father was such a big shot. Suddenly, forced to look for a job, he found interviews scarce. A real estate firm in Seabrook hired him, but he lasted only eight months.

To survive the overhead, he shared office space with other lawyers. To pay bills, he volunteered for every court-appointed indigent case on the docket. Ruiz County was too small for a public defender, and the indigent cases were parceled out by the judges. His eagerness to be in the courtroom cost him dearly when the Russo murder stunned the town. Every other lawyer either left or hid, and Tyler was appointed to represent Quincy Miller, who was presumed guilty the day of his arrest.

For a twenty-eight-year-old lawyer with limited courtroom experience, his defense was nothing short of masterful. He fought fiercely, contested every piece of evidence, brawled with the State's witnesses, and believed firmly in his client's innocence.

The first time I read the trial transcript I was amused by his brashness in the courtroom. By the third reading, though, I realized that his scorched-earth defense probably alienated the jury. Regardless, the kid had enormous potential as a trial lawyer.

Then he quit the law.

WE DRIFT ALONG the edge of Paradise Island and dock at a resort. As we walk along the pier toward the hotel, Tyler says, "We're thinking about buying this place. It's for sale. I want to branch out and get away from shopping centers. My father-in-law is more conservative."

A Florida real estate developer who moves conservatively?

I nod as if I find this fascinating. Money talk gives me a migraine. Anything to do with finance, markets, hedge funds, private equity, venture capital, basis points, real estate, bonds, etc., and I glaze over. Since I don't have two nickels to rub together, I really don't care how others plot their fortunes.

We amble through the lobby like a couple of tourists from Akron and take the elevator to the third floor where Tyler has a large suite. I follow him to a terrace with a lovely view of the beach and ocean beyond. He fetches two beers from a fridge and we sit down for a talk.

He begins with "I admire you, Post, for what you're doing. I really do. I walked away from Quincy because I had no choice, but I've never believed he killed Keith Russo. I still think of him often."

"Who did?"

He exhales and takes a long drink from his bottle. He gazes at the ocean. We are under a large umbrella on a terrace, with no sign of human activity anywhere in the vicinity except for some distant laughter on the beach. He looks at me and asks, "Are you wearing a wire, Post?"

Not today. Thankfully.

"Come on, Tyler. I'm not a cop."

"You didn't answer my question."

"No. I'm not wearing a wire. You need a strip search?"

He nods and says, "Yes."

I nod back, no problem. I step away from the table and strip down to my boxers. He watches closely, and when I've gone far enough he says, "That's good."

I get dressed and return to my seat and my beer.

He says, "Sorry about that, Post, but I can't be too careful. You'll understand later."

I raise both hands and say, "Look, Tyler, I have no idea what you have on your mind, so I'll just shut up and you do the talking, okay? I know you realize that everything is deathly confidential. The people who killed Keith Russo are still around, somewhere, and they're afraid of the truth. You can trust me, okay?"

He nods and says, "I think so. You asked me who killed Russo, and the answer is I don't know. I have a good theory, in fact an excellent one, and when I tell my story I think you'll agree."

I take a swig and say, "I'm all ears."

He takes a deep breath and tries to relax. Alcohol is important here and I drain my bottle. He gets two more beers from the fridge, then leans back in his chair and gazes across the ocean. "I knew Keith Russo, and pretty well. He was about ten years older and going places, already tired of the small town and dreaming of something bigger. I wasn't particularly fond of him, no one was really. He and his wife were making some money repping drug dealers in Tampa, even had an apartment down there. Lots of rumors around Seabrook that they were planning to pull up stakes, leave the backwater, and step into the big leagues. He and Diana kept to themselves, like they were a cut above the rest of us small-time ham-and-eggers. Occasionally, they were forced to get their hands dirty when things were slow—divorces, bankruptcies, wills and deeds—but that work was beneath them. The job Keith did for Quincy in his divorce was pathetic and Quincy was rightly ticked-off. They picked the perfect stooge, didn't they, Post? Disgruntled client goes berserk and kills lazy lawyer."

"Their plan worked."

"Yes it did. The town was shocked. Quincy got arrested and everybody breathed easier. All the lawyers hid, everyone but me, and I got the call. Had no choice. At first I figured he was guilty, but he soon convinced me otherwise. I took the case and it ruined my law practice."

"You did a marvelous job at trial."

He waves me off. "I don't care anymore. That was another life." He leans in close on his elbows, as if things are now even more serious. "This is what happened to me, Post. I've never told anyone this story, not even my wife, and you can't repeat it. Not that you'll want to because it's too dangerous. But here's what happened. After the trial I was emotionally and physically exhausted. I was also disgusted with the trial and the verdict and I hated the system. But after a few weeks some of the fire returned because I had to do the appeal. I worked on it day and night and convinced myself that I could sway the Florida Supreme Court, something that rarely happens."

He takes a drink and studies the ocean. "And the bad guys were watching me. I just knew it. I became paranoid about my phones, apartment, office, car, everything. There were two anonymous phone calls and both times a really eerie male voice said, 'Back off.' That's it. Just, 'Back off.' I couldn't report this to the police because I didn't trust them. Pfitzner was in control of everything and he was the enemy. Hell, he was probably the voice on the other end.

"About five or six months after the trial, while I was working on the appeal, two of my law school buddies knew I needed to get away, so they planned a bonefishing trip to Belize. Ever tried bonefishing?"

I've never heard of bonefishing. "No."

"It's a blast. You stalk 'em in the saltwater flats, great here in the Bahamas and throughout Central America. Belize has some of the best. My buddies invited me down and I needed a break. Bonefishing is a real boys' adventure—no wives, no girlfriends, plenty of drinking. So I went. The second night there, we went to a beach party not far from our fishing lodge. Lots of locals, some women, plenty of gringos there to fish and drink. Things got pretty rowdy. We were chugging beers and rum punch but not to the point of blacking out. We weren't college-hammered, but my drink got spiked and someone took me away. To where I don't know, will never know. I woke up on the floor of a concrete cell with no windows. Hot as hell, a sauna. My head was splitting and I needed to throw up. There was a small bottle of water on the floor and I gulped it down. I had been stripped down to my boxers. I sat there on the hot floor for hours and waited. Then the door opened and two really nasty boys with handguns came after me. They slapped me around, blindfolded me, and tied my wrists together, then marched me for probably half an hour down a dirt path. I was stumbling and dying of thirst, and every ten steps or so one of the thugs cussed me in Spanish and pushed me forward. When we stopped they tied a rope to my wrist, stretched my arms above my head, and yanked me up. It hurt like hell and led to shoulder surgery a year later, but I wasn't thinking about later. I bounced off wooden beams as I went up and finally stopped at the top of a tower where they pulled off my blindfold and allowed me to soak in the scenery. We were at the edge of a pond or a swampy bayou or something, about the size of a football field. The water was thick and brown and filled with crocodiles. Lots of crocodiles. With me on the deck were three more heavily armed dudes who weren't very friendly, and two skinny kids who couldn't have been more than eighteen. They were dark-skinned and completely naked. A zip line of sorts ran from the tower, dipped across the pond, and was tied off at a tree on the other side. If not for the crocs, it might have been a fun summertime swimming hole with a zip line. If not for the crocs. My head was pounding and my heart was about to explode. They picked up a burlap sack filled with bloody chickens and hitched it to the zip line, then released it. As it swung down to the water it dripped blood, and this really excited the crocodiles. When the sack stopped over the center of the pond, one of the guards pulled a cord and the dead chickens dropped in a heap on top of the crocs. They must have been starving because they went crazy.

"With the appetizer served, it was time for the entrée. They grabbed the first skinny Latino boy and hitched his wrists to the zip line. He screamed as they kicked him off the tower and screamed even louder as he flew across the pond. When he stopped in the center, his toes were about ten feet above the crocs. The poor boy was crying and screaming. It was awful, just awful. Slowly, a guard turned a crank and down he went. He kicked frantically, as you can imagine. He kicked and screamed for his life but soon his feet were in the water, and the crocs began ripping apart his flesh and bones. The guard kept turning the crank, the boy went farther down. I watched a human being eaten alive."

He takes a drink and studies the ocean. "Post, there is no way to describe the fear, the absolute horror of watching something as indescribable as that and knowing you're waiting in a very short line. I wet my boxers. I thought I was going to faint. I wanted to jump but the guards had us. Fear as few people have ever known it. Facing a firing squad must be awful, but at least the killing is over in a flash. Being eaten alive, well.

"Anyway, as they were hitching up the second boy I realized what was obvious—that I had been chosen to go last so I could suffer the nightmare of watching the first two.

"Something else happened. I heard laughter off to my right, on the other side of a small building. Male voices, laughing at the sport, and I wondered how often these good ole boys met here for fun and games. I made a move toward the edge of the platform but a guard yanked me by the hair and threw me against the railing. These guys were burly and nasty and I wasn't really strong enough to resist, not that it would have worked. I tried to look away but the guard grabbed my hair again and hissed, 'Look! You look!'

"They shoved the second boy off the tower. He screamed even louder, and when they dangled him above the crocodiles he kicked and bawled something about 'Maria! Maria!' When they began to lower him I closed my eyes. The sounds of his flesh ripping and bones cracking were sickening. I finally fainted but it didn't help my cause. They slapped me viciously, pulled me to my feet, hitched me to the zip line, and shoved me off the tower. I heard the laughter again. When I stopped above the middle of the pond, I glanced down. I told myself not to but I couldn't help it. Nothing but blood, bone fragments, body parts, and all those frenzied crocodiles wanting more. When I realized I was descending, I thought about my mother and sister and how they would never know what happened to me. And it was good that they would never know. I didn't scream or yell or cry, but I couldn't stop kicking. When the first fat croc lunged for my foot, I heard a loud voice call out in Spanish. I began my ascent.

"They lowered me from the tower and put on the blindfold. I was too weak to walk so they found a golf cart. I was thrown back into the same cell where I curled into a ball on the concrete floor and cried and sweated for at least an hour before the guards returned. One knocked me down and pinned my arm against my back while the other injected me with a drug. When I woke up I was back in Belize, in the bed of a pickup truck driven by two cops. We stopped at the jail and I followed them inside. One gave me a cup of coffee while the other explained that my two friends were very worried about me. They had been told that I was in jail for public drunkenness, and that would be the best story to stick with.

"Once my head cleared and I was back at the fishing lodge, I talked to my buddies and tried to put together a time line. I told them I'd been in jail, no big deal, just another adventure. The abduction lasted for about forty hours and I'm sure it involved a boat, a helicopter, and an airplane, but my memory was shot. The drugs. I couldn't wait to get out of Belize and back home. I'll never again subject myself to the jurisdiction of a third world country. I quit bonefishing too."

He stops and gulps some more beer. I'm too stunned to say anything but manage to mumble, "That's insane."

"It still causes nightmares. I have to fib to my wife when I wake up yelling. It's always just under the surface."

All I can do is shake my head.

"Back in Seabrook, I was a mess. I couldn't eat or sleep, couldn't stay at the office. I locked myself in my bedroom and tried to nap, always with a loaded gun. I was exhausted to the point of collapse because I couldn't sleep. I saw those two boys over and over. I heard their screams, their anguished cries, the horrifying frenzy of the hungry crocs, bones breaking, and laughter off in the distance. I thought about suicide, Post, I really did."

He drains his bottle and goes to the fridge for more. He sits down and continues, "Somehow, I convinced myself that it was all a dream caused by too much booze and a spiked drink. A month passed and I slowly began to pull things together. Then this arrived in the mail."

He reaches for a file I had not noticed. As he opens it he says, "Post, I've never shown this to anyone." He hands me an 8x10 color photo. It's Tyler, in his boxers, dangling from the zip line with his feet just inches above the raging open mouth and jagged teeth of a large crocodile. The terror in his face is indescribable. It's a close shot, with nothing in the background to indicate place or time.

I gawk at it, then look at Tyler. He's wiping a tear from a cheek and says in a weak voice, "Look, I need to make a call, okay? It's business. Grab another beer and I'll be back in fifteen minutes. There's more to the story."

23

I put the photo back in the file and leave it on the table, never to see it again, I hope. I walk to the edge of the terrace and gaze at the ocean. There are too many wild thoughts spinning around to grab just one and analyze it. But fear dominates them all. Fear that drove Tyler out of the profession. Fear that keeps his secrets buried. Fear that weakens my knees some twenty years after his abduction.

I'm lost in my thoughts and do not hear him return to the terrace. He startles me with "What's your main thought right now, Post?" He's standing beside me with black coffee in a paper cup.

"Why didn't they just kill you? No one would ever know."

"The obvious question and one that I've had twenty years to think about. My best answer is that they needed me. They had their conviction. Quincy was headed to prison forever. They must have had some concern about his appeal, and since I was writing it they wanted me to back off. And I did. I raised all the obvious legal issues on appeal, but I really toned down the language. I took a knee, Post. I mailed it in. You've read it, right?"

"Sure, I've read everything. I thought your brief was sound."

The Guardians

"Legally, yes, but I was going through the motions. Not that it would've mattered. The Florida Supreme Court was not going to reverse his conviction regardless of what I wrote. Quincy had no idea. He thought I was still raging against his injustice, but I backed off."

"The Court affirmed unanimously."

"No surprise there. I filed the usual perfunctory appeal to the U.S. Supreme Court. Denied as always. And I told Quincy it was over."

"And that's why you didn't ask for post-conviction relief?"

"That, plus there was no new evidence at that time. I threw in the towel and walked away. Needless to say, I wasn't getting paid at that point. Two years later, Quincy filed his own motions from prison, got one of the jailhouse lawyers to help him, but they went nowhere."

He turns and walks back to the table and takes his seat. He places the file in an empty chair. I join him and we sit for a long, silent spell. Finally, he says, "Just think of the logistics, Post. They knew I was going fishing in Belize, knew where I would be staying, so they must have been listening to my phones. This was before the Internet, so no e-mails to hack. Think of the manpower it took to spike my drink, drag me away, load me up in a boat or plane and take me to their little camp where they made sport out of feeding their enemies to the crocodiles. The zip line was pretty elaborate, the crocs plentiful and hungry."

"A well-organized gang."

"Yes, one with plenty of money, resources, contacts with local police, maybe border agents, everything the best narco-traffickers need. They certainly made a believer out of me. I finished the appeal, but I was a wreck. I finally got

163

some counseling, told my therapist I'd been threatened by
people who could make good with their threats, and that I
was cracking up over it. He got me through it and I eventually packed up and left town. You need any more proof that
Quincy didn't kill Russo?"

"No, and I really didn't need this."

"This is a secret that will never be told, Post. And this is
the reason I'm not getting involved with anyone's efforts to
help Quincy."

"So you know more than you're telling?"

He considers this while he sips coffee. "Let's just say that I
know some things."

"What can you tell me about Brad Pfitzner? I assume you
knew him pretty well back then."

"There were suspicions about Pfitzner back then, but they
were always whispered. A few of the lawyers who worked the
criminal beat, including me, heard more of the gossip than
the others. There was a small port on the Gulf called Poley's
Inlet. It was in Ruiz County, thus under his control. The rumors were that he allowed the drugs to come in there and get
warehoused in remote parts of the county before being dis-
tributed north toward Atlanta. Again, only rumors. Pfitzner
was never caught, never charged. After I left, I watched from
a distance and kept in touch with a couple of lawyer friends in
Seabrook. The Feds never got their hands on Brad."

"And Kenny Taft?"

"Taft was killed not long before I left town. There were
rumors that the murder did not go down the way Pfitzner
described. Again, like Russo, Pfitzner was in charge of the
investigation and could write the story any way he wanted.
He made a big production of losing one of his own men. Big

funeral, procession, cops from all over lining the streets. A glorious send-off for a fallen soldier."

"Is the Taft angle important?" I ask. He goes silent and studies the ocean. To me, the answer becomes obvious, but he says, "I don't know. Might be something there."

I'm not going to push him. I've already gotten far more than I expected, and we'll talk again. I note his reluctance to discuss Kenny Taft and decide to move on.

"So why take out Keith Russo?" I ask.

He shrugs as if the answer should now be obvious. "He did something to upset the gang and they hit him. The quickest way to catch a bullet is to rat out. Maybe the DEA pressured him and flipped him. With Russo out of the way and Quincy taking the fall, it was soon business as usual. They wanted the conviction to stand, and I decided to go bonefishing."

"Pfitzner retired to the Keys where he lives in a nice condo appraised by the county at one point six million," I say. "Not bad for a sheriff who earned sixty thousand at his peak."

"And didn't finish high school so probably not too savvy of an investor. I'll bet most of his loot is buried offshore. Be careful where you dig, Post. You might find things you wish you'd left alone."

"Digging is part of my job."

"But not mine. This is all history for me. I have a good life, with a beautiful wife and three teenagers. I'm not getting involved after today. Good luck and all that, but I don't want to see you again."

"Understood. Thanks for the meeting."

"This suite is yours if you want. If you stay, you can take a cab back to the airport in the morning."

"Thanks, but I'll leave with you."

24

According to Section 13A-10-129 of the Alabama Code of Criminal Conduct, a person who "removes or alters physical evidence" from an official proceeding is guilty of tampering. And, though it is only a Class A misdemeanor, it can be punishable by up to one year in jail and a fine of $5,000. Normally, in a misdemeanor case, the complaining party, in this case the DA Chad Falwright, would simply file an affidavit accusing me of the crime and ask the sheriff to issue a warrant for my arrest.

But Chad is frightened these days because the greatest achievement of his lackluster career is about to become his biggest screwup. He is up for reelection next year, not that anybody really wants his job, and if it becomes known that he prosecuted and almost executed Duke Russell for someone else's murder, then he *might* lose some votes. So Chad is fighting back, and hard. Instead of pursuing the lofty goal of finding the truth and unraveling an injustice, he attacks me because I'm trying to prove him wrong and exonerate an innocent man.

To prove his toughness, he convenes a grand jury in Verona and gets an indictment charging me with tampering. He calls Jim Bizko with *The Birmingham News* and squawks about this major accomplishment. But Bizko despises Chad and asks why he refuses to submit all seven pubic hairs for DNA testing. Bizko does not report the indictment.

My pal in Alabama is Steve Rosenberg, a radical lawyer from New York who moved south and remains noticeably unassimilated in his strange surroundings. He runs a nonprofit in Birmingham and defends dozens of death penalty cases.

Rosenberg calls Chad and they engage in an extensive cuss fight, and not for the first time. When the dust settles, it is agreed that I will surrender myself to Chad in his office, get processed, and immediately appear before a judge to discuss bail. There is a chance that I could spend a night or two in jail but this does not worry me. If my clients can endure decades in horrible prisons, I can certainly survive a brief stint in a county joint.

This is my first indictment and I'm quite proud of it. I have a book on my shelf about noted lawyers who were thrown in jail fighting for their clients, and I would be honored to join them. Rosenberg once spent a week behind bars for contempt in Mississippi. He still laughs about it, says he picked up some new clients.

We meet in front of the courthouse and embrace. Steve is pushing sixty and looks more radical with age. His thick gray hair is shoulder length and unkempt. He has added an earring and a small tattoo across his carotid artery. He grew up a brawler in Brooklyn and practices law like a street fighter. He's fearless and likes nothing more than charging into old courthouses in backwater towns throughout the South and mixing it up with the locals.

"All of this for one lousy pubic hair?" he laughs. "I could've loaned you one of mine."

"More than likely it would be too gray," I reply.

"Ridiculous. Just ridiculous." We enter the courthouse and walk upstairs to Chad's office. The sheriff is waiting with two deputies, one of whom is holding a camera. In a show of real hospitality, the locals have agreed to go through the motions in the courthouse and avoid the jail, for now anyway. I sent them a set of my fingerprints two days ago. I pose for my mug shot, thank the sheriff, who seems bored with it all, and wait for Chad. When we are finally shown into his office, no one makes even the slightest effort to shake hands. Rosenberg and I thoroughly loathe this guy and he feels the same toward us. As we struggle with the preliminary chatter, it is obvious that he is preoccupied, even nervous.

We soon understand why. At 1:00 p.m., we enter the main courtroom and take our seats at the defense table. Chad assumes the other one with a couple of assistants. The courtroom is the domain of the Honorable Leon Raney, a crusty old fossil who presided over Duke's trial and never gave the kid a break. There are no spectators. No one cares. It's just a pubic hair taken by an innocence lawyer from Georgia. Chad's dream of generating a bit of publicity fails again.

Instead of a grouchy old white man in a black robe, a young and very pretty black lady in a maroon robe appears on the bench, and, with a smile, says good afternoon. Judge Marlowe informs us that Judge Raney has taken a leave of absence because of a stroke last week, and that she will be pinch-hitting until he returns. She is from Birmingham and has been sent in by special orders from the Alabama Supreme

Court. We begin to understand why Chad is so nervous. His home-field advantage has been annulled by an honest referee.

Judge Marlowe's first order of business is my initial appearance and the issue of my bail. She nods at the court reporter, goes on the record, and begins, pleasantly, with "I've read the indictment and frankly, Mr. Falwright, there's not much to this case. Surely you have better things to do. Mr. Rosenberg, does your client still have possession of the pubic hair that was DNA tested?"

Rosenberg is on his feet. "Sure does, Judge. It's right here on the table and we would like to return it to Mr. Falwright, or whoever has the evidence file these days. My client didn't tamper with or steal anything. He simply borrowed one of the pubic hairs. He was forced to, Your Honor, because Mr. Falwright refuses to do DNA testing."

"Let me see it," she says.

Rosenberg picks up a small plastic bag and hands it to her. Without opening it, she looks, strains, finally sees something, and puts it down. She frowns and shakes her head and says to Falwright, "You gotta be kidding."

Chad stumbles to his feet and begins stuttering. He's been the DA here for twenty years, and for his entire career he's had the protection of a like-minded right-winger with little sympathy for those accused of crimes. Leon Raney was his predecessor in the DA's office. Suddenly, Chad is forced to play on a level field and he does not know the rules.

"This is a serious matter, Your Honor," he wails with fake indignation. "The defendant, Mr. Post, admits he stole the evidence from the files, files that are protected, files that are sacrosanct." Chad loves big words and often tries to impress juries with them, but, reading the trial transcript, he often gets them wrong.

She replies, "Well, if I read the record correctly, the pubic hair in question was gone for over a year before you or anyone else realized it was missing, and it came to your attention only when Mr. Post told you about it."

"We can't guard all of the old files, Your Honor—"

She raises a hand and cuts him off. "Mr. Rosenberg, do you have a motion?"

"Yes ma'am. I move to dismiss this charge against Mr. Post."

"So ordered," she says immediately.

Chad's mouth falls open and he manages to grunt before falling, loudly, into his chair. She glares at him with a look that frightens me, and I've just been cleared.

She picks up another stack of papers and says, "Now, Mr. Rosenberg, I have before me your petition for post-conviction relief filed two months ago on behalf of Duke Russell. Since I am the presiding judge, and will be for an unknown period of time, I am inclined to proceed with this petition. Are you prepared to do so?"

Rosenberg and I are on the verge of some serious laughter. "Yes ma'am," he replies at full throttle.

Chad has turned pale and is once again struggling to get to his feet. "Mr. Falwright?" she asks.

"No way, Judge. Come on. The State has not even filed a response. How can we proceed?"

"You'll proceed if I tell you to proceed. The State has had two months to respond, so what's taking so long? These delays are unfair and unconscionable. Have a seat, please." She nods at Rosenberg and both lawyers sit down. Everyone takes a deep breath.

She clears her throat and says, "At issue here is a simple request by the defense to DNA test all seven pubic hairs taken from the crime scene. The defense is willing to bear the expense of the testing. DNA is now used every day to both include and exclude suspects and defendants. Yet, as I understand it, the State, through your office, Mr. Falwright, is refusing to allow testing. Why? What are you afraid of? If the testing excludes Duke Russell, then we're looking at a wrongful conviction. If it nails Mr. Russell, you will have plenty of ammunition to argue he received a fair trial. I've read the file, Mr. Falwright, all fourteen hundred pages of the trial transcript and everything else. The conviction of Mr. Russell was based on bite-mark and hair analysis, both of which have been proven, time and again, to be wildly unreliable. I have doubts about this conviction, Mr. Falwright, and I'm ordering DNA testing for all seven hairs."

"I'll appeal that order," Chad says without bothering to stand.

"I'm sorry. Are you trying to address the court?"

Chad stands again and says, "I will appeal such an order."

"Of course you will. Why are you so opposed to DNA testing, Mr. Falwright?"

Rosenberg and I exchange looks of sheer disbelief, with no small amount of humor thrown in. In our business, we rarely have the upper hand and almost never see a judge peel skin off a prosecutor. Our astonishment is hard to conceal.

Chad, still standing, manages to say, "It's just not necessary, Your Honor. Duke Russell was convicted in a fair trial by fair-minded jurors in this very courtroom. We're just wasting time."

"I'm not wasting time, Mr. Falwright. But I believe you are. You're stalling and trying to avoid the inevitable. This tampering charge is further proof of that. I've ordered the testing, and if you appeal my order you will only waste more time. I suggest you cooperate and let's get it done."

She glares at Chad with a withering look that rattles him. When he can't think of anything to say, she wraps up the hearing with "I want all seven pubic hairs on this desk within the hour. It would be awfully convenient for them to simply disappear."

"Judge, please," Chad tries to protest. She raps the gavel and says, "Court's adjourned."

CHAD, OF COURSE, does not cooperate. He waits until the last possible moment to appeal her order, and the issue is sent to the state supreme court where it could languish for a year or so. Up there the Supremes have no deadline forcing them to rule on such matters and they are notoriously slow, especially in post-conviction relief cases. Years ago they affirmed Duke's conviction after his trial and set a date for his execution, then they denied his first effort at relief. Most appellate judges, state and federal, despise these cases because they drag on for decades. And once they decide that a defendant is guilty, they rarely change their minds, regardless of new evidence.

And so we wait. Rosenberg and I discuss the strategy of pushing hard for a hearing before Judge Marlowe. Our fear is that old Judge Raney might recover and take his job back, though this is unlikely. He's in his early eighties, golden years for a federal judge but a bit long in the tooth for an elected one. However, we are faced with the obvious reality that without DNA testing we cannot prevail.

I return to Holman and death row to visit with Duke. It's been over three months since I last saw him and delivered the news that we had found the real killer. That euphoric moment has long since passed. These days his moods swing from raw anger to deep depression. Our phone conversations have not been pleasant.

Prison is a nightmare for those who deserve it. For those who don't, it is a daily struggle to maintain some level of sanity. For those who suddenly learn that there is proof of their innocence yet they remain locked up, the situation is literally maddening.

25

I'm driving on a two-lane highway, headed east in either Mississippi or Alabama, it's hard to say because these pine forests all look the same. Savannah is the destination in general. I haven't been home in three weeks and I need a break. My cell buzzes and the ID says it's Glenn Colacurci, the old lawyer in Seabrook.

It's not him but rather his comely little secretary, Bea, and she wants to know when I'll be back in the area. Glenn wants to talk but would rather meet somewhere other than Seabrook.

Three days later, I walk into The Bull, a popular bar in Gainesville. In a booth near the back, I see Bea as she waves and begins scooting out. Seated across from her and spiffed up nicely is Attorney Colacurci. Blue seersucker suit, starched white shirt, striped bow tie, suspenders.

Bea excuses herself and I take her seat. The waitress informs us that the bartender just happens to be concocting his own special recipe of sangria and we really should try it. We order two glasses.

"I love Gainesville," Glenn says. "I spent seven years here in another lifetime. Great town. Great university. What's your school, Post? Can't remember."

I don't recall mentioning it to him. "Tennessee, under-grad. Good ole Rocky Top."

He offers a slight grimace at this, says, "Not my favorite song."

"And I'm not much of a Gator fan either."

"Of course not." We've managed to skip the weather, which in the South consumes at least the first five minutes of every casual conversation between two men before the sub-ject turns to football, which goes on for an average of fifteen minutes. I am often almost rude in my desire to avoid wasting all this time.

"Let's skip the football, Glenn. That's not why we're here."

The waitress delivers two impressive glasses of pinkish sangria on ice.

When she's gone he says, "No, it's not. My girl found your petition online and printed me a copy. Not much of a com-puter man myself. Interesting reading. Well reasoned, well argued, very convincing."

"Thank you. That's what we do."

"Got me to thinking back some twenty years ago. After Kenny Taft got murdered, there was some speculation that that episode did not go down like Pfitzner said. A lot of ru-mors that Taft got ambushed by his own men, Pfitzner's boys. Perhaps our fine sheriff was involved in the drug trade, as you suspect. Perhaps Taft knew too much. At any rate, that case has been cold for twenty years. No sign of the killers, no evidence at all."

I nod politely as he warms up. I hit my straw and he fol-lows my lead.

"Taft's partner was a boy named Brace Gilmer, who walked away with minor injuries, seems like he may have been nicked by a bullet, but nothing serious. I knew his mother, an old client from an old lawsuit. Gilmer left town not long after the killing and never came back. Years ago I bumped into his mother and we had a nice chat. She told me then, must've been fifteen years ago, that Brace believed that he was also a target that night and just got lucky. He and Taft were the same age, twenty-seven, and got on well. Taft was the only black deputy and didn't have many friends. He also knew something about the Russo murder, at least according to Gilmer. Have you talked to him by chance?"

"We have not." We can't find him. Vicki can usually track down anyone in twenty-four hours, but so far Brace Gilmer has eluded us.

"Didn't think so. His mother moved away sometime back. I found her last week in a retirement home near Winter Haven. She's older than me and in bad health, but we had a nice chat on the phone. You want to talk to Gilmer."

"Probably," I say with restraint. Gilmer is at the top of my list these days.

Glenn slides over one of his business cards. On the back is scribbled the name: *Bruce Gilmer.* The address is in Sun Valley.

"Idaho?" I ask.

"He was in the Marines and met a girl from there. His mother thinks he may not be too talkative. He got scared and left town a long time ago."

"And changed his name."

"Looks like it."

"Why would the guy's mother give out his address if he doesn't want to talk?" I ask.

He circles an index finger around his ear to indicate she's crazy. "I suppose I caught her on a good day." He laughs like he's really clever and pulls long and hard on his straw. I take a sip. His big nose is red and his eyes leak like a drinker's. I start to feel the alcohol.

He continues, "And so a few weeks ago I was having drinks with another old-fart lawyer in Seabrook, guy you don't know. We used to be partners back in the day but he quit after his wife died and left him some money. I told him about meeting you and about your theories and such, and I gave him a copy of your petition. He says he always suspected Pfitzner got the wrong man because Pfitzner wanted the wrong man. Keith knew too much and had to be disposed of. Frankly though, Post, I just don't remember conversations like that at the time of the murder."

This old gossip is of no benefit at all. After a town rushes to judgment, it's only natural that some people take the time to reflect as the years pass. Most folks, though, are just relieved that somebody got convicted and the case is closed.

I have what I need and am unlikely to gather any more useful information. As he drains his glass, his eyelids begin to droop. He probably drinks his lunch most days and naps throughout the afternoon.

We shake hands and say goodbye like old friends. I offer to get the check, but he's decided to have some more sangria. As I'm walking away, Bea appears out of nowhere, and with a big smile says she'll see me later.

KENNY TAFT LEFT behind a pregnant wife, Sybil, and a two-year-old child. After his death, Sybil returned to her hometown of Ocala, became a schoolteacher, remarried, and had another child.

Like nightfall, Frankie eases into town and finds her home, a nice split-level in the suburbs. Vicki has done her research and we know that Sybil is married to a high school principal. Their home is assessed at $170,000 and taxes last year were $18,000. There is one mortgage that is eight years old. Both vehicles have bank loans. Evidently, she and her husband live a quiet life in a nice section of town.

And Sybil does not wish to disturb her life. On the phone, she tells Frankie that she does not want to talk about her deceased husband. The tragedy of Kenny's murder was twenty-plus years ago and it took her a long time to get over it. The fact that the killers have never been found only makes it worse. No, she knows nothing that was not known back then. Frankie presses a little and she gets upset. The line goes dead. He reports to me and we decide to back off, for now.

DRIVING NONSTOP FOR three days from Savannah to Boise would have been easier than flying there. Because of weather somewhere in between, I sit in the Atlanta airport for thirteen hours as flights fall like dominoes. I camp out near a bar and watch the stranded walk in and, hours later, stagger out. Once again, I am thankful that alcohol is not my temptation. I eventually make it to Minneapolis where I am informed that my flight to Boise is overbooked. I stand by and stand by and am finally awarded the last seat. We arrive in Boise at 2:30 a.m. and, of course, the rental car I reserved is not available because the rental desk is closed.

Other than the frustration, though, this is not a big deal. I have no appointment in Sun Valley. Bruce Gilmer does not know I'm on my way.

Leave it to Vicki to find a really cheap motel in this famous resort area. At dawn I drag myself into a small room in a run-down tourist trap next door in Ketchum, and sleep for hours.

Gilmer is employed by a Sun Valley resort as a golf course manager. We don't know much about him, but since there are no divorce records for either Brace or Bruce Gilmer we are assuming he is still married to the same woman. Nor could Vicki find any official record of Brace legally changing his name to Bruce. Regardless, he did a nice job of leaving Seabrook behind some twenty years ago. He's now forty-seven, a year younger than me.

Driving from Ketchum to Sun Valley, I can't take my eyes off the mountains and the scenery. The weather is a dream. It was ninety-five and sticky when I left Savannah. Here it's about thirty degrees cooler and if there is humidity I can't feel it.

The resort is exclusive, for members only, and this is tricky. But the collar always helps. I put it on and stop at the gate. I tell the guard that I have an appointment with Bruce Gilmer. He checks a clipboard as cars line up behind me. Most are probably golfers eager to tee off. He finally gives me a pass and waves me through.

At the pro shop I ask for Mr. Gilmer and get directions. His office is in a building hidden from view and surrounded by tractors, mowers, and irrigation equipment. I ask a laborer and he points to a man standing under a terrace talking on the phone. I ease behind him and wait. When the phone is put away, I step up and say, "Excuse me, are you Bruce Gilmer?"

He turns, faces me, immediately notices the collar, and assumes I'm a minister of some variety instead of a nosy lawyer digging through his past.

"I am. And you are?"

"Cullen Post, with Guardian Ministries," I say as I hand him my card. I've done this so often my timing is perfect.

He studies the card, slowly extends a hand, says, "Nice to meet you."

"And you."

"What can I do for you?" he asks with a smile. After all, the guy works in a service business. The customer first and all that.

"I'm an Episcopal priest and I'm also a lawyer, an innocence lawyer. I work with clients who have been wrongfully convicted and I try to get them out of prison. Men like Quincy Miller. He's my client now. Can I have a few minutes of your time?"

The smile vanishes and he glances around. "To talk about what?"

"Kenny Taft."

He sort of grunts and sort of laughs as his shoulders sag. He blinks a few times as if in disbelief and mumbles, "You gotta be kidding."

"Look, I'm one of the good guys, okay? I'm not here to frighten you or blow your cover. Kenny Taft knew something about the murder of Keith Russo and maybe he took it to his grave, maybe he didn't. I'm just chasing leads, Mr. Gilmer."

"It's Bruce." He nods to a door and says, "Let's step into my office."

Thankfully, he has no secretary. He spends his time outdoors, and his office has the cluttered look of a man who would rather repair a sprinkler head than type a letter.

There's junk everywhere and old calendars tacked to the walls. He points to a chair and falls into one behind his metal desk.

"How'd you find me?" he asks.

"Just happened to be in the area."

"No. Seriously."

"Well, you're not exactly hiding, Bruce. And what happened to Brace?"

"How much do you know?"

"A ton. I know Quincy Miller didn't kill Keith Russo. His murder was a gang hit, drug dealers, and Pfitzner was probably covering for the gang. I doubt I'll ever find the man who pulled the trigger, but I don't have to. My job is to prove Quincy didn't do it."

"Good luck with that." He takes off his cap and runs his fingers through his hair.

"They're all long shots, but we win more than we lose. I've walked eight of my clients out of prison."

"And this is all you do?"

"You got it. I have six clients right now, including Quincy. Did you know him, by chance?"

"No. He grew up in Seabrook, same as Kenny Taft, but I'm from Alachua. Never met the man."

"So you didn't work on the murder investigation?"

"Oh no, couldn't get near it. Pfitzner was in charge and he kept it all to himself."

"Did you know Russo?"

"Not really. I knew who he was, saw him in court from time to time. It's a small town. You're convinced he wasn't killed by Quincy Miller?"

"One hundred percent."

He ponders this for a moment. His eye and hand movements are slow. He never blinks. He's over the shock of someone from his past tracking him down and does not appear to be concerned.

I say, "I have a question, Bruce. Are you still hiding?"

He smiles and replies, "Not really. It's been a long time, you know? My wife and I left in a hurry, sort of in the middle of the night, eager to leave the place behind, and for the first couple of years I kept looking over my shoulder."

"But why? Why did you leave and what were you afraid of?"

"You know, Post, I'm not sure I want to talk about this. I don't know you, you don't know me. I left my baggage behind in Seabrook and it can stay there for all I care."

"Understood. But why would I repeat any of this to anyone else? You were not a witness in Quincy's case. I couldn't drag you back to Seabrook if I wanted to. You have nothing to say in court."

"Then why are you here?"

"Because I believe Kenny Taft knew something about the Russo murder and I'm desperate to find out."

"Kenny can't talk."

"Granted. But did he ever tell you something about Russo?"

He thinks long and hard and begins shaking his head. "I don't remember anything," he says, but I doubt he's telling the truth. He's uncomfortable here so he does what is expected and moves to another subject. "A gang hit, like a contract killing?"

"Something like that."

"How can you be so sure? I thought there was no doubt Miller killed the lawyer."

How can I be sure? The visual of Tyler hanging just inches above the crocs flashes through my mind. "I can't tell you everything I know, Bruce. I'm a lawyer and most of my work is confidential."

"If you say so. Look, I'm pretty busy right now." He glances at his watch and does a lame job of acting as though he's now pressed for time. He suddenly wants me out of the room.

"Sure," I say. "I'll be around for a few days, taking some time off. Can we talk again?"

"Talk about what?"

"I'd like to know what happened the night Kenny got killed."

"How would that benefit your client?"

"You never know, Bruce. My job is to keep digging. You have my number."

26

I take a lift to the top of Bald Mountain and slowly hike down 5,000 feet. I am pathetically out of shape and have many excuses for it. Number one is my nomadic lifestyle, which prevents any chance of a daily workout in a nice gym. The low-end motels Vicki finds do not advertise such amenities. Number two is the fact that I spend far too much time sitting and not standing or walking. At forty-eight my hips are beginning to ache and I know it's from endless hours behind the wheel. On the plus side, I eat and drink as little as possible and have never touched tobacco. My last physical was two years ago and the doctor said everything looked fine. Years ago he told me that the secret to a long healthy life is to consume as little food as possible. Exercise is important but cannot reverse the damaging effects of too many calories. I have tried to follow his advice.

So to celebrate the hike I stop at a lovely lodge near the base and consume a cheeseburger and two beers while basking in the sun. I'm sure this place can be frightening in the winter, but in mid-July it is heavenly.

I call Bruce Gilmer's office number and get voice mail. I'll pester him today and tomorrow, then leave town. I can't see making this journey again. Future conversations will be by phone, if they happen at all.

I find a library in Ketchum and make myself at home. I have a stack of materials to read, including Guardian's assessment of a potential new client in North Carolina. Joey Barr has spent seven years in prison for a rape he claims he didn't do. His victim agrees. Both have sworn that their relations were completely consensual. Joey is black, the girl white, and when they were seventeen they were caught in bed by her father, a rough character. He pressured her to file charges, point the finger and keep doing so until Joey was convicted by an all-white jury. The girl's mother, who had divorced the girl's father and despised the man, took up Joey's cause after he was sent away. Mother and daughter have spent the past five years trying to convince the appellate courts and anyone else who might listen that Joey is innocent.

Such is the nature of my daily reading. I haven't had the luxury of finishing a novel in years.

The brain trust at Guardian believes that we are about to walk Duke Russell out of prison, so it's time to think about reloading our docket.

I'm in a quiet reading room on the main floor of the Ketchum public library, with papers strewn about a small table, as if I own the place, when my phone vibrates. Bruce is getting off work and wants to talk.

HE DRIVES A golf cart along an asphalt path and we wind around the course. It's busy, with golfers hacking away on a perfect cloudless day. He stops on a ridge overlooking a gorgeous fairway and puts on the brake.

"Just beautiful," I say, absorbing the mountains in the distance.

"You play?" he asks.

"No. Never have. I assume you have a low handicap."

"At one time, yes, but not so much now. Not enough time. A round takes four hours and it's hard to squeeze it in. I talked to my lawyer this morning. He's down there on the tenth green."

"What did he have to say?" I ask.

"Not much. Here's the deal, Post. I'm not going to say anything that might get me involved, not that I know anything to begin with. I'm not signing an affidavit and I'll ignore any subpoena. No court in Florida can touch me anyway."

"I'm not asking for any of that."

"Good. You said you wanted to talk about the night we were ambushed. How much do you know?"

"We have a copy of the file from the Florida state police. Freedom of Information stuff. So we know the basics, know what you said to the investigators."

"Good. I didn't tell them everything, as you might guess. I got nicked in the shoulder and was in the hospital for a couple of days before I talked to anyone. Had time to think. You see, Post, I'm sure Pfitzner set up the ambush and sent us in. I'm sure Kenny was the target, but they also tried to kill me too, and they would have but I got lucky."

"Lucky?"

He holds up a hand as if to say, "Hang on."

"It was a narrow gravel road with thick woods on both sides. Very dark, three a.m. We got hit from both sides and the rear, so there were several bad boys with guns. Man, it was awful. We were riding along having a laugh, not too

186

worried about anything, and in a flash the rear window got blown out, bullets were popping through the side windows, all hell broke loose. I don't remember stopping the car but I did, slammed it in park, then slid out the door and into a ditch, bullets smacking my door and ricocheting everywhere. I heard Kenny when he got hit. Back of the head. I had my service revolver loaded and cocked, but it was pitch black. As suddenly as it started, it stopped. I could hear men moving in the woods. The thugs were not leaving. They were getting closer. I peeked through some weeds, saw a silhouette, and fired. Nailed him. I was a good shot, Post, back in the day. He screamed and yelled something, and, Post, it was not in Spanish. No sir. I know a cracker when I hear one, and that poor bastard grew up within fifty miles of Seabrook. They suddenly had a problem—a badly wounded comrade, maybe even a dead one. He needed help but where could they go? Wasn't my problem, really. But they backed off, retreated, vanished in the woods. I waited and waited and noticed blood on my left arm. After a few minutes, could've been five, could've been thirty, I crawled around the car and found Kenny. What a mess. Bullet entered from the rear, exit wound took half of his face. Killed instantly. He was also hit in the torso several times. I got his gun, crawled along the ditch for twenty or so feet, made a little nest, and dug in. I listened for a long time and heard nothing but the sounds of the night. No moon, nothing but blackness. According to the dispatcher's log, I called in at 4:02, said we'd been ambushed. Kenny was dead. Pfitzner was the first one there, which seemed really odd. Just like he was the first one at Russo's office."

"He was probably in the woods directing things," I say.

"Probably so. They took me to the hospital and treated my wound, nothing bad. Just got grazed. But I asked for some meds and they knocked me out. I told the doctors I didn't want to talk to anyone for a day or two and they protected me. When Pfitzner finally came in, along with the State boys, I didn't tell the part about nailing one of the thugs, a dude whose mother tongue was definitely not Spanish."

"Why not?"

"Pfitzner wanted both of us dead, Post. He wanted to eliminate Kenny because Kenny knew something, and since I was along for the ride it was necessary to rub me out too. Couldn't run the risk of leaving behind a witness. Think about that, Post. A sheriff elected by the people and trusted by the entire community sends two of his men into an ambush with the plan to get both of them killed. That's Bradley Pfitzner."

"He's still alive, you know?"

"I don't care. My dealings with him were over twenty years ago."

"What did you tell him in the hospital?"

"Everything but the part about me nailing one of his thugs. I've never told anyone that, and I'll deny it tomorrow if you repeat it."

"So you're still afraid?"

"No, Post. I'm not afraid. I'm just not risking any trouble here."

"No word from the guy you hit?"

"Nothing. It was before the Internet and searching was more difficult. I dug enough to learn that there were two shooting victims admitted to Tampa's public hospital on that date. One was shot by an intruder who was caught. The other

188

guy was found dead in an alley. I couldn't prove anything so I lost interest. About that time, my wife and I decided to leave town."

"How did Pfitzner treat you afterwards?"

"The same. He was always very professional, the perfect cop, a good leader who believed in discipline. He gave me a month of paid leave after Kenny's funeral and did everything he could to show concern. That's why he was so treacherous. The community admired him and no one believed he was corrupt."

"Was it known among his men?"

"We had our suspicions. Pfitzner had two pit bulls who ran things, Chip and Dip. They were brothers, a couple of real leg-breakers who did the dirty work. Arnie had a mouth full of oversized teeth and one of his front ones was chipped; thus, he was called Chip behind his back. Amos had smaller teeth but a fat lower lip that was always packed with a thick wad of smokeless tobacco; thus Dip. Below them were a few members of their team who were in on the action, the drug payoffs, but they kept all that separate from the routine business of protecting the county. Again, Pfitzner did a good job as sheriff. At some point, long before I arrived, he succumbed to the temptation of drug money. He protected the port, allowed the stuff to come in, provided safe zones to store it, and so on. I'm sure he made a mint, and I'm sure Chip and Dip and the others got their share. The rest of us had good salaries and benefits."

He waves at a golf cart and two attractive ladies wave back. He follows them around a fairway, then veers over a small bridge to a secluded hideaway under some trees. When we are settled in, I ask, "So what did Kenny know?"

"I don't know, he never said. He dropped a hint one time but never finished the conversation. You're familiar with the fire that destroyed a bunch of evidence, including stuff from the Russo murder?"

"Yes, I've seen the report."

"When Kenny was a kid he wanted to be a spy. Sort of odd for a black kid in a small town in Florida, but he loved spy books and spy magazines. The CIA never called so he became a cop. He was really good with technology and gadgets. An example: He had a friend who thought his wife was fooling around. He asked for help, and Kenny, in a matter of minutes, rigged up a phone tap in the guy's utility room. It recorded every phone call and the guy checked the tape every day. Before long he heard his beloved cooing with her Romeo and planning their next rendezvous. Kenny's friend caught 'em in bed and beat the shit out of the guy. Slapped her around too. Kenny was right proud of himself."

"So what did he hear?"

"Something about the evidence getting destroyed. A few days before the Russo murder there was a rape out in the county, white on white, and the victim said she never saw the guy's face but knew he was white. The favorite suspect was a nephew of Chip and Dip's. The rape kit was stored with the other stuff because there was no room in the old headquarters. When it burned, the rape kit was destroyed, along with other valuable proof. Kenny and I were drinking coffee late one night, taking a break, and he said something to the effect that the fire was no accident. I wanted to follow up but we got a call and took off. I asked him about it later and he said he overheard a conversation between Chip and Dip about burning the building."

He stops talking and there is a long pause. When I realize he's finished with his story, I ease in with "Nothing else?"

"That's all I have, Post, I swear. Over the years I've speculated that Kenny had probably wired the phones around the office. He suspected Pfitzner and his gang were in on the drug loot and wanted the proof. DEA was poking around and there was talk about the Feds coming in. Could we all get busted? Would Pfitzner sing and blame us? I don't know, just my best guess, but I think Kenny was listening and he heard something."

"That's a pretty wild theory."

"Yes it is."

"And you have no idea what he may have heard?"

"Nothing, Post. No clue."

He starts the cart and we continue our tour of the course. Every turn reveals another scenic vista of mountains and valleys. We cross rushing streams on narrow wooden bridges. At the thirteenth tee box he introduces me to his lawyer who asks how things are going. We say all is well and he hurries off with his buddies, much more concerned with his game than any of his client's business. At the clubhouse, I thank Gilmer for his time and hospitality. We promise to talk in the near future but both know that will not happen.

It's been a long, interesting trip but not that productive. However, in this business that's not at all unusual. If Kenny Taft knew something, he took it to his grave.

191

27

Under Florida law, petitions for post-conviction relief must be filed in the county where the defendant is incarcerated instead of where he was convicted. Since Quincy is staying these days at the Garvin Correctional Institute, which is half an hour away from the small town of Peckham, which is at least an hour from civilization, his case comes under the jurisdiction of a rural circuit court ruled by a judge with a dim view of post-conviction relief. I really can't blame him. His docket is packed with all manner of junk claims filed by jailhouse lawyers toiling away inside the prison just down the road.

The Poinsett County courthouse is a tacky, modern creation designed by someone who didn't get paid much. The main courtroom is dark, windowless, and with low ceilings that create a sense of claustrophobia. The worn carpet is a dark maroon. The wood panels and furniture are stained a dark brown. I've been in at least a hundred courtrooms in a dozen states, and this is by far the most depressing and dungeon-like.

The State is represented by the Attorney General, a man I'll never meet because he has about a thousand underlings between him and me. Poor Carmen Hidalgo drew the short straw and got stuck with Quincy's petition. Five years ago she was in law school at Stetson, ranked in the middle of her class. Our file on her is thin because we don't need to know much. Her response to our petition was nothing more than a stock answer with some boilerplate and all the names changed.

She fully expects to win, especially given the attitude of the guy on the bench. The Honorable Jerry Plank has been mailing it in for years and dreaming of retirement. He generously set aside one full day for our hearing, but it's not eight hours of work. Because no one cares about a case that is now twenty-three years old, the courtroom is empty. Even the two clerks look bored.

However, we are watching and waiting. Frankie Tatum sits alone six rows back, behind us, and Vicki Gourley sits alone five rows back, behind the State. Both are wearing tiny video cameras that can be activated with their phones. There is no security at the door. Again, no one in this town or county has ever heard of Quincy Miller. If our efforts are being monitored by the bad guys, whoever "they" may be, this could be their first chance to see us in action. Courtrooms are public areas. Anyone can come and go at will.

My co-counsel is Susan Ashley Gross, the warrior from the Central Florida Innocence Project. Seven years ago, Susan Ashley was with me when we walked Larry Dale Kline out of prison in Miami. He was Guardian's second exoneree, her first. I would ask Susan Ashley to marry me today but she's fifteen years younger and happily engaged at the moment.

Last week I filed a motion asking that the defendant be allowed to sit through the hearing. Quincy's presence is not necessary but I thought he might enjoy a day in the sun. Not surprisingly, Judge Plank said no. He has ruled against us on every pre-hearing matter, and we fully expect him to deny any post-conviction relief. Mazy is already working on our appeal.

It's almost ten when Judge Plank finally emerges from a hidden door behind the bench and assumes his perch. A bailiff recites his standard admonitions as we stand awkwardly. I glance around and count heads. In addition to Vicki and Frankie, there are four other spectators, and I ask myself how they could possibly care about this hearing. No one in Quincy's family knows about it. Except for one brother, no family member has contacted Quincy in years. Keith Russo has been dead for twenty-three years, and as far as his family is concerned the killer was locked away a long time ago.

One white male is about fifty and wears an expensive suit. One white male is about forty and wears a black denim shirt. One white male is about seventy and has the look of the bored courthouse regular who'll sit through anything. The fourth is a white female on the front row behind us and is holding a notepad, as if reporting. We filed our petition weeks ago and have not received a single inquiry from the press. I can't imagine who would be covering a hearing in a forgotten case in East Nowhere, Florida.

Susan Ashley Gross calls to the stand Dr. Kyle Benderschmidt from VCU. His opinions and findings are memorialized in a thick affidavit we filed with our petition, but we decided to spend the money and produce him live. His credentials are impeccable, and as Susan Ashley is walking him through his résumé, Judge Plank looks at Carmen Hidalgo and says, "Do you have any serious objections to this man's credentials?"

She stands and says simply, "No."

"Good. Then he is accepted as an expert in the field of bloodstain analysis. Proceed."

Using four of the 8x10 color enlargements that were used at trial, Susan Ashley leads our witness through an examination of the flashlight and the tiny specks of red matter on its lens.

Judge Plank interrupts with "And what happened to this flashlight? It was not presented at trial, right?"

The witness shrugs because he can't testify about it. Susan Ashley says, "Your Honor, according to the trial transcript, the sheriff testified that it was destroyed in a fire about a month after the murder, along with other evidence the police kept in storage."

"There's no trace of it?"

"Not to our knowledge, Your Honor. The State's expert, Mr. Norwood, examined these very photographs and gave the opinion that the lens of the flashlight was spattered with the blood from the victim. By then, the flashlight was long gone."

"So, if I understand your position, the flashlight was the only real link between Mr. Miller and the crime scene, and when the flashlight was found in the trunk of his car he became the prime suspect. And when the jury was presented with this evidence, it deemed it sufficient for a guilty verdict."

"That's correct, Your Honor."

"Proceed."

Benderschmidt continues with his criticism of Norwood's misguided testimony. It was not based on science, because Norwood did not understand the science behind blood spatter. Benderschmidt uses the word "irresponsible" several times to describe what Norwood told the jury. It was irresponsible to suggest the killer held the flashlight with one hand as he fired the 12-gauge shotgun with the other. There was no proof of this. No proof of where Keith was sitting or standing when he was shot. No proof of where the killer was. It was irresponsible to say that the specks were actually blood, given the small amount present. It was irresponsible to even use the flashlight, because it was not taken from the crime scene.

After an hour, Judge Plank is exhausted and needs a break. It's not clear if he is actually sleepy though he does seem to glaze over. Frankie quietly moves to the back row and sits next to the aisle. As the recess is called, and Plank disappears, the spectators rise and leave the courtroom. As they do, Frankie catches all of them on video.

After a smoke and a pee and probably a quick nap, Judge Plank reluctantly returns for more and Benderschmidt gets back on the stand. During his evaluation, he began to doubt whether the back spatter, the alleged bloody specks on the lens, was really blown backward and away from the victim. Using a diagram of Russo's office and other photos from the scene, Benderschmidt testifies that based on the location of the door and the likely position of the gunman, and based on the location of Keith's body and the enormous amount of blood and matter on the walls and shelves behind it, it appears unlikely that the impact of the two shotgun blasts would have blown blood toward the killer. To buttress this opinion, Benderschmidt produces some photos of other crime scenes involving 12-gauge shotgun victims.

It's gory stuff, and after a few minutes His Honor has had enough. "Let's move on, Ms. Gross. I'm not sure photos from other crimes are beneficial here."

He's probably right. On cross-examination, Carmen Hidalgo goes through the motions and scores only when she gets Benderschmidt to admit that bloodstain experts often disagree, as do all experts.

As the witness leaves the stand, Judge Plank looks at his watch as if he's had a long, hard morning, and he says, "Let's break for lunch. Back at two, and hopefully you will have something new, Ms. Gross." He raps his gavel and disappears, and I suspect he has already reached his conclusion.

In Florida, as in almost all states, post-conviction relief is considered only when new evidence is found. Not better evidence. Not more credible evidence. Quincy's jury heard from Norwood, an alleged expert on bloodstains, and though his qualifications and his opinions were viciously attacked by young Tyler Townsend, the jury unanimously believed him.

With Kyle Benderschmidt and Tobias Black, our second bloodstain expert, we are in effect presenting evidence that is only better—but not new. Judge Plank's comment is quite revealing.

AS THE MAN in the nice suit and the man in the black denim shirt leave the courthouse, separately, they are being watched. We hired two private detectives to help monitor things. Frankie has already briefed them and is talking on the phone. Vicki is sitting in one of only two diners close to the courthouse, waiting. I go to the other diner and sit at the counter. Frankie emerges from the courthouse and walks to his car in a nearby parking lot. Mr. Nice Suit gets into a slick black Mercedes sedan with Florida tags. Mr. Black Denim gets into a green BMW with Florida tags. They leave downtown two minutes apart and both pull into the parking lot at a shopping center on the main highway. Black Denim gets into the Mercedes and away they go, leaving bright red flags everywhere. Sloppy.

When I get word, I hustle over to the other diner where Vicki is camped out in a booth with an untouched order of fries in a basket. She's on the phone to Frankie. The Mercedes is headed south on Highway 19 and our tail has eased in behind it. Our man calls back with the tag number, and Vicki goes to work. We order iced tea and salads. Frankie arrives a few minutes later.

We have seen the enemy.

The Mercedes is registered to a Mr. Nash Cooley, of Miami. Vicki e-mails this info to Mazy at home and both women are burning up their keyboards. Within minutes we know that Cooley is a partner in a firm that specializes in criminal defense. I call two lawyers I know in Miami. Susan Ashley Gross, who's eating a sandwich in the courtroom, calls her contacts. Mazy calls a lawyer she knows in Miami. Vicki pecks away. Frankie enjoys his tuna melt and fries.

Cooley and Black Denim park at a fast-food place in the town of Eustis, population 18,000 and twenty minutes away. What is obvious becomes even more so. The two men eased into town to watch the hearing, did not want to be seen together or recognized in any way, and sneaked off for a bite. As they dine, our tail exchanges cars with his colleague. When Cooley leaves Eustis and heads our way, he is being followed at a distance by another car.

Cooley is a partner in a twelve-member firm with a long history of representing drug dealers. Not surprisingly, it is a low-profile firm with a sparse website. They don't advertise because they don't need to. Cooley is fifty-two, law school at Miami, a clean record with no bar complaints. His photo on-line needs to be updated because he appears at least ten years younger, but this is not unusual. After our first cursory round of research, we find only one interesting story about the firm. In 1991, the guy who founded the firm was found dead in his pool with his throat slashed. The murder remains unsolved. Probably just another disgruntled client.

TWO P.M. COMES and goes with no sign of Judge Plank. Perhaps we should ask one of the clerks to check and see if he is (1) alive, or (2) just napping again. Nash Cooley enters and sits near the back, oblivious to the fact that we know the names of his children and where they go to college. Black Denim enters a moment later and sits far away from Cooley. So amateurish.

Using the services of a high-tech security firm in Fort Lau-derdale, we sent a video frame of Black Denim and paid for turnaround service. The firm's facial recognition technology was primed to run the frame through the firm's many data banks, but that was unnecessary. The first data bank was the Florida Department of Corrections, and the search lasted for all of eleven minutes. Black Denim is Mickey Mercado, age 43, address in Coral Gables, a convicted felon with dual citizenship—Mexican and American. When Mercado was nineteen he got shipped away for six years for, of course, traf-ficking. In 1994, he was arrested and tried for murder. The jury hung and he walked.

As we wait for Judge Plank, Vicki is still in the diner, ordering coffee and raging through the Internet. She will tell us later that Mercado is a self-employed private security consultant. Whatever that means.

Their identifications are stunning, and as we sit peacefully in the courtroom it's hard not to turn around, call them by name, and say something like "What the hell are you doing here?" But we are much too seasoned for anything like that. When possible, never let the enemy know what you know. Right now, Cooley and Mickey have no idea that we have their names, home addresses, license plate and Social Security numbers, and places of employment, and we are still digging. Of course, we assume that they have a file on me and Guardian and its meager staff. Frankie is nothing but a shadow and will never be caught. He's in the hallway outside the courtroom, watching and moving. There are few blacks in this town and he is always conscious of getting looks.

When Judge Plank appears at 2:17, he instructs Susan Ashley to call our next witness. There are no surprises in these hearings so everyone knows Zeke Huffey is back in Florida. The surprise was that he agreed to testify live if we would pay his airfare. That, and I had to swear in writing that the statute of limitations has run on perjury so he cannot be prosecuted.

These days Zeke is just happy to be free. It won't last long and we know it, but at least he's saying all the right things about going straight. Taking the oath, he swears to tell the truth, something he's done many times in courtrooms before commencing to lie like a polished jailhouse snitch. He tells his story about chatting with his cellie Quincy Miller, who bragged about blowing off the head of his lawyer and tossing the 12-gauge in the Gulf. Zeke says that in return for his bogus testimony his drug charges were greatly reduced and he was sentenced to time served. Yes, he feels bad about what he did to Quincy and has always wanted to make amends.

Zeke makes a decent witness but his problem is obvious. He's lied so many times that no one can be certain, especially His Honor, if he's telling the truth now. Nonetheless, his testimony is crucial to our efforts because the recantations of witnesses do constitute new evidence. With Zeke's live testimony and Carrie Holland's affidavit, we have enough ammo to argue long and hard that Quincy's trial was not fair. If we are successful in getting a new trial, we can then present much better scientific evidence to the jury. Neither Norwood nor anyone like him will get near the courtroom. Our dream is getting the facts before a new jury.

On cross, Carmen Hidalgo has far too much fun leading Zeke through his long and colorful career as a jailhouse informant. She has certified court records from five trials over the past twenty-six years in which Zeke lied to juries so he could walk. He admits to lying in that one but not the other one. He gets confused and can't remember which lie he told in that case. It's painful to sit through and His Honor is quickly tiring, but the bloodletting continues. Ms. Hidalgo hits her stride and surprises us with her courtroom presence.

By 3:30, Judge Plank is yawning and squinting and obviously checking out. He's exhausted and trying desperately to stay awake. I whisper to Susan Ashley to wrap things up and let's get out of here.

28

The day after Vicki and I return to Savannah, we gather in the conference room with Mazy to assess the case. Florida, like Alabama, does not impose a deadline on judges in post-conviction matters, so old Plank might die before he decides anything. We suspect he's already made up his mind, but he'll take plenty of time before he rules. There's nothing we can do to prod him along, and it would be counterproductive to try to do so.

We are assuming that we are being watched at some level and this provokes a spirited discussion. We agree that all digital files and communications must be upgraded and heavily secured. This will cost about $30,000, cash that's not in our beleaguered budget. The bad guys have unlimited money and can buy the best surveillance.

I seriously doubt that they will snoop around Savannah and watch our movements. That would only bore them and yield no useful information. However, we agree that we must become more vigilant and vary our routines. They could have easily followed me to Nassau and tracked me as I met with Tyler Townsend. Same for Sun Valley and Bruce Gilmer. But those trips were before we filed our petition and before our names were officially entered.

Of Nash Cooley, we have learned more. We have public data regarding his autos, real estate, and both divorces. Suffice to say he makes a lot of money and likes to spend it. His home in Coral Gables is assessed at $2.2 million. He has at least three cars titled in his name, all German imports. His firm operates out of a sparkling new high-rise in downtown Miami, with branches on Grand Cayman and in Mexico City. According to a friend of Susan Ashley's, some drug lawyers in south Florida are known to take fees offshore. They are rarely caught, but occasionally the Feds will bust one for tax evasion. This source says that Varick & Valencia has been in the dirty business for a long time and is quite adept at advising its clients on the more sanitary ways of laundering money. Two of the firm's senior partners are veteran courtroom brawlers with many victories to their credit. In 1994, they defended Mickey Mercado on a murder charge and hung the jury.

I cannot understand the logic of Nash Cooley making the six-hour drive to watch our post-conviction hearing. If he wanted a good look at me, he could have gone to our website, simple as it is. Same for Susan Ashley. All of the petitions, motions, briefs, and rulings are public record, easily findable online. And why would he run the risk of being spotted? Granted, the risk was quite low in that backward part of the state, but nonetheless he got himself identified by us. I can assume only that Cooley was there because a client ordered him there.

Mickey Mercado is a career thug who has probably worked for a cartel his entire adult life. Which cartel, we are not certain. He and two others were charged with murdering another drug trafficker in a deal gone bad, but the Feds couldn't make it stick.

Now he's trailing me?

I make the point to the ladies that looking over our shoulders will not help Quincy Miller. Our job is to prove him innocent, and not necessarily to identify the guy who pulled the trigger.

I have not told the ladies everything. I seldom do. The story of Tyler and the crocodiles is one I'll keep to myself. That image never goes away.

Our discussion about Tyler goes on throughout most of the day as we go back and forth with ideas and arguments. On the one hand I feel compelled to reach out again and at least warn him that our efforts are now being monitored. On the other hand, though, the mere act of contacting him could potentially place him in danger. The same goes for Gilmer, but he does not know as much as Tyler.

At the end of the day we decide it's an important risk to take. I go online and return to From Under Patty's Porch where I pay twenty bucks for another month and send a message that will erase itself in five minutes:

Nassau again—important.

Five minutes pass with no response. I send the same message four times over the next three hours and hear nothing.

After dark, I leave the office and walk a few blocks in sweltering heat. The days are long and humid, and the town is crowded with tourists. As usual, Luther Hodges is waiting on his porch, eager to get out of the house.

"Hello Padre," I call out.

"Hello, my son." We embrace on the sidewalk, exchange lighthearted insults about gray hair and waistlines, and start walking. After a few minutes I realize something is bothering him.

"Texas will kill another one tomorrow," he explains.

"Sorry to hear."

Luther is a tireless abolitionist whose simple message has always been: Since we can all agree that it's wrong to kill, why do we allow the State to kill? When an execution appears on the horizon, he and his fellow abolitionists write the usual letters, make calls, post comments online, and occasionally go to the prison to protest. He spends hours in prayer and grieves for murderers he's never met.

We're not in the mood for a fancy meal so we duck into a sandwich shop. He pays for mine, as always, and as soon as we are seated he grins and says, "Now, tell me the latest on Quincy's case."

SINCE GUARDIAN BEGAN its work, we have opened eighteen cases, eight of which resulted in exonerations. One client was executed. Six are current. Three we closed when we became convinced our clients were indeed guilty. When we make a mistake we cut our losses and move on.

With eighteen cases we have learned that, sooner or later, we'll get a lucky break. His name is Len Duckworth and he lives at Sea Island, about an hour south of Savannah. He drove up, walked into our headquarters, saw no one at the reception desk, stuck his head into Vicki's room, and said hello. Vicki was polite, as always, but very busy. Within minutes, though, she was calling for me. "This could be important," she says. We eventually settle in the conference room upstairs with a fresh pot of coffee. Vicki and Mazy take notes and I just listen.

Duckworth is about seventy, tanned and trim, the epitome of a comfortable retiree with plenty of time for golf and tennis. He and his wife moved to Sea Island a few years back and are trying to stay busy. He's from Ohio, she's from Chicago, both prefer warm weather. He was an FBI agent in 1973 when Congress created the Drug Enforcement Agency, which sounded more exciting than his desk job. He switched agencies and spent his career with the DEA, including twelve years in charge of north Florida.

For months now we've been trying with no success to obtain DEA records from the 1980s. But, like the FBI and ATF, the DEA is tenacious about protecting its archives. One of Vicki's FOIA requests came back with a letter in which every word was redacted except for the "a's" and "the's."

This is indeed a lucky day. Duckworth says, "I know a lot about the drug business back then. Some things I can talk about, some I cannot."

I say, "I'm curious about why you came here. We've been trying to get DEA files and notes for the past seven months, with no luck."

"You won't get much because DEA always hides behind the excuse that its investigations are active and ongoing. It doesn't matter how old or inactive a case might be, the DEA's procedure is to give you nothing. And they'll go to court to protect their information. That's the way we operated."

"How much can you tell us?" I ask.

"Well, I can talk about the murder of Keith Russo because that case was closed over twenty years ago and because it wasn't a DEA matter. I knew Keith, knew him well because we flipped him. He was one of our informants and that's what got him killed."

Vicki, Mazy, and I look at each other as this settles in. The only person on the planet who can confirm that Keith Russo was an informant is sitting in one of our old mismatched chairs and calmly sipping coffee.

"Who killed him?" I ask tentatively.

"Don't know, but it wasn't Quincy Miller. It was a hit from the cartel."

"Which cartel?"

He pauses and takes a sip of coffee. "You ask me why I came here. I heard about your efforts to exonerate Miller and I applaud what you're doing. They got the wrong guy because they wanted the wrong guy. I have a lot of background I can share without divulging confidential stuff. Primarily, though, I just wanted to get out of the house. My wife is shopping today around the corner and we'll meet for a nice lunch later."

I say, "We're all ears and we have all day."

"Okay, first a bit of history. By the mid 1970s, when the DEA was created, cocaine was raging across the country and coming in by the ton in ships, planes, trucks, you name it. The demand was insatiable, profits were enormous, and the growers and traffickers could barely keep up. They built huge organizations throughout Central and South America and stashed their money in Caribbean banks. Florida, with eight hundred miles of beaches and dozens of ports, became the preferred point of entry. Miami became the playground for the traffickers. South Florida was controlled by a Colombian cartel, one that is still in business. I was not involved down there. My section was from Orlando north, and by 1980 the Saltillo Cartel out of Mexico ran most of the cocaine. Saltillo is still around but it got merged with a bigger outfit. Most of its leaders got butchered in a drug war. These gangs are always up and down and the casualties are breathtaking. The savagery is unbelievable. I won't bore you."

"Please don't," Vicki says.

I have another quick visual of Tyler and the crocodile feast, and say, "We have a fair amount of background on Sheriff Pfitzner and what went on in Ruiz County."

He smiles and shakes his head, as if reminded of an old friend. "And we never caught that guy. He was the only sheriff that we knew of in north Florida who was in bed with the cartel. We had him in our sights when Russo got hit. Things changed after that. Some of our crucial informants got lockjaw."

"How'd you flip Russo?" I ask.

"Keith was an interesting guy. Very ambitious. Tired of the small town. Wanted to make a lot of money. Damned good lawyer. He had some drug clients in the Tampa–St. Pete area and sort of made a name for himself. An informant told us that he was taking big fees in cash, reporting some or none, even moving money offshore. We watched his tax returns for a couple of years and it was obvious he was spending a lot more than he was making on Main Street in Seabrook. So we met with him and threatened him with an indictment for evasion. He knew he was guilty and didn't want to lose everything. He was also guilty of laundering money for some of his clients, primarily the Saltillo boys. He did this by using offshore shell companies to buy Florida real estate and doing all the paperwork. Not terribly complicated stuff, but he knew what he was doing."

"Did his wife know he was an informant?"

Another smile, another sip. Duckworth could tell war stories for hours. "This is where it gets really fun. Keith liked the ladies. He was careful not to chase 'em in Seabrook, but Tampa was another story. He and Diana kept an apartment there, ostensibly for reasons related to their work, but Keith used it for other reasons. Before we flipped him, we got warrants and had bugs in the apartment, office, even at home. We were listening to everything, including Keith's calls to his girls. Then, we got a real shock. Seems as though Diana decided to play the same game. Her dude was one of her drug clients, a pretty boy who worked in Miami for the Saltillo Cartel. Ramon Vasquez was his name. There were a couple of times when Keith was in Tampa hard at work and Ramon sneaked into Seabrook to visit Diana. Anyway, you can imagine what kind of shape the marriage was in. So, to answer your question, we were never sure if Keith told his wife about being an informant. We warned him not to, of course."

"What happened to Diana?" Vicki asks.

"Somehow the cartel found out about Keith working for us. I strongly suspect that another informant, a double agent, one of our guys, sold the information. It's a dirty business with loyalties that can change daily. Hard cash and the fear of being burned alive can flip a lot of people. They took out Keith, and Diana eventually left town."

"And Ramon?" asks Mazy.

"He and Diana hooked up in Tampa for a while, then kept moving south. We didn't know for sure back then but we suspected he sort of semiretired from his trafficking career and stayed out of trouble. Last I heard, they were still together somewhere in the Caribbean."

"With plenty of money," I say.

"Yes, with plenty of money."

"Was she involved with the murder?" Mazy asks.

209

"That has never been proven. You know about the life insurance and the joint bank accounts, but that's not too unusual."

I ask, "Why didn't you bust Pfitzner and the cartel?"

"Well, after the murder, the case evaporated. We were within a month or two of a huge bust that would have produced a lot of indictments, including some charges against Pfitzner. We had been patient, too patient, really, but we were fighting with the U.S. Attorney's office down there. They were overworked and so on. We couldn't get the lawyers fired up. You know how they are. After the murder, our informants vanished and the case fell apart. The cartel got spooked and pulled back for a while. Pfitzner eventually retired. I was moved to Mobile where I finished my career."

"Who would the cartel use to do the killing?" Mazy asks.

"Oh, they have plenty of gun thugs, and these guys are not always sophisticated assassins. They're brutes who'd rather cut off a man's head with an axe than put a bullet in it. A couple of shotgun blasts to the face is tame for these boys. Their murders are messy because they want them to be. If they leave behind clues, they don't care. You're never going to find them because they're back in Mexico, or Panama. Somewhere in the jungle."

Mazy says, "But the Russo crime scene was clean, right? No clues left behind."

"Yes, but Pfitzner was in charge of the investigation."

I say, "I'm not sure I understand why you couldn't nail Pfitzner. You say you knew he was guarding the port, storing the coke, protecting the dealers, and you had informants, including Keith. Why couldn't you bust him?"

Duckworth takes a deep breath and locks his hands behind his head. He stares at the ceiling, keeps a smile on his face, replies, "That is probably the biggest disappointment of my career. We really wanted that guy. One of us, a law enforcement man, on the take and in bed with the nastiest people you could ever meet. Pumping cocaine into Atlanta, Birmingham, Memphis, Nashville, all over the Southeast. And we could've done it. We had infiltrated. We had built the case. We had the evidence. It was the U.S. Attorney in Jacksonville. We just could not get him to move fast enough and take it to the grand jury. He insisted on running the show and didn't know what he was doing. Then Russo got hit. I still think about that guy, the U.S. Attorney. He later ran for Congress and I couldn't wait to vote against him. Last I heard, he was chasing ambulances with his smarmy face on billboards."

Mazy asks, "And you say this cartel is still around?"

"Most of it is, or at least it was when I retired. I've been out of the loop for the past five years."

Mazy says, "Okay, let's talk about the people who ordered the hit on Russo. Where are they now?"

"Don't know. I'm sure some are dead, some are in prison, some have retired to their mansions around the world. And some are still trafficking."

"Are they watching us?" Vicki asks.

Duckworth leans forward and takes a sip. He thinks about this for a long moment because he appreciates our concern. Finally, he says, "I can only speculate, obviously. But, yes, they are watching at some level. They do not want Quincy Miller exonerated, to say the least. I have a question for you," he says, looking at me. "If your client walks, will the murder case be reopened?"

"Probably not. In about half of our cases we manage to identify the real perpetrator, the other half we do not. Here, it looks highly unlikely. The case is old. The evidence is gone. The real killer is, as you say, living well somewhere far away."

"Or he's dead," Duckworth says. "Gun thugs don't last long in the cartels."

"So why are they watching us?" Vicki asks.

"Why not? You're easy to watch. The court filings are public. Why not keep up with things?"

I ask, "Ever hear of a Miami drug lawyer named Nash Cooley?"

"I don't think so. Is he with a firm?"

"Varick and Valencia."

"Oh sure. They've been around for years. Well known in the trade. Why do you ask?"

"Nash Cooley was in the courtroom last week when we argued our motion."

"So you know him?"

"No, but we identified him. He was with a guy named Mickey Mercado, one of his clients."

Being a good cop, he wants to ask how we identified the two, but he lets it go. He smiles and says, "Yes, I'd be careful if I were you. It's safe to assume they're watching."

29

According to Steve Rosenberg, Judge Marlowe has more clout than we gave her credit for. He suspects she lobbied the Alabama Court of Appeals to move at what could be a record pace. Barely two months after the hearing in Verona, the court unanimously affirms Judge Marlowe's command to DNA test the seven pubic hairs. And they order the testing to be paid for by the office of the Honorable Chad Falwright. Two detectives from the state police drive the evidence to the same lab in Durham that we used to test the saliva of Mark Carter. I stare at my phone for three days until it buzzes with a call from Her Honor herself.

With perfect unaccented diction and in the most beautiful female voice I've ever heard, she says, "Well, Mr. Post, it appears as though you are correct. Your client has been excluded by DNA testing. All seven pubic hairs once belonged to Mr. Carter."

I'm in Vicki's office and my face says it all. I close my eyes for a moment as Vicki quietly hugs Mazy.

Her Honor continues, "Today is Tuesday. Can you be here for a hearing on Thursday?"

"Of course. And thank you, Judge Marlowe."

"Don't thank me, Mr. Post. Our judicial system owes an enormous debt of gratitude to you."

These are the moments we live for. Alabama came within two hours of killing an innocent man. Duke Russell would be cold in his grave if not for us and our work and our commitment to undoing wrongful convictions.

But we'll celebrate later. I leave immediately and head west toward Alabama, phoning nonstop. Chad doesn't want to talk and of course he's far too busy at the moment. Since he'll try to screw things up again, and since he's incompetent to begin with, we're worried about the apprehension of Mark Carter. To our knowledge Carter knows nothing about the DNA testing. Steve Rosenberg convinces the Attorney General to call Chad and get him in line. The AG also agrees to notify the state police and ask them to keep an eye on Carter.

LATE WEDNESDAY MORNING, Duke Russell is lying on his bunk, the same one he's had for the past ten years, reading a paperback and minding his own business when a guard looks through the bars and says, "Hey Duke. Time to go, man."

"Go where?"

"Goin' home. A judge wants to see you in Verona. Leavin' in twenty minutes. Get packed." The guard shoves a cheap duffel through the bars and Duke begins stuffing in his assets: socks, T-shirts, boxers, two pairs of sneakers, toiletries. He owns eight paperbacks, and since he's read each at least five times he decides to leave them for the next guy. Same for his small black-and-white TV and rotating fan. By the time he walks out of his cell, in handcuffs but no leg irons, his comrades are cheering and clapping. Near the front door the other guards have gathered to slap him on the back and wish him well. Several walk him outside where a white prison van is waiting. As he leaves death row he refuses to look back. At Holman's administration building, he is transferred to a county patrol car and whisked away. Once outside the prison, the car stops and the deputy in the front passenger's seat gets out. He opens a rear door, unlocks the handcuffs, and asks Duke if he would like something to eat. Duke thanks him but declines. His emotions are overwhelming his appetite.

Four hours later, he arrives at the county jail where I'm waiting with Steve Rosenberg and a lawyer from Atlanta. We've convinced the sheriff that Duke is about to be released because he is in fact innocent, so the sheriff is cooperating. He allows us to use his cramped office for our little meeting. I explain what I know to my client, which is not everything. Tomorrow, Judge Marlowe plans to vacate his conviction and order his release from custody. Idiot Chad is threatening to re-file charges against not only Duke but Mark Carter as well. His bizarre new theory is that the two of them tag-teamed the rape and murder of Emily Broone.

The two of them have never met. As outrageous as this sounds, it is not surprising. When boxed-in and bleeding, prosecutors often become wildly creative with new theories of guilt. The fact that Mark Carter's name was never mentioned at Duke's trial ten years ago will kill this nonsense. Judge Marlowe is on the warpath and will not listen to it. And, the Alabama Attorney General is putting pressure on Chad to back off.

Nonetheless, he has the power to re-file charges and it is something to worry about. He could have Duke arrested not long after he's released. As I try to explain these legal vagaries to my client, he becomes too emotional to talk. We leave him with the sheriff, who takes him to the nicest cell for his last night in captivity.

Steve and I drive to Birmingham and have drinks with Jim Bizko of *The Birmingham News*. He's rabid with the story and has circulated the gossip among his colleagues. Tomorrow, he promises us, will be a circus.

We have a late dinner and find a cheap motel, one far away from Verona. We do not feel safe staying there. The victim's family is large and has many friends, and we've had anonymous phone threats. They too are part of the business.

BEFORE DAWN, Mark Carter is arrested by the state police and taken to a jail in a county next door. The sheriff tells us this as we enter the courtroom and prepare for the hearing. As we wait, and as a crowd gathers, I look out a window and notice brightly painted television vans in front of the court-house. At 8:30, Chad Falwright arrives with his little gang and says good morning. I ask him if he still plans to re-indict my client. He smiles smugly and says no. He is thoroughly beaten, and at some point during the night, probably after a tense phone chat with the Attorney General, he decided to call it quits.

Duke arrives with his uniformed escorts and he's all smiles. He's wearing an oversized navy jacket, a white shirt, and a tie with a knot as big as a fist. He looks splendid and is already savoring the moment. His mother is on the front row behind us, along with at least a dozen relatives. Across the aisle is Jim Bizko and several reporters. Judge Marlowe is allowing still photography, and cameras are clicking.

She assumes the bench promptly at nine and says good morning. "Before we get started, I have been asked by Sheriff Pilley to inform the public and the press that a resident of this county, a man named Mark Carter, was arrested this morning at his home in Bayliss and charged with the rape and murder of Emily Broone. He remains in custody and will appear in this courtroom in about an hour. Mr. Post, I believe you have a motion."

I rise with a smile and say, "Yes, Your Honor. On behalf of my client, Duke Russell, I ask that his conviction entered in this case be vacated and that he be released immediately."

"And what is the basis of this motion?"

"DNA testing, Your Honor. We have obtained DNA testing on the seven pubic hairs found at the crime scene. Mr. Russell is excluded. All seven originated from Mr. Carter."

"And as I understand the facts, Mr. Carter was the last person seen with the victim while she was still alive, is that so?" She asks this as she glares at Chad.

"That is correct, Your Honor," I say with suppressed glee. "And Mr. Carter was never considered a serious suspect by the police or the prosecutor."

"Thank you. Mr. Falwright, do you oppose this motion?"

He rises quickly and almost whispers, "The State does not."

She reshuffles some papers and takes her time. Finally, she says, "Mr. Russell, would you please stand?"

He gets to his feet and looks at her as if bewildered. She clears her throat and says, "Mr. Russell, your convictions for rape and capital murder are hereby vacated and dismissed. Forever, and they cannot be brought back. I was not involved in your trial, obviously, but I do consider it a privilege to be involved here today with your exoneration. A grave miscarriage of justice has occurred and you have paid a dear price. You were wrongfully convicted by the State of Alabama and incarcerated for a decade. Years that can never be replaced. On behalf of the State, I say that I'm sorry, and I realize my apology does not even begin to heal your wounds. However, it is my hope that one day soon you will remember the apology and take some small measure of comfort in it. I wish you a long happy life with this nightmare behind you. Mr. Russell, you are free to go."

There are gasps and shrieks behind us as his family hears this. Duke leans forward and places both hands on the table. I stand and put an arm around him as he sobs. For some reason I notice how frail and thin he is in someone's old sports coat.

Chad hits a side door and makes his escape, too cowardly to walk over and offer an apology of his own. He'll probably spend the rest of his career lying about how Duke got off on one of those technicalities.

Outside the courtroom, we face the cameras and answer questions. Duke says little. He just wants to go home and eat his uncle's barbeque ribs. I don't have much to say either. Most lawyers dream of these moments, but to me they are bittersweet. On the one hand there is immense satisfaction in saving an innocent man. But on the other, there is anger and frustration with a system that allows wrongful convictions. Almost all can be avoided.

Why are we expected to celebrate after an innocent man is freed?

I navigate through the crowd and walk with my client to a small room where Jim Bizko is waiting. I promised him an exclusive, and Duke and I unload. Bizko starts with questions about his near miss with the executioner seven months earlier, and before long we're laughing about Duke's last meal and his frantic efforts to finish his steak and cake before returning to his cell. The laughter feels good and comes easily, as do the tears.

AFTER HALF AN hour, I leave them and return to the courtroom where the crowd is loitering and waiting for the next bit of drama. Judge Marlowe assumes the bench and everyone takes a seat. She nods and a bailiff opens a side door. Mark Carter appears in handcuffs and the standard orange jumpsuit. He glances around, sees the crowd, finds his family on the front row, then looks away. He takes a seat at the defense table and stares down as his boots catch his attention.

Judge Marlowe looks at him and asks, "Are you Mark Carter?"

He nods.

"Please stand when I address you and answer in a clear voice."

He reluctantly gets to his feet as if he's in control of the moment. "I am."

"Do you have a lawyer?"

"Nope."

"Can you afford one?"

"Depends on how much one might cost."

"Very well. I'll appoint one for now and he'll meet you over in the jail. We'll come back next week and try again. In the meantime you will be held without bail. Have a seat."

He sits and I ease forward to the defense table. I lean down and in a low voice say, "Hey, Mark, I'm the guy who called you the night they almost killed Duke. Remember the call?"

He glares and since he's cuffed and can't throw a punch, he looks as though he might spit.

"Anyway, I called you a cowardly scumbag because you were willing to let another man die for your crime. And I promised I'd see you in court."

"Who are you?" he snarls.

A bailiff is moving toward us and I back away.

IN A BRIEF ceremony, the staff at Guardian hangs a large, framed color photo of Duke Russell on the wall with the other eight exonerees. It is a handsome portrait we paid for. Our client is posing outdoors at his mother's home, leaning on a white board fence with a fishing rod at his side. A big smile. The contented face of a man happy to be free and young enough to enjoy another life. A life we've given him.

We pause and pat ourselves on the back, then return to our work.

30

Quincy thinks I'm here because I'm his lawyer and part of my job is to see my clients at every opportunity. This is my fourth visit and I bring him up to date. Of course we have heard nothing from Judge Plank just down the road, and Quincy does not understand why we can't file a complaint and make the old fossil do something. I describe Zeke Huffey's performance in court and pass along the guy's apology for helping send Quincy to prison for the rest of his life. Quincy is unmoved. We kill two hours covering the same material.

Leaving the prison, I head south on a county road that soon expands to four then six lanes as Orlando looms. Watching the rearview mirror has become a habit that I hate, but I can't make myself stop. I know there's no one back there. If they are listening and watching they wouldn't do it with such an antiquated method. They might hack phones and computers and who knows what else, but they wouldn't waste their time chasing me in my little Ford SUV. I take a quick exit onto a busy thoroughfare, then another quick turn and wheel into the vast parking lot of a suburban mall. I park between two cars, walk inside like an average shopper, and hike at least half a mile to a sprawling Nike store where, at exactly 2:15, I find a rack of men's running shirts. Tyler Townsend waits on the other side of the rack. He's wearing a golf cap from a country club and a pair of fake tortoiseshell glasses.

Glancing around, he says softly, "This better be good."

I examine a shirt and say, "We have seen the enemy. And I think you should know about it."

"I'm listening," he says without looking at me.

I tell him about the hearing in front of Judge Plank, the appearance of Nash Cooley and Mickey Mercado, and their clumsy efforts to avoid being seen together. Tyler does not recognize either name.

A kid with a big smile approaches and asks if we need help. I politely wave him off.

I give Tyler all the background we have on both Mercado and Cooley. I summarize what Len Duckworth told us about the DEA and the cartel.

"You suspected Russo was an informant, didn't you?" I ask.

"Well, he was killed for a reason. Either his wife had him knocked off for the life insurance, which no one really ever believed, or he got in too thick with some of his shady clients. I've always figured it was the work of the drug gang. That's how they handle informants, like those two boys I described down in Belize, or wherever it was. Remember the photo, Post? Me on the zip line?"

"I think about it all the time."

"And so do I. Look, Post, if they're watching you then we ain't gonna be pals no more. I don't want to see you again." He takes a step back, glaring at me. "Nothing, Post, you hear? No contact whatsoever."

I nod and say, "Got it."

At the door he scans the mall, as if he might see a couple of thugs with large guns, then walks away as nonchalantly as possible. He quickens his pace and is soon out of sight, and I realize how utterly terrified he is by the past.

The question is: How terrified should we be of the present?

The answer arrives within hours.

WE SELECT OUR cases with great care, and once engaged we investigate and litigate with diligence. Our goal is to find the truth and exonerate our clients, something we've now done nine times in the past twelve years. However, it has never occurred to me that our efforts to save a client might get one killed.

IT WAS A prison beating with all the markings of an ambush, and as such it will be difficult to get the facts. Witnesses are unreliable if they come forward at all. Guards often see nothing. The administration has every reason to cover up and to slant its version in a way most favorable to the prison.

Not long after I said goodbye to Quincy that morning, he was jumped by two men in a walkway between a machine shop and a gymnasium. He was stabbed by a shank and beaten severely by blunt instruments, and left for dead. A guard eventually walked by, saw him lying in a pool of blood, and called for help. He was loaded into an ambulance and taken to the nearest hospital and from there was rushed to Mercy Hospital in Orlando. Tests revealed a fractured skull, swollen brain, broken jaw, splintered shoulder and collarbone, missing teeth, and so on, and three deep stab wounds. He was given six pints of blood and put on life support. When the prison finally called our office in Savannah, Vicki was informed that he was "critical" and not expected to survive.

I was on the Jacksonville bypass when she called me with the news. I forgot all the other clutter in my brain and turned around. Quincy has no family to speak of. Right now, he needs his lawyer.

I HAVE SPENT half of my career hanging around prisons, and I've become accustomed to the violent culture but not calloused by it, because caged men will always invent new ways to harm one another.

But I've never considered the possibility of an innocence case being derailed from inside the prison by rubbing out the prospective exoneree. It's a brilliant move!

If Quincy dies, we close the file and move on. This is not an established policy at Guardian because we've never been confronted with such a death, but with an endless supply of cases to choose from, we cannot justify our time in trying to exonerate anyone posthumously. I'm sure they know that. Whoever "they" might be. For purposes of my own lengthy monologues behind the wheel, I suppose I could refer to them as the Saltillo gang, or something like that. But "they" works better.

So they are watching our court filings. Perhaps they are trailing us occasionally, maybe hacking a bit and eavesdropping. And they certainly know about us and our recent victory in Alabama. They know we have a track record, that we can litigate, that we are tenacious. They also know that

Quincy did not kill Keith Russo and they don't like us digging for the truth. They do not want to openly confront us, or frighten or intimidate, not now anyway, because that would verify their existence, and it would probably require them to commit another crime, something they would like to avoid. A fire, or a bomb, or a bullet could make for a mess and leave clues.

The easiest way to stop the investigation is to simply take out Quincy. Order a hit from inside the prison where they already have friends or know some tough guys who will work cheap for cash or favors. Killings there are so routine anyway.

I rarely spend time reviewing the prison records of my clients. Since they are innocent, they tend to behave themselves, avoid gangs and drugs, take whatever educational courses are available, work, read, and help other inmates. Quincy finished high school in Seabrook in 1978 but could not afford college. In prison, he has accumulated over a hundred hours of credits. He has no serious disciplinary violations. He helps younger inmates avoid gangs. I can't imagine Quincy making enemies. He lifts weights, has learned karate, and in general can take care of himself. It would require more than one healthy young man to bring him down, and I'll bet he inflicted some damage of his own before he fell.

Sitting in Orlando traffic, I call the prison for the fourth time and ask to speak to the warden. There is no way he'll take my call, but I want him to know I'll be there soon enough. I make a dozen calls. Vicki is hounding the hospital for information, of which there is little, and she relays this to me. I call Frankie and tell him to head south. I finally get Quincy's brother, Marvis, who is working construction in Miami and can't get away. He is the only relative who cares about Quincy and has visited him regularly for the past twenty-three years. He is shaken and wants to know who would do this to Quincy. I have no answers.

The collar usually works in hospitals so I put it on in the parking deck. ICU is on the second floor and I bluff my way past a busy nurse. Two huge young men—one white, the other black—are sitting on stools next to a room with glass walls. They are prison guards and wear the gaudy black-and-tan uniforms that I've seen around the Garvin Correctional Institute. They are bored and seriously out of place. I decide to be nice and introduce myself as Quincy's lawyer.

Not surprisingly, they know virtually nothing. They were not at the scene, did not see the victim until he was in the ambulance, and were ordered to follow the ambulance and make sure the prisoner remains secure.

Quincy Miller is certainly secure. He is strapped down to a bed that sits high in the center of the room, surrounded by tubes, monitors, drips, machines. A ventilator hums away as it pumps oxygen through a tracheotomy tube and keeps him alive. His face is covered with thick gauze with tubes poked through it.

The white guard is telling me that he has flatlined three times in the past two hours. Folks came running from all directions. The black guard confirms this and adds that it's just a matter of time, at least in his opinion.

Our small talk quickly runs out of gas. These boys don't know if they are supposed to sleep on the floor, find a motel room, or go back to the prison. The office is closed there and they can't find their boss. I offer the shrewd observation that the prisoner is going nowhere.

One of the doctors happens by and notices my collar. We step away for a quiet word. I try to quickly explain that the patient has no family, that he has been in prison for almost twenty-three years for someone else's crime, and that as his lawyer I'm sort of in charge. He's in a hurry and doesn't need all this. He says the patient received multiple injuries, the most serious of which is severe trauma to the brain. Using pentobarbital, they put him in a medically induced coma to relieve pressure on the brain. If he survives, he faces a lot of surgery. The upper left jaw, collarbones, and left shoulder will be rebuilt. Maybe his nose. One knife wound pierced a lung. His right eye could be badly damaged. At this early moment, there is no way to predict the level of permanent brain impairment, though it will probably be "substantial—if he makes it."

I get the uneducated impression that the doctor is clicking through a mental checklist of Quincy's injuries, and since he'll die anyway, why name them all?

I ask about his chances, and the doctor shrugs and says, "One in a hundred." Like a gambler in Vegas.

AFTER DARK, MY two buddies in uniform have had enough. They are tired of doing nothing, tired of getting in the way, tired of the frowns from the nurses, and tired of guarding a prisoner who couldn't possibly make a run for it. They're also hungry, and judging by their bulging waistlines their dinner hour is not to be trifled with. I convince them that I plan to spend the night in the visitors' lounge down the hall, and if anything happens to Quincy I'll call their cell phones. I say goodbye with the promise that their prisoner is locked away for the night.

There are no seats or chairs near the beds in ICU. Visitors are not welcome. It's okay to stop by for a look, or a word if the loved one is able to talk, but the nurses are fairly aggressive about keeping the place as dark and quiet as possible.

I make a nest in the lounge around the corner and try to read. Dinner is machine food, which is seriously underrated. I nap, unload a barrage of e-mails, read some more. At midnight, I tiptoe back to Quincy's room. His ECG is causing concern and there is a team around his bed.

Could this be the end? In some ways, I hope so. I don't want Quincy to die, but then I don't want him living like a vegetable either. I purge these thoughts and say a prayer for him and his medical team. I back into a corner and watch through the glass wall as heroic doctors and nurses work frantically to save the life of a man Florida tried its best to kill. An innocent man robbed of his freedom by a crooked system.

I struggle with my emotions as I ask myself: Is Guardian responsible for this? Would Quincy be here if we had declined to take his case? No, he would not. His dream of freedom, as well as our desire to help him, made him a target.

I bury my face in my hands and weep.

31

There are two sofas in the ICU lounge, neither designed to be slept on by an adult. Across the room, one is being used by a mother whose teenaged son was gruesomely injured in a motorcycle accident. I have prayed with her twice. The other sofa is where I wrestle with a hard pillow and nap fitfully until about 3:00 a.m., when I think of something that should have been obvious earlier. I sit up in the dimly lit room and say to myself: "Great. Dumbass. Why have you just now thought of this?"

Assuming the attack on Quincy was ordered from someone on the outside, then isn't he in more danger now than he was in prison? Anyone can walk into the hospital, take the elevator to the second floor, breeze past the ICU nurses at the front desk with a plausible story, and gain immediate access to Quincy's room.

I calm down and admit my paranoia. There are no assassins on the way, because "they" believe "they" have already taken care of Quincy. And rightfully so.

Sleep is impossible. Around 5:30 a doctor and a nurse enter the lounge and huddle with the mother. Her son died twenty minutes ago. Since I am the nearest minister I get dragged into this drama. They leave me holding her hand and calling relatives.

Quincy hangs on. The morning rounds start early and I meet with another doctor. There is no change and little hope. I explain to him that I think my client could be in danger. He was attacked by some people who obviously want him dead—it wasn't a routine prison brawl—and the hospital needs to know this. I ask him to notify the staff and those in charge of security. He seems to understand but makes no promises.

At 7:00, I call Susan Ashley of the Central Florida Innocence Project and tell her about Quincy. We brainstorm for half an hour and agree that the FBI should be notified. She knows who to call. We also discuss the strategy of running to federal court and suing Florida and its Department of Corrections. We would seek an immediate injunction ordering the warden at Garvin to investigate the attack and open his files. I call Mazy and we have a similar conversation. As usual, she's cautious but never shy about filing suit in federal court. An hour later, Mazy, Susan Ashley, and I have a conference call and decide to do nothing for a few hours. All strategies will change if Quincy dies.

I'm in the hallway on the phone when a doctor sees me and approaches. I end the call and ask what's going on.

He says gravely, "The EEG is showing a steady decrease in brain activity. His heart rate is down, twenty beats a minute. We're getting down to the end and we need someone to talk to."

"About pulling the plug?"

"That's not really a medical term but it'll do. You say he has no family."

"He has a brother who's trying to get here. It's his decision, I guess."

"Mr. Miller is a ward of the state, correct?"

"He's an inmate in a state prison, has been for over twenty years. Please don't tell me the warden gets to make the decision."

"Absent a family member, yes."

"Shit! If the prison gets to pull the plug then no inmate is safe. Let's wait for the brother, okay? I'm hoping he'll be here by noon."

"Okay. You may want to think about last rites."

"I'm Episcopalian, not Catholic. We don't do last rites."

"Well, then do whatever you're supposed to do just before death."

"Thanks."

As he walks away, I see the same two prison guards emerge from the elevator, and I greet them like old friends. They're back for another day with nothing to do but sit. Yesterday I thought they were totally worthless, but now I'm glad to see them. We need more uniforms around here.

I offer to buy them breakfast in the basement cafeteria and suspect they've never declined food. Over waffles and sausage they manage to laugh about their problems. The warden called them in first thing this morning for an ass-chewing. He was angry because they left the prisoner without authority to do so. They are now on thirty days' probation with demerits on file.

They've heard no gossip about the attack, and as long as they're sitting around the hospital doing little they will continue to hear nothing. However, the place where Quincy was jumped is known to be one of the few areas of the

John Grisham

prison yard unmonitored by surveillance cameras. There have been other assaults there. The black guard, Mosby, says he knew of Quincy many years back before he was assigned to another unit. The white guard, Crabtree, never heard of him, but then there are almost two thousand inmates at Garvin.

Though they know very little, they are enjoying the importance of being vaguely connected to such an exciting event. I confide in them that I believe the attack was ordered from the outside and that Quincy is now an even easier target. He must be protected.

When we return to ICU there are two uniformed hospital security guards milling about, frowning at everyone as if the President was back there on life support. There are now four young men with weapons on duty, and while none of them could sprint to first base without collapsing, their presence is comforting. I chat with a doctor who says nothing has changed, and I leave the hospital before anyone can ask me if Quincy's machines should be turned off.

I find a cheap motel, shower, brush my teeth, do a partial change of clothing, then race away toward Garvin. Susan Ashley has been hounding the warden's secretary without success. My plans to barge into his office and demand answers are blocked at the check-in office where I am denied entry to the prison. I hang around for an hour and threaten everyone who will listen, but it's futile. Prisons are secure for many reasons.

Back at the hospital, I chat with a nurse I've been flirting with and she says his vitals have improved slightly. His brother, Marvis, can't leave his job in Miami. No one from the prison will take or return calls.

For lunch I flip a coin and Mosby wins. Crabtree orders a ham-on-rye and stays behind to protect Quincy. Mosby and I stroll down to the cafeteria and load our trays with leftover lasagna and vegetables straight from the can. There's a crowd and we squeeze into the last table, one that presses against his stomach. He's only thirty, grossly overweight, and I want to ask him how large he plans to be in ten years. Or twenty? Does he realize that at the rate he's expanding he'll be diabetic by the age of forty? But, as always, I keep these questions to myself.

He is intrigued by our work and keeps looking at the collar. So I regale him with slightly embellished stories of the men we've walked out of prison. I talk about Quincy and make the case for his innocence. Mosby seems to believe me, though he really doesn't care. He's just a kid from the country working for twelve bucks an hour because he needs the job. He hates it—hates the fact that he works behind fencing and razor wire; hates the danger of herding criminals who constantly scheme of ways to escape; hates the bureaucracy and endless rules; hates the violence; hates the warden; hates the constant stress and pressure. All for twelve bucks an hour. His wife cleans offices while her mother keeps their three kids.

Vicki has found three newspaper stories about corrupt guards at Garvin. Two years ago, eight were fired for selling drugs, vodka, porn, and the favorite—cell phones. One inmate was caught with four phones and was retailing them to his customers. He confessed that his cousin stole them on the outside and bribed a guard to sneak them in. One of the sacked guards was quoted: "We can't live on twelve dollars an hour so we gotta do something."

233

Over dessert—chocolate pie for him, coffee for me—I say, "Look, Mosby, I've been inside about a hundred prisons, so I've learned a few things. And I know that someone saw Quincy get jumped. Right?"

He nods and says, "More than likely."

"For something really bad, a rape or a knifing, you have to find the right guard who'll look the other way, right?"

He smiles and keeps nodding. I push on, "Last year there were two murders at Garvin. Either on your watch?"

"Nope."

"They catch the guys?"

"First one they did. Second guy got his throat cut while he was asleep. Still unsolved, probably stay that way."

"Look, Mosby, it's important for me to find out who jumped Quincy. You and I know damned well that there's a guard or two involved. I'll bet one was looking out during the attack. Right?"

"Probably." He takes a bite of pie and looks away. After he swallows he says, "Everything's for sale in prison, Post. You know that."

"I want names, Mosby. The names of the men who beat Quincy. How much will it cost?"

He leans in lower and tries to adjust his stomach. "I don't have the names, I swear. So I'll have to get them and I'll have to pay the guy. He might have to pay another guy. See what I mean. I'd like a few bucks too."

"Sure, but can I please remind you that we're a nonprofit with no money?"

"You got five thousand dollars?"

I frown as if he's asked for a million, but five is the right figure. Some of the men in the gossip chain are prisoners who think in terms of the basics: better food, drugs, a new color television, some condoms, softer toilet paper. Some are guards who need a thousand dollars for auto repairs.

"Maybe," I say. "This needs to happen fast."

"What will you do with the names?" he asks as he shovels in the last chunk of pie.

"Why do you care? It's probably a couple of lifers who'll just get more time."

"Probably so," he says with his mouth full.

"So, we have a deal? You start digging and I'll find some money."

"Deal."

"And let's keep it quiet, Mosby. I don't want Crabtree poking around. Besides, he'll probably want some of the fee, right?"

"Right. Not sure I trust him."

"I'm not sure I do either."

We return to ICU and give Crabtree his sandwich. He's sitting with an Orlando city policeman, a big talker who tells us that he has been ordered to hang around for a few days. There are plenty of uniforms milling around, and I begin to feel better about Quincy's safety.

32

Twenty-eight hours have passed since the beating, and after five or six flatlining episodes, Quincy's monitors have begun to stabilize. Though he certainly doesn't know it, there is slightly more activity in his brain, and his heart is a bit stronger. However, this does not inspire optimism among his doctors.

I'm sick of the hospital and need to escape, but I can't get too far from the patient. I spend hours on my sofa in the lounge, on the phone, online, anything to kill time. Mazy and I decide to wait another day before contacting the FBI. The federal lawsuit can wait too, though we're having second thoughts about it. There is still no word from the warden, no contact with the prison.

Mosby and Crabtree are instructed to leave at 5:00 p.m. They are replaced by a gray-haired veteran named Holloway, who isn't very friendly. He seems perturbed at being relegated to hallway monitoring and doesn't say much. Whatever. At least we have another armed guard on duty. I'm tired of talking to people anyway.

Marvis Miller arrives early in the evening and I walk him to the room to see his brother. He is immediately emotional and I back away. He stands at the foot of the bed, afraid to touch anything, and stares at the mountain of gauze that is Quincy's face. A nurse needs some information from him and I return to the lounge to kill more time.

I have dinner with Marvis, my third meal of the day in the cafeteria. He is six years younger than Quincy and has always idolized his big brother. They have two sisters but don't speak to them. The family split after Quincy's conviction when the sisters assumed he was guilty, the jury said so, and they cut all ties. This upset Marvis, who has always believed his brother was framed and who felt strongly that he needed the family's support more than ever.

After we choke down the food, we choose to sit and drink coffee rather than to reenter the stultifying dreariness of the visitors' lounge. I explain my fears about Quincy's safety. I offer my rather speculative theory that the attack was ordered by someone connected to his conviction, someone who's afraid of our investigation. I offer a lame apology for what has happened, but he will have none of it. He is grateful for our efforts and says so repeatedly. He has always dreamed of his big brother walking victoriously out of prison, an innocent man. Marvis is a lot like Quincy, easygoing, likeable, believable, a decent man trying to survive a tough life. There are flashes of bitterness at a system that robbed his brother, but there is also a lot of hope that a grievous wrong will someday be made right.

Eventually we drag ourselves upstairs and I yield my sofa. I go to the motel, shower, and fall asleep.

MOSBY, MEET Frankie Tatum. The rendezvous takes place in a honky-tonk on the outskirts of Deltona, far away from

Mosby's world. He says he once frequented the place in his youth but is sure no one will recognize him now. As always, Frankie scopes it out before they meet. It's almost midnight on a Thursday and the place is deserted and quiet. It takes a couple of beers for them to relax with each other.

Give Frankie two beers with a brother in friendly surroundings and he can be trusted.

"I need six thousand cash," Mosby says. They're at a table in the rear, near an empty pool table. The two guys at the bar cannot hear a word.

"We can do that," Frankie says. "What do we get for the money?"

"I have a piece of paper with three names. The first two are convicted killers pulling hard time, parole is way down the road, if ever. They did the number on Quincy. The third name is the guard who was close by and didn't see a thing. Probably the lookout. There's no video. They picked a spot that is unmonitored. Don't know why Quincy was in the vicinity because most inmates know better. A guy got raped there two months ago. Maybe Quincy figured he was too tough to mess with and just got careless. You'll have to ask him if you get the chance."

"How much do you know about the two thugs?"

"Both are white, tough dudes in a tough gang, the Aryan Deacons. The first name is a guy I used to see every day when I worked his unit. From Dade County, nothing but trouble. The second name is unknown to me. There are two thousand prisoners at Garvin and thankfully I don't know them all."

"Any chance it was a gang matter?"

"I doubt it. The gangs are always at war, but Quincy stayed away from them, from what I'm told."

Frankie takes a sip from his bottle and pulls a white envelope from a coat pocket. He places it on the table and says, "Here's five thousand."

"I said six," Mosby says without reaching for the money.

From another pocket, Frankie pulls out a roll of bills and keeps it below the table. He counts quickly and hands over ten $100 bills. "That's six."

Mosby gives him the scrap of paper with one hand while taking the cash and the envelope with the other. Frankie unfolds the paper and looks at the three names.

Mosby says, "There's something else. Quincy didn't go down easy. He landed some punches while he was able. The first name there survived with a crushed nose. He was treated at the infirmary this afternoon, said he got in a fight. Happens all the time and few questions are asked. His face will be messed up for a few days so I'd move fast. A little confirmation."

"Thanks. Anything else?"

"Yeah, I won't be going back to the hospital. They're alternating guards now and we're always shorthanded. Tell Mr. Post I appreciate the business."

"Will do. And we appreciate it too."

I GIVE MAZY the first name, Vicki the second, while I pursue all three. Fifteen minutes after Frankie said goodbye to Mosby, our three computers are raging through the Internet.

Robert Earl Lane was convicted of first-degree murder for the killing of his girlfriend seventeen years ago in Dade County. Prior to that, he served three years for assaulting a police officer. Jon Drummik killed his grandmother for $60

239

in cash, money he needed to buy crack. He pled guilty in Sarasota in 1998 and avoided a capital trial. Both have been at Garvin Correctional Institute for about ten years, and since their prison files are confidential we can't find much. Mazy can usually hack into almost anything, but we decide to avoid breaking the law. Likewise, prison gangs such as the Aryan Deacons are not known to keep much in the way of records, so there is no way to verify their membership.

The guard is Adam Stone, white male, thirty-four years old, resident of a little hick town half an hour from the prison. At 2:15 a.m., Frankie finds Stone's home and calls in the license plate numbers of his car and pickup truck. At 3:00 a.m., the team at Guardian has a conference call and all info is exchanged. We put together a plan to dig deep into the backgrounds of Lane and Drummik and learn as much as possible about the Aryan Deacons in Florida.

Our theory is that the hit on Quincy was ordered, and paid for, by someone on the outside. Lane and Drummik had nothing to do with the Russo murder. They're just a couple of hard-timers doing the job for a few bucks. The fact that their victim was black made the attack more enjoyable.

At 5:00 a.m. I return to the hospital and find the visitors' lounge empty. I'm stopped at the ICU desk by a nurse, so at least someone is awake. I ask about Marvis Miller, and she nods toward Quincy's room. Marvis is asleep on a rollaway cot, protecting his brother. There are no other guards or cops around. The nurse explains that last night around midnight Marvis became upset at the lack of vigilance and demanded the cot. Her boss agreed and they rolled one into Quincy's room. I thank her and ask, "How's the patient?"

She shrugs and says, "Hanging on."

An hour later, Marvis stumbles forth, rubbing his eyes and happy to see me. We find some stale coffee and sit in folding chairs in the hallway, watching the parade of nurses and doctors doing their early rounds. One group motions for us to join them at Quincy's door, and we are informed that his vitals continue to show slight improvement. They plan to keep him in a coma for several more days.

Marvis is worried about losing his job and needs to leave. We embrace at the elevator and I promise to call if there is a change. He promises to return as soon as possible, but he's almost five hours away.

Two heavily equipped Orlando policemen appear and I chat them up. They plan to hang around for an hour or so until a prison guard arrives.

At 7:30 I get an e-mail from the prison. The warden has a few spare minutes to grant me an audience.

I ARRIVE AT Garvin forty-five minutes before my ten o'clock appointment. I try to explain to the staff at check-in that I have a meeting with the warden, but I'm treated like every other lawyer there to see a client. Nothing is easy in a prison. Rules are entrenched, or they are amended on the fly—whatever it takes to waste more time. I'm finally fetched by a guard in a golf cart and we go for a spin toward the administration building.

The warden is a large black guy with a real swagger. Twenty years ago he played football at Florida State and was drafted into the NFL where he lasted ten games before blowing out a knee. His office is adorned with color photos of him in uniforms, and autographed footballs, and table lamps made of helmets. Looks like he played for the Packers. He sits behind a massive desk that's covered with files and paperwork, the domain of an important man. To his left stands the prison lawyer, a pale white bureaucrat who holds a notepad and stares at me as if he just might drag me into court for some reason, or no reason at all.

"I've got about fifteen minutes," the warden begins pleasantly. His name is Odell Herman. On the walls there are at least three framed jerseys of different colors with the name HERMAN across the back. You'd think the guy made the Hall of Fame.

"Thanks for your time," I reply like a real smartass. "I'd like to know what happened to my client, Quincy Miller."

"We're investigating and can't talk about it yet. Right, Mr. Burch?"

Mr. Burch offers a lawyerly nod to confirm this.

"Do you know who attacked him?" I ask.

"We have suspects, but, again I can't talk about it right now."

"Okay, I'll play along. Without divulging names, do you know who did it?"

Herman looks at Burch, who shakes his head.

"No sir, we don't have that information yet."

At this point the meeting is over. They are covering up and will give me nothing.

"Okay. Do you know if a guard was involved in the attack in any way?"

"Of course not," Herman says with irritation. How dare I suggest something so outrageous.

"So, as of today, three days after the attack, you don't know who did it and you claim that no one working for the prison was involved. Is that correct?"

"That's what I said."

I abruptly stand and head for the door. "There were two thugs who attacked my client. The first is Robert Earl Lane. Check him out. Right now his eyes are swollen shut, bluish in color because his nose was broken by Quincy. Lane was treated at your infirmary a few hours after the assault. We'll subpoena the records so don't lose them."

Herman's mouth opens but no words escape. Lawyer Burch frowns and looks thoroughly confused.

I open the door, pause, and conclude with "There's more to the story. It will all come out when I bust your ass in federal court."

I slam it behind me.

33

The Orlando office of the FBI is located in a four-level modern building in the suburb of Maitland. Susan Ashley and I arrive early for a three o'clock meeting with the powers that be. She has spent the past two days making contacts and jockeying for the appointment. She has also sent along a short summary of our file on Quincy Miller. We have no idea which special agent we'll meet, but we are optimistic that we'll find someone willing to listen.

Her name is Agnes Nolton, early forties and with enough clout to have a nice corner office. Along the way we pass dozens of agents in cramped cubbyholes, so it's readily apparent that Agent Nolton has some seniority. In her office we are joined by Special Agent Lujewski, who looks like he should still be in college. After coffee is served and the pleasantries are finished, I am invited to do the talking.

I quickly summarize Guardian's work on behalf of Quincy Miller and give the opinion that he was framed by a drug gang, with a lot of help from the ex-sheriff of Ruiz County. Now that we're pushing for post-conviction relief, those responsible for the murder of Keith Russo are feeling the heat. I give the names of Nash Cooley, the drug lawyer in Miami, and Mickey

Mercado, one of his henchmen. I speculate that these two along with other unknowns are responsible for the rather brilliant idea of ending our investigation by eliminating our client.

"Would that work?" Nolton asks. "If your client dies, what happens to the case?"

"Yes, it would work," I reply. "Our mission is to get innocent people out of prison. We don't have the time or resources to litigate from the grave."

She nods in agreement and I continue. I describe Quincy and make much of the fact that he was not involved with gang activity; thus, there should have been no reason for the Aryans to attack him.

"So, we're talking about a contract killing?" she asks.

"Yes, murder for hire, a federal offense."

It's obvious, at least to me, that Nolton is intrigued by the case. Lujewski keeps a poker face but misses nothing. He opens a laptop and starts pecking.

I continue, "And, we have the names of the two assailants, both convicted murderers. You've heard of the Aryan Deacons?"

Nolton smiles and likes it even more. A drug gang, a Mexican cartel at that, a crooked sheriff, the murder of a lawyer at his desk, a wrongful conviction, and now an attempted contract killing to stop an effort at exoneration. Not your everyday case.

"Sure," she says. "But we're too busy putting people in prison to worry about what happens once they get there. Do you plan to give me the names?"

"What will you do with them?"

She ponders this as she takes a sip of coffee and glances at Lujewski. He stops pecking and says, "The Aryan Deacons spun off from the Aryan Brotherhood, the largest white prison gang in the U.S. The Dekes' membership is estimated at ten thousand, though recordkeeping is spotty. Typical gang activity—drugs, food, sex, cell phones. Their alumni—the few who get out—remain members and carry on criminal activity. Pretty nasty bunch of boys."

Nolton says to me, "Again, we have our hands full on this side of the wall."

I say, "There's also a prison guard who's probably involved. White guy who looked the other way. He could be the weak link because he has more to lose."

She says, "I like the way you think, Post."

"We're in the same business, sort of. You solve crimes to lock people up. I solve crimes to get people out."

IT WAS A typical workday for Adam Stone. He punched in at 7:59 a.m., and spent fifteen minutes at his locker drinking coffee and eating a doughnut with two other guards. He was in no hurry to report to Unit E for another stressful day of supervising criminals who would kill him if given half a chance. A few of the men he liked, and he enjoyed their banter. Others he despised, or even hated. Especially the blacks. Stone had been raised in a rough, rural area where few blacks lived or felt welcome. His father was a bitter racist who despised all minorities and blamed them for his lack of upward mobility in life. His mother claimed to have been sexually assaulted by a black athlete in high school, though no charges were ever filed. As a child, Adam was taught to avoid blacks when possible and to speak to them only in unpleasant terms.

As a prison guard, though, he had no choice. Seventy percent of the population at Garvin was black or brown, as were most of the guards. For the seven years Adam had worked there, his racism had only deepened. He saw them at their worst—caged men who had always been discriminated against and abused were in charge of an environment they controlled. Their retribution was often sickening. For protection, the whites needed their own gangs. He secretly admired the Aryans. Outnumbered and constantly threatened, they survived by swearing blood oaths to one another. Their brand of violence was often breathtaking. Three years earlier, they had attacked two black guards with razor-sharp shanks, then hid the bodies and watched them bleed to death.

During the day, Adam made his rounds, escorted prisoners to the infirmary and back, spent an obligatory hour watching surveillance cameras, stretched his thirty-minute lunch break into an hour, and punched out at 4:30. Eight hours of work without breaking a sweat, at twelve dollars each.

He has no way of knowing that agents working for the federal government spent the day digging through his life.

Two of them trail him as he leaves the prison. He is driving his pride and joy, a late-model Ram monster truck with over-sized tires, black rims, not a speck of dirt anywhere. It is costing him $650 a month with years to go. His wife drives a late-model Toyota sedan at $300 a month. Their home is mortgaged to the tune of $135,000. Their bank records, obtained by warrant, show balances of almost $9,000 in checking and savings. In summary, Adam and his wife, who works as a part-time clerk in an insurance office, are living far above their meager means.

He stops for gas at a country store and goes inside to pay. When he returns, two gentlemen in jeans and sneakers are

247

waiting. They quickly give their names, mention the FBI, flash badges, and say they would like to talk. For a tough guy who feels even tougher in his uniform, Adam is weak at the knees. Beads of sweat ripple across his forehead.

He follows them a mile to an abandoned school with an empty gravel lot. Under an old oak, next to what was once a playground, he leans on the edge of a wooden picnic table and tries to sound relaxed. "What can I do for you fellas?"

Agent Frost says, "Just a few questions."

"Go right ahead," Adam says with a drippy smile. He wipes his large forehead with the back of a sleeve.

Agent Thagard says, "We know you're a guard at Garvin, been there for what, seven years?"

"Yes sir. Something like that."

"You know an inmate by the name of Quincy Miller?"

Adam frowns and looks at the tree limbs as if searching deeply. A shake of the head and a quite unconvincing no. "Don't believe so. Lot of inmates at Garvin."

Frost asks, "How about Robert Earl Lane and Jon Drummik? Ever meet those guys?"

A quick cooperative smile and "Sure, they're both in Unit E. That's where I'm stationed for now."

Thagard says, "Quincy Miller, who's black, was beaten unconscious three days ago in the alley between the gym and the shop, next to Unit E. He was stabbed at least three times and left for dead. You were on duty when the attack occurred. Know anything about it?"

"I may have heard about it."

"How could you not hear about it?" Frost snaps sharply and takes a step closer.

"A lot of fights at Garvin," Adam says defensively.

Thagard asks, "You didn't see Lane and Drummik attack Quincy Miller?"

"No."

"We have an informant who says you did. Says you were right there, but the reason you didn't see anything was because you didn't want to. Says you were the lookout. Says you're well known as one of the Deacons' favorite gofers."

Adam exhales mightily as if sucker punched in the gut. He wipes his forehead again and tries in vain to smile as if amused. "No way, man, no way."

Thagard says, "Let's cut the bullshit, Adam. We have search warrants and we have collected all of your financial crap. We know you have nine thousand dollars in the bank, which is quite impressive for a guy making twelve bucks an hour and whose wife makes ten for part-time work, a guy with two kids, a guy who's never inherited shit from a relative, a guy who spends at least two thousand a month just on nice wheels and a nice house, not to mention groceries and the phone bills. You're living way above your means, Adam, and we know, from our informant, that you pick up extra dough running drugs for the Deacons. We can prove that in a court tomorrow."

They could not, but Adam certainly didn't know the difference.

Frost takes the hand-off smoothly with "You're going to be indicted, Adam, federal court. The U.S. Attorney in Orlando is working on it now, grand jury comes in tomorrow. But we're not going after the guards. Most of them peddle goods back and forth, pick up some extra cash. The warden doesn't really care because he wants his inmates stoned. They behave better when they have trouble walking. You know the drill, Adam. We couldn't care less about the contraband. We're on to something much more important. The attack on Quincy Miller was a contract for hire, a hit ordered by someone on the outside. That makes it a conspiracy, and that makes it federal."

Adam's eyes water and he wipes them with a forearm. "I ain't done nothing. You can't indict me."

Frost says, "Gee, we've never heard that before."

Thagard says, "The U.S. Attorney will grind you to a pulp, Adam. You don't stand a chance. He'll make sure the prison fires you immediately. There goes your salary, there go your bribes, all that cash. Then you'll lose this cute little monster truck with the fat tires and ghetto rims, and your house, and, shit, Adam, it's going to be awful."

"You're full of shit," he says, trying to get tough but his voice cracks. They almost feel sorry for him. "You can't do this."

Frost says, "Oh, we do it all the time, Adam. If you're indicted, it'll take two years to get you to trial, more if the U.S. Attorney so chooses. He doesn't care if you're guilty or innocent, he just wants to ruin you if you don't cooperate."

Adam's head jerks back as his eyes grow big. "Cooperate?"

Frost and Thagard exchange grave looks as if they're not sure they should proceed. Thagard leans in and says, "You're a small fish, Adam. Always have been, always will be. The U.S. Attorney couldn't care less about you and your dipshit little bribery scheme. He wants the Deacons, and he wants to know who paid for the hit on Quincy Miller. You play ball with us, we play ball with you."

"You want me to snitch?"

"No. We want you to inform. Big difference. Gather information from your buddies, pass it along to us. You find out who ordered the hit and we'll forget about an indictment."

"They'll kill me," he says, and finally bursts into tears. He sobs loudly into his hands as Frost and Thagard look around. Cars pass on the county road but no one bothers to look.

After a few minutes, he pulls himself together. Thagard says, "They will not kill you, Adam, because they will not know what you're doing. We handle informants all the time, we know the game."

Frost says, "And, if things get too dangerous, Adam, we'll get you out and get you a job in a federal joint. Twice the pay, twice the benefits."

Adam looks at them with red eyes and asks, "Can we keep this quiet? I mean, no one can know about this, not even my wife."

With the word "we" a deal is struck. Frost says, "Of course, Adam. You think we tell folks about our confidential informants? Come on, man. We wrote the book on handling informants."

For a long time nothing is said as Adam stares at the gravel and occasionally wipes fluids from his face. They watch him and are almost sympathetic. He says, "Can I think about this? Gimme some time."

"No," Frost says. "We don't have time. Things are moving fast, Adam. If Quincy dies then you'll be on the hook for capital murder, federal style."

"What's the charge now?"

"Attempted murder. Conspiracy. Thirty years max, and the U.S. Attorney will go for every last day of it."

He shakes his head and appears ready for more tears. His voice breaks as he says, "And if I play ball, as you like to say?"

"No indictment. You walk, Adam. Don't be a fool."

Frost closes the deal with "This is one of those life-altering moments, Adam. You make the right decision right now and your life goes on. The bad one, and you're gonna be locked up with the same savages you've been guarding."

Adam stands and bends at the waist, belches. "Excuse me," he says and walks to the edge of the old playground where he begins retching. Frost and Thagard turn and look toward the road. Adam kneels behind a large bush and vomits loudly for a spell. When he's finished he shuffles back and sits at the picnic table. His shirt is soaked with sweat, and his cheap brown tie is specked with his lunch.

"Okay," he says hoarsely. "What's the first order of business?"

Frost doesn't hesitate. "Do either Lane or Drummik have a cell phone?"

"I know Drummik does. I took it to him."

"Where did you get it?"

Adam hesitates before plunging in. When he says what he's about to say, there is no turning back. "There's a man named Mayhall, don't know his first name, don't know if Mayhall is real or fake, don't know where he lives or where he comes from. I see him once or twice a month. He comes here with the goodies for his boys inside Garvin. Cell phones and dope, usually pills and meth, cheap drugs. I take the stuff in and deliver to the right people. He pays me a thousand bucks a month in cash, plus a little stash of dope to sell on my own. I'm not the only guard who does this. When you earn twelve an hour it's hard to survive."

Thagard says, "We get that. How many Aryan Deacons in Garvin?"

"Twenty-five or thirty. The Brotherhood has more."

"How many guards service the Deacons?"

"I'm the only one I know of. Certain guards take care of certain groups. I doubt if Mayhall would want anyone else involved. He gets what he wants with me."

"Has he served time?"

"I'm sure he has. You can't join the Deacons unless you're in prison."

Frost asks, "Can you get Drummik's cell phone?"

Adam shrugs and smiles as if he's quite clever. "Sure. Cell phones are prized possessions and sometimes they get stolen. I'll go to Drummik's cell when he's out on the yard, make it look like a theft."

"How soon?" Thagard asks.

"Tomorrow."

"Okay, do it. We'll track his calls and we'll give you a replacement."

Frost asks, "Will this Mayhall character get suspicious if Drummik finds another phone?"

Adam thinks for a moment. Things are still not quite clear. He shakes his head and says, "I doubt it. These guys buy, sell, trade, steal, barter, you name it."

Thagard leans down and sticks out a hand. "Okay, Adam, we got a deal, right?"

Adam reluctantly shakes his hand.

Frost says, "And your phones are tapped too, Adam. We're monitoring everything, so no stupid moves, okay?"

They left him at the picnic table, staring into the distance and wondering how his life could change so fast.

34

With the FBI throwing its weight around, Quincy is moved to a corner room that is more secure. Two surveillance cameras are mounted prominently above his door. The hospital staff is on high alert and its guards are more of a presence. The prison sends one over each day for a few hours of hallway monitoring, and Orlando police officers enjoy stopping by to flirt with the nurses.

Quincy's condition improves each day and we slowly begin to believe that he will not die. I'm on a first-name basis with his doctors and staff by now and everybody is pulling for my client. He is as secure as possible, so I decide to hit the road. The place is driving me crazy. Who doesn't hate sitting around a hospital? Savannah is five hours away and I've never been so homesick.

Somewhere around St. Augustine, Susan Ashley calls with the news that old Judge Jerry Plank has entered an order denying our petition for post-conviction relief. His decision is expected; the surprise is that he woke up long enough to do something. We were anticipating a wait of at least a year, but he disposed of it in two months. This is actually good news because it speeds along our appeal to the state supreme court.

I don't want to pull over and read his opinion, Susan Ashley says it's very brief. A two-page order in which Plank says we provided no new evidence, in spite of the recantations from Zeke Huffey and Carrie Holland. Whatever. We were expecting to lose at the circuit court level. I cuss for a few minutes in traffic then settle down. There are times, many times, when I despise judges, especially blind ones and old ones and white ones, almost all of whom cut their teeth in prosecutors' offices and have no sympathy for anyone accused of a crime. To them, everybody who is charged is guilty and needs time in jail. The system works beautifully and justice always prevails.

When my rant is over, I call Mazy as she's reading the order. We discuss the appeal and she will drop everything and get it ready. When I arrive at the office late in the afternoon, she has a first draft prepared. We discuss it over coffee with Vicki and I tell stories about the events in Orlando.

ADAM STONE MADE a clean swap with Jon Drummik's phone. He took the old one as he ransacked the cell, and the following day handed a new one to Drummik. The FBI is scrambling to track old calls and listening to the new ones. They are confident that their targets will walk into the trap. They have no information on Mayhall, or at least none they can share with me, but they plan to watch him closely the next time he meets with Adam.

For three straight days before the attack on Quincy, Drummik called a cell phone in Delray Beach, north of Boca Raton. The day after the attack, he made only one call, to the same number. However, the trail ended when the number fizzled. It was a burner, a disposable phone with a thirty-day plan that was paid for by cash at a Best Buy store. Its owner is being very careful.

Adam does not have Mayhall's phone number; has never had it. There is nothing to track until Mayhall calls, and he finally does. The FBI grabs the incoming number from Adam's phone and follows it to another cell phone, also in Delray Beach. The puzzle is coming together. Monitoring the phone signal, the FBI picks up Mayhall's scent as he buzzes along Interstate 95 headed north. The car he's driving is registered to one Skip DiLuca of Delray Beach. White male, age fifty-one, four-time felon with manslaughter his worst sin, paroled three years earlier from a Florida prison, currently managing a shop selling used motorcycles.

DiLuca, aka Mayhall, arranges to meet Adam after work at a bar in Orange City, forty-five minutes from the prison. Adam says they always meet at the same place and have a quick beer as they talk shop. To avoid suspicion, Adam changes into street clothes. His handlers tape a small wire to his chest. He arrives first, selects a table, does a mike check, all bugs are working. An FBI crew is listening in the back of a van parked in the street behind the bar.

After a few curt pleasantries, the real conversation begins:

DILUCA: They didn't kill Miller. What happened?
ADAM: Well, several things went wrong. First, Miller
knows how to fight and went crazy. Robert Earl Lane
has a busted nose. Took a few minutes to subdue him,
too much time. Once they had him down they couldn't
finish him off before another guard saw them. They
didn't cut him enough.
DILUCA: Where were you?

ADAM: I was there, man, right where I was supposed to be. I know my turf. The ambush worked perfectly, just couldn't get the guy down.

DILUCA: Well, he ain't dead, and that's a problem. We got paid for a job that's not finished. The gentlemen I'm dealing with are not happy.

ADAM: Not my fault. I did what I was supposed to do. Can't you get him at the hospital?

DILUCA: Maybe. We've had a look, lots of uniforms in the way. His condition improves each day so our end of the deal stinks more and more. We were supposed to take him out, plain and simple. You tell Drummik and Lane that I'm really pissed about their lousy job. They promised me they could do it.

ADAM: How much heat are you taking?

DILUCA: I'll deal with it.

Their conversation is brief, and when they finish their beers, they step outside. DiLuca hands Adam a brown paper grocery bag with $1,000 in cash, two new cell phones, and a supply of drugs. He leaves without saying goodbye and hurries away. Adam waits until he is out of sight, then tells his handlers DiLuca is gone. He drives around the block and meets them on a side street.

Technically, legally, the FBI has the goods for an indictment against DiLuca, Adam, Drummik, and Lane for a contract killing, or an attempted one. But the two inmates are already locked up. Adam is too valuable as an informant. And DiLuca can lead them to the real catch.

Twenty minutes down the road, DiLuca sees blue lights in his mirror. He checks his speedometer and knows damned well he is not violating the law. He is on parole and treasures his freedom; thus, he sticks to the rules, or at least the rules of the road. A county officer takes his license and registration, and spends half an hour calling it in. DiLuca begins to squirm. When the officer returns, he asks, rudely, "You been drinking?"

"One beer," DiLuca answers truthfully.

"That's what they all say."

Another county car with flashing lights arrives, and parks in front of DiLuca's car. Two officers get out and glare at him as if he has just murdered some children. The three huddle and kill more time as DiLuca fumes. Finally, he is ordered out of the car.

"What the hell for?" he demands as he closes his door. He should not have. Two officers grab him and force him across the hood of his car while another slaps on handcuffs.

"You were swerving recklessly," the first officer says.

"The hell I was," DiLuca snaps.

"Just shut up."

They search his pockets, take his phone and wallet, and toss him rather roughly into the back seat of the first patrol car. As he is taken away, an officer calls a wrecker, then calls the FBI. At the station, DiLuca is placed in a holding room where he is forced to pose for a mug shot, then left to sit for the next four hours.

A federal magistrate on standby in Orlando quickly approves two search warrants; one for DiLuca's apartment, the other for his car. FBI agents enter the apartment in Delray Beach and go to work. It is a one-bedroom apartment with sparse, cheap furnishings and no evidence whatsoever of a woman. The kitchen counters are covered with dirty dishes. Laundry is piled in the hallway. The refrigerator has nothing more than beer, water, and cold cuts. The coffee table in the den is littered with hardcore porn magazines. A laptop is found in a tiny office and carried outside to a van where a technician copies the hard drive. Two burners are found, opened, analyzed, tapped, and put back on the desk. Listening devices are hidden throughout the apartment. After two hours the team is finished, and while normally it would be fastidious in rearranging things, DiLuca is such a slob it would be impossible for him or anyone else to notice that a surveillance team had spent the evening rummaging through his apartment.

Another team goes through his car and finds nothing important but another burner. Evidently, DiLuca has no permanent cell phone number. Digging through the cheap phone, the technician hits pay dirt in the Contacts file. DiLuca has only ten numbers in memory, and one is for Mickey Mercado, the operative who showed up in court to eavesdrop on our motion for post-conviction relief. In the Recents file, there are twenty-two incoming and outgoing calls from and to Mercado in the past two weeks.

A GPS monitor is attached to the inside of his rear bumper so the car cannot escape surveillance. At 10:00 p.m., the county sheriff enters the holding room and apologizes to DiLuca. He explains that there was a bank robbery near Naples earlier in the day and the getaway car matched DiLuca's. They suspected him, but now realize they were wrong. He is free to go.

DiLuca is not gracious and forgiving, and leaves as quickly as possible. He is suspicious and decides not to return to Delray Beach. He is also wary of using his burner so he makes no calls. He drives two hours to Sarasota and checks into a budget motel.

The next morning, the same federal magistrate issues a warrant authorizing the search of the apartment of Mercado and the electronic surveillance of his telephones. Another warrant directs his cell phone provider to open its records. However, before the bugging is complete, DiLuca calls Mercado from a pay phone. He is then tracked from Sarasota to Coral Gables where his trail is picked up by a team of FBI agents. He finally parks at an Afghan kebob restaurant on Dolphin Avenue and goes inside. Fifteen minutes later, a young female agent saunters inside for a bite and identifies DiLuca eating with Mickey Mercado.

DILUCA'S CHILLING COMMENT to Adam that they had "had a look" at Quincy in the hospital ratchets up the security there. Quincy is moved again, to another corner room, and he is never left unwatched.

AGENT AGNES NOLTON keeps me abreast of these developments, though I do not know everything. I caution her against using our phones, and we use encrypted e-mails. She is confident that (1) Quincy will be protected, and (2) they will soon ensnare Mercado in their conspiracy. One source of concern is that he has dual citizenship and can come and go as he pleases. If he becomes suspicious, he might simply run home and never be seen again. Nolton believes that nailing Mercado will be our ultimate prize. The conspirators above him, the real criminals, are probably not in the U.S. and virtually immune from prosecution.

With the FBI fully on board, and with our client still alive, we can return our attention to exonerating him.

35

The sangria is calling. Glenn Colacurci is thirsty and wants to meet again at The Bull in Gainesville. After two days of trying to rest in Savannah, I head south again and the adventure continues. Quincy has been eased out of his coma and is fairly alert. His vitals improve each day and his doctors are talking about moving him out of ICU and into a private room where they can begin planning the surgeries to mend his bones. They repeatedly assure me that security is tight, so I'm not compelled to hustle down for more hours of sitting in the hall and staring at my feet.

I get to The Bull minutes after 4:00 p.m. and Glenn's tall glass is already half empty. His large fleshy nose is turning pink, a shade that almost matches the drink. I order the same and look around for his cute little secretary who I catch myself thinking about more than I should. I don't see Bea.

Glenn has read about Quincy's problems and wants the inside scoop. Since I've known a hundred small-town windbag lawyers like him, I reveal nothing new. As with most prison beatings, details are sparse and sketchy. In a grave conspiratorial whisper he informs me that the local weekly newspaper in Ruiz County is now following Quincy's case and our efforts to exonerate him. I absorb this in rapt attention and pass on the opportunity to tell him that Vicki is monitoring half the newspapers—weekly and daily—in the State of Florida. She keeps a running record of every word printed about the case. We live on the Internet. Glenn stumbles across it once a week.

This meeting has a purpose, other than drinking, and after half an hour I realize that the sangria is the oil of conversation. He smacks his lips, brushes his mouth with a sleeve, and finally gets down to business. "So, I gotta tell you, Post, I've been thinking about this case night and day. Really into it, you know. This all happened on my watch, back in my glory days when I was in the state senate and also ran the biggest law firm in the county, and, well, you know, I thought I was really in the loop. I figured Pfitzner was working both sides of the street, but we stayed in our lanes, if you know what I mean. He ran his show, got his votes, I did the same. When Keith got his head blown off and your boy got convicted for it, well, I was satisfied. I wanted the death penalty. The whole town was relieved. Looking back, though . . ."

He sees the waiter, flags him over, drains the dregs from his glass, and orders another round. I have at least six inches of liquid left in mine. With plenty of time on the clock, this could spiral into one sloppy afternoon.

He catches his breath and continues. "Looking back, though, things don't add up. I'm kin to half the county and represented the other half. Last time I ran for reelection I got eighty percent of the vote and I was pissed about the lost twenty. There's an old deputy, won't give you the name, but he used to run cases for me. I'd pay him in cash and give him a cut when we settled. Did the same for ambulance drivers and tow truck operators. Had 'em all on the payroll. Anyway, the deputy is still around, lives near the Gulf, and I've been talking to him. He retired years ago, health's in the tank but hell he's pushing eighty. He worked on Pfitzner's staff and managed to stay on his good side. He did the light stuff—traffic, football games, school events. Wasn't much of a cop but didn't want to be. Just enjoyed the uniform and the paycheck. Says you're right, says Pfitzner was on the take with the drug traffickers, says it was known throughout the force. Pfitzner had these two brothers—"

"Chip and Dip."

He pauses and flashes a smile with his yellow teeth. "You're pretty good, Post."

"We are thorough."

"Anyway, Chip and Dip ran things for Pfitzner and held everybody in line. The inner circle kept the money and thought they were keeping the secrets too, but, of course, it's a small town."

The waiter returns with two jugs of hooch and looks at my first, virtually untouched, as if to say, "Let's go, pal, this is a real bar." I give him a smirk and take a long pull on the straw. Glenn does the same, and after a noisy swallow says, "The deputy tells me Kenny Taft was not killed by some random gang of drug thugs, not at all. He says some of the deputies back then strongly suspected Pfitzner set up the ambush, says he needed to put the clamps on Taft, who knew something. He says it worked just swell but with one minor hitch. A man got shot. Evidently, either Kenny Taft or Brace Gilmer managed to get off a lucky round and one of the gun thugs went down. The story goes that he bled out on the way to the hospital and they dumped his body behind a queer joint in Tampa. Just another unsolved murder. Luckily for Pfitzner, the guy was not a deputy and not from Seabrook so no red flags were raised. Any of this sound familiar, Post?"

I shake my head no. I will not repeat anything Bruce Gilmer told me in Idaho.

Another long pull and he's energized for more narrative. "So the obvious question is why did Pfitzner want to get rid of Kenny Taft."

"That's the puzzle," I say helpfully.

"Well, the rumor is that Kenny Taft got wind of the plan to burn the shed where the cops stored crime scene stuff, and that Taft removed several boxes of evidence before the fire. No one knew this, of course, and once he had the goods he was afraid to do anything with them. He must've said too much and word filtered back to Pfitzner, who set up the ambush."

"Several boxes?" I ask as my mouth immediately goes dry and my heart starts pounding. I drink sangria to calm myself.

"That's the rumor, Post. Don't know what was destroyed in the fire and don't know what was removed by Kenny Taft. Just rumors. There was a missing flashlight, as I recall. I've read your post-conviction petition, saw where you lost last week, and anyway the flashlight was presumed to have been destroyed. Right, Post?"

"That's right."

"Maybe it wasn't destroyed."

"That's interesting," I manage to say with calmness. "Does the rumor cover the part that reveals what Kenny did with the boxes of evidence?"

"No, it doesn't. But interestingly enough, the rumor says that during his funeral service, which was fit for a five-star

265

general, Pfitzner had two of his men go through Kenny's house inch by inch looking for the boxes. They have never been found, according to the rumor."

"But you have a hunch, right?"

"No, but I'm working on it, Post. I have lots of sources, old and new, and I'm on the prowl. Just thought you'd like to know."

"And you're not worried?" I ask.

"Worried about what?"

"Worried that you might discover something that has been well hidden. Quincy Miller didn't kill Keith Russo. The murder was ordered by a drug gang with Pfitzner's blessing and cover-up. The gang is still around and ten days ago they tried to kill Quincy in prison. They don't like our way of digging up the past, and they won't like yours either."

He laughs and says, "I'm too old to worry, Post. Plus, I'm having too much fun."

"Then why are we hiding in a bar in Gainesville?"

"Because there aren't any decent bars in Seabrook, which is probably a good thing for a guy like me. Besides, this is my college town. Love the place. Are you worried, Post?"

"Let's just say that I'm being careful."

36

The file on Mickey Mercado gets thicker. With warrants, his income tax returns are obtained and scoured. He lists his occupation as a security consultant, a sole proprietor as opposed to a partnership or corporation. His business address is in the same building as Varick & Valencia, Nash Cooley's law firm. Last year's reported gross income was slightly more than $200,000, with deductions for a mortgage and a couple of nice cars. He's single, divorced, with no dependents. No charitable activities at all.

The FBI has no interest in wasting its time pursuing prison guards who peddle dope or prison gangs at war with each other. But Special Agent Agnes Nolton can't resist the scenario of a crime boss hiring the Aryan Deacons to kill an innocent man whose lawyers are trying to exonerate him. She makes the decision to roll the dice in a big way and put Skip DiLuca in a vice. It is a high-risk, high-reward strategy.

With the cooperation of the U.S. Attorney, she appears before a federal grand jury and presents the evidence. Jon Drummik, Robert Earl Lane, Adam Stone, and Skip DiLuca are indicted for the attempted contract killing and aggravated assault of Quincy Miller. The indictments are sealed, and the FBI waits in ambush.

I'm waiting too, hanging around Quincy's new hospital room and helping to nurse him back to good health. Our conversations are brief because talking quickly tires him. He remembers nothing about the attack. As for his short-term memory, there's not much there.

ADAM STONE checks in. Mr. Mayhall is on the way with more contraband and cash. Because of his near-arrest last time, May-hall decides to change meeting places. He picks a taco joint at the northern edge of Sanford, population 50,000. Adam arrives first in street clothes, gets a table with a view of the parking lot, and helps himself to some tacos. He has been told by the FBI that Mayhall, real name DiLuca, is now driving a new silver Lexus that he has just leased. Adam munches away and watches for the Lexus. It arrives fifteen minutes late and parks next to Adam's monster truck. DiLuca gets out and walks hurriedly to the restaurant's side door, but he never makes it. Two agents in dark suits materialize from nowhere and block his path. They flash badges and point to a black SUV waiting by a dumpster. DiLuca knows it would be foolish to resist or to say anything. He drops his head and slumps his shoulders as they lead him away. Once again he's managed to screw up his life in the free world. Once again he feels the tight clamp of metal handcuffs.

Adam is the only person inside the restaurant to witness the drama. He is not pleased by the events. His world just got rocked again. He's been promised by the FBI that his indict-ment will be tossed in return for his cooperation. He's been promised a better job. But who carries out these promises?

The plan, as far as he knows, is to grab DiLuca before he can squeal to anyone. Thus, the Deacons should not learn of his arrest, nor should they have any way of knowing that Adam, their favorite gofer and mule, is now an informant. But Adam knows that in prison loyalties change by the day and secrets are hard to keep. He fears for his life and wants another job.

He finishes a taco and watches the SUV drive away. Immediately, a tow truck arrives and takes the new Lexus. When things are back to normal, Adam finishes his last taco and walks to his truck, suspecting that he too will soon be arrested. Or, worse, shanked and left to bleed out.

FOR ALMOST AN hour, Skip DiLuca rides in the rear seat with cuffs firmly around his wrists, and says not a word. The agent seated next to him doesn't speak either. Nor do the two up front. The side windows are heavily tinted so that those inside barely see out, and those outside certainly cannot see the passengers.

The SUV winds and putters through traffic and finally makes its way to the rear of the FBI building in Maitland. DiLuca is walked up two flights of stairs and marched to a windowless room where more agents are waiting. He's shoved into a chair and his cuffs are removed. No fewer than six agents are in the room, an impressive show of force. Skip wonders if all this muscle is really necessary. If he made a break for it, where would he go? Relax, everybody.

A woman walks in and the men stiffen. She sits across from Skip, but the men stay on their feet, at the ready. She says, "Mr. DiLuca, my name is Agnes Nolton, Special Agent, FBI, and you're under arrest for the attempted contract killing of

Quincy Miller, and for aggravated assault, and a few other less significant crimes. We just searched your car and found three hundred capsules of crystal meth, so we'll add those charges later. Here's your indictment. Have a look."

She slides across the indictment and DiLuca takes his time reading it. He's not impressed and reads with a smug look, as if checking box scores. When he's finished, he gently places it on the table and offers her a drippy smile. She hands him another sheet of paper with his Miranda rights. He reads them and signs at the bottom. He's done this dance before.

She says, "We'll turn you over to the jailers in a moment, but first I'd like to have a little chat. Do you want a lawyer?"

"No, I want two lawyers. Maybe three."

"You need them. We can stop now and provide you with counsel tomorrow. But, if that happens, then we cannot have my little chat, and that will be very bad for you."

"I'm listening," he says calmly.

"You have an extensive criminal record and you're now facing another thirty years on all counts. You're fifty-one, so you'll die behind bars."

"Thank you."

"Don't mention it. Frankly, you're not much of a target and we have better things to do than fret over the games played by prison gangs. But a contract killing is another matter. Somebody paid for it. You tell us who, how much, all the details, and we can guarantee a light sentence for you and years of freedom thereafter. That is, if you stay out of trouble, which seems doubtful."

"Thanks."

"Don't mention it. We're offering a sweet deal, Mr. Di-Luca, and the offer expires in exactly forty-three minutes."

She glances at her watch as she says this. "You can't leave this room and you certainly cannot call anyone."

"I'll pass. I'm not a snitch, not a rat."

"Of course not, didn't mean to imply. But let's not kid ourselves. You're not exactly the president of the Rotary Club either. Look in the mirror, Skip. Face the truth. You're nothing but a con, a crook, a criminal with a rap sheet, a member of a violent gang, a racist, a long-time loser with a history of doing stupid things. Now you've been caught bribing a guard and hauling dope for your fellow Deacons. Pretty stupid, Skip. Why in hell can't you do something smart in your life? Do you really want to spend the next thirty years locked up with those animals? And it's federal, Skip, and not a camp. We'll make sure you get a U.S. Pen."

"Come on."

"A U.S. Pen, Skip, the worst of the worst. For the next thirty years. Garvin was a picnic compared to where you're headed."

Skip takes a deep breath and studies the ceiling. He's not afraid of prison, not even a U.S. Pen. He's spent most of his life behind the fence and he survived, at times even prospered. His brothers are there, all sworn together in a vicious but protective gang. No work, no bills to pay. Three meals a day. Plenty of drugs, especially for a gang member. Lots of sex if one is so inclined.

However, he's just met a lady he's quite fond of, his first romance in many years. She's a bit older, not rich but with some means, and they've talked of living together and taking a trip. Skip can't go far because he's on parole; a passport is only a dream. But she's given him a glimpse of another life, and he really doesn't want to go back to prison.

Because he's such an experienced con, he knows how to play the game. This tough gal can find some room to negotiate. He asks, "So how much time are we talking about?"

"As I said, thirty years."

"With a deal?"

"Three to five."

"I can't survive three to five. The answer is no."

"If you can't survive three to five, how can you expect to survive thirty?"

"I've been there, okay? I know the turf."

"Indeed you do."

Nolton stands and glares at him. "I'll be back in thirty minutes, Skip. Right now you're wasting my time."

He asks, "Can I have some coffee?"

Nolton spreads her arms and says, "Coffee? I don't have any coffee. Anybody here got coffee?" The other six agents look around as if searching for coffee. Finding none, they shake their heads. She marches out of the room and someone closes the door. Three agents remain. The largest one parks himself by the door in a heavy chair and begins deleting voice mails. The other two sit at the table with Skip and immediately find urgent work with their cell phones. The room is silent and Skip pretends to nod off.

Fifteen minutes later the door opens and Nolton walks in. She doesn't sit but looks down at Skip and says, "We just picked up Mickey Mercado in Coral Gables and we're getting ready to offer him the deal of a lifetime. If he takes it first, you're screwed and our offer is off the table. Think fast, Skip, if that's possible."

She turns around and marches out again. Skip manages to keep a poker face as his bowels grind and he feels nauseous. His vision blurs as his head spins. They not only know about Mercado, but now they have him! This is overwhelming. Skip glances around and notices the two agents at the table watching his every move. He is breathing heavier and he cannot stop it. His forehead turns wet. They make notes on their phones and send messages.

A moment passes and he does not retch. He keeps swallowing hard and another moment passes.

Ten minutes later she's back. She sits this time, a clear indication that she plans to really squeeze his balls. She begins pleasantly with "You're a fool, Skip. Any con in your shoes who can't take this deal is a fool."

"Thank you. Let's talk about witness protection."

She doesn't smile but she is obviously pleased as they take a giant step in the right direction. She says, "We can talk about it, but I'm not sure it will work in this case."

"You can make it work. You do it all the time."

"Indeed we do. So, hypothetically speaking, if we agree to stash you away, what do we get right now? On this table? Obviously we have Mercado. Was he your immediate contact? Was there someone above him? How many names can you give us? How much money? Who got it?"

DiLuca nods and looks around the room. He hates ratting and he has spent his career brutally punishing informants. However, there comes a time when a man has to worry about himself. He says, "I will tell you everything I know, but I want a deal in writing. Now. On this table, as you say. I don't trust you, you don't trust me."

"Fair enough. We have a standard short-form agreement that we've used for years. It's been approved by various defense lawyers. We can fill in a few blanks and see what happens."

DILUCA IS TAKEN to another room and placed before a large desktop computer. He types his own statement:

About six weeks ago, I was approached by a man who identified himself as Mickey Mercado, said he was from Miami. He actually knocked on the door of my apartment, which was odd because very few people know me or know where I live. As it turned out, he knew a lot about me. We went to a cafe around the corner and had our first meeting. He knew I was a Deacon and had spent time at Garvin. He knew all about my criminal record. I was a bit rattled by this and so I started asking him a bunch of questions. He said he was a security consultant. I asked what the hell that means, and he said he worked for various clients primarily in the Caribbean and so on and he was pretty vague. I asked him how I could be sure he wasn't some kind of cop or agent or some such prick who was trying to suck me into a trap. I asked if he was wearing a wire. He laughed and assured me he was not. Anyway, we swapped phone numbers and he invited me to visit his office, see his operation. He swore he was legit. A few days later, I drove to downtown Miami, went up about 35 floors, and met him in his office. Nice view of the water. Has a secretary and some staff. No name on the door, though. We had a cup of coffee, talked

for an hour. He asked if I still had contacts inside
Garvin. I said yes. He asked how difficult it would be
to take out another prisoner in Garvin. I asked if he
was talking about a contract. He said yes, or something
like that. Said there was an inmate who needed to be
"extinguished" because of some vague bad deal with a
client of Mercado's. He did not give me a name and I
did not say yes to the contract. I left and drove home.
In the meantime, I dug through the internet and found
very little about Mercado. But I was almost convinced
he was not a cop. Our third meeting took place in a
bar in Boca. That's where we cut the deal. He asked
how much it would cost. I said $50,000, which was a
big rip-off since you can get a guy rubbed out in prison
for much less. But he didn't seem to mind. He told
me the target was Quincy Miller, a lifer. I didn't ask
what Miller had done and Mercado didn't offer. It was
just a business deal as far as I was concerned. I called
Jon Drummik, the leader of the Dekes at Garvin, and
he arranged it all. He would use Robert Earl Lane,
probably the most dangerous man there, black or white.
They would get $5000 each up front, another $5000
when the job was finished. I planned to pocket the
rest and screw them. You can't take cash to prison, so
I had to arrange payment in cash to Drummik's son
and Lane's brother. At our fourth meeting, Mercado
gave me $25,000 in cash. I doubted I would ever see
the other half, regardless of what happened to Quincy
Miller. But I didn't care. $25,000 is gravy for a prison
murder. I then met with Adam Stone, our mule,
and planned the killing. He delivered messages to

Drummik and Lane. The attack was well done but they didn't finish the job. Stone said another guard got in the way or something. Mercado was furious at the bad result and refused to pay the rest of the money. I kept $15,000 cash.

Mercado never mentioned his client's name. He was my sole contact. Frankly, I didn't inquire since I figured it's best to know as little as possible in a deal like that. If I had asked, I'm sure Mercado would have ducked the question.

A friend of mine in Miami, a former trafficker, says Mercado is sort of a semi-legit operator who is often hired by traffickers to fix problems. I have met with him twice since the attack on Miller but both meetings were not productive. He asked if I thought it might be possible to get to Miller in the hospital. I went there and looked around but didn't like what I saw. Mercado wants me to monitor Miller's recovery and find a way to finish the job.

Skip DiLuca

WITH THE CONSPIRACY to kill Quincy still active, the FBI must make a decision. It prefers to watch Mercado and hope he leads to bigger fish, perhaps even using DiLuca as bait. However, as long as Mercado is on the loose and planning to finish off Quincy, the danger is real. The safest route is to arrest Mercado and apply pressure, though no one within the Bureau expects him to talk or cooperate.

DiLuca is kept in jail, in solitary, under surveillance, and far from any form of communication. He's still a career criminal who cannot be trusted. No one would be surprised if he contacted Mercado if given the chance. And he would certainly make sure Jon Drummik and Robert Earl Lane knew that Adam Stone is a rat.

Agnes Nolton makes the decision to arrest Mercado, and to get Adam Stone away from Garvin. Plans are immediately made to move him and his family to another town, one near a federal prison where a better job is waiting. Plans are also in the works to send DiLuca to a camp where surgeons will alter his looks and give him a new name.

ONCE AGAIN, PATIENCE pays dividends. Using a Honduran passport and the name "Alberto Gomez," Mercado books a flight from Miami to San Juan, and from there he rides an Air Caribbean commuter to the island of Martinique, French West Indies. The locals scramble to pick up his trail in Fort-de-France, the capital, and he is watched as he takes a cab to the Oriole Bay Resort, a lush and secluded getaway on the side of a mountain. Two hours later, a government jet lands at the same airport and FBI agents hustle to waiting cars. The resort, though, is booked. It has only twenty-five quite expensive rooms and they're all taken. The agents check in to the nearest hotel, three miles away.

MERCADO MOVES SLOWLY around the resort. He has lunch alone by the pool and drinks in the corner of a tiki bar with a view of the foot traffic. The other guests are high-end Europeans with their mix of languages, and none raise suspicions. Late in the afternoon, he walks along a narrow path

fifty yards up the mountain to a sprawling bungalow where a
porter serves him a drink on the terrace. The sparkling blue
Caribbean stretches for miles below him. He lights a Cuban
cigar and enjoys the view.

The man of the house is Ramon Vasquez and he eventually
wanders onto the terrace. The woman of the house is Diana,
his longtime mate, though Mercado has never met nor seen
her. Diana waits and watches from a bedroom window.

Ramon pulls up a chair. They do not shake hands. "What
happened?"

Mercado shrugs as if there are no problems. "Not sure.
The job wasn't finished on the inside." They speak in soft,
rapid Spanish.

"Obviously. Is there a plan to complete the deal?"

"Is that what you want?"

"Very much so. Our boys are not happy at all and they
want this problem to go away. They, we, thought you could
be trusted for something this simple. You said it would be
easy. You were wrong, and we want the deal closed."

"Okay. I'll work on a plan, but it most certainly will not
be easy. Not this time."

The porter brings Ramon a glass of ice water. He waves
off a cigar. They chat for half an hour before Mercado is
excused. He eases back to the resort, suns by the pool, entertains a young lady during the evening, and has dinner alone
in the elegant dining room.

The following day, Mercado uses a Bolivian passport and
returns to San Juan.

37

There are only two incorporated municipalities in Ruiz County: Seabrook, population 11,000, and the much smaller village of Dillon, population 2,300. Dillon is to the north and farther inland, rather remote and seemingly forgotten by time. There are few decent jobs in Dillon and not much in the way of commerce. Most of the young people leave out of necessity and a desire to survive. Prospering is rarely thought of. Those left behind, young and old, muddle along, living off whatever meager wages they can find and checks from the government.

While the county is 80 percent white, Dillon is half and half. Last year its small high school graduated sixty-one seniors, thirty of whom were black. Kenny Taft finished there, in 1981, as had his two older siblings. The family lived a few miles out from Dillon in an old farmhouse Kenny's father bought at a foreclosure before he was born.

Vicki has put together a spotty history of the Tafts, and they have seen more than their share of suffering. From old obituaries, we know that Kenny's father died at fifty-eight, cause unknown. Next in line was Kenny, who was murdered at the age of twenty-seven. A year later, his older brother was killed in an auto accident. Two years later, his older sister, Ramona, died at the age of thirty-six, cause unknown. Mrs. Vida Taft, having outlived her husband and all three children, was committed to a state mental hospital in 1996, but the court records are not clear about what happened after that. Commitment proceedings are confidential in Florida, as in most states. At some point she was released, because she died "peacefully at home," according to the obit in the Seabrook weekly. No will has ever been probated for her or her husband so it's safe to assume they never signed one. The old farmhouse and the five acres around it are now owned by a dozen grandchildren, most of whom have fled the area. Last year Ruiz County assessed the property at $33,000, and it's not clear who paid the $290 in taxes to prevent a foreclosure.

Frankie finds the house at the end of a gravel road. A dead end. It has obviously been abandoned for some time. Weeds are growing through the sagging planks of the front porch. Some shutters have fallen to the ground, others hang by rusty nails. A thick padlock secures the front door, the same around back. No windows have been broken. The tin roof looks sturdy.

Frankie walks around it once and that's enough. He carefully steps through the weeds and returns to his truck. He's been sniffing around Dillon for two days and thinks he's found a decent suspect.

Riley Taft's day job is chief custodian at the Dillon Middle School, but his real vocation is ministering to his congregation. He's the pastor of the Red Banks Baptist Church a few miles farther out in the country. Most Tafts are buried there, some with simple headstones, some without. His flock numbers fewer than a hundred and cannot afford a full-time pastor.

Thus, the custodial job. After some phone calls, he agrees to meet Frankie at the church late in the afternoon.

Riley is young, late thirties, thickset and easygoing with a wide smile. He walks Frankie through the cemetery and shows him the Taft section. His father, the oldest child, is buried between Kenny and their mother. He narrates the family tragedies: his grandfather dead at fifty-eight from some mysterious poisoning; Kenny murdered; his father killed instantly on a highway; his aunt dead from leukemia at thirty-six. Vida Taft died twelve years ago at seventy-seven. "Poor woman went crazy," Riley says with wet eyes. "Buried her three children and went off the deep end. Really off."

"Your grandmother?"

"Yep. So why do you wanna know about the family?"

Frankie has already gone through the song and dance about Guardian, our mission, our successes, and our representation of Quincy Miller. He says, "We think Kenny's murder didn't go down the way the sheriff said."

This gets no reaction. Riley nods to the back of the small church and says, "Let's get something to drink." They walk past the tombstones and markers of other Tafts and leave the cemetery. Through a rear door they step into the church's narrow fellowship hall. Riley opens a fridge in a corner and pulls out two small plastic bottles of lemonade.

"Thanks," Frankie says, and they settle into folding chairs.

"So what's this new theory?" Riley asks.

"You've never heard of one?"

"No, never. When Kenny got killed it was the end of the world. I was about fifteen or sixteen, tenth grade I think, and Kenny was more of a big brother than an uncle. I worshipped him. He was the family's pride. Real smart, going places, we thought. He was proud to be a cop but he wanted to move on up. God, how I loved Kenny. We all did. Everybody did. Had a pretty wife, Sybil, a sweet lady. And a baby. Everything going his way and then he's murdered. When I heard the news I fell to the floor and bawled like a baby. I wanted to die too. Just put me in the grave with him. It was just awful." His eyes water and he takes a long swallow. "But we always believed he stumbled across some drug dealers and got shot. Now, twenty-plus years later you're here to tell me something different. Right?"

"Yes. We believe Kenny was ambushed by men working for Sheriff Pfitzner, who was counting his money with the drug dealers. Kenny knew too much and Pfitzner got suspicious."

It takes a second or two for this to sink in, but Riley absorbs it well. It's a shock, really, but he wants to hear more. "What's this got to do with Quincy Miller?" he asks.

"Pfitzner was behind the murder of Keith Russo, the lawyer. Russo made some money as a drug lawyer, got flipped by the DEA and became an informant. Pfitzner found out about it, arranged the murder, and did a near flawless job of pinning it on Quincy Miller. Kenny knew something about the murder, and it cost him his life."

Riley smiles and shakes his head and says, "This is pretty wild."

"You've never heard this gossip?"

"Never. You gotta understand, Mr. Tatum, that Seabrook is only fifteen miles from here, but it might as well be a hundred. Dillon is its own world. A sad little place, really. Folk here just barely hang on, barely get by. We got our own challenges and we don't have time to worry about what's happening over in Seabrook, or anywhere else for that matter."

"I understand that," Frankie says and takes a sip.

"So, you did fourteen years for somebody else's murder?" Riley asks in disbelief.

"Yes, fourteen years, three months, eleven days. And Reverend Post came to the rescue. It's brutal, Riley, locked up and forgotten when you know you're innocent. That's why we're working so hard for Quincy and our other clients. As you know, brother, lots of our people are locked up for stuff they didn't do."

"You got that right." They drink in solidarity.

Frankie presses on. "There might be a chance, probably a slight one, that Kenny had possession of some evidence that was stored behind Pfitzner's office in Seabrook. His former partner told us this recently. Kenny got wind of a plan to burn the building and destroy the evidence, and he removed some stuff before the fire. If Pfitzner indeed ambushed Kenny, then why did he want him dead? It was because Kenny knew something. Kenny had the evidence. There was no other reason, or at least none that we've come across, that explains Pfitzner's motive."

Riley is enjoying the story. He says, "So the big question is—what did Kenny do with the evidence? That's why you're here, right?"

"You got it. It's doubtful Kenny would take it home, because that could have endangered his family. Plus he was living in a rental house."

"And his wife wasn't too happy there. It was out on Secretary Road, east of Seabrook. Sybil wanted to move to some other place."

"By the way, we found Sybil in Ocala and she will not talk to us. Not a word."

"A nice lady, always had a smile for me, anyway. I haven't seen Sybil in years, don't suppose I ever will. So, Mr. Tatum—"

"Please, Frankie."

"So, Frankie, you're thinking Kenny might have brought the stuff back to the home place, just down the road, and hid it there, right?"

"The list of possible hiding places is short, Riley. If Kenny had something to hide, something valuable, he would have wanted to keep it somewhere safe and accessible. Makes sense, right? Does the old house have an attic or a basement?"

Riley shakes his head. "There's no basement. I'm not sure but I think there's an attic. Never seen it, never been up there." He takes a sip and says, "This seems like a real goose chase to me, Frankie."

Frankie laughs and says, "Oh, we specialize in goose chases. We waste tons of time digging through haystacks. But, occasionally, we find something."

Riley finishes his lemonade, slowly gets to his feet, and begins pacing around the room as if suddenly burdened. He stops and looks down at Frankie and says, "You can't go into that house. It's too dangerous."

"It's been abandoned for years."

"By real people, but there are plenty of folk moving around. Spirits, ghosts, the place is haunted, Frankie. I've seen it for myself. I'm a poor man with a few bucks in the bank, but I wouldn't walk into that house at high noon with a gun in my hand for a thousand dollars cash. Nobody in our family will either."

Riley's eyes are wide with fear and his finger shakes as he points it at Frankie, who is momentarily dumbstruck. Riley walks to the fridge, pulls out two more bottles, hands one to Frankie and sits down. He breathes deeply as he closes his eyes, as if gathering strength for a long-winded tale. Finally, he begins, "Vida, my grandmother, was raised by her grandmother in a Negro settlement ten miles from here. It's gone now. Vida was born in 1925. Her grandmother was born back in the 1870s when a lot of folk still had kin who were born in slavery. Her grandmother practiced witchcraft and African voodoo, which was common back then. Her religion was a mix of Christian gospel and old-world spiritualism. She was a midwife and the local nurse who could whip up salves and ointments and herbal teas to cure just about anything. Vida was profoundly influenced by this woman and throughout her life she, too, considered herself to be a spiritual master, though she knew better than to use the word 'witch.' Are you with me, Frankie?"

He was, but they were wasting time now. Frankie nodded earnestly and said, "Sure. Fascinating."

"I'm giving you the quick version, but there's a big thick book about Vida. She was a frightening woman. She loved her kids and grandkids and ruled the family, but she had a dark, mysterious side too. I'll give you one story. Her daughter, Ramona, my aunt, died at thirty-six, you saw her tombstone. When Ramona was young, about fourteen or so, she was raped by a boy from Dillon, a bad kid. Everybody knew him. The family was upset as you might guess, but didn't want to go to the sheriff. Vida didn't trust the white man's justice. She said she would handle things herself. Kenny found her one night, at midnight under a full moon, in the backyard

285

going through some voodoo ritual. She was tapping a small drum, with gourds around her neck and snakeskins around her bare feet, and chanting in an unknown tongue. Later, she told Kenny that she put a hex on the boy who raped Ramona. Word got out and everybody, well at least all the black folk, in Dillon knew the boy was cursed. A few months later he got burned alive in a car wreck, and from then on people ran from Vida. She was much feared."

Frankie absorbs this without a word.

"Over the years she got crazier, and we finally had no choice. We hired a lawyer in Seabrook to get her committed. She was furious with the family and threatened us. Threatened the lawyer and the judge. We were terrified. They couldn't do anything with her at the asylum and she talked her way out. She told us to stay away from her and the house, and we did."

Frankie manages to say, "She died in 1998, according to the obituary."

"That was the year, no one knows the day. My cousin Wendell got concerned and went to the house, found her lying peacefully in the middle of her bed, sheets pulled up to her chin. Dead for days. She left a note with instructions to bury her next to her children, with no funeral or ceremony. She also wrote that her last act on this earth was to put a curse on the house. Sad to say, but we were relieved when she died. We buried her in a hurry, in a thunderstorm, a quick service with just the family, and the moment we lowered her into the ground lightning hit a tree in the cemetery and we jumped out of our skin. I've never been so scared in my life, and never so happy to see a casket get covered with dirt."

Riley takes a long drink and wipes his mouth with the back of a hand. "That was my grandmother, Vida. We called her Granny, but most of the kids around here called her Voo-doo behind her back."

In a voice as firm as possible, Frankie says, "We need to see the attic."

"You're crazy, man."

"Who's got the key?"

"I do, but I haven't stepped inside in years. The electricity was cut off long ago, but you can sometimes see lights at night. Lights moving around. Only a fool would walk through those doors."

"I need some air." They step outside into the heat and walk to their vehicles. Riley says, "You know, this is weird. Kenny's been dead for twenty years and nobody from the outside has shown any interest. Now, in less than a week, you and two others come snooping around."

"Two others?"

"Two white dudes showed up last week, asking questions about Kenny. Where did he grow up? Where did he live? Where is he buried? I didn't like them and I played dumb, gave 'em nothing."

"Where were they from?"

"I didn't ask. I got the impression they wouldn't tell me anyway."

38

Quincy's first surgery is a six-hour repair job piecing together a shoulder and collarbone. It goes well and the doctors are pleased. I sit with him for hours as he recovers. His battered body is mending well and some of his memory is returning, though the attack is still a black hole. I do not tell him what we know about Drummik and Robert Earl Lane, or Adam Stone and Skip DiLuca. He's heavily medicated and is not ready for the rest of the story.

There is a guard of some variety sitting by his door around the clock, often more than one. Hospital security, prison guards, Orlando police, and FBI. They take turns and I enjoy chatting them up. It breaks the monotony. I often marvel at the cost of it all. Fifty thousand dollars a year to keep him in prison, for twenty-three years now. A drop in the bucket to what the taxpayers are now spending to keep him alive and fix up his wounds. Not to mention the security. Millions, and all wasted on an innocent man who should never have been incarcerated in the first place.

I'm napping on the rollaway cot in his room early one morning when my phone buzzes. Agent Nolton asks if I'm in town. She has something to show me. I drive to her office and follow her to a large conference room where a tech guy is waiting.

He dims the lights and, still standing, we look at a large screen. A face appears—Hispanic male, age about sixty, ruggedly handsome with fierce dark eyes and a salt-and-pepper beard. Agnes says, "Name is Ramon Vasquez, longtime senior management in the Saltillo Cartel, sort of semiretired now."

"The name is familiar," I say.

"Hang on." She clicks and another image appears, an aerial of a small resort tucked into the side of a mountain that is surrounded by the bluest water in the world. "This is where he spends most of his time. The island is Martinique, French West Indies. The getaway is called Oriole Bay Resort, owned by one of a million faceless companies domiciled in Panama." She splits the screen and the face of Mickey Mercado appears. "Three days ago our friend here used a Honduran passport to fly to Martinique where he met with Vasquez at the resort. We showed up but couldn't get in, and that was probably a good thing. The next day Mercado used a Bolivian passport to return to Miami through San Juan."

It hits hard. "Vasquez was the boyfriend of Diana Russo," I say.

"Still is. They've been together since about the time of her dear husband's untimely death." She clicks again. Mercado disappears and half of the screen is black. The other half is still the island. "No pictures of Diana. According to what we've been able to piece together, and I won't bore you with stories of how shaky intelligence can be anywhere in the Caribbean, they spend most of their time living in luxurious seclusion at their resort. She sort of runs the place but keeps an extremely low profile. They also travel a lot, all over the world. DEA is not sure if their travels are related to trafficking, or if they just want to get off the island. They think Vasquez is past his prime but still does a little consulting. Could be that the Russo murder happened on his watch and he's expected to clean up the mess. Or, it could be that he is still active in the business. Whatever he does, he's extremely careful."

I back to a chair, fall into it, and mumble, "So she was involved."

"Well, we don't know for sure, but she suddenly looks a lot guiltier. She renounced her American citizenship fifteen years ago and became a full-fledged citizen of Panama. Probably cost her fifty grand. New name is Diana Sanchez but I'll bet she has others. Who knows how many passports. No record that she and Ramon have ever officially tied the knot. Apparently, they have not reproduced. Seen enough?"

"Is there more?"

"Oh yes."

THE FBI WAS monitoring Mercado and was preparing to arrest him when he made an inexplicable blunder. He picked up the wrong phone and made a call to a number that cannot be traced. The conversation, though, was recorded. Mercado suggested to the man on the other end that they meet at a crab shack in Key Largo for lunch the following day. Moving with a speed that is remarkable and makes me happy to be on the same side as the FBI, Nolton got a warrant and her agents arrived first. They photographed Mercado in the parking lot, filmed him eating crabs with his contact, and photographed both as they got into their cars. The late-model Volvo SUV is registered to Bradley Pfitzner.

On film, he looks to be in decent shape, with a gray goatee and waves of gray hair. Retiring in luxury seems to be suiting him well. He's almost eighty years old, but moves like a much younger man.

Nolton says, "Congratulations, Post. We finally have the link."

I am too stunned to speak. She says, "Of course we can't indict Pfitzner for having lunch, but we'll get warrants and we'll know when he takes a pee."

I say, "Be careful. He's pretty savvy."

"Yes, but even the smartest criminals do dumb things. Meeting with Mercado is a gift."

"No clue that Pfitzner has any contact with DiLuca?" I ask.

"None whatsoever. I'll bet my paycheck that Pfitzner does not even know DiLuca's name. Mercado moves in the dark world where he knew about the Aryans and arranged the hit. Pfitzner probably supplied the cash, but we'll never prove it unless Mercado sings. And guys like him do not rat."

I'm overwhelmed and struggle to keep things in order. My first reaction is "What a train wreck. In the span of three days Mercado leads you to Ramon and Diana Russo, and then to Bradley Pfitzner."

Agnes nods along, quite proud of their progress but too businesslike to gloat. "Some of the puzzle is coming together, but there's a long way to go. Gotta run. I'll keep you posted." She's off to another meeting, and the tech guy leaves me alone in the room. For a long time I sit in the dim light and stare at the wall and try to process these bombshells. Agnes is right in that we suddenly know a lot more about the conspiracy to murder Keith, but how much can be proven? And how much can help Quincy?

I finally leave the room and the building and drive back to the hospital where I find Marvis sitting with his brother. He tells me he talked his boss into a few days of vacation and he'll be around. This is welcome news and I hurry back to the motel and gather my things. I'm inching out of town in traffic when inspiration hits so hard I'm almost compelled to pull over and walk around my car. I keep driving as a simple yet beautiful plan takes shape. Then I call my new best friend, Special Agent Agnes Nolton.

"What's up?" she says crisply after I hold for ten minutes.

"The only way to nail Pfitzner is to suck him into the conspiracy," I say.

"Sounds like entrapment."

"Close, but it might just work."

"I'm listening."

"Have you already packed off DiLuca to parts unknown?"

"No. He's still around."

"We need one more job before he vanishes."

AT HIALEAH PARK, DiLuca takes a seat in the grandstand far away from other spectators. He holds a racing sheet as if ready to start betting on the horses. He's wired with the latest bug, which can pick up a deer snorting thirty yards away. Mercado appears twenty minutes later and sits next to him. They buy two beers from a vendor and watch the next race.

Finally, DiLuca says, "I have a plan. They moved Miller again, between surgeries. He continues to improve but he ain't leaving for some time. The guards are rotating and there's always somebody watching his door. The prison sends a few boys over now and then. That's where the plan begins.

292

We borrow a guard's uniform from Stone and one of my boys puts it on. He eases in late at night. On cue there's a bomb threat at the hospital, maybe we'll blow up something in the basement, nobody gets hurt. Typically, the hospital will go berserk. Active shooter drill and all that craziness. In the melee, our boy gets to Miller. We'll use an EpiPen needle, get one from the pharmacy, and load it with something like ricin or cyanide. Jab him in the leg and he's gone in five minutes. If he's awake, he won't be able to react in time, but they keep him knocked out a lot. We'll do it late at night when more than likely he'll be asleep. Our man walks out and disappears into the confusion."

Mercado sips his beer and frowns. "I don't know. Sounds awfully risky."

"It is, but it's a risk I'm willing to take. For a fee."

"I thought there were cameras everywhere."

"Above the door, but not in the room. Our guy gets in because he's a guard. Once inside, he'll do the deed in seconds and then join the chaos. If he gets his picture taken, no big deal. No one in hell will ever know who he is. I'll have him on a plane within an hour."

"But Miller's in a hospital, surrounded by good doctors."

"True, but by the time they identify the toxin he'll be dead. Trust me on this. I poisoned three men in prison and did it with homemade juice."

"I don't know. I'll have to think about it."

"It's no sweat for you, Mickey. Except for the cash. If our boy screws up and gets caught, he won't talk. I promise. If Miller survives, you keep the other half. But prison hits are cheap. This ain't prison."

"How much?"

"A hundred grand. Half now, half after his funeral. Plus the other twenty-five grand from the first hit."

"That's pretty steep."

"It'll take four men, me and three others, including the bomb maker. It's far more complicated than shanking some stiff in prison."

"That's a lot of money."

"You want him dead or not?"

"He's supposed to be dead already but your thugs screwed up."

"Dead or not?"

"It's too much money."

"It's chump change to your boys."

"I'll think about it."

Across the track and next to the paddocks, a crew in the back of a delivery van films every movement as the bug captures every word.

PFITZNER TAKES LONG walks with his second wife, fishes with a buddy in a sleek thirty-two-foot Grady-White, and plays golf every Monday and Wednesday in the same foursome. From all indications—dress, home, cars, nice restaurants, clubs—he is quite affluent. They watch him but they do not go into his house—too many security cameras. He has an iPhone that he uses for normal conversations, and he has at least one burner for the more sensitive calls. For eleven days he ventures no farther than the golf course or the marina.

On the twelfth day, he leaves Marathon, driving north along Highway 1. By the time he reaches Key Colony Beach the plan is activated. It is ramped up when Mercado leaves

Coral Gables, headed his way. He arrives in Key Largo first and parks in the lot outside Snook's Bayside Restaurant. Two agents in shorts and floral-print shirts ease in and take a table near the water, thirty feet from Mercado's table. Ten minutes later, Pfitzner arrives in his Volvo and goes inside without his gym bag, one of several mistakes.

As Mercado and Pfitzner dine on seafood salads, the bag is removed from the Volvo. Inside are five stacks of $100 bills wrapped tightly with rubber bands. Not fresh new banknotes, but bills that have been stashed for some time. A total of $50,000. Two stacks are removed and replaced with newer bills whose serial numbers have been recorded. The gym bag is returned to the rear floorboard of the Volvo. Two more agents arrive, rounding out the team of ten.

When lunch is over, Pfitzner pays the bill with an American Express card. He and Mercado exit and step into the sun. They hesitate by the Volvo as Pfitzner unlocks the door, opens it, grabs the gym bag, and, without unzipping it and looking inside, hands it to Mercado, who takes it so nonchalantly it's clear he's done it before. Before Mercado can take one step, a loud voice yells, "Freeze! FBI!"

Bradley Pfitzner faints and falls hard into the car next to his Volvo. He crumples to the asphalt as the agents swarm Mercado, take the bag, and slap on cuffs. When Bradley stands, he's dazed and there is a cut above his left ear. An agent wipes it roughly with a paper towel as the two suspects are loaded up for the ride to Miami.

39

The following day, Agent Nolton calls with the news that Skip DiLuca is on a plane headed to Mars with a new identity and the chance for a new life. His girlfriend plans to join him later. Agnes passes along the latest with Pfitzner and Mercado, but nothing has changed. Not surprisingly, Nash Cooley's law firm is representing both, so the prosecution will soon grind to a halt while the lawyers gum up the system. Both defendants are trying to get out on bond but the federal magistrate won't budge.

Her voice is more relaxed, and she ends the conversation with "Why haven't you asked me to dinner?"

Any pause would show weakness so I immediately say, "How about dinner?" In my usual state of cluelessness around the opposite sex, I had not bothered to notice if she wears a wedding band. I would guess her age at forty-two. I seem to remember photos of children in her office.

"You're on," she says. "Where shall we meet?"

"It's your city," I say, on my heels. The only food I've eaten in Orlando has been in the basement cafeteria of Mercy Hospital. It's dreadful, but cheap. I desperately try to remember the balance on my last credit card statement. Can I afford to take her to a nice restaurant?

"Where are you staying?" she asks.

"At the hospital. It doesn't matter. I have a car." I'm staying in a cheap motel in a sketchy part of town, a place I would never mention. And my car? It's really a little Ford SUV with bald tires and a million miles on the odometer. It hits me that Agnes knows this. I'm sure the FBI has checked me out. One look at my wheels and she'll prefer to "meet" at the restaurant rather than go through the formality of me picking her up. I like the way she thinks.

"There's a place called Christner's on Lee Road. Let's meet there. And Dutch treat."

I like her even more. I may even fall in love with her. "If you insist."

With a law degree and eighteen years of seniority, her salary is around $120,000, or more than mine, Vicki's, and Mazy's combined. In fact, Vicki and I really don't consider ourselves on salary. We each extract $2,000 a month to survive, and give ourselves a bonus at Christmas if there's anything left in the bank.

I'm sure Agnes realizes that I live in poverty.

I dress in my only clean shirt and well-used khakis. She breezes in from the office and, as always, is well put-together. We have a glass of wine at the bar then retire to our table. After we order another glass of wine, she says, "No shoptalk. Let's talk about your divorce."

I chuckle at her abruptness, though I've come to expect it. "How'd you know?"

"Just guessing. You go first and talk about yours, then I'll talk about mine, and in doing so we'll avoid talking about work."

Well, I say, it was a long time ago, and I launch into my past. Law school, courting Brooke, marriage, the career as a public defender, my nervous breakdown that led to seminary and a new career, the calling to help the innocent.

The waiter hovers and we order salads and pasta dishes.

She's had two divorces, actually. A minor one that followed a terrible first marriage, and a major one that was settled less than two years ago. He was a corporate executive who was transferred a lot. She wanted her career and got tired of moving. It was a painful split because they loved each other. Their two teenagers are still trying to cope.

Agnes is intrigued by my work, and I'm happy to talk about our exonerees and our current cases. We eat and drink and talk and enjoy a delightful meal. I'm thrilled to be in the presence of an attractive and intelligent woman, and also to be dining outside the hospital cafeteria. She seems to crave conversation that is unrelated to her work.

But over tiramisu and coffee, we drift back to pressing matters. We are baffled by the actions of Bradley Pfitzner. For many years now he has lived a comfortable life far away from the scene of his crimes. He never came within a mile of being indicted. He was suspected and investigated but too smart and lucky to get caught. He walked away with his money and laundered it nicely. His hands are clean. He did a fine job of putting Quincy away and making sure Kenny Taft would never squeal. Why would he now run the risk of entangling himself in a plot to kill our efforts by killing Quincy?

Agnes speculates he was acting on behalf of the cartel. Perhaps, but why would the cartel, and Pfitzner too for that matter, care if we walk Quincy out of prison? We are no closer to identifying the hired gun who murdered Russo twenty-three years ago. And if by some miracle we learn his name, it will take three more miracles to link him to the cartel. Exonerating Quincy does not equate to solving that murder.

Agnes speculates that Pfitzner and the cartel assumed the hit in prison would be easy and leave no clues. Just find a couple of tough guys pulling hard time and promise a little cash. Once Quincy was buried, we would close the file and go away.

We agree that Pfitzner in his old age probably got spooked when he realized someone with credibility was digging into a matter he considered stone cold. He knows our case has merit, and he knows from our reputation that we are tenacious and usually successful. Walking Quincy out of prison would leave many unanswered questions. Hauling him out in a hearse would bury those questions.

There is also the real possibility that Pfitzner believed himself to be immune from any reckoning. For years he was the law. He operated above it, below it, within and without, did whatever he pleased while keeping the voters content. He retired with a fortune and considers himself quite clever. If one more crime was needed, and one as straightforward as a prison hit, then he could certainly pull it off and never worry again.

Agnes entertains me with tales of incredible blunders by otherwise smart criminals. She says she could fill a book with such stories.

We speculate and second-guess and talk about our pasts late into the evening, thoroughly enjoying the long conversation. The other diners clear out, though we hardly notice. When the waiter gives us the look, we realize the restaurant is empty. We split the check, shake hands at the door, and agree to do it again.

40

When the FBI sank its fangs into Adam Stone and Skip DiLuca, I realized that Quincy Miller has one beautiful civil lawsuit. With the active complicity of a state employee, Stone, the assault became an intentional tort far more actionable than the garden-variety prison beating. The State of Florida became liable and has no way out. I discussed this at length with Susan Ashley Gross, our co-counsel, and she recommended, hands down, a trial lawyer named Bill Cannon, of Fort Lauderdale.

There is no shortage of tort stars in Florida. The state's laws are plaintiff-friendly. Its juries are educated and historically generous. Most of its judges, at least those in the urban areas, lean toward the victims. These factors have spawned an aggressive and successful trial bar. Just observe the billboards along any busy Florida highway and you'll almost wish you could get injured. Switch on early morning television and you're bombarded with hawkers who feel your pain.

Bill Cannon doesn't advertise because he doesn't need to. His stellar reputation is national. He's spent the past twenty-five years in courtrooms and convinced juries to fork over a billion dollars in verdicts. The ambulance chasers who roam the streets bring him their cases. He sifts through their nets and selects the best ones.

I decide to hire him for other reasons. First, he believes in the cause and donates generously to Susan Ashley's innocence group. Second, he believes in pro bono and expects his partners and associates to donate 10 percent of their time representing the less fortunate. Though he now zips around in his own jet, he grew up poor and remembers the pain of getting stepped on when his family was wrongfully evicted.

Three days after Mercado and Pfitzner are arrested, Cannon files on behalf of Quincy a $50 million federal lawsuit against the Florida Department of Corrections, Mickey Mercado, and Bradley Pfitzner. The lawsuit also names Robert Earl Lane and Jon Drummik, the assailants, along with Adam Stone and Skip DiLuca, but they will be dismissed later. Immediately after filing the lawsuit, Cannon convinces a magistrate to freeze the bank accounts and all other assets of Mercado and Pfitzner before the money slips away and disappears into the Caribbean.

With search warrants, the FBI assaults Mercado's fancy condo in Coral Gables. They find some handguns, temporary phones, a cash box with only $5,000, and a laptop with little valuable information. Mercado lived in fear and avoided leaving tracks. However, two bank statements lead the FBI to three accounts totaling about $400,000. A similar raid on his office nets little more. Agnes assumes Mercado kept his goodies offshore in shady banks.

Pfitzner wasn't quite so oily. A raid on his home was temporarily slowed when his wife went nuts and tried to block the doors. She was finally subdued with handcuffs and threatened with jail. Bank records lead to three accounts in Miami where the good-ole-boy sheriff has almost $3 million in cash. A money market account has slightly over $1 million. Not bad for a small-town sheriff.

Agnes thinks there's more. Ditto for Cannon. If Pfitzner was brazen enough to keep $4 million in dirty dollars in U.S. banks, imagine what he stashed offshore. And Cannon knows how to find it. While the FBI starts leaning on Caribbean banks, Cannon hires a forensic accounting firm that specializes in tracking dirty money funneled out of the country.

As confident as he is, Cannon does not make predictions. He is, however, confident that his new client will recover a substantial amount in damages, minus, of course, the obligatory 40 percent off the top that stays with the law firm. I am silently hopeful that Guardian might get a few bucks to pay its utility bills, but that rarely happens.

Quincy, though, is not thinking about money these days. He's too busy trying to walk. The doctors have operated on a shoulder, both collarbones, a jaw, and he has thick plaster on the top half of his torso and around one wrist. They have implanted three new teeth and braced his nose. He is in constant pain but tries gamely not to mention it. He has tubes draining one lung and one side of his brain. He is so medicated it's difficult to determine how well his brain is working, but he is determined to get out of bed and move around. He growls at his physical therapists when their sessions end. He wants more—more walking, bending, massages, rubdowns, more challenges. He's tired of the hospital but has no place to go. Garvin has nothing to offer as rehab and the health care is far below sub-par. When he's wide awake he quarrels with me about getting him exonerated so he doesn't have to return to Garvin.

41

Word has spread through the family, and some of the Tafts are not happy with the idea of anyone poking around into Vida's haunted house. The feeling is that she hexed it before she died and filled it with angry spirits who can't get out. Unlocking the doors now could release all kinds of evil, with most of it undoubtedly aimed at her descendants. She died holding a hard grudge against those who sent her to the asylum. She was crazy as a coot in her final days but that didn't stop her from blanketing the family with curses. According to Frankie, one strain of African witchcraft believes that curses die with the witch, but another says they can last forever. No living Taft wants to find out.

Frankie and I are riding in his shiny pickup toward Dillon. He's driving, I'm texting. On the console between us is a 9-millimeter Glock, properly purchased and registered by him. If we gain entry into the house, he plans to take it with him.

"You don't really believe in all that witchcraft stuff, do you Frankie?" I ask.

"I don't know. Wait till you see the house. You won't be so eager to go inside."

"So, you're worried about ghosts and goblins, stuff like that?"

"Keep laughing, boss." He touches the Glock with his right hand. "You'll wish you had one of these."

"You can't shoot a ghost, can you?"

"Never had to. But, just in case."

"Well, you go in first, with the gun, and I'll follow, okay?"

"We'll see. If we get that far."

We pass through the sad little town of Dillon and wind our way deeper into the country. At the end of a gravel drive there is an old pickup parked in front of the dilapidated house. As we slow to a stop, Frankie says, "There it is. The guy on the right is Riley, my buddy. Don't know but I guess the other guy is his cousin Wendell. He could be the troublemaker."

Wendell is about forty, a working man in dirty boots and jeans. He does not smile during the introductions and handshaking, nor does Riley. It is immediately obvious that a lot has been said and these two have issues. After a minute's worth of small talk, Riley asks me, "So, what's your plan here? What do you want?"

"We would like to go into the house and look around," I say. "I'm sure you know why we're here."

"Look, Mr. Post," Wendell begins respectfully, "I know that house inside and out. I lived here off and on as a kid. I found Vida when she died. And not long after she was gone I tried to live here with my wife and kids. Couldn't do it. The place is haunted. Vida said she put a hex on it and, believe me, she did. Now, you're looking for some boxes, and I'm telling you you're not likely to find anything. I think there's a small attic but I never saw it. We were too afraid to go up there."

"Then let's have a look," I say, as confidently as possible. "You guys stay here while Frankie and I poke around."

Riley and Wendell exchange hard looks. Riley says, "It ain't that easy, Mr. Post. Nobody wants those doors opened."

"Nobody? As in?" I ask.

"As in the family," Wendell says with an edge. "We got some cousins around here, others scattered, and no one wants this place disturbed. You never knew Vida, but I'm telling you she's still around and she's not to be trifled with." There is trepidation in his voice.

"I respect that," I say, but I only *sound* sincere.

A breeze that only a second ago did not exist rustles through a willow tree with limbs overhanging the house. As if on cue, something grinds and squeaks on the back side of the roof and my arms instantly are covered with goose bumps. All four of us gawk at the house and take deep breaths.

We need to keep talking. I say, "Look, fellas, this is nothing more than the old needle in the haystack. No one knows for sure if Kenny Taft really took some evidence before the fire. If he did, then no one has a clue what he did with the stuff. It could be here in the attic, but chances are it disappeared somewhere else years ago. This is probably a waste of time, but we chase every lead. We just want to look around and then we'll leave. Promise."

"What if you find something?" Wendell asks.

"We'll call the sheriff and turn it in. Maybe it can help us. But, regardless, it's nothing that has any value to the family." With these poor folks, the idea of some family jewels hidden in the attic is ludicrous.

305

Wendell takes a step back, walks around as if deep in thought, leans on the fender of a car, spits, crosses his arms against his chest, says, "I don't think so."

Riley says, "Right now, Wendell's got more support than I do. If he says no, then the answer is no."

I spread my hands and say, "One hour. Just give us one hour and you'll never see us again."

Wendell shakes his head. Riley watches him, says to Frankie, "Sorry."

I give both of them a look of disgust. This is probably a shakedown, so let's get it over with. I say, "All right. Look, this property is assessed by Ruiz County at $33,000. That's roughly one hundred dollars each day for the entire year. We, Guardian Ministries, will lease the house and these premises for one day for two hundred dollars. From nine tomorrow morning until five tomorrow afternoon. With an option to extend one extra day at the same rate. What do you say?"

The Tafts absorb this and scratch their chins. "Sounds low," Wendell says.

"How about five hundred a day?" Riley asks. "I think we can live with that."

"Come on, Riley. We're a nonprofit with no money. We can't just pull cash out of our pockets. Three hundred."

"Four hundred, take it or leave it."

"Okay. Agreed. Under Florida law, any agreement dealing with land must be in writing. I'll get a one-page lease contract and let's meet back here at nine in the morning. Deal?"

Riley seems pleased. Wendell barely nods his head. Yes.

*　*　*

WE LEAVE DILLON as fast as possible and share a few laughs along the way. Frankie drops me off near my car on Main Street in Seabrook, and heads east. He's staying in a motel somewhere between here and Gainesville, but as always the details are vague.

I enter the law offices of Glenn Colacurci a few minutes after five, and I hear him roaring on the phone somewhere in the rear. Bea, his lovely assistant, finally emerges and flashes that smile. I follow her back and find Glenn at his desk, piles of paperwork scattered on and around it. He leaps to his feet, thrusts out a hand, and says hello as if I'm his prodigal son. Almost as quickly, he glances at his watch, as if he has no idea what time it is, and says, "Well I'll be damned, it's five o'clock somewhere and it's five o'clock here. What'll it be?"

"Just a beer," I say, keeping it on the light side.

"A beer and a double," he says to Bea, who slinks away. "Come on, come on," he says, pointing to his sofa. He waddles over with his cane and falls into an ancient, dusty pile of leather. I sit on the sagging sofa and shove a quilt out of the way. I assume he naps here each afternoon as he snores off his liquid lunch. With both hands on the heel of his cane, and his chin resting on his knuckles, he smiles wickedly and says, "I can't believe Pfitzner's really in jail."

"Neither can I. It's a gift."

"Tell me about it."

Assuming again that anything I say will be repeated at the coffee shop in the morning, I breeze through the quick version of the FBI's fine work nailing an unnamed prison guard and his unnamed contact with the prison gang. This led to an operative working for the drug dealers, and he led to Pfitzner, who stepped into the trap with all the naivete of a small-time shoplifter. Now he's facing thirty years.

Bea brings our drinks and we say, "Cheers." His liquid is brown and there isn't much ice in his glass. He smacks his lips as if parched, and says, "So what brings you to town?"

"I'd like to meet with the sheriff, Wink Castle, tomorrow if I can find him. We're having conversations about reopening the investigation, especially now that we know Pfitzner tried to kill Quincy." There is enough truth in this to explain why I'm in town. "Plus, I am curious about you. Last time we met in Gainesville you seemed to be having a good time digging through the case. Any more surprises?"

"Not really, been busy elsewhere." He waves an arm at the landfill on his desk as if he's pulling eighteen-hour days. "Any luck with the Kenny Taft angle?"

"Well, sort of. I need to retain your services for a bit of legal work."

"Paternity, DUI, divorce, murder? You name it, you're at the right place." He roars at his own humor and I laugh along. He's been using that same line for at least fifty years.

I get serious and explain our contacts with the Taft family and our plans to search the house. I hand him a $100 bill and make him take it. He's now my lawyer and we shake hands. Everything is now confidential, or should be. I need a simple one-page lease that will impress the Taft family, along with a check drawn on Glenn's trust account. I'm sure the family would prefer cash, but I prefer paperwork. If evidence is found in the house, the chain of custody will be hopelessly complicated and documentation will be crucial. Sipping our drinks, Glenn and I discuss this like a couple of seasoned lawyers analyzing a unique problem. He's pretty savvy and sees a couple of potential problems I haven't thought of. When his glass is empty, he summons Bea for another round. When she brings them, he instructs her to take notes in shorthand, just like in the old days. We hammer out the basics and she retires to her desk.

He says, "I noticed you staring at her legs."

"Guilty. Something wrong with that?"

"Not at all. She's a dear. Her mother, Mae Lee, runs my house, and for dinner every Tuesday prepares the most exquisite spring rolls you've ever tasted. Tonight's your lucky night."

I smile and nod. I have no other plans.

"Plus, my old pal Archie is coming over. I may have mentioned him before. Indeed, I think I did over sangria at The Bull. We're contemporaries, practiced here decades ago. His wife died, left him some dough, so he quit the law, big mistake. He's been bored for the last ten years, lives alone with little to do. Retirement's a bad gig, Post. I think he has a crush on Mae Lee. Anyway, Archie loves spring rolls and is good for tall tales. And he's a wine snot with a big cellar. He'll bring the good stuff. You do wine?"

"Not really." If he could only imagine my balance sheet.

His last ice cube is down to a sliver and he rattles it around, ready for more. Bea returns with two copies of a rough draft. We make a few changes and she leaves to print the final draft.

GLENN'S HOME IS on a shady street four blocks off Main. I drive around for a few minutes to kill time, then park in the drive behind an old Mercedes I assume is owned by Archie. I hear them laughing around the corner and head to the backyard. They are already on the porch, reared back in overstuffed wicker rockers while two vintage ceiling fans rattle above. Archie keeps his seat as introductions are made. He's at least as old as Glenn and not the picture of health. Both have long scraggly hair that may have once been considered cool or nonconformist. Both are dressed in badly aged seer-sucker suits, no ties. Both wear geezer sneakers. At least Archie doesn't need a cane. His enthusiasm for wine has given him a permanent red nose. Glenn sticks with his bourbon but Archie and I try a Sancerre he's brought over. Mae Lee is as pretty as her daughter and serves us our drinks.

Before long, Archie cannot restrain himself. He says, "So, Post, are you responsible for Pfitzner getting locked up?"

I deflect any credit and tell the story from the viewpoint of a guy on the sideline watching it unfold, with a bit of inside scoop from the Feds. Seems as though Archie often clashed with Pfitzner back in the day and has no use at all for the man. He simply cannot believe that after all these years the crook is behind bars.

Archie tells the story of a client whose car broke down in Seabrook. The cops found a gun under the front seat, and for some reason determined that the kid was a cop killer. Pfitzner got involved and backed up his men. Archie told Pfitzner not to bother the kid in jail, but he was interrogated anyway. The cops beat a confession out of the boy and he served five years in prison. For a disabled car. Archie practically spews venom at Pfitzner by the end of the narrative.

The stories flow as these two old warriors repeat tales they've told many times. I mostly listen, but as lawyers they are interested in Guardian's work, so I tell a few stories but keep them brief. There is no mention of the Taft family and my real purpose for being in town. My highly paid counsel keeps our confidences. Archie opens another bottle of Sancerre. Mae Lee sets a pretty table on the veranda, with wisteria and verbena crawling along the trellises above it. Another ceiling fan pushes the warm air around. Archie thinks a Chablis would be more appropriate and fetches a bottle. Glenn, whose taste buds must be numb, switches to wine.

The spring rolls are indeed delicious. There is a large platter of them, and, fueled by the alcohol and the dearth of good food lately, I pig out. Archie keeps pouring, and when Glenn notices my feeble attempts to cut back he says, "Oh hell, drink up. You can sleep here. I have plenty of beds. Archie always stays. Who wants that drunk on the road at this time of night?"

"A menace to society," Archie agrees.

For dessert, Mae Lee brings a platter of sweet egg buns—soft little things filled with a mix of egg yolks and sugar. Archie has a Sauternes for the course and goes on and on about the pairing. He and Glenn pass on coffee, primarily because it lacks alcohol, and before long a small humidor appears on the table. They pick through it like kids in a candy store. I cannot remember my last cigar but I do recall turning green after a few puffs. Nonetheless, I am not about to shy away from the challenge. I ask for something on the milder side and Glenn hands me a Cohiba something or other, a certified real Cuban. We shuffle and stagger back to the rockers and blow clouds of smoke into the backyard.

Archie was one of the few lawyers who got on well with Diana Russo, and he talks about her. He never suspected she was involved in her husband's murder. I listen intently but say nothing. He, like everybody else in Seabrook, assumed Quincy was the killer and was relieved when he was convicted. As the clock ticks and the conversation lags, they cannot believe how wrong they were. Nor can they believe that Bradley Pfitzner is in jail and not likely to get out.

Gratifying, yes. But Quincy is still a convicted killer and we have a long way to go.

The last time I glance at my watch it's almost midnight. But I refuse to make a move until they do. They are at least twenty-five years older and have far more experience with serious drinking. I gamely hang on as Archie switches to brandy and I take one too. Mercifully, Glenn begins snoring, and at some point I nod off.

42

Of course, the weather turns foul. It hasn't rained in north Florida in two weeks, there's even talk of a drought, but the day breaks dark and turbulent as we hustle through Dillon, Frankie at the wheel and me gritting my teeth and swallowing hard.

"You sure you're okay, boss?" he asks, for at least the third time.

"What are you getting at, Frankie?" I snap. "I've already confessed. I had a long night, too much to drink, too much to eat, a rather nasty cigar, and I slept on the porch like a dead man until a really big cat pounced on my chest at three in the morning and scared the hell out of me. How was I to know it was his rocker? Neither of us could go back to sleep. So, yes, I have some cobwebs. My eyes are leaking. I'm covered with cat hair. And I feel like death warmed over. There."

"Nauseous?"

"Not yet. But I'll let you know. How about you? Excited about exploring a haunted house, one hexed by an African witch doctor?"

"Can't wait." He touches his Glock and grins, thoroughly enjoying my physical agony.

Riley and Wendell are waiting at the house. The wind is howling and the rain will begin soon enough. I hand them each a copy of the lease and quickly go over the basics. They are more interested in the money, so I hand them a check made payable to both and drawn on the Colacurci Law Firm's trust account.

"How 'bout cash?" Wendell says, frowning at the check.

I give a lawyerly frown and reply, "Can't do cash for a real estate transaction." I'm not sure if this is true in Florida but I project the voice of authority.

From the bed of his truck, Frankie removes an eight-foot stepladder and a shiny new crowbar purchased yesterday. I hold two flashlights and a can of insect repellent. We move through the tall weeds to the remains of the front porch steps and stare at the house. Wendell points and says, "Two rooms over two rooms, den and one bedroom downstairs. Stairs to the right, in the den. Two bedrooms up. Over that you might find an attic, you might not. Again, I've never been up there, never wanted to go. Never even asked about it, really. Around back is an addition added sometime later. That's the kitchen and a bathroom, with nothing above it. It's all yours, fellas."

I am determined not to show the slightest reticence as I begin spraying my arms and legs with the repellent. I'm assuming the place is filled with ticks and spiders and nasty little bugs I've never heard of. I hand the can to Frankie, who sprays himself. He sets the ladder by the door for the time being. We're not sure if we'll need it.

With a reluctance that seems overly dramatic but is probably real, Riley steps forward with a key and twists it into the heavy padlock. It springs and the lock falls loose. He backs

The Guardians

away quickly. Both Tafts seem ready to bolt. Lightning hits not far away and we're startled. The skies rumble as the dark clouds swirl. Being the brave one, I shove the front door with my foot and it creaks open. We take a breath and are relieved when nothing ominous emerges. I turn to Riley and Wendell and say, "See you guys in a minute."

Suddenly, the door slams shut with a loud crack. Frankie yelps a frantic "Shit!" as I jump out of my skin. Both Tafts retreat, wide-eyed, mouths open. I give a fake laugh as if to say "Damn this is fun," then step forward and open the door again.

We wait. Nothing emerges. No one slams the door again. I switch on my flashlight and Frankie does the same. He has his in his left hand, the crowbar in his right, the Glock in a hip pocket. One glance at his face and it's obvious he's terrified. And this from a man who survived fourteen years in prison. I jam the door open and we step inside. Vida died thirteen years ago and supposedly the house has been off-limits, but someone has helped themselves to most of the furniture. The smell is not bad, just thick and musty. The wooden floors are mildewed and molded and I can feel myself inhaling all manner of deadly bacteria. With our lights, we scan the bedroom on the left. A mattress is layered with dust and dirt. I assume this is where she died. The filthy floor is covered with broken lampshades, old clothing, books and newspapers. We take a few steps into the den and scan it with our lights. A television from the 1960s with a cracked screen. Peeling wallpaper. Layers of dust and crud and spiderwebs spun everywhere.

As we shine our lights up the narrow staircase and prepare to go up, a heavy rain hits the tin roof and the noise is deafening. The wind kicks up and rattles the walls.

315

I take three steps up, Frankie is on my heels, and suddenly the front door slams again. We are enclosed, with whatever spirits Vida left behind. I pause but only for a second. I'm the leader of this expedition, the brave one, and I cannot show fear though my unsettled bowels are turning flips and my heart is about to explode.

How much fun will I have recounting this episode to Vicki and Mazy?

Add this to the list of all the things they didn't mention in law school.

We make it to the top of the stairway and the heat hits like a sauna, a hot sticky fog we could probably see if things weren't so dark. The rain and wind are pounding the roof and windows and making a tremendous racket. We step into the bedroom on the right, a small space no more than twelve feet square, with a mattress, a broken chair, and a rug in tatters. We light the ceiling, looking for a sign of a door or entry point to the attic, but see nothing. It's all pine, once painted white but peeling badly. In a corner, something moves and knocks over a jar. I shine it with my light and say, "Back off. It's a snake!" A long, thick black one, probably not poisonous but at the moment who cares? It's not coiled but slinking around, not headed our way, probably just confused by the interruption.

I don't mess with snakes but nor am I deathly afraid of them. Frankie, however, is, and he pulls out the Glock.

"Don't shoot," I say above the din. We freeze and keep the snake in our beams for a long time as our shirts begin to cling to our backs and we breathe even heavier. Slowly, it slithers under the rug and we can't see it anymore.

The rain slackens and we collect ourselves. "How do you feel about spiders?" I ask over my shoulder.

"Shut your mouth!"

"Be careful, because they are everywhere."

As we backtrack out of the room, still scanning the floor for the snake or others, a ferocious clap of lightning hits nearby, and in that instant I know that if I don't die at the hands of an evil spirit or venomous animal, I'm certain to die of cardiac arrest. Sweat drips from my eyebrows. Our shirts are completely soaked. In the other bedroom, there is a small cot with what looks like an old green army blanket bunched on it. No other furniture or furnishings. Wallpaper sags from the walls. I glance out the window, and through the sheets of rain I can barely make out the image of Riley and Wendell sitting in the truck, riding out the storm, watching the house as wipers sweep the windshield, no doubt with the doors locked to protect them from spirits.

We kick junk out of the way to check for snakes, then turn our attention to the ceiling. Again, there is no sign of an opening to an attic above. I suppose it's possible that Kenny Taft hid his boxes up there and sealed them off for good, or at least until he one day returned for them. How the hell am I supposed to know what he did?

Frankie notices a ceramic knob to a smaller door, probably a closet. He points at it, calling it to my attention, but obviously prefers that I open it. I grab it, jiggle it, yank it hard, and as it flies open I am suddenly face-to-face with a human skeleton. Frankie feels faint and falls to one knee. I step away and begin vomiting, finally.

A squall line batters the house even harder, and for a long time we listen to the sounds of the storm. I do feel somewhat better after purging my system of spring rolls, beer, wine, brandy, and everything else. Frankie pulls himself together and we slowly return our lights to the closet. The skeleton is hanging from a plastic cord of some sort, and its toes barely touch the floor. Below it is a puddle of black, oily goo. Probably what's left of the blood and organs after many years of decay. It doesn't appear to be a hanging. The cord is around the chest and under the arms, as opposed to the neck, so that the skull lists to the left and the vacant eye sockets are cast downward, as if permanently ignoring all interlopers.

Just what Ruiz County needs—another cold case. What better place to hide your victim than a house so haunted its owners are too afraid to enter. Or, perhaps it could have been a suicide. This is a case we will happily hand over to Sheriff Castle and his boys. It's someone else's problem.

I close the door and turn the knob as firmly as possible.

So we have two choices. We can go to work in the bedroom with the live snake, or stay here with the quite dead human in the closet. We take the second one. Frankie manages to reach a ceiling board with the end of his crowbar and rips it down. Our lease does not give us the right to damage the house, but does anyone really care? Two of its owners are sitting out there in a truck too terrified to step through the front door. We have a job to do and I'm already tired. As Frankie begins ripping down another board, I carefully thread my way down the stairs and reopen the front door. I nod at Riley and Wendell though the rain is too thick for eye contact. I grab the ladder and take it upstairs.

When Frankie yanks down the fourth board, a box of old fruit jars comes crashing down and shatters around our feet. "Beautiful!" I yell. "There is storage up there." Inspired, Frankie rips boards with a fury and before long a third of the bedroom ceiling has been reduced to debris, which I toss in a corner. We're not coming back and I don't care how we leave the place.

I position the ladder and gingerly climb through the gap in the ceiling. When I'm waist-high in the attic I scan it with my light. It's windowless, pitch-black, cramped and musty, no more than four feet in height. For an old attic, it is surprisingly uncluttered, evidence that its owners were not consumers; evidence too that Kenny may have sealed it off over twenty years ago.

It's impossible to stand, so Frankie and I slowly crawl on all fours. The rain is pounding the tin roof just inches above our heads. We have to scream at each other. He goes one way, I go the other, very slowly. Crawling, we fight our way through thick spiderwebs and watch every square inch for another snake. I pass a neat stack of one-by-six pine planks, probably left over from construction a hundred years ago. There is a pile of old newspapers, the top one dated March of 1965.

Frankie yells and I scurry over like a rat, the dust already caked on the knees of my jeans.

He has pulled back a shredded blanket enough to reveal three identical cardboard boxes. He points his light at a label on one and I lean in to within inches. The faded ink is handwritten, but the info is clear: *Ruiz County Sheriff's Department—Evidence File QM 14.* All three boxes are sealed with a thick brown packing tape.

With my cell phone I take a dozen dark photos of the three boxes before they are moved an inch. To protect them, Kenny was smart enough to place them across three two-by-four planks to keep them off the floor in the event of rain leakage. The attic, though, seems remarkably sealed, and if it can stay dry in a deluge like this, the roof is working fine.

The boxes are not at all heavy. We gently scoot them to the opening. I go down first and Frankie hands them to me. When they are in the bedroom, I take more photos of the scene. With snakes and skeletons around, our exit is swift. The front porch is falling in and wet with rain, so we keep the boxes just inside the front door and wait for the weather to break.

43

Ruiz County is grouped with two others to form Florida's 22nd Judicial District. The current elected prosecutor is one Patrick McCutcheon, a Seabrook lawyer with offices in the courthouse. Eighteen years ago, when McCutcheon finished law school, he took an associate's position with the busy law offices of the Honorable Glenn Colacurci. When his career took a turn toward politics, they parted ways amicably.

Glenn assures me, "I can talk to the boy."

He can and he does. And while he's getting McCutcheon's attention, I work the phones tracking down Sheriff Castle, always a busy man. However, when I finally convince him my adventures earlier that morning were real, and that I have in my possession three boxes of old evidence Bradley Pfitzner tried to burn, I get his full attention.

Glenn, with no sign whatsoever of having been excessive the night before, seizes the moment with gusto and wants to take over. At 2:00 p.m. we gather in his office—me, Frankie Tatum, Patrick McCutcheon, Sheriff Castle, and Bea in one corner taking notes.

My correspondence with McCutcheon has all been written and cordial. Almost a year ago I made the routine request

321

that he reopen Quincy's case, and he politely declined, which was no surprise. I also asked Castle to reopen the investigation, but he had little interest. Since then I have e-mailed each summaries of the latest developments, so they are informed. Or should be. I assume they have reviewed my materials. I also assume they were much too busy until Pfitzner was arrested. That stunning event got their attention.

Now, they are captivated. Their sudden interest is piqued by three lost and found boxes of evidence.

It takes an awkward moment for me to establish who's in charge. Glenn would like nothing better than to hold court, but I politely shove him aside. Without explaining how or why we became interested in Kenny Taft, I walk them through our contact with the family, the lease, the payment, and the morning's adventures in the old house. Bea enlarged the photos of the boxes as they sat in the attic, and I pass these around.

"Have they been opened?" the sheriff asks.

"No. They are still sealed," I reply.

"Where are they?"

"I'm not saying right now. First, we need to reach an agreement about how to proceed. No agreement, no evidence."

"Those boxes belong to my department," Castle says.

"I'm not sure about that," I reply. "Maybe, maybe not. You and your department didn't know about them until two hours ago. There is no open investigation because you declined to get involved, remember?"

McCutcheon needs to assert himself so he says, "I agree with the sheriff. If the evidence was stolen from his department, regardless of when, then it belongs to him."

Glenn also needs to assert himself and he scolds his former associate. "His department, Patrick, tried to destroy the stuff twenty years ago. Thank God Post found it. Look, you're already playing tug-of-war. We need to agree here and proceed together. I represent Mr. Post and his organization, and you have to forgive him if he seems rather possessive of this evidence. There could be something in there that exonerates his client. Given the track record here in Seabrook, he has a right to be concerned. Everybody take a deep breath."

We do, then I say, "I suggest we agree on a plan, and then we open the boxes together, all on video of course. If the flashlight is there, gentlemen, then I want the option of keeping it and having it analyzed by our experts, Dr. Kyle Benderschmidt and Dr. Tobias Black. I believe you guys have copies of their reports. Once they are finished with their work, I will hand it over so you can take it to the state crime lab."

"Are you saying your experts are better than the State of Florida's?" Castle asked.

"Damned right I am. If you will recall, the State put on the stand a quack by the name of Paul Norwood. His work has been completely debunked over the past decade, but he did a number on Quincy. He's now out of business. Sorry, fellas, but I'm not trusting the State here."

"I'm sure our crime lab can handle this," McCutcheon says. "Norwood did not work for the State back then."

When McCutcheon speaks, Glenn feels obligated to fire back. "You're not listening, Patrick. My client is calling the shots. If you can't agree, then you don't see the evidence. He takes it with him and we go to Plan B."

"Which is?"

"Well, we haven't worked out all of the details, but Plan B certainly includes Mr. Post leaving town with the boxes and having the evidence analyzed by independent experts. You'll be cut out. Is that what you want?"

I stand and glare at Castle and McCutcheon. "I'm not really here to negotiate. I don't like your tone. I don't like your attitude. The boxes are safely tucked away, hidden again, and I'll fetch them when I'm ready." I walk to the door and open it when McCutcheon says, "Wait."

THE BOXES HAVE been dusted off but still show their age. They're sitting side by side in the middle of Glenn's long conference room table. A video camera on a tripod is aimed at them. We crowd around and gawk at them. I touch the first one and say, "I'm assuming QM is Quincy Miller. Would you like to do the honors?" I ask the sheriff, then hand over a small penknife. I also give him a pair of thin surgical gloves, which he obligingly puts on. Bea turns on the video recorder as Frankie begins filming with his phone.

Castle takes the knife and runs the blade through the packing tape along the top, then the sides. As he pulls open the flap, we strain to see what's inside. The first item is a clear plastic bag filled with what appears to be a white shirt covered in blood. Without opening it, Castle lifts it for the cameras, looks at a tag, and reads, "Crime scene, Russo, February 16, 1988."

He places it on the table. The shirt inside the bag appears to be jagged in places. The blood is almost black, twenty-three years later.

Next is another clear plastic bag with what looks like a pair of dress slacks wadded up and stuffed in. There are black stains. Castle reads the tag—the same information.

Next is a letter-sized box wrapped in a black trash-can liner. He carefully removes the plastic, sits the box on the table, and opens it. One by one he removes sheets of smudged copy paper, a yellow legal pad, notecards, and four cheap pens and two unused pencils. The tag says it's materials taken from Russo's desk. Everything is bloodstained.

One by one, he removes four lawbooks, all stained. The tag says they were taken from Keith's bookshelves.

Next is a cardboard box about twelve inches square. It is snug inside a plastic freezer bag, which in turn is zipped inside another one. Castle carefully removes the plastic, and, as if we know what's coming, he pauses a second as we stare at the brown box. It is not taped shut but has a fold-in latch. Slowly, he opens it and removes yet another plastic ziplock bag. He places it on the table. Inside is a small black flashlight, about a foot long and with a two-inch lens.

"Let's not open that," I say, with my heart in my throat.

Castle nods his agreement.

Glenn assumes command of his office and says, "Gentlemen, let's have a seat and determine where we are."

We move to one end of the table and sit down. Frankie moves to the other end and puts away his phone. Bea says, "I'm still recording."

"Let it run," I say. I want every word on the record.

For several minutes, the four of us sit in various states of repose and try to gather our thoughts. I look at the flashlight, then look away, unable to comprehend its presence, unable to fully process what it might mean. Finally, McCutcheon says, "I have a question, Post."

"Go."

"You've been living with this case for almost a year now. We have not. So, what's your best theory as to why Pfitzner wanted to destroy this evidence?"

I say, "Well, I believe there is only one explanation, and Kyle Benderschmidt helped me arrive at it. As he said, there was a smart law man at work here, and a devious one. The flashlight was planted by Pfitzner and it was carefully photographed. You've seen the pictures. Pfitzner knew he could find a quack like Paul Norwood who would look at them, without ever examining the flashlight, and feed the jury the prosecution's theory that it was used by the killer, Quincy, to fire away in the dark. The reason Pfitzner wanted the flashlight to disappear was that he was afraid that another expert, one with better training than Norwood, might examine it for the defense and tell the truth. Pfitzner also knew that a black guy in a white town would be much easier to convict."

They chew on this for another long gap. Again, McCutcheon breaks the silence with "What's your plan, Post?"

I reply, "I was not expecting so much blood. It's a gift, really. So, ideally, I first take the flashlight to Benderschmidt for an exam. He cannot do his work here because he has an extensive lab at VCU."

McCutcheon says, "And if the blood on the flashlight matches the blood on the clothing, then Quincy is linked to the crime, right?"

"Possibly, but that won't happen. The flashlight was a plant by Pfitzner and was not at the scene of the crime. I guarantee it."

Glenn needs to insert himself. He says to McCutcheon, "Well, the way I see it, we have two issues. The first is exoneration, the second is the prosecution of the real killer. The first is pressing, the second may never happen. Sure, Pfitzner is in jail, but linking him to the actual murder still looks like a long shot. You agree, Post?"

"Yes, and I'm not concerned with that right now. He gave us a gift and he's locked away for a long time. I want Quincy Miller out of prison as soon as humanly possible, and I want your help. I've been down this road before, and when the district attorney cooperates things go much faster."

"Come on, Patrick," Glenn scolds. "The writing is on the wall. This boy got screwed by this county twenty-three years ago. It's time to make things right."

Sheriff Castle smiles and says, "I'm listening. We'll reopen as soon as you get the test results."

I would like to lunge across the table and hug him.

McCutcheon says, "It's a deal. I only ask that everything is photographed, videoed, and preserved. I may need it for another trial one day."

"Of course," I say.

Castle says, "Now, about those other two boxes."

Glenn sticks his cane into the floor, jumps to his feet, says, "Let's have a look. There might be some dirt on me in there."

We laugh nervously and get to our feet. Frankie clears his throat and says, "Hey boss, don't forget about that closet."

I had forgotten. I look at the sheriff and say, "Sorry to complicate matters, Sheriff, but we stumbled across something else in the Taft house, in a closet upstairs. I'm not sure you can call it a dead body or a corpse because it's nothing but a skeleton. All bones. Probably been there for years."

Castle frowns and says, "Great. Just what I need."

"We didn't touch it, but we didn't notice any bullet holes in the skull. Could be just another suicide."

John Grisham

"I like the way you think, Post."

"And there was no clothing at all. Anyway, we didn't tell the Tafts, so it's all yours."

"Thanks for nothing."

44

Glenn invites Frankie and me to another round of Chinese food on the porch, but we beg off. I leave Seabrook late in the afternoon, with Frankie close on my tail as if to help guard my valuable cargo. It's on the seat next to me where I can keep an eye on it. One little box with the flashlight, yet to be touched for the first time in decades, and one plastic bag holding a bloody shirt. We drive nonstop for three hours and get to Savannah just after dark. I lock the evidence in my apartment for the night so I can sleep beside it. Vicki is roasting a chicken, and Frankie and I are starving.

Over dinner, we debate driving versus flying to Richmond. I don't want to fly because I don't like the idea of subjecting our evidence to airport security. A bored agent could have a blast with our bloody shirt. The idea of another one fiddling with the flashlight is terrifying.

So we leave at five in the morning, in Frankie's roomy and much more reliable pickup, with him behind the wheel and me trying to nap for the first leg. He starts nodding off just over the state line in South Carolina and I take the wheel. We pick up an R&B station out of Florence and sing along with Marvin Gaye. For breakfast we get biscuits and coffee at a fast-food drive-in window and eat on the road. We can't help but laugh about where we were exactly twenty-four hours earlier. In the attic, terrified and expecting to be attacked by evil spirits. When Frankie recalls my violent vomiting when the skeleton almost jumped out of the closet, he laughs so hard he cannot eat. I remind him that he practically fainted. He admits he took a knee and actually grabbed for his Glock.

It's almost 4:00 p.m. when we arrive in downtown Richmond. Kyle Benderschmidt has cleared the deck and his team is waiting. We follow him to a large room in his suite of labs. He introduces us to two colleagues and two technicians, and all five pull on surgical gloves. Two video cameras, one suspended directly above the table, the other mounted at one end, are activated. Frankie and I take a step back, but we'll miss nothing because the eye-in-the-sky broadcasts simultaneously to a high-def screen on the wall in front of us.

Kyle addresses the camera at the end of the table and gives the names of everyone in the room, as well as the date, place, and purpose of the exam. He casually narrates what he's doing as he removes the box from the plastic bag, opens it slowly, and removes the smaller bag holding the flashlight. He unzips it and places the prize on a white ceramic board, three feet square. With a ruler he measures its length—eleven inches. He explains to his audience that the black casing is some type of light metal, probably aluminum, with a textured surface that is not smooth. He assumes it will be difficult to find fingerprints. For a moment he becomes a professor and informs us that latent prints can remain on a smooth surface for decades if left untouched. Or, they can disappear quickly if the surface is exposed to the elements. He begins unscrewing the cap to remove the batteries, and specks of rust fall from the grooves. He softly shakes the flashlight and two D batteries reluctantly drop out. He does not touch them but says that batteries often have fingerprints. Smart burglars and other criminals almost always wipe off their flashlights, but often forget about the batteries.

I've never thought of this. Frankie and I exchange glances. Breaking news to us.

Kyle introduces a colleague named Max, who happens to be the better fingerprint guy. Max takes charge of the narrating as he leans over the two batteries and explains that since they are primarily black in color he will use a fine white powder, similar to talcum. With a small brush and a deft stroke he applies the powder to the batteries and says it will stick to the body oils left behind by the skin, should there be any. Nothing at first. He gently rolls the batteries over and applies more powder. "Bingo," he says. "Looks like a thumbprint."

My knees turn to rubber and I need to sit down. But I can't do it because everyone is now looking at me. Benderschmidt says, "What about it, Counselor? Probably not a good idea to proceed with the print, right?"

I struggle to collect my wits. I convinced myself months ago that we would never find the killer. But—didn't we just find his thumbprint?

I say, "Yes, let's stop with the print. It's probably headed for the courtroom, and I'd feel better if the Florida crime lab crew lifts it."

"Agreed," Kyle says. Max is nodding too. These guys are too professional to screw up evidence.

I have an idea. "Can we photograph it and send it to them now?"

"Sure," Kyle says with a shrug and nods to a technician. He looks at me and says, "I suppose you're rather eager to ID someone, right?"

"That's correct, if it's possible."

The technician rolls in a contraption that is described as a high-resolution camera with an unpronounceable name, and they spend the next thirty minutes taking close-ups of the thumbprint. I call Wink Castle in Seabrook and get his contact with the state crime lab. He wants to know if we've made any progress and I say nothing yet.

When the camera is gone, Kyle places the batteries in plastic containers and turns his attention to the lens. I've looked at the photographs a thousand times and know that there are eight specks of what was believed to be Russo's blood. Three of them are slightly larger and measure close to one-eighth of an inch in diameter. Kyle plans to remove the largest of these three and do a series of tests. Because the blood has been dried for almost twenty-three years, it will not be easy to lift. Working like a team of neurosurgeons, he and Max take off the cap and place the lens in a large clear petri dish. Kyle keeps up his narration. Using a small syringe, he discharges a drop of distilled water directly onto the largest speck of blood. Frankie and I are watching this on the screen.

The water mixes well, and a drop of pinkish liquid rolls off the lens and into the petri dish. Benderschmidt and Max nod in agreement. They are pleased with the sample. They peel off their surgical gloves as a technician takes it away.

Kyle says to me, "We'll take a small sample of the blood from the shirt and compare things. Then we'll run some tests, diagnose the samples. It'll take some time. We'll work tonight."

What am I supposed to say? I would prefer to have the results, and favorable ones at that, right now, but I thank him and Max. Frankie and I leave the building and roam around downtown Richmond looking for a café. Over iced tea and sandwiches we try to talk of things unrelated to blood, but it's impossible. If the sample from the flashlight matches the stains from the shirt, then the truth is unclear and there are still unanswered questions.

However, if the samples came from different sources, Quincy will walk. If he's able. Eventually.

And the thumbprint? It will not automatically lead to the guy who pulled the trigger unless it can be proven that the flashlight was at the scene. If the samples don't match, the flashlight wasn't there but was planted in Quincy's trunk by Pfitzner. Or so we speculate.

During the long drive from Savannah to Richmond, Frankie and I debated whether we should inform the Tafts that there is a skeleton in one of their closets. When we told Sheriff Castle, he showed little interest. On the one hand, the Tafts may have a relative who vanished years ago and this could solve the mystery. But on the other hand, they're already so spooked by the place it's hard to believe they'll have much interest in yet another haunted death.

Over coffee, we decide that the story is too good to leave alone. Frankie pulls up the number for Riley Taft and gives him a call. Riley is just leaving work at the school and is surprised to learn that we are already so far away with the evidence. Frankie explains that most of it is now in the possession of the sheriff, but we took what we needed. He asks if the family has any stories about folks disappearing, say in the past ten years or so.

Riley wants to know why this is important.

With a grin and a glow in his eyes, Frankie tells the story of what else we found in the house yesterday morning. In the closet of the east bedroom there is a skeleton, fully intact with a plastic rope around its chest holding it in place. Probably not a suicide. Possibly a murder but not by hanging, though little is certain.

As Riley reacts in shock, Frankie grins and almost chuckles. They go back and forth as Riley accuses Frankie of pulling his leg. Frankie warms to the story and says that the truth is easy to prove. Just go have a look. And, furthermore, he and Wendell should enter the house as soon as possible and retrieve the skeleton for a proper burial.

Riley howls at this and begins cursing. After he settles down, Frankie apologizes for bearing bad news, but just thought they would want to know. The sheriff may contact them soon and want to look around.

Frankie listens, grins, says, "No, no, Riley, I wouldn't burn it."

Riley rails and at one point Frankie pulls the phone away from his ear. Over and over he says, "Now, come on, Riley, don't burn it."

When he ends the call he's convinced the house is about to be torched by its owners.

45

We have to wait until almost 11:00 a.m. when Dr. Benderschmidt finishes his lectures and returns to his office. Frankie and I are waiting there, fully caffeinated. He strides in with a smile and says, "You win!" He falls into his chair, fiddles with his bow tie, and is delighted to deliver the wonderful news. "There's no match. There's not even human blood. Oh, there's plenty on Russo's shirt, type O like fifty percent of us, but that's all we know. As I said, we're not a DNA lab here, and, thankfully, you don't need one. The blood on the flashlight came from an animal, most likely a rabbit or a similar small mammal. In my report I'll go into the science with all the vocabulary and terms, but not now. I'm running behind because I was up all night with this file. I'm catching a flight in two hours. You don't look surprised, Post."

"I'm not surprised, Doc. Just relieved to know the truth."

"He'll walk, right?"

"It's never that easy. You know the drill. It'll take months of knife-fighting in court to walk him out, but we're going to win. Thanks to you."

"You did the grunt work, Post. I'm just a scientist."

"And the thumbprint?"

"The good news is that it's not Quincy's. The bad news is that it's not Pfitzner's either. As of now it's unknown, but the Florida crime lab is still digging. They ran it through their systems last night, got nothing. Which probably means the person who handled the battery does not have prints on file. So it could be anybody. Pfitzner's wife, his housekeeper, one of his office boys. Somebody you've never heard of and will never find."

Frankie says, "But it doesn't matter, right? If the flashlight was not at the scene, then the real killer didn't use it."

"That's correct," Kyle says. "So what happened? I suspect Pfitzner killed a rabbit, got a blood sample, and doused the flashlight. Me, I'd use a large syringe from the drugstore and spray the lens from about five feet away. It would spatter nicely enough. He let it dry, handled it with gloves, stuck it in a pocket, got a warrant for Quincy's car, planted it. He knew of Paul Norwood, the so-called expert, and made sure the prosecutor hired him. Norwood would say anything for a fee, and he rolled into town with a thick résumé and convinced the, shall we say, unsophisticated jurors. Mostly white, as I recall."

"Eleven to one," I add.

"Sensational murder, the thirst for justice, the perfect suspect with motive, and an ingenious frame job. Quincy barely escaped the death penalty and got sent away forever. Twenty-three years later, the truth is discovered by you, Post. You deserve a medal."

"Thanks, Doc, but we don't do medals. Just exonerations."

"It's been a real pleasure. A fantastic case. I'll be there when you need me."

★   ★   ★

LEAVING RICHMOND, I call my favorite nurse, who hands the phone to Quincy. I keep it simple and explain that we now have valuable evidence that will one day exonerate him. I downplay our chances of a quick release and caution that the next few months will see a lot of legal maneuvering to get him out. He is pleased, grateful, and subdued.

He was attacked thirteen weeks ago and makes progress every day. He comprehends more and his words come quicker, his vocabulary expands. One major problem we're having with him is that he does not understand that his rehab should go as slowly as possible. For him, getting well enough to be discharged means returning to prison. I have repeatedly tried to impress upon his medical team the importance of taking their time. But the patient is tired of going slow, tired of the hospital, tired of surgeries and needles and tubes. He wants to get up and run.

As Frankie drives south, I have long conversations with Mazy, Susan Ashley, and Bill Cannon. There are so many ideas that Mazy patches together a conference call and the entire team brainstorms for an hour. She has the most brilliant idea of the moment, a trick play she has been contemplating for some time. Under Florida law, petitions for post-conviction relief must be filed in the county where the inmate is housed. Thus, old Judge Plank gets inundated with frivolous paperwork, because Garvin is right down the road in rural Poinsett County. He is too jaded by this to feel sympathy, and wouldn't recognize new evidence if it bit him in the ass.

As of today, though, Quincy is not incarcerated at Garvin. He's hospitalized in downtown Orlando, the center of Orange County, population 1.5 million and home to forty-three different circuit judges. If we file a new petition in Orange County it will be assailed by the State, which will claim that we're simply forum-shopping, but there is nothing to lose. If we prevail, we will present our new evidence before a new judge, one from a metropolitan area with some diversity. If we lose, we bounce back to old Plank for another go. First, though, we must dismiss our appeal of Plank's denial of our first petition. It's been sitting untouched in the supreme court in Tallahassee for three months.

Mazy and I spend the next two days putting together an amended petition and dismissing the first one. We get the good news that the Florida state crime lab has reached the same conclusions as Kyle Benderschmidt.

There is no news from the Tafts and that skeleton in their closet.

If we kept champagne around the office, we might just pop a cork when my favorite nurse calls from Orlando and says (1) Quincy has an infection from one of the knife wounds, and (2) his jaw has not healed correctly and he needs another surgery.

I end the conversation with "Please don't let him out."

WE FILE IMMEDIATELY in circuit court in Orange County, Susan Ashley's backyard. The court is secretive about how cases are assigned among the judges, so we do not know who we'll draw. The State of Florida takes two weeks to respond, and does so with a rather terse little motion to dismiss that's hardly worth the effort.

Susan Ashley asks for an expedited hearing, and we learn that our judge is the Honorable Ansh Kumar, a thirty-eight-year-old second-generation American whose parents immigrated from India. We were praying for diversity and we got it. He grants our request for the hearing, a good sign, and I hustle down to Orlando. I'm riding with Frankie in his truck because he thinks my little Ford is not safe anymore, especially when I'm weaving while yelling into the phone. So he drives and I try not to yell.

Frankie is crucial these days for another reason. Not surprisingly, he's become close to Quincy and spends hours with him at the hospital. Together they watch ballgames, eat fast food, and in general terrorize the staff. The nurses know that both men have served long sentences for crimes they did not commit, so they let them by with some good-natured sexual bantering. Frankie tells me that some of the nurses can dish it out as fast as the boys.

Once again, the State of Florida sends down Carmen Hidalgo to carry the ball. She's one of a thousand lawyers in the Attorney General's office, and again drew the short straw. Old innocence cases are not highly sought-after by the State's top litigators.

We gather for what should be a brief hearing in a modern courtroom on the third floor of a downtown high-rise, the new judicial building that Orange County is quite proud of. Judge Kumar welcomes the lawyers with a warm smile and orders us to get on with it.

Carmen goes first and presents a nice argument that the state statute is clear and requires all such petitions for post-conviction relief to be filed in the county where the inmate is incarcerated. Susan Ashley counters with the argument that our client may still be assigned to Garvin, but he isn't there. For the past fifteen weeks he's been here, in Orlando, with no discharge date in sight. This issue has been briefed by both sides, and it is immediately obvious that Judge Kumar has read not only the briefs, but our thick petition as well.

After listening patiently, he says, "Ms. Hidalgo, it appears as though the defendant has caught the State in a rather unique little loophole. The statute does not say a word about where to file this petition when the defendant is temporarily removed from the prison where he or she is housed. Looks like they gotcha!"

"But, Your Honor . . ."

Judge Kumar slowly raises both hands and offers a warm smile. "Please be seated, Ms. Hidalgo. Thank you. Now, first, I'm keeping this case for several reasons. First and most important, I'm not convinced that the statute requires that this petition be filed in Poinsett County. Second, I'm intrigued by the facts, especially in light of recent developments. I've read everything—the defendant's first and second petitions, the State's responses, the federal lawsuit filed against the former sheriff of Ruiz County and others, the indictments against those who allegedly conspired to carry out a contract killing in prison. I've read it all. And the third reason I'm keeping this case is because there seems to be a good chance that Quincy Miller has spent the past twenty-three years in prison for a murder committed by someone else. I assure you I have not made up my mind and I am looking forward to a full evidentiary hearing on this petition. Ms. Gross, when can you be ready for a full hearing?"

Without standing, Susan Ashley says, "Tomorrow."

"And Ms. Hidalgo?"

"Your Honor, please, we haven't even filed our answer yet."

"Oh, I think you have. You filed one for the previous petition. It's already in your computer. Just update it a bit and get it re-filed here immediately, Ms. Hidalgo. The hearing will be three weeks from today, in this courtroom."

The following day, Ms. Hidalgo sprints to the state supreme court with an expedited appeal of Kumar's ruling. A week later, the Florida Supremes issue a two-sentence ruling that sides with us. We're headed for a showdown, and this time it appears as though we now have a judge who will listen.

46

Bill Cannon makes an offer that surprises us. He would like to do the honors and take charge of the courtroom when we present our petition for post-conviction relief. He views it as an excellent tune-up for the federal lawsuit that is still months away. He's itching for a fight and wants to hear the witnesses in person. Susan Ashley is only thirty-three and has limited experience in the courtroom, though she is bright and quick on her feet. I'd rate her at Double-A. Cannon, by reputation, is already in the Hall of Fame. She is delighted to yield the floor and honored to sit in the second chair. Since I'm a potential witness, I relinquish my role as a lawyer, without a twinge of regret. I still have a front row seat.

Sensing a win for the home team, Vicki and Mazy take a few days off and drive to Orlando for the occasion. Frankie sits with them on the front row. All the Guardians are present. And there's more. The Reverend Luther Hodges has also made the trip from Savannah to watch us in action. He has followed the case from the day we signed on and has spent many hours in prayer for Quincy. Glenn Colacurci arrives adorned in pink seersucker and with pretty Bea at his side. I doubt if he's been praying that much. Sitting with him is

Patrick McCutcheon who, according to Glenn, has made the decision not to retry Quincy should we prevail with our petition.

Susan Ashley has been working the press and the case is generating publicity. The story of an old corrupt sheriff conspiring to knock off an innocent man he put in prison over twenty years ago is too good to miss. And now that the innocent man is pushing hard for his release while the sheriff is locked away adds layers to the plot. There are reporters scattered around the courtroom, along with twenty or so spectators. Every courtroom, regardless of its size or location, attracts its regulars—the curious who have nothing better to do.

Judge Kumar assumes the bench without ceremony and welcomes everyone. He looks around and does not see the prisoner. Two days ago, he granted our request to allow Quincy to attend his own hearing. So far he has done everything we've asked of him.

"Bring him in," he says to a bailiff. A door beside the jury box opens and a deputy enters. Quincy walks behind him with a cane, no cuffs. He's wearing a white shirt and tan slacks that I bought him yesterday. He wanted to wear a tie for the first time in twenty-three years, but I said it wasn't necessary. There would be no jury, just a judge who probably wasn't wearing a tie under his black robe. He's at least forty pounds thinner and his motor skills have not fully recovered, but, damn, he looks great. He glances around, at first confused and uncertain, and who could blame him, but then he sees me and smiles. He shuffles our way as the deputy leads him to a seat between Susan Ashley and Bill Cannon. I'm ensconced behind them next to the bar. I pat Quincy on the shoulder and tell him how nice he looks. He turns and looks at me with watery eyes. This brief foray into freedom is already overwhelming.

We're in a brawl with the Department of Corrections over what to do with him. His doctors are finished for now and ready to discharge, which means a one-way ticket back to Garvin. Susan Ashley has requested a transfer to a minimum security unit near Fort Myers with rehab facilities. His doctors have generously provided letters and memos supporting his needs for more rehab. We are vehemently arguing that Garvin is a dangerous place for all prisoners in general but for Quincy in particular. Bill Cannon is barking away at the bureaucrats in Corrections in Tallahassee. However, since he currently has them all on the ropes with his $50 million lawsuit, they are not being cooperative. Odell Herman, the warden at Garvin, says that Quincy will be placed in PC—protective custody—like this is really something generous. PC is nothing more than solitary confinement.

What Quincy needs is another infection, but since the last one almost killed him I keep this to myself. He's been in the hospital for nineteen weeks, and he's said to Frankie several times that at this point he prefers prison.

We prefer nothing less than freedom, and it will happen. The timing is not clear.

Bill Cannon rises and walks to the podium to address the court. He's fifty-four years old, with thick and styled gray hair, a black suit, and the confidence of a courtroom master who can extract anything he wants from a jury, or a judge. His voice is a rich baritone that I'm sure he worked on decades ago. His elocution is perfect. He begins by saying that we are on the brink of finding the truth, the foundation of the greatest legal system in the world. The truth about who did or did not kill Keith Russo. The truth that was covered up long ago in a small corrupt town in north Florida. The truth that was deliberately buried by bad men. But now, after decades, after putting an innocent man away for twenty-three years, the truth is at hand.

Cannon doesn't need notes, doesn't stop to look down at a yellow legal pad. There are no gaps, no "uh's" or "ah's" or fragmented sentences. The man speaks off the cuff in polished prose! And he's mastered a strategy learned by few lawyers, even the most skilled advocates: he is succinct, does not repeat himself, and is brief. He lays out our case and tells Judge Kumar what we are about to prove. In less than ten minutes he sets the tone and leaves little doubt that he is on a mission and will not be denied.

Carmen Hidalgo responds by reminding the court that the jury has spoken. Quincy Miller was given a fair trial many years ago and the jury unanimously convicted him. He came within one vote of getting the death penalty. Why should we relitigate old cases? Our system is strained and overworked and not designed to keep cases alive for decades. If we allow all convicted murderers to create new facts and allege new evidence, then what good is the first trial anyway?

She is even briefer.

Cannon decides to begin with drama and calls to the stand Wink Castle, Sheriff of Ruiz County. Wink brings with him a small cardboard box. After he's sworn, Cannon takes him through the process of describing what's in it. A clear plastic bag holds the flashlight, and it's laid on the table next to the court reporter. Wink describes how it came into his possession. Cannon rolls a video of us in Glenn's office opening the boxes. It's a fun story and we all enjoy it, especially His Honor. Castle gives what little he knows of the history, including the mysterious fire. He is proud to inform the court that things have been modernized in Ruiz County under his watch.

In other words, the drug dealers are gone. We're all clean now!

On cross-examination, Carmen Hidalgo scores a few minor points by forcing Castle to admit that the evidence boxes were missing for many years; thus, there is a huge gap in the chain of custody. This could be crucial if the flashlight is used in a subsequent criminal trial, but it's useless now. When she's finished, Judge Kumar inserts himself into the action by asking Wink, "Has this flashlight been examined by the state crime lab?"

Wink says yes.

"Do you have a copy of their report?"

"No sir. Not yet."

"Do you know the name of the criminologist in charge of this evidence?"

"Yes sir."

"Good. I want you to call him right now and tell him that I expect him here tomorrow morning."

"Will do, sir."

I'm called as the second witness and sworn to tell the truth. This is the fourth time in my career that I've taken the stand, and courtrooms look far different from the inside of the witness box. All eyes are on the witness, who tries to focus and relax as his heart hammers away. Instantly, there is the hesitation to speak because the wrong words might tumble out. Be truthful. Be convincing. Be clear. All the standard advice

I give to my witnesses is distant, at least for the moment. Thankfully, I have a brilliant trial lawyer on my side and we've rehearsed my little routine. I can't imagine sitting up here trying to sell some half-baked tale with a guy like Cannon throwing grenades at me.

I tell a highly amended story of finding the flashlight, leaving out huge chapters along the way. Nothing about Tyler Townsend in Nassau, or Bruce Gilmer in Idaho; nothing about e-mails that evaporated in five minutes; nothing about African voodoo or a real skeleton in a closet. I rely on a rumor passed along by an old lawyer who'd heard that perhaps Kenny Taft knew too much and got himself killed. So I went to the Taft family and started digging. Got lucky. On a big screen, Cannon produces photos of the dilapidated house, and some of the dark ones I took in the attic, and another video of Frankie hauling the boxes out of the haunted house. I recount our trip to Richmond with the evidence and the meeting with Dr. Benderschmidt.

On cross, Carmen Hidalgo asks a series of questions designed to cast more doubt upon the chain of custody. No, I do not know how long the boxes were in the attic, nor do I know who put them there, nor do I know for sure if Kenny Taft actually removed them himself before the fire, nor do I know if anyone helped him, nor do I know if he opened the boxes and tampered with the evidence. My responses are polite and professional. She's just doing her job and doesn't want to be here.

She presses me on the source of the rumors about Kenny Taft, and I explain that I have confidential sources to protect. Sure, I know more than I'm offering at this time, but I am, after all, a lawyer and understand confidentiality. She asks His

Honor to instruct me to answer her questions. Cannon objects and delivers a mini-lecture on the sanctity of a lawyer's work product. Judge Kumar denies her request and I return to my chair behind Quincy.

Dr. Kyle Benderschmidt is in the courtroom and eager to leave it. Bill Cannon calls him as our next witness and begins the tedious qualification process. After a few minutes, Judge Kumar looks at Carmen Hidalgo and asks, "Do you really want to question his qualifications?"

"No, Your Honor. The State will accept his credentials."

"Thank you." Kumar is not rushing anyone and seems to enjoy being in control. With only three years under his belt, he seems quite accomplished and confident.

Cannon bypasses the flawed testimony the jury heard from Paul Norwood—it's briefed extensively by Mazy—and instead drills into the real proof. Now that we have the flashlight and the spatter, we no longer have to guess. On the big screen Benderschmidt presents photos taken by him recently and compares them to the trial exhibits used twenty-three years ago. The specks have faded in color over time, even though the lens was apparently shielded from light. He identifies the three largest ones and points to his sample. More enlarged photos, more forensic jargon. Benderschmidt launches into what quickly becomes a tedious science lesson. Maybe this is because my gene pool runs shallow with science and math, but whether I'm bored or not is insignificant. His Honor is absorbing it.

Kyle begins with the basics: human blood cells are different from animal blood cells. Two large images appear on the screen and Benderschmidt goes into professor mode. The image on the left is a greatly enlarged red blood cell taken from blood on the lens. The image on the right looks similar and is a red blood cell taken from a rabbit, a small mammal. Humans are mammals and their red blood cells are similar in that they do not have nuclei. Reptiles and birds have nucleated red blood cells, we do not. The professor taps his laptop, the images change, and we are lost in the world of red blood cells. The cell's nucleus is small and round and serves as the cell's command center. It controls the cell's growth and reproduction. It is surrounded by a membrane. And on and on.

Attached to our petition was Benderschmidt's full report, including pages of impenetrable stuff on cells and blood. I confess that I have not read it entirely, but something tells me Judge Kumar has.

The bottom line: Animal red blood cells vary greatly among species. He is almost certain that the blood on the lens of the flashlight found in Quincy's car by Bradley Pfitzner came from a small mammal. He is emphatically certain that it is not human blood.

We did not bother with DNA testing the two samples because there was no reason to. We know that the blood on Keith's shirt was indeed his. We know that the blood on the lens was not.

Watching Cannon and Benderschmidt tag-team through the testimony is like watching a finely choreographed dance routine. And they had never met until yesterday. If I were defending the $50 million lawsuit roaring down the pike, I would start talking settlement.

It's almost 1:00 p.m. when Benderschmidt finishes off the rote series of lame questions tossed up by Carmen. Judging by his rail-thin frame, His Honor cares little about lunch, but the rest of us are weak with hunger. We break for an hour and a half. Frankie and I drive Kyle to the airport, stopping for a quick drive-through burger along the way. He wants to know as soon as possible when there is a ruling. He loves his work and loves this case and is desperate for an exoneration. Bad science convicted Quincy, and Kyle wants to clean up the mess.

FOR THE PAST seven months, Zeke Huffey has enjoyed his freedom so much that he's managed to avoid another arrest. He's on probation in Arkansas and can't leave the state without permission from his parole officer. He says he's clean and sober and determined to remain so. A nonprofit loaned him a thousand dollars for his initial survival, and he's working part-time at a car wash, a burger place, and a lawn maintenance company. He is surviving and has repaid almost half of his loan. Guardian bought him a plane ticket, and he takes the stand looking tanned and healthier.

His performance in the first hearing before Ole Judge Plank was exemplary. He owned his lies and, while blaming Pfitzner and a bad system, said he knew what he was doing. He had been planted as a snitch and had delivered beautifully. Now, though, he deeply regrets his lies. In a poignant moment that catches everybody off guard, Zeke looks across the courtroom at Quincy and says, "I did it, Quincy. I did it to save my own skin, and I sure wish I hadn't done it. I lied to save me and to send you away. I'm so sorry, Quincy. I'm not asking for forgiveness, because if I was you I wouldn't forgive me. I'm just saying I'm sorry for what I did."

Quincy nods but does not respond. He will tell me later that he wanted to say something, to offer forgiveness, but he was afraid to speak in court without permission.

Zeke gets roughed-up on cross when Carmen zeros in on his colorful history of lying in court. When did the lying stop, or has it? Why should anyone believe that you're not lying now? And so on. But he survived this before and he handles it well. More than once he says, "Yes ma'am, I admit I've lied before, but I'm not lying now. I swear."

Our next witness is Carrie Holland Pruitt. It took some work to convince Carrie and Buck to make the long drive to Orlando, but when Guardian generously threw in a family package of tickets to Disney World the deal was sealed. Mind you, Guardian cannot afford such family packages to Disney World, but Vicki, as always, somehow found the money.

With Bill Cannon in complete control, Carrie recalls her sad history in the prosecution of Quincy Miller. She did not see a black man running away from the scene, holding what appeared to be a stick, or something. Indeed, she didn't see anything. Didn't hear anything. She was coerced into lying at trial by Sheriff Pfitzner and Forrest Burkhead, the former prosecutor. She told her lies, and the following day Pfitzner gave her a thousand dollars in cash, told her to catch the next bus, and threatened to jail her for perjury if she ever returned to Florida.

After the first sentence or two of her testimony, her eyes begin to water. Before long her voice cracks. Halfway through it's a tear-fest as she lays claim to her lies and says she's sorry. She was a confused kid back then, doing drugs and dating a bad boyfriend, a cop, and she needed the money. Now, she's been clean and sober for fifteen years and never misses a day of work. But she has thought about Quincy many times. She sobs and we wait for her to get control. Buck is on the front row, wiping his cheeks too.

Judge Kumar calls for a recess and we break for an hour.

His clerk apologizes and says he is tending to an urgent matter in chambers. Marvis Miller arrives and huddles with his brother while a guard watches from a distance. I sit with Mazy and Vicki and analyze the testimony so far. A reporter wants a word but I decline.

At 4:30, we convene again and Bill Cannon calls our last witness for the day. I have just informed Quincy to lessen the shock. When Cannon says the name "June Walker," Quincy turns and stares at me. I smile and nod reassuringly.

Frankie does not tire easily, especially when stalking people of color who need to cooperate with us. Over the months he gradually cultivated a relationship with Otis Walker in Tallahassee, and from there got to know June. They resisted at first and were still upset by the fact that Quincy's lawyers had painted such an unflattering picture of his first wife. But with time, Frankie managed to impress upon June and Otis that old lies should be corrected if you're given the chance. Quincy didn't kill anybody, yet June had helped the real killers, a bunch of white men.

She rises from the third row and walks with a purpose to the witness stand where she is sworn in by the clerk. I've spent time with June and tried to impress upon her that there will be nothing easy about sitting in a courtroom and admitting to perjury. I've also assured her that she cannot and will not be prosecuted for it.

She nods at Quincy and grits her teeth. Bring it on. She gives her name and address and says that her first husband was Quincy Miller. They had three children together before the marriage flamed out in a bitter divorce. She's on our side and Bill Cannon treats her with respect. He lifts some papers from his desk and addresses her.

"Now, Mrs. Walker, I direct your attention back many years ago to the murder trial of your ex-husband, Quincy Miller. In that trial you testified on behalf of the prosecution, and in doing so you made a series of statements. I would like to go through them, okay?"

She nods and says quietly, "Yes sir."

Cannon adjusts his reading glasses and looks at the trial transcript. "The prosecutor asked you this question: 'Did the defendant Quincy Miller own a twelve-gauge shotgun?' And your response was, 'I think so. He had some pistols. I don't know much about guns, but, yes, Quincy had a big shotgun.'

"Now, Mrs. Walker, was your answer truthful?"

"No sir, it was not. I never saw a shotgun around our house, never knew Quincy to have one."

"Okay. The second statement. The prosecutor asked you this question: 'Did the defendant enjoy hunting and fishing?' And your response: 'Yes sir, he didn't hunt much but went out to the woods from time to time with his friends, usually shooting birds and rabbits.'

"Now, Mrs. Walker, was your answer truthful?"

"No, it was not. I never knew Quincy to go hunting. He liked to fish with his uncle a little, but no hunting."

"Okay, third statement. The prosecutor handed you a color photograph of a flashlight and asked if you had ever seen Quincy with one like it. Your response: 'Yes sir, this looks like the one he kept in his car.'

"Now, Mrs. Walker, was your answer truthful?"

"No, it was not. I never saw a flashlight like that one, not that I can remember anyway, and I sure never saw Quincy with one like it."

"Thank you, Mrs. Walker. Last question. At trial the prosecutor asked you if Quincy was in the vicinity of Seabrook on the night Keith Russo was murdered. Your response: 'I think so. Somebody said they saw him out at Pounder's Store.'

"Mrs. Walker, was your answer truthful?"

She starts to answer but her voice fails her. She swallows hard, looks directly at her ex-husband, clenches her jaw, and says, "No sir, it wasn't truthful. I never heard anybody say anything about Quincy being around that night."

Cannon says, "Thank you," and tosses the papers on his table. Carmen Hidalgo slowly gets to her feet as if uncertain how to proceed. She hesitates as she studies the witness and realizes that she cannot score a single point here. She acts frustrated and says, "The State has nothing, Your Honor."

Judge Kumar says, "Thank you, Mrs. Walker. You are excused."

June can't leave the witness stand fast enough. In front of me, Quincy suddenly shoves back his chair and gets to his feet. Without his cane he steps behind Bill Cannon and limps toward June. She slows a step as if frightened, and for a second the rest of us are frozen as a disaster unfolds. Then Quincy throws his arms open wide and June walks into them. He hugs her as they both burst into tears. Two people who once produced three children but grew to hate one another embrace in front of strangers. "I'm so sorry," she whispers over and over. "It's all right," he whispers right back. "It's all right."

47

Vicki and Mazy are eager to meet Quincy. They have lived with his case for a long time and know a lot about his life, but they've never had the chance to say hello. We retreat from the courthouse and gather at Mercy Hospital where he is still a patient and a prisoner. His room now is in a new annex where the rehab facilities are housed, but we meet him in the basement cafeteria. His guard is an Orlando policeman who sits far away, bored.

After twenty-three years of prison food, he does not complain about the bad food they sell in this cafeteria. He wants a sandwich and chips and I fetch it for him as he, Vicki, and Mazy rattle on about the day's adventures in court. Frankie sits next to him, always ready to assist. Luther Hodges is close by, absorbing the moment and happy to be included. Quincy wants us to join him for dinner but we have committed to other plans later in the evening.

He is still moved by his encounter with June. He has hated her for so long and so hard that he is stunned by the speed with which he forgave her. Sitting there listening to her confess her lies, something came over him, maybe the Holy Spirit, and he just couldn't hate anymore. He closed his eyes and asked God to take away all of his hate, and in a flash a huge burden left his shoulders. He could actually feel the release as he exhaled. He forgave Zeke Huffey, and he forgave Carrie Holland, and he feels wonderfully, beautifully unburdened.

Luther Hodges smiles and nods. It's his kind of message.

Quincy nibbles at his sandwich, eats a few chips, says his appetite has yet to return. He weighed 142 yesterday, far below his fighting weight of 180. He wants to know what will happen tomorrow, but I'd rather not speculate. I assume Judge Kumar will finish with the witnesses, take the case under consideration, and issue a ruling in weeks or months. He gives every impression of being sympathetic, but I learned years ago to always expect the worst. And to never expect justice to be swift.

After an hour of nonstop chatter, the guard says our time is up. We all hug Quincy and promise to see him in the morning.

BILL CANNON's law firm has offices in the largest six cities in Florida. The partner who runs the Orlando office is a medical malpractice assassin whose name, Cordell Jollie, invokes horror among incompetent doctors. He has financially wrecked many of them and is far from finished. His verdicts and settlements have provided him the means to buy a mansion in a ritzy section of Orlando, an exclusive neighborhood with gates and shaded streets lined with outrageous homes. We pull into a circular drive and notice parked to one side a Bentley, a Porsche, and a Mercedes coupe. Jollie's fleet is worth more than Guardian's annual budget. And parked proudly in front is an old Beetle, no doubt owned by Susan Ashley Gross, who has already arrived.

Normally, we at Guardian would have declined a dinner invitation to such an address, but it is next to impossible to say no to Bill Cannon. Besides, we are just nosy enough to want to see a home that we would otherwise only glimpse in a magazine. A dude in a tux greets us at the front door—my first-ever encounter with a real butler. We follow him through a massive parlor with vaulted ceilings, a room bigger than most reasonable homes, and we are suddenly conscious about our clothes.

Frankie had the presence of mind to pass on the invitation. He, Quincy, and Luther Hodges plan to watch a baseball game on television.

We forget about our clothes when Cordell himself rushes in from another room in a T-shirt, dirty golf shorts, and flip-flops. He's holding a beer in a green bottle and pumps our hands with vigorous introductions. Bill Cannon appears, also in shorts, and we follow them through the cavernous dwelling to a rear terrace that overlooks a pool large enough to race skiffs. A pool house at the far end can easily sleep fifteen. A gentleman in all whites takes our drink orders as we are directed to a shaded sitting area under creaking fans. Susan Ashley is sipping white wine as she waits for us.

"I'd introduce y'all to my wife but she left last month," Cordell says loudly as he falls into a wicker rocker. "Third divorce."

"I thought it was four," Cannon says seriously.

"Could be. I think I'm done." It's easy to get the impression that Cordell plays hard, works hard, parties hard, and keeps nothing inside. "She wants this house but there's that little prenup thing she signed right before the wedding."

"Can we talk about something else?" Cannon says. "Our law firm lives in fear of Cordell's next divorce."

What, exactly, are we supposed to talk about at this point? "We had a good day in court," I say. "Thanks to Bill." Vicki, Mazy, and Susan Ashley are wide-eyed and seemingly afraid to speak.

Cannon says, "It always helps when the facts are on your side."

"Damn right," Cordell adds. "I love this case. I'm on the firm's litigation committee and from the moment Bill pitched this case I said, 'Hell yes.'"

"What's a litigation committee?" I ask. Cordell is on our side, and he has a big mouth so there's a chance we can learn a lot.

He says, "Every lawsuit we file has to be screened by a committee made up of the managing partners of the six offices. We see a lot of crap and we also see a lot of good cases that are either unwinnable or too expensive. For us to take a case there has to be a good chance of recovery of at least ten million bucks. That simple. If we don't see the potential for ten million, then we pass. Quincy, he's looking at more than that. You have the complicity of the State of Florida, with no caps on damages. You have four million already frozen in the sheriff's bank accounts, with more parked offshore. And you have the cartel."

"The cartel?" I ask.

Mr. All-Whites returns with a silver tray and hands down our drinks. Beer for me. White wine for Mazy. And white wine for Vicki as well, which is probably the second time she has not said no since I've known her.

Bill says, "It's not a new angle, but it's something we haven't tried before. We've associated a firm out of Mexico City that stalks the assets of narco-traffickers. It's dicey work, as you might guess, but they've had some success in attaching bank accounts and freezing property. The Saltillo Cartel has some new faces, primarily because the old ones got blown away, but some of the principals are still known. Our plans are to get a big judgment here and enforce it anywhere we can find the assets."

"Seems like suing a cartel would be somewhat dangerous," I say.

Cordell laughs and says, "Probably not as bad as suing tobacco companies, gun makers, or big pharma. Not to mention crooked doctors and their insurance companies."

Mazy says, "Are you saying that Quincy Miller will get at least ten million dollars?" She asks this slowly, as if in disbelief.

Cannon laughs and says, "No, we never make guarantees. Too many things can go wrong. It's litigation and so it's always a roll of the dice. The State will want to settle but Pfitzner will not. He'll go down swinging and trying like hell to protect his money. He has good lawyers, but he'll be fighting from inside of a prison. I'm saying that Quincy's case has that much potential, minus, of course, the matter of our fees."

"Hear, hear," Cordell says as he drains his bottle.

"How long will it take?" Vicki asks.

Bill and Cordell look at each other and shrug. Bill says, "Two, maybe three years. Nash Cooley's firm knows how to litigate so it will be a fair fistfight."

I watch Susan Ashley as she follows this closely. Like Guardian, her nonprofit cannot split attorneys' fees with real law firms, but she told me in confidence that Bill Cannon promised to donate 10 percent of the legal fees to the Central Florida Innocence Project. She, in turn, promised me half of whatever they get. For a second my mind goes crazy as our Mexican lawyers garnish Caribbean bank accounts filled with huge sums of money that gets whacked as it trickles down, but at the very end there is little Guardian Ministries waiting with its hand out for a few thousand bucks.

There is a direct correlation between the amount of money we raise and the number of innocent people we exonerate. If we were to catch a windfall, we would probably restructure and add personnel. Maybe I can buy a new set of tires, or better yet, upgrade to a nicer used vehicle.

The alcohol helps and we are able to relax and forget about our poverty as drinks are freshened and dinner preparations are made. Litigators on booze can spin fascinating yarns, and Cordell entertains us with one about an ex-CIA spy he hired and planted deep inside a medical malpractice insurance company. The guy was responsible for three exorbitant verdicts and retired without getting caught.

Cannon tells one about getting his first million-dollar verdict at the age of twenty-eight, still a record in Florida.

Back to Cordell, who's reminded of his first airplane crash.

It's a relief when Mr. All-Whites informs us dinner is served. We move to one of the dining rooms inside the mansion where the temperature is much cooler.

48

The Honorable Ansh Kumar takes the bench with another smile and says good morning. We're all in our proper places, eager for the day to begin and anxious about what might happen next. He looks down at Bill Cannon and says, "After we adjourned yesterday, I contacted the state crime lab in Tallahassee and spoke with the director. He said the analyst, a Mr. Tasca, would be here at ten a.m. Mr. Cannon, do you have another witness?"

Bill stands and says, "Maybe, Your Honor. Agnes Nolton is a special agent with the FBI office here in Orlando and she is in charge of the investigation into the brutal attack on Quincy Miller almost five months ago. She is prepared to testify about that investigation and its relevance to this case."

I had an early breakfast with Agnes and she is willing to help in any way. However, we are doubtful Judge Kumar will see the need for her testimony, restricted as it would be.

He knows this is coming because I mentioned it during a recess yesterday. He thinks about it for a long moment. Carmen Hidalgo rises slowly and says, "Your Honor, may it please the court, I'm having trouble understanding why this testimony can help us here. The FBI had nothing to do with the investigation into the murder of Keith Russo, nor the prosecution of Quincy Miller. Seems like a waste of time to me."

"I tend to agree. I've read the indictments, the lawsuit, the press coverage, so I know something about the conspiracy to murder Mr. Miller. Thank you, Agent Nolton, for your willingness to testify, but you will not be needed."

I glance back at Agnes and she is smiling.

His Honor taps the gavel and calls for a recess until 10:00.

MR. TASCA HAS been studying blood for the State of Florida for thirty-one years. Both sides stipulate to his credentials. Carmen does so because he is the State's expert. We do so because we want his testimony. Carmen refuses to question him on direct examination. She says this is our petition, not hers. No problem, says Bill Cannon, as he jumps into the testimony.

It's over in a matter of minutes. Bill asks, "Mr. Tasca, you have tested the blood taken from the shirt and you have analyzed the blood sample from the flashlight lens, correct?"

"That's correct."

"And have you read the report prepared by Dr. Kyle Benderschmidt?"

"Yes, I have."

"Do you know Dr. Benderschmidt?"

"I do. He's quite well known in our field."

"Do you agree with his conclusion that the blood on the shirt came from a human and the blood on the flashlight lens came from an animal?"

"Yes, there's no doubt about it."

362

Cannon then does something that I do not recall seeing before in a courtroom. He starts laughing. Laughing at the absurdity of eliciting further testimony. Laughing at the paucity of the evidence against our client. Laughing at the State of Florida and its pathetic efforts to uphold a bad conviction. He waves his arms and asks, "What are we doing here, Judge? The only physical evidence linking our client to the crime scene is that flashlight. Now we know it wasn't there. It was never owned by our client. It wasn't recovered from the crime scene."

"Any more witnesses, Mr. Cannon?"

Still amused, Bill shakes his head and walks from the podium.

The Judge asks, "Ms. Hidalgo, any witnesses?"

She waves him off and is ready to sprint to the nearest door.

"Closing remarks from the attorneys?"

Bill stops at our table and says, "No, Your Honor, we believe enough has been said and we urge the court to rule quickly. Quincy Miller has been released by his doctors and is scheduled to be returned to prison tomorrow. That is a travesty. He has no business in prison, now or twenty years ago. He was wrongfully convicted by the State of Florida and he should be set free. Justice delayed is justice denied."

How many times have I heard that? Waiting is one of the hazards in this business. I've seen a dozen courts sit on cases involving innocent men as if time doesn't matter, and I've wished a hundred times that some pompous judge could be forced to spend a weekend in jail. Just three nights, and it would do wonders for his work ethic.

"We'll adjourn until one p.m.," His Honor says with a smile.

CANNON HOPS INTO a limousine and races away to the airport where his private jet is waiting to whisk him to a settlement conference in Houston, where he and his gang will carve up a drug company they caught fudging its R&D. He's almost giddy in anticipation.

The rest of our team huddles in a café somewhere in the depths of the judicial building. Luther Hodges joins us for the first round of coffee. A large clock on one wall gives the time as 10:20 and it appears as though the second hand has stopped. A reporter butts in and asks if Quincy will answer some questions. I say no, then step into the hallway and chat with her.

During the second round, Mazy asks, "So what can go wrong?"

Lots of things. We are convinced Judge Kumar is about to vacate the conviction and sentence. There is no other reason for him to reconvene court at 1:00 p.m. If he planned to rule against Quincy, he would simply wait a few days and mail it in. The hearing clearly went our way. The proof is on our side. The judge is friendly, or has been so far. The State has all but given up. I suspect that Kumar wants some of the glory.

However, he could remand Quincy back to prison for processing. Or send the case back to Ruiz County and order Quincy held there until the locals screw it up again. He could order Quincy back to jail in Orlando pending the appeal of his order by the State. I do not anticipate walking him out the front door as the cameras roll.

The clock barely moves and I try to avoid looking at it. We nibble on sandwiches at noon just to pass the time. At 12:45 we return to the courtroom and wait some more.

At 1:15 Judge Kumar assumes the bench and calls for order. He nods at the court reporter and asks, "Anything from counsel?"

Susan Ashley shakes her head no for our side as Carmen does the same.

He begins reading: "We are here on a petition for post-conviction relief filed under Rule 3.850 by the defendant, Quincy Miller, asking this court to vacate his conviction for murder many years ago in the 22nd Judicial District. Florida law is clear that relief can only be granted if new evidence is shown to the court, evidence that could not have been obtained by due diligence in the original proceedings. And it is not sufficient to make an allegation that there is new evidence, but it must also be proven that the new evidence would have altered the outcome. Examples of new evidence can be recantations of witnesses, discovery of exculpatory evidence, or the finding of new witnesses who were unknown at the time of the trial.

"In this case, the recantations of three witnesses—Zeke Huffey, Carrie Holland Pruitt, and June Walker—provide clear proof that their testimonies at trial were compromised and inaccurate. The court finds them to be strong, credible witnesses now. The only physical evidence linking Quincy Miller to the murder scene was allegedly the flashlight, and it was not available at trial. Its discovery by the defense team was remarkable. The analysis of the blood spatter by experts on both sides proves that it was not at the crime scene, but probably planted in the trunk of the defendant's car. The flashlight is exculpatory evidence of the highest order.

"Therefore, the conviction for murder is vacated and the sentence is commuted effective immediately. I suppose there is the chance that Mr. Miller could be indicted and tried again in Ruiz County, though I doubt this. If so, that will be another proceeding for another day. Mr. Miller, would you please stand with your attorneys?"

Quincy forgets about his cane and jumps to his feet. I grab his left elbow as Susan Ashley grabs his right one. His Honor continues, "Mr. Miller, the people responsible for your wrongful conviction over twenty years ago are not in this courtroom today. I'm told some are dead. Others are scattered. I doubt they will ever be held accountable for this miscarriage of justice. I don't have the power to pursue them. Before you go, though, I'm compelled to at least acknowledge that you have been badly mistreated by our legal system, and since I'm a part of it, I apologize for what has happened to you. I will help with your formal exoneration efforts in any way possible, including the matter of compensation. Good luck to you, sir. You are free to go."

Quincy nods and mumbles, "Thank you."

His knees are weak and he sits and buries his face in his hands. We gather around him—Susan Ashley, Marvis, Mazy, Vicki, Frankie—and for a long time little is said as we all have a good cry. Everybody but Frankie, a guy who did not shed a tear when he walked out of prison after fourteen years.

Judge Kumar eases over without his robe and we thank him profusely. He could have waited a month, or six, or a couple of years, and he could have ruled against Quincy and sent us into the appellate orbit where nothing is certain and time means little. It is unlikely he'll have another chance to free an innocent man after two decades in prison, so he is savoring the moment. Quincy gets to his feet for a hug. And once the hugging begins it is contagious.

This is our tenth exoneration, second in the past year, and each time I look at the cameras and reporters I struggle with what to say. Quincy goes first and talks about being grateful and so on. He says he has no plans, hasn't had time to make any, and just wants some ribs and a beer. I decide to take the high road and not blame those at fault. I thank Judge Kumar for his courage in doing what was right and just. I've learned that the more questions you take the more chances you have to screw up, so after ten minutes I thank them and we leave.

Frankie has pulled his pickup to the curb on a side street. I tell Vicki and Mazy that we'll meet in Savannah in a few hours, then get in the front passenger seat. Quincy crawls in the rear seat and asks, "What the hell is this?"

"Called a club cab," Frankie says, easing away.

"It's all the rage, for white boys anyway," I say.

"I know dudes driving these," Frankie says defensively.

"Just drive, man," Quincy says, soaking up the freedom.

"You want to run by Garvin and get your things?" I ask.

They both laugh. "I might need a new lawyer, Post," Quincy says.

"Go ahead. He can't work any cheaper than me."

Quincy leans forward on the console. "Say, Post, we ain't talked about this yet, but how much do I get from the State, you know, for the exoneration part of this?"

"Fifty thousand a year for each year served. Over a million bucks."

"When do I get it?"

"It'll take a few months."

"But it's guaranteed, right?"

"Practically."

"How much is your cut?"

"Zero."

"Come on."

Frankie says, "No, it's true. Georgia paid me a bunch of money and Post wouldn't take any of it."

It dawns on me that I'm in the presence of two black millionaires, though their fortunes were earned in ways that defy description.

Quincy leans back, exhales, laughs, says, "I can't believe this. Woke up this morning and had no idea, figured they'd haul me back to prison. Where we going, Post?"

"We're getting out of Florida before someone changes his mind. Don't ask who. I don't know who or where or how or why, but let's go hide in Savannah for a few days."

"You mean, somebody might be looking for me?"

"I don't think so, but let's play it safe."

"What about Marvis?"

"I told him to meet us in Savannah. We're eating ribs tonight and I know just the place."

"I want some ribs, a beer, and a woman."

"Well, I can handle the first two," I say. Frankie cuts his eyes at me as if he might have some ideas about the third.

After half an hour of freedom, Quincy wants to stop at a burger place along the busy highway. We go in and I pay for sodas and fries. He picks a table near the front window where he tries to explain what it's like to sit and eat like a normal person. Free to enter and leave. Free to order anything on the menu. Free to walk to the restroom without asking for permission and not worrying about bad things in there. The poor guy's emotions are a mess and he cries easily.

Back in the truck, we join the crush on Interstate 95 and slog our way up the East Coast. We allow Quincy to select the music and he likes early Motown. Fine with me. He's fascinated with Frankie's life and wants to know how he survived the first few months out of prison. Frankie warns him about the money and all the new friends he is likely to attract. Then Quincy dozes off and there is nothing but music. We navigate around Jacksonville and are within twenty miles of the Georgia line when Frankie mumbles, "Dammit."

I turn around and see blue lights. My heart sinks as Quincy wakes up and sees the lights. "Were you speeding?" I ask.

"I guess so. Wasn't paying much attention."

A second car with lights joins the first but, oddly, the troopers remain in their cars. This cannot be good. I reach into my briefcase, remove a collar, and put it on.

"Oh, so you're a preacher now," Quincy says. "Better start praying."

Frankie asks, "Got another one of those?"

"Sure." I hand him a collar, and since he's never worn one before I help get it adjusted properly around his neck.

Finally, the cop in the first car gets out and approaches on the driver's side. He's black, with aviator shades, Smokey's hat, the works. Fit and trim and unsmiling, a real hard-ass. Frankie lowers his window and the cop stares at him, sort of startled.

"Why are you driving this?" he asks.

Frankie shrugs, says nothing.

"I was expecting some Georgia cracker. Now I got a black reverend." He looks across at me, takes in my collar. "And a white one too."

He glances into the rear seat and sees Quincy—eyes closed, deep in prayer.

"Registration and license, please." Frankie hands them over and the trooper goes back to his cruiser. Minutes drag by and we say nothing. When he approaches again, Frankie lowers the window and the officer hands over the registration card and driver's license.

He says, "God told me to let you go."

"Praise the Lord," Quincy gushes from the back seat.

"A black preacher driving a pickup truck with a white preacher riding shotgun speeding down the interstate. I'm sure there's a story here."

I hand him one of my business cards and point to Quincy. "This guy just got out of prison after twenty-three years. We proved he was innocent down in Orlando and the judge let him walk. We're taking him to Savannah for a few days."

"Twenty-three years."

"And I served fourteen in Georgia, for somebody else's murder," Frankie says.

He looks at me and says, "You?"

"They haven't convicted me yet."

He hands the card back, says, "Follow me." He gets in his car, keeps the blue lights on, guns the engine, takes the lead, and within seconds we're doing eighty miles an hour with a full escort.

AUTHOR'S NOTE

Inspiration came from two sources: one, a character; the other, a plot.

First, the character. About fifteen years ago I was researching a case in Oklahoma when I stumbled upon a box of documents marked for Centurion Ministries. I knew very little about innocence work back then and I'd never heard of Centurion. I asked around and eventually made my way to its offices in Princeton, New Jersey.

James McCloskey founded Centurion Ministries in 1980 while he was a divinity student. Working as a prison chaplain, he met an inmate who insisted that he was innocent. Jim eventually came to believe him and went to work to prove his innocence. His exoneration inspired Jim to take another case, and then another. For almost forty years, Jim has traveled the country, usually alone, digging for lost clues and elusive witnesses, and searching for the truth.

To date, sixty-three men and women owe their freedom to Jim and the dedicated team at Centurion Ministries. Their website tells a much richer story. Take a look, and if you have a few spare bucks, send them a check. More money equals more innocent people exonerated.

The plot of *The Guardians* is based on a real story, sad to say, and it involves a Texas inmate named Joe Bryan. Thirty years ago, Joe was wrongly convicted of murdering his wife, a horrible crime that occurred at night while Joe was sleeping in his hotel room two hours away. The investigation was botched from the beginning. The real killer was never identified, but strong evidence points to a former policeman who committed suicide in 1996.

The prosecution could not establish a motive for Joe killing his wife because he had none. There were no cracks in the marriage. The only physical evidence supposedly linking him to the crime was a mysterious flashlight found in the trunk of his car. An expert told the jury that the tiny specks found on its lens were "back spatter," and belonged to the victim. Thus, the expert testified, the flashlight was present at the crime scene, even though it was not recovered from it.

The expert's testimony was overreaching, speculative, and not based on science. He was also allowed to theorize that Joe probably took a shower after the murder to remove bloodstains but offered no proof of this. The expert has since backed away from those opinions.

Joe should have been exonerated and freed years ago, but it hasn't happened. His case languishes before the Texas Court of Criminal Appeals. He's seventy-nine years old and his health is failing. On April 4, 2019, he was denied parole for the seventh time.

In May of 2018, *The New York Times Magazine* and ProPublica copublished a two-part series about Joe's case. It is investigative reporting at its finest. The journalist, Pamela Colloff, did a masterful job of digging into all aspects of the crime and prosecution, and the breakdown in the judicial system.

So, thanks to Jim McCloskey and Joe Bryan for their stories. One great regret is that Jim did not have the chance to discover Joe's case thirty years ago. Thanks to Pamela Colloff for her fine work and for bringing the story to the attention of a much wider audience.

Thanks also to Paul Casteleiro, Kate Germond, Bryan Stephenson, Mark Mesler, Maddy deLone, and Deirdre Enright.